"*Atmospheric, haunting, gritty and compelling, with the authenticity only someone who has experienced war can accurately convey. I can't remember the last time a book made me cry. This novel gives the Hanham family life again and ensures their story will not be forgotten... Highly recommended.*"

Carole McEntee-Taylor, Author of Military History and Historical Fiction.

"*Hanham vividly captures the unbreakable bond between three brothers and their wider family from the outbreak of The First World War, their enlistment and training, to the stark reality of fighting on the front line. In this book Andrew masterfully brings to life one of countless untold family sagas. Not only does he get inside the minds of these courageous brothers and comrades enduring the complexities of life in the trenches and beyond, but he also depicts the uncertainty and harrowing effects the war had on their loved ones back at home... I highly recommend this book.*"

Rowley Gregg MC, CEO of *Remember and There But Not There* charity.

Hanham

By Andrew Wood

"For Mum and Dad. Without your love and support this would not have been possible. I am eternally grateful."

"All the letters and documents used in this book are genuine correspondence from the Hanham family and events are based on diary extracts and factual accounts."

- Andrew Wood, author of Hanham

Hanham

The Ploegsteert Memorial is situated just off the Rue De Messines in the small Belgian town of Ploegsteert. Two large stone lions are permanent sentinels at the entrance to the stone structure within, its thick stone colonnades and curved panels reminiscent of an ancient Greek temple. It is a magnificent homage to the eleven thousand, four hundred and forty-seven names that adorn the panels. These are the names of British and Empire soldiers with no known grave, a memorial to the missing, to men whose bodies were never recovered amid the horror of war.

Listed on panel ten are one hundred and ninety-two names from the 13th Battalion The London Regiment, *The Kensington Battalion.* Among them is the name Hanham…

Neuve Chapelle, France – 11ᵗʰ March 1915

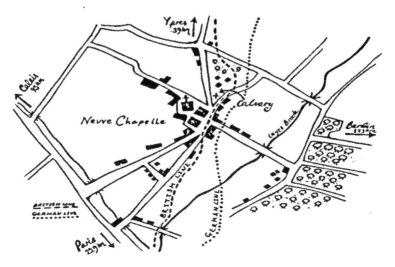

STUART woke suddenly to the sound of rifle fire cracking over his head. Heavy bullets hit the dirt with dull thuds and sparked aggressively off the rubble and buildings around him. Immediately the warm, peaceful embrace of scant sleep became cold, wet reality and weakened by fatigue he rolled onto his knees frantically searching for his rifle. His mouth was dry, and his head throbbed violently in pain. In the grey light of pre-dawn, he prayed he was still dreaming.

"Here they go again!" shouted the man next to him firing wildly, "This time they mean business!"

Fear ripped Stuart from his delirium, alert now as if icy water had been thrown into his face. "Keep the fire going lads! Don't let them get around us!" roared Stuart as he climbed to his feet and hunched into a run down the line of his Platoon. His legs were stiff with cold but instinctively he was in search of Lieutenant Harding, his Platoon

Commander. He found him fifty metres away directing fire to the east.

"We can't stay here much longer, sir, they forced us to use most of our ammunition last night and we have no sign of resupply," said Stuart, trying his hardest to impress upon his commander the severity of their predicament. Both men flinched as incoming fire spat shrapnel from the walls around them.

"Sergeant Hanham, it's the same across the Company! Re-enforcements are on the way!" replied Harding. His soft young features turned harder and brazen, fair hair darkened by mud and sweat under his officer's cap and his voice pitched high with the pressure of command. Stuart nodded his acknowledgement and continued up the line. A few men were hunkered down behind a low stone wall doing their best to separate individual rounds from a belt of ammunition to be passed out among the men. Stuart nodded and smiled reassuringly to one of the young men whose face was washed with fear and hands shaking. The remainder of his platoon was returning fire towards the German line, teeth clenched in terrified anger.

As Stuart finished the check of his men, firing from the enemy trench ceased and the world became silent for a short, eerie moment. Suddenly a flare erupted from the German position and broke the lull. As it fizzed bright and high into the grey sky all the Kensington men followed its flight with wide, fearful eyes. Their bodies froze in terror. "They mean to shell us again lads, find some cover but keep your eyes peeled! They may try and move round!" yelled Stuart as he ran back down the line of his men in a desperate search for cover. Around him men were curling up into tight balls and others searched for safety among the rubble and destroyed houses. As the first guns in the distance blazed in a dull chorus

Stuart managed to find a small bit of cover behind a shallow wall but it was not adequate for his large frame, one side of his flank was exposed, it would have to do. Already the deathly whistles could be heard above him.

The first few shells landed a hundred yards to the rear of the Kensington line and sprayed shrapnel at the unoccupied end of the village. The second volley landed fifty yards to the front of the men. Close enough to violently shake the ground beneath them and shower them all in mud, bricks and explosive heat. The third was more accurate and smashed directly into where soldiers from the Royal Irish Rifles were occupying the front line. Screams from the wounded added to the orchestra of war and Stuart's hands, lamely cupped around his ears, did little to dampen the noise. There was nothing he could do but wait and pray that the shelling did not spread to the left and account for Kensington lives. His prayer went unanswered. Soon cries for stretcher-bearers were passed down but there was nothing they could do while the ferocious shelling continued. Stuart felt helpless and as the ground shook around him he could only grit his teeth and remain fixed in a tight ball of despair. His brain flicked violently through all the images of his life; of family and friends, living and dead, summer days in Kent countryside fishing with his brothers and visions of his mother, sisters and beloved Emily waiting nervously at home. He began to sob.

After a period of time that felt like years the shelling ceased and the dust began to settle. The light rain that had been a fine, cold curtain mixed with the dust in the air and formed a stone paste on the uniforms of the men occupying the line, their hair and eyelashes were thick with grime. Stuart was unscathed but disoriented by the ringing in his ears and unsteady on his feet as he ran along encouraging his men out of their poorly protected positions and back onto the firing line. The morning was dull and damp, the sun's brightness only just pierced the gloom. Stuart could now see the enemy line of trenches. Out of them grey figures started to appear and, goaded by shouts and whistle blasts, they swarmed towards Stuart and the British frontline. "Here they come!" screamed one man further down. Men who had been hunched down to avoid the raking enemy machine gun fire stood up bravely and started firing into the approaching mass of uniformed men.

At first the German advance seemed to falter under the weight of fire coming from the British line and the first out of their trench fell lamely onto their faces. They soon gathered momentum and came on at a menacing pace. A British artillery officer fired a flare up into the sky to signal the British guns to start firing from the rear, but it seemed to Stuart they might soon be overwhelmed. Undaunted, the Kensington men kept firing and Stuart ran along the line, encouraging his men. Two were wounded by machine gun fire and immediately they withdrew from the firing line to make a dash for the aid station in the village but a third was not so lucky. As he was struck in the side of the head by a bullet from a German machine gun, the pale pink and grey of his brain showered the man next to him, sections of bright white skull clung to the muck. The soldier covered in his friend's mess looked in shock at the limp body on the floor and the tangled mess of hair and blood on the side of his tunic. Stuart saw in his face the startled fear that was the prelude to a breakdown, so he dashed over and pointed the man's rifle forcefully in the direction of the approaching enemy. "Keep firing Jack! Let them have it!" yelled Stuart into his ear and as his comrade returned fire, Stuart pulled from his tunic the matted mess that seconds before had held the complex mind of his friend.

A few moments later British shells started to fall onto the advancing enemy in front of the Kensington line. Apart from a thin layer of slippery mud the ground over which the Germans were advancing was solid, so the exploding shells wreaked gruesome havoc. Large hot fragments of shrapnel flew through the air severing limbs and heads and German bodies were thrown like rag dolls into the air and fell back to earth, limp and lifeless as their attack came to an end. Some men started to cheer at the spectacle, but Stuart turned away, he had no desire to witness such carnage.

*

Later that morning, the Kensingtons were relieved by men from the Devonshire Regiment so they made their way back through the village to an area where they could regroup. Stuart's head was pounding as he marched toward the rear, he hadn't had any water for over twelve hours and suddenly he was aware of the painful hunger in his belly. The distant gunfire and shouting had dulled so he turned and looked up the road towards the village. The old stone crucifix remained eerily untouched by war. Its holy presence saddened him, immediately he thought of home and of his family. The last time he had seen this cross, just the day before, his brother was still with him unharmed but now, for the first time in his life, he questioned the presence of God. He looked at it angrily before sadness and the prickling of tears in his eyes forced his attention to the road.

Over the next hour Stuart and the other platoon sergeants tried to help the officers in B Company organise their men and account for those missing or dead. By ten o'clock the sun had risen high in the sky and broken through the clouds. It was warm on the backs of the Kensington men who had formed up behind an old barn and waited for instructions. Silently they brushed the baked mud from their clothing and rubbed their dirty faces clean.

Next to Stuart an officer from A Company read through their nominal role, Stuart stood in front of his platoon and the remainder of B Company waiting their turn to answer. He was looking to the floor in deep contemplation, his brow furrowed in anger. He stood apart from the rest and under a lone cloud of despair, aggressively he brushed the dry dirt from his tunic and trousers as names were called by a senior officer.

"French?"

"Sir"

"Green?"

"Sir"

"Goldman?"

"Sir"

"Hanham?"

There was no answer from the assembled men of A Company. Some of the men looked at Stuart at the mention of his brother's name but he didn't catch their eye or show any sign of acknowledgement. Instead he looked at the floor and watched a beetle struggle through the dewy grass, he hoped the beetle would take his focus, but he only saw the faces of his brothers. "Private Hanham?" asked the officer again.

"Hit, sir, yesterday afternoon," replied a man from the ranks.

Stuart could not control his emotions. He felt a revolting churn in his stomach and his big heart began to ache in his chest. He felt his body start to shake and his bright blue eyes moisten in sadness but conscious of the many sets of eyes piercing his back he turned his sadness to anger. He lifted his great boot into the air, and with clenched jaw, slammed it down hard on the beetle moving innocently through the grass in front of him. He felt its small body crack under his foot and without permission turned and walked away behind the barn, no one stopped him. Once out of sight Stuart walked slow and unsteady before eventually, he collapsed down in the sun, he took a cigarette out of his tobacco tin and lit it with a single match. Tears were flowing freely from his eyes over the large bags that now seemed a permanent feature on his weathered face. His belly was tight in hunger and pain as he took a big draw from his cigarette and turned his face towards the bright sky.

Stuart could not believe he was the only brother left out here fighting. He tried to pretend for a moment it was all a dream and that he would once again be back home together with the family, but the reality was choking and harsh. He had known deep down the war would be like this, he knew back in August life wouldn't be the same again. He had hoped to be wrong, but he wasn't and the usual pride he felt in being wise and knowledgeable was nowhere to be found. Only sadness flooded like venom around his aching body as he remembered the happier times at home and the hope of what could have been.

Kensington, London – August 1911

BASIL and Eva were uncomfortably hot and shining with sweat as they dropped their luggage in the hallway of 184 Holland Road. They had carried their heavy bags all the way from Hammersmith station through the blazing heat of August so the cool tiled entrance to the house was sweet relief and it felt like a deep cave. Eva hung her hat on the large iron hook, ran a hand through her wiry grey hair and wiped her wrinkled brow with a white cloth, she arched her back and sighed with pleasure. Basil loosened his tie and removed his jacket silently before helping his mother with her cream summer jacket, she was portlier now than she had been when they lived in the countryside, so a lot of her clothes were tight.

"I don't know about you, but I could certainly do with a cup of tea," said Eva as she raised her hand to her youngest son's cheek and pinched it hard, breaking his fatigued gaze. "... And it looks like you could use one too."

"Mother!" said Basil, brushing her hand away in frustrated teenage embarrassment. Eva chuckled, removed her white lace gloves and waddled down the hall towards the kitchen. Basil turned to the mirror next to him and looked into his own bright blue eyes staring back, he used his crinkled shirt sleeve to wipe the sweat from his brow before following Eva into the kitchen.

"Looks like Stuart has made some fresh lemonade, would you prefer a glass of that B?" asked Eva as Basil entered the kitchen.

"Sounds great," replied Basil. He looked into the garden where he could see the familiar shape of Stuart laid flat on the lawn soaking in the sun like a reptile. A smile broke across his face as he passed his mother and headed out through the open door to join his brother. Eva called him back.

"Please take the cases up the stairs B, you know how I struggle." Basil turned to her with a frown and was about to speak out, but he thought better of it. He knew very well she could manage, she was from Inverness in the freezing north of Scotland and had been the archetypal matriarch of the Hanham family even before the death of her husband, Abdiel in 1908. She was the strongest woman they knew but enjoyed making her boys carry out such tasks to cement her authority. Basil as the youngest, and not yet eighteen, was still a boy under her spell. It wasn't worth an argument, so he quickly obeyed and ran back through the hallway to fetch the luggage.

Out in the garden Stuart and his friend John Green were shirtless, casually laying on the grass and enjoying the August sun. They each had in their hands a glass of lemonade and on plates next to them were the crumbs of sandwiches. They were both covered in oil from a dismantled motorbike on the patio. Green was the first to see Eva and he stood up respectfully as she stepped into the sun. Stuart remained propped up on his right elbow and looked over to see why his friend was so startled. "Mother," said Stuart, once he realised she was home. "How was your time in the country?" Stuart levered his broad, athletic frame up to welcome his mother formally.

Before saying a word, Eva surveyed her garden like a detective entering the scene of a brutal crime. She noticed a couple of chairs from the dining room, oily rags strewn across the floor and a large round tin full of engine oil under the carcass of Stuart's motorcycle. A short moment later Basil bounded through the door of the kitchen and broke the silence, Stuart welcomed his brother home. "Hello B old boy, catch any more fish since your last letter?"

"A few, too hot for them now though," said Basil with a smile as he made his way over to shake hands with Green. "Hello John," he said, offering his hand. John Green was a member of the same Territorial Army Regiment as Stuart, the one he was keen to join himself next year, when he was old enough. The 13th Battalion of The London Regiment, *The Kensingtons*.

Eva had still said nothing. "Don't worry mother, we will have cleaned up by tonight. We weren't expecting you until tomorrow afternoon." Stuart raised his eyebrows in a way that suggested innocence and spread his thick arms wide inviting her in for a hug. Eva, not interested in getting covered in oil and sweat, raised her hand gracefully to decline the offer. She turned her attention to Green.

"Mr Green?"

"We've actually met before Ma'am, at our passing out parade," said Green. She hadn't remembered him, but he looked a nice boy, dark and distinguished.

"So, what is wrong with the old girl now?" asked Basil, gesturing towards the motorcycle that lay dismembered. He had shaken the boyishness from his voice, the presence of his eldest brother always made Basil act beyond his years.

"Nothing B, she's running great, but John said he would help me change the oil. Probably overdue some new blood in her veins," said Stuart. "John here is rather the man to see when it comes to motors." Basil looked towards Green and raised his eyebrows in respect. He too loved the complexities of machines and was excited about the prospect of putting it back together, he assumed Stuart would let him help.

"My father has a few old ones that keep failing, I learnt out of necessity I suppose," said Green to Eva but she simply smiled politely and made to sit down. Basil, sleeves rolled up and crouched next to the bike, was looking in wonder at the engine and the parts laid out on the floor. He tucked his tie into his shirt to keep it safe from the oil and grime.

"Change your clothes if you are going to play with that machine," said Eva with her head back in the chair and eyes closed to the sun.

"I will, I'm just looking for now." Basil resented her making him feel like a child in front of Stuart and his friend. Green headed over to Basil, crouched next to him and started to explain the different components. Basil, with his relentless need to impress, was eager to learn.

Eva took a long drink from her lemonade, it was cold and bitter and quenched her thirst wonderfully. She put the glass down with a contented sigh and turned to Stuart, propped up on his elbows, head back lolling in the sun like a cat. "So where is your brother? Where is Eric?"

Stuart squinted. "He was here this morning, we went to church together, but he left with some of his friends and we came home to fix the bike," said Stuart, relaxed and enjoying the heat on his body.

"Do you think he'll be home this evening?"

"I should think so, he didn't have much money with him so he can't drink all day." Stuart returned his head to the back of his neck and closed his eyes to the sky. Eva exhaled and took another sip from her lemonade. Eric would often spend his Sunday drinking after church and on a sunny day like today he would be in the Red Lion, playing cards and singing songs in the garden. She hoped it was a phase, he hadn't long been old enough to drink and she feared too much mention of it would only push him further down that road, such was the character of her middle son.

"There is a letter from K on the table," said Stuart.

"What did she say?"

"She said she has another show lined up after this one and that Stella and Frank are well. Frank is on tour soon with the Coldstream Band." Eva leant back in her chair and relaxed her eyes and aching muscles, comfortable in the warming glare of a peaceful London sun and happy in knowledge her two daughters were well.

After a short rest Eva talked of her trip and Stuart listened as she recounted news and stories from her visit to Kent, the place where all the Hanham children were born and spent their childhood, before she went to wash and unpack. At about six o'clock, as the sun crept behind the buildings, the front door was flung open with a bang as Eric returned home. "Ah the Mater and B return!" he announced as he sauntered through the kitchen into the garden. He walked confidently onto the patio and lifted his younger brother in a boyish embrace and show of strength that Basil hated. He and Eric were only thirteen months apart, but Eric was without a doubt the elder. He was broader, stronger and carefree, Basil was taller and leaner, timid and reserved, but their bond was strong and lasting.

"You whiff of ale and fags old man!" said Basil clasping an oily rag to his face to mask the smell from Eric's mouth, hair and clothes. Unperturbed Eric turned to Green and Stuart next to the nearly assembled bike.

"How are you, John?"

"Well thank you Eric, this old girl will be like new when we are finished."

"Good to hear, I'll take it out for a spin." Eric flashed a cheeky grin at Stuart.

"Touch it and I'll take *YOU* apart!" snapped Stuart with a smile.

Eric returned his attention to Basil "How was the old place? Did you visit all the favourite haunts? This old boy says you caught a basket load of fish." Eric jerked his thumb in Stuart's direction.

"We had a pleasant time, E, it's not changed at all. Some of the chaps were asking after you, Reg and Hastings took me for a drink." Basil looked around to make sure Eva wasn't in earshot.

"Glad to hear it, I hope you gave them my best?"

"I did, I also said they should come and visit soon, seeing as you can't peel yourself away from city life." Basil smiled.

"Yes! Good man, let's hope they do," said Eric as Eva, hearing the commotion and taking a break from her unpacking, entered the garden. "Mater!" Eric ran towards her, lifted her up and spun her around. She knew he had been drinking and could now smell the ale and cigarettes on his breath, in his dark hair and on his clothes. He put her down gently, despite his eagerness he knew she was no longer a young woman and was getting fragile with age.

"Goodness Eric! You really smell of ale."

Eva placed both her arms on his broad chest and pushed him gently away from her. She looked into his bright grey eyes and could see the glazed expression. She didn't mind drinking but having seen the damage cheap whisky did in her childhood town of Inverness, she insisted on moderation. Stuart had abstained from alcohol and Basil's hero like worship of him led Eva to believe that Abdiel's passion for drink had, presently, only been passed to Eric.

"Just a few Sunday beers with friends, Mater. They are all good sorts," said Eric leading Eva back into the house, a big arm around her shoulder. "Tell me all about your visit…"

Andrew Wood

76 Amesbury Avenue, London – 5th August 1914

IT seemed like a normal Wednesday in August. The sun was bright in the sky and the city heat was close and stifling, relieved only slightly by the occasional, refreshing breeze from the west. People conducting their normal business around Streatham masked a deadly undercurrent. The cauldron of European politics had been simmering furiously and, in the thrumming heat of summer, events in Sarajevo had forced it to boil over. Britain had declared war on the industrial might of Germany. Today was no normal day at all.

At a quarter past six Eric bounded through the door, he was sweating through his shirt and with hair matted to his brow it was obvious he had been running. He dropped his satchel in the hallway and shouted into the house. "Stuart! Stuart are you here?" He could hear movement on the floorboards above his head, Basil had rushed out of his room and stood at the top of the stairs, "...B! Old boy, have you heard the news?"

"Of course I have!" replied Basil, running down the stairs, almost falling in the excitement. He didn't know the correct gesture when he reached Eric. Should they embrace, shake hands? He settled on a firm handshake.

"Where is Stuart? I need you both to get me into your lot, I'm not going over there with anyone else and God help me I'm not missing out on this!" said Eric as he wiped the sweat from his brow with his shirt.

"What about work?"

"Old Talbot can find someone else. Plus, all the boys are going to join up eventually, no one will want to miss out on this," replied Eric as he pushed past Basil and headed toward the kitchen.

15

Hanham

The house at 76 Amesbury Avenue was very different to 184 Holland Road. In comparison, it was tiny, but it had enough rooms for the boys if Basil and Eric shared. Kathleen was living in a small flat with an actress friend on a month-to-month basis, she was happy and enjoyed the flexibility it afforded her. Sometimes she would stay with her sister Stella and husband Frank who had a small basement flat near Camden Town. The reason for the move was hard for Eva and the family. Abdiel's unexpected death in October 1908 had left them with little money but they were well looked after by his Uncle Charles who had been like a father to Abdiel. It was Charles who encouraged the move from Kent to London and it was he who had ensured the family were looked after. His death in 1912 left Eva and the boys in some financial peril so they moved to the smaller house in Streatham in early 1913. Even so, Basil was forced to get a job before the end of his accountancy studies and Eric's income from building work was required. Stuart did his best to help out where he could, but no one begrudged him his lack of contribution. When he finished his law studies, he would become the main provider for the Hanham family and life would regain some financial balance. Regardless, "76" was a fine home and the area suited the Hanham family, who had felt a little out of their social depth in Kensington.

Amesbury Avenue was a terraced street, red brick and full of character with tiny front gardens that had been lovingly adorned with hanging baskets. Large trees lined the street which, in summer, bloomed a beautiful green and purple and in the autumn, burned red and gold.

It wasn't until after seven o'clock that Stuart returned home. He entered the house casually, dropped his bag by the front door and bent down to open the large brass buckle of the main compartment. He removed a book that he needed for study that evening. As he walked towards the kitchen, he heard his brothers talking, stopped and returned the book to his bag by the door. He wouldn't need the information on its pages for a while to come.

He entered the kitchen to the smell of boiling ham, Eva was at the worktop under the small window at the far end chopping vegetables, her sturdy frame facing away from him. Basil and Eric were talking loudly together hunched over a newspaper with their back to Stuart.

"Good evening, all." Eric and Basil looked up, quickly silenced by his entrance. Eva turned slowly with a reserved smile and sad eyes.

"Stuart, old boy, I assume you've heard," said Eric.

"Of course I have E, it is all anyone can talk about." Stuart loosened his tie and stepped down the single stone step into the kitchen.

"E wants to join the Kensingtons, he wants us to get him in," said Basil, calmly. Stuart's relaxed and assured demeanour always made Basil act mature. Eric's carefree attitude would make Basil excited and rebellious at times but when the three were together it was Stuart's respectful, grown up attitude that won over the younger boy. Basil had always been in awe of his eldest brother. Stuart said nothing.

"Well, old man, can you speak to someone?" asked Eric.

"I am sure we can sort something." Stuart was non-committal. He didn't know what the process would be so didn't want to promise anything to Eric that would prove to be impossible - the lawyer in him.

"What about you? You're coming, right?"

Eva, who had been listening, paused for a second or two before continuing to chop. Stuart noticed her reaction so ignored his brother's question. Eric wasn't completely naïve, he saw Stuart look at Eva and understood why he didn't answer. He looked back at Stuart and winked. Stuart nodded back.

"How are you mother?" asked Stuart. Eva turned to face him, drying her hands on her apron. Her face was heavy with worry and looked aged in the darker light of the kitchen.

"I don't quite know what to say, my dear. It is a lot to take in, don't you think?"

Stuart raised his eyebrows and nodded in agreement. "Indeed, it is. You were right to say it would end up like this."

"Sadly, yes." Eva turned back to the worktop and shovelled the roughly chopped vegetables into a pot of boiling water. She placed the lid on the pot and left the room, touching Stuart gently on the shoulder as she went.

Eric waited for a moment after Eva had gone and then quietly asked Stuart his plan. Stuart leant towards his brothers who mirrored him.

"Of course I'm going, law school will be here when we get back. I'm not missing out on this and besides, someone needs to look after you two."

Eric threw his head back and laughed. Basil was slightly annoyed Stuart had insinuated he needed *looking after* but he was glad Stuart would be there. He smiled and sat back in his chair.

The Hanham brothers were going to war. This was not a normal day at all.

*

The next day Stuart, Eric and Basil woke early and had a small breakfast of eggs and sausage that Eva prepared for them. They were shaking with excitement but did not want to seem too eager in front of their mother who, unknown to the boys, had endured a sleepless night of prayer. She hoped this would all soon prove to be the flexing of government muscles and a reasonable solution would be reached.

At just after seven o'clock the three boys left the house and set out towards Kensington Town Hall, temporary Headquarters of The Kensington Battalion. Stuart and Basil travelled in their khaki uniform, each carrying a holdall full of spare kit and equipment they might need if they were to head off straight away. Eric, smartly dressed in a dark suit, carried a small suitcase of useful things Stuart had helped him pack.

Kensington Town Hall was a hive of activity. There were men in uniform and civilian dress spilling out into the street, laughing and joking. Basil, enjoying the fact Eric was a little nervous about entering his world, headed straight for the closest group of men he knew and shook their hands excitedly. Stuart, acknowledging nods and salutations stuck with Eric and went with him to find out where the new recruits were to start their enlistment process, he thought he might have to vouch for him and was expecting to have to give Eric a good reference.

Just up the steps of the south entrance Stuart saw Sergeant Major Hockley with a clipboard and a furrowed brow. He was standing next to a long line of unfamiliar men dressed in smart civilian attire, the magnificent building behind him added grandeur to his formidable presence.

"Morning, sir," said Stuart, bracing to attention in front of Hockley. Eric stood there, a little shocked by Stuart's display of obedience and respect. For some reason he had not thought about the disciplined nature of the Army and, for the first time, he was afraid.

"Morning, Hanham," said Hockley, eyeing Eric with suspicion. "And who is this then?" Stuart relaxed his posture, formalities over.

"This is my brother Eric. He wants to join up with us, do you know where I should send him, sir?"

"Leave him here with me, we'll have him processed." Eric thought Hockley might reach out and shake his hand but instead he returned his attention to his clipboard.

Stuart turned towards Eric, he could see his brother was now more than a little nervous and was relishing it. "See you on the other side, E, Sergeant Major Hockley will look after you now." He winked at Eric and punched him hard on the arm. Eric smiled and restrained himself from retaliation as he watched Stuart head back down towards where Basil was stood laughing with a group of men. Eric was envious, he now wished he hadn't been so quick in saying no to joining up with Basil in 1912, if he had he wouldn't now be left alone with an intimidating stranger. Eric turned slowly towards Hockley who was looking straight at him. His deep brown eyes, bristling moustache and hard fatherly features made Eric jump. He stood there wide eyed and embarrassed.

"Name and date of birth, boy," Hockley's tone was slow and patronising.

"Hanham, Eric Abdiel – 20th September 1892." Eric tried in vain not to appear worried or scared.

"Good lad," said Hockley with a smile and a wink. "Wait here and you'll be processed." Perhaps he was human after all, thought Eric, as Hockley inspected his clipboard again.

*

The enlistment process was easy for Eric, but he would have to return the next day to sign some official documents. In the meantime, new recruits like him were subjected to a medical, sized off for their uniform, issued equipment and completed endless forms. Once finished they were given a welcome address by Lieutenant Colonel Lewis, the Commanding Officer. By the end of the day they were all but fully serving members of the 13th *'Kensington'* Battalion of the London Regiment.

Already enlisted men like Stuart and Basil paraded with their companies and signed paperwork to say they were happy to be embodied and serve overseas. Some men were selected to leave immediately and set up the training depot at Abbots Langley in Hertfordshire. Most were sent home and told to report back in a week when they would begin their training.

Stuart and Basil waited for Eric before heading home together in the warm embrace of early evening. The three men were children again, as if on their way home from school for the summer. They lost themselves in youthful fantasy, choosing to forget that soldiers are sometimes called upon to give their lives. However, on the balmy evening of the 6th of August 1914 it was they who had chosen adventure. They would kill a few Germans perhaps, win a medal or two and return heroes to a world they had saved from the teeth of a hungry imperial wolf. In their minds were images from the Boer War and the great conquests of the Empire when British soldiers arrogantly laid waste to armies unable to match their strength and stamina. Even Stuart in his wisdom was ignorant in that moment to the incredible human cost of these seemingly *glorious* campaigns. For the moment, they were young, free and alive and were relishing being the tip of Britain's powerful sword.

However, in the last few steps to 76 they steadied themselves like teenagers trying to hide the influence of alcohol. They dropped their cases to check their uniforms, adjusted their caps smartly and entered the house as if there was a senior officer inside. It was nearly eight o'clock and the evening had grown cloudy and dark, the house even darker and oddly foreboding. The boys, hushed like naughty children, dropped their kit bags in the hall and headed towards the kitchen where they could hear voices, their hobnail boots clicking and scratching loudly along the tiled floor.

Sat at the table in the kitchen were Kathleen and Eva. Kathleen looked up into Stuart's bright blue eyes when he entered, the others filed in behind him. Eric was sheepish, suddenly embarrassed by his new uniform, he removed his hat.

"Good evening, K," said Stuart leaning down to kiss her cheek, "and to you Mother," kissing her also. Basil and Eric followed suit.

"Mother says you're all going off together. Is that true?" asked Kathleen. She was calm and matter of fact. Her thick brown hair was loose around her shoulders and her hazel eyes shone like amber jewels in the fading light.

"It's true, K," said Basil in excitement. "Eric is even in the same Platoon as us."

Stuart sat at the top of the rustic table and Basil on the side closest to the door, opposite Kathleen. Eric jumped up onto the work surface and bit into an apple he took from the bowl next to him. "Well I think it is good you're all going together. You'll promise to look after them, won't you Basil?" said Eva with a smile, gently touching Basil's arm.

"I will, Mother." Basil removed his hat and placed it on the table, fiddling proudly with the badge on the front he had a broad smile on his face.

"And law school, Stuart?" asked Kathleen.

"Most of us that can will be going I think. It might add a year to my studies, but I wouldn't want to miss out on this."

"Basil? Eric? What about your jobs?"

"Well, K, I guess we are soldiers for the foreseeable," said Eric, casual as ever, taking another bite from his apple. Basil turned to him and smiled in agreeable pride.

"I see, well, I do worry about Mother," said Kathleen placing a hand on Eva's shoulder. "Who will pay the rates?"

"I'll be fine dear, and I know your father would be most proud of you boys. I know he would wish for The Lord to watch over you all," said Eva, raising her hands skyward in a submissive gesture. It seemed she had decided to be strong, despite her heart breaking into three separate pieces at the thought of her sons going off to war.

"Thank you, I know he would too and don't worry, we'll be sending money back here and you'll be able to pick it up at the post office," said Stuart, placing a hand on Eva's arm. Eric and Basil nodded with him.

Eric then spoke, his mouth full of apple, "Perhaps you should move in here K? Just while we are all away."

Kathleen sat up in her chair. "Mother? Would that be something you'd like?"

Kathleen had not remained at home with Eva long after the Hanham family move to London. She had become an actress quickly, so worked long and demanding hours that meant she was rarely at home when they had lived on Holland Road. Now the family lived in the smaller house on Amesbury Avenue, Eva didn't have a room for her eldest daughter, so Kathleen had been living with friends in the fashionable quarters of the city amongst artist and musicians.

Eva reached with both hands and laid them gently on Kathleen's in a loving grasp. "I would like that very much indeed." There was emotion in her voice. Kathleen looked away with a smile, pleased and embarrassed by her mother's deep love. She wondered whether Eva would have been too proud to ask her to move back without the suggestion from one of the boys and smiled in respect of her stubbornness.

"A good idea," said Stuart. Eric nodded, juice from the apple in his mouth flowed down to his chin.

Eva steadied herself, she was going to be strong. "Well, I think we should have a nice lunch on Sunday. Are you boys around or do you have to rush off straight away?"

"No, we are around. We don't parade until next Thursday," said Basil.

"Wednesday," said Stuart, correcting him.

"Well then, this Sunday we'll have a nice lunch. Kathleen, can you make it?"

"Of course," Kathleen wore a heartfelt smile, she was still flushed with emotion.

"Wonderful. Perhaps you could ask Stella too? It would be lovely to have all my children under one roof."

"Of course I will, I'll ask her tonight. I don't think her, or Frank have any plans."

"Very well, after church on Sunday," said Eva, standing to walk away down the hall. "And Eric, my dear, they are cooking apples."

Eric spat out what remained of the bitter apple in his mouth and the room erupted in laughter.

76 Amesbury Avenue, London – 9th August 1914

EVA and the boys arrived back at 76 shortly after one o'clock, it was such a lovely day that Eva had wanted to walk from the church of St. Pauls in Hammersmith. Although some way from Streatham they had made friends there and the boys were members of the church club so they attended whenever they could. On the walk home Basil made a few jokes at Eric's expense, adding that he'd soon be walking longer distances with a heavy pack. Eric laughed it off letting Basil have these jibes, if Basil could manage all the physical aspects of soldering then he could too. Stuart spent a lot of their walk in silence but did occasionally raise the topic of finances and tried to reassure Eva she would be well looked after. Eva wasn't too concerned about money, she knew she would manage, her main concern was the well-being of her boys off to war.

When they arrived home some children were playing football in the street. They shouted out for Eric to join in and he duly did, loosening his tie and throwing his hat to Basil who looked on enviously at Eric's popularity, even among the children in their road. Stuart opened the door to the smell of thyme, garlic and roast beef and they entered the house to sounds of birds and laughter from outside. Kathleen came to greet them in the hallway. Her face was shining red and some of her dark hair was stuck to sweat on her brow. The skin on her rounded chin creased in a wide, welcoming smile.

"Smells good, K," said Basil as he hung up Eric's hat and Eva's jacket before removing his own.

"I thought I'd get a head start on dinner," she said, directing her answer towards Eva who she embraced.

"It does indeed smell rather good, dear. Where did you get the beef?"

"From the butchers in Brixton, the one by the station. I bought it on my way over."

"But I got us a chicken at the market yesterday." Eva sounded slightly put out by Kathleen's intervention.

"I saw mother, we'll cook that later so it will keep. I thought it would be nice to have a good bit of beef today." Kathleen put a reassuring hand on Eva's shoulder and smiled at her mother. Eva nodded.

"A wonderful idea," said Eva as Eric crashed through the door, hot and sweating.

"Is that roast beef I smell?"

"It is," said Kathleen, proud of her impact on the day.

"Won't argue with that, K," said Eric, pushing past Basil and Stuart to greet his sister with a kiss on the cheek.

"I'm doing dinner for three o'clock," she said, walking back into the kitchen.

At just before three Eric rang the dinner bell from the bottom of the stairs and in the most formal tone he could conjure called his mother down to dinner. "Mrs Hanham, Lady of Streatham, your Sunday dinner awaits you." Kathleen chuckled as she walked into the front room with a large bowl of potatoes, but she was concerned Stella had still not arrived. Basil was placing serving spoons into the bowls of fine-looking vegetables and Stuart was rearranging the cutlery after Eric's poor attempt. He looked up at Kathleen concerned, Kathleen frowned angrily at him and shrugged her shoulders in despair.

Eva came down the stairs regally and Eric bowed like a maître d' as she entered the dining room. It made her smile. She took a deep breath in expectation, but a quick survey of the room showed the places set for Stella and Frank were empty. Eva tried to keep her emotions in check, but it was clear in her face she was disappointed. She quickly regrouped. "Kathleen my dear this looks wonderful. What a perfect Sunday meal." She was hurting badly but managed to sound sincere, she had so desperately wanted the whole family to be present. Since Stella had married Frank in October of 1910 she had seen far less of her which, although expected once a woman took a husband, made her sad. She wished they could both be here today to see the boys off.

"Quite so. And I'm very hungry," said Eric, still trying to act the fool to relive the tension. It was the only way he knew how, and it usually worked.

Basil was stood at his place next to his mother at the head of the table closest to the door. Eric was opposite him, Kathleen by his side. Stuart stood at the other head of the table but made his way round next to Basil in a feeble attempt to make it less obvious two seats were vacant.

"Shall we say grace mother?" asked Stuart.

"Why don't you do it, dear," said Eva, head bowed in preparation.

Stuart held out his hands to Basil and Kathleen and lowered his head to pray. The others did the same, completing the circle. Stuart paused for a moment to gather his thoughts and to come up with an apt grace for the occasion. He didn't want to mention the war or family, that would have been too much for Eva, so he decided to keep his grace simple.

"Our Father, who-" Stuart was cut off by four loud knocks on the window. They all looked up to see Stella wide eyed, face flushed red with exertion, guilty grin of the tardy. Frank was stood behind her in a shirt and tie holding up a bottle of wine.

"Don't start without us!" called Stella through the open window. Eva put her hands over her mouth and started to cry.

The Hanham house was fizzing with happiness and warm with love that afternoon. They talked about life, London and the exciting worlds that were growing in its new bohemian heart. They discussed music, dance and theatre, all the things Eva loved so dearly, and argued over politics and current affairs until the subject was banned. Frank explained angrily how he as army bandsman was not allowed to join the fighting arms and how he would be needed for public events and the drive for war bonds. They gossiped about family friends, much to the embarrassment of Kathleen, when Stella casually revealed her sister had been spending a great deal of time with Howard Boundford. Kathleen's bright pink face was clear indication she had intended to keep him a secret for a while longer at least.

Eva and the Hanham family could not have wished for a better afternoon. Politics, war and the frustrations of life were far away, and the warm glow of summer kept spirits high. As Stella and Frank said their goodbyes none of them could possibly have known this would be the last time the Hanham family were together.

Kensington Town Hall – 12th August 1914

STUART looked at his watch and tensed, the empty feeling of panic in his gut. It was already approaching seven-thirty and they had to make it to Kensington Town Hall for eight, an impossible feat now.

"Sorry Mother but we have to leave," said Stuart, trying in vain to remain calm. Basil sensed his haste so shovelled the last of his eggs into his mouth as he stood but Eric looked up confused from his seat at the table.

"We have to go now, E. We're already late," said Stuart with a glare that made Eric drain his cup of tea and gather his khaki peaked cap from the table. The three boys made their way towards the door where their equipment and belongings had been stacked.

"Looks like we can't help you with the dishes, Mater!" said Eric as he hauled his pack onto his back and adjusted his uniform, a cheeky smile spread across his handsome young face.

"It's ok, I'll sort it boys. You all get off," replied Eva as she shooed them out the door. Outside on the street she pulled each of their faces down to her level and kissed them on the cheek. She patted Stuart and Eric on the arm but gave Basil a loving pinch of his cheek, his eyes were wide and full of concern.

"Go on, I'll sort it all out. You mustn't be too late."

Eva watched her sons run awkwardly down the hill to the Streatham Road, large packs bouncing ungainly on their backs as they waved farewell to their mother and home. She waited until they had turned the corner before she returned to the house and closed the door. Instantly, she dropped to the floor and wept into her hands. She had been so strong for them over the last few days while they prepared for training and the war beyond. She had marvelled at Basil's meticulous nature, the way he packed, unpacked and then re-packed in his own precise way. She smiled at how Eric's nonchalance had angered Basil and she was impressed, as always, by the calm, organised nature in which Stuart had sorted his equipment, postponed his studies and cleaned his room for Kathleen to move home. They were so different in their approach to life but together they left her for war and she couldn't hold back the searing pain of motherly anguish any longer. She cried hysterically until her body was weak and her mind stretched beyond thought, in a daze she went up to bed to rest.

*

The boys arrived at Kensington Town Hall nearly an hour late and were concerned they would be reprimanded on the very first day of their adventure, but they need not have worried. While there was some order there was also a mob feel to proceedings and a strange sense of calm. Men were spilling out into the street with their packs laid in piles around them. Motor vehicles and horse drawn carts using the street were forced to move slowly past the increasing number of uniformed men who looked at them with an air of authority, claiming their right of way. Senior Officers would periodically shout a name from of one of the high windows, their elevated position in the beautiful grey stone building adding weight to their rank. A senior man down below would relay the name and if the man in question were present, he would dash through the grand doors and up the marble stairs to receive his orders or sign a form.

Stuart and Basil nudged their way into a group of friends, but Eric hung back, he was new to this mob and felt a little uneasy. All three had tried to appear as if they were not panicked or exhausted after their run from the station but failed miserably.

"Bloody hell, Basil! What happened to you?" asked Davison, a stocky soldier with strong brow and pale blue eyes. Basil was showing the results of physical exertion slightly more than his brothers.

"We were running late," said Stuart, wiping the sweat from his brow with a handkerchief.

"Ah you've got plenty of time, not leaving here until eleven. Lots of lads still to turn up," said Green, sucking from his cigarette.

"You must be Eric," said Davison reaching for Eric's hand. "Welcome to B Company." He offered Eric a cigarette which he took gratefully, the friendly gesture put him at ease.

"Word is we're billeted nearby for a few days and heading off Sunday. Big parade planned," whispered Green to Stuart like it was secret information to which he was not supposed to be privy. Stuart nodded slowly in careful acknowledgement and Eric pretended he hadn't heard.

They stood around for a while longer, Basil excitedly introduced Eric to others. He was happy for Basil to have so many friends of his own, he always thought he had provided the friends Basil now called his closest. After an hour of idle gossip, speculation about the training to come and their deployment to the continent there was a shout from steps of the town hall's grand entrance that made Eric jump. "Right men! Fall in!... Hurry up!" Screamed the figure from the shade of the doorway. He seemed to take up all the space of the large double doors, standing bolt upright with golden buttons shining through the morning gloom he looked like a bear in soldiers clothing. "… If you don't know how to do that, just find a line and stand in the bugger!" A ripple of laughter came from the crowd. "Officers kindly make your way inside. Sergeants fall in!" The officers continued their conversations as they walked into the building and there was a shuffle in the ranks as men found a place in the mass of bodies. "Company Sergeant Majors to the rear." Eric noticed an intense moment of quiet as they hurried to their place. "Turn to your left! Quick march!

The men stepped off, but it was shabby and not the smart disciplined movement most were used to, new recruits like Eric had no experience of marching with heavy packs so no step was called to confuse matters further.

"That's the Regimental Sergeant Major or RSM," said Davison who was marching on Eric's left. "Word is he saw off more than a few Boer in South Africa."

"That's *Sir* to you and yeah, don't fuck with him," said another man just in front, the men around them chuckled quietly. Eric was intimidated by it all but strangely excited by his first couple of hours in the army.

The battalion made its way down the cobbled roads and wide hot streets, studs from hobnail boots crashing loudly but far from in unison. There were sporadic cheers from bystanders along the way and for men like Eric, the excitement, kindled by the first experience of marching in a large body of men, only grew. Eventually they turned into the Elizabethan grandeur of Holland House and as they marched towards the front of the building Eric couldn't help but marvel at the regal dwelling. The morning sun illuminated its red bricks and grey stone trim. The walled courtyard and ominous frontage reminded him of a castle but the bright flowers and the arched tops to the main building gave it a foreign, imperial feel. Around the gardens he noticed large tents had been erected and soldiers were scurrying around.

The men were called to halt and some of the new recruits that instinctively removed their packs were quickly reprimanded. "Who told you to remove your kit?" screamed one Sergeant Major from behind. Eric was thankful he hadn't removed his and as he looked towards Stuart, standing to his right, he saw him wink at him. Eric could tell Stuart was enjoying his unease.

*

The next few days disappeared in a surreal haze of training and activity. Eric, and his fellow new additions, were taught equipment and uniform husbandry, how to march as a formed body of men and how to strip, clean and fire their rifles. They were subjected to some vigorous physical training that consisted of quick marches through the streets of Kensington and Hammersmith. Eric found this to be enjoyable as he was athletic and strong, fit from a childhood in the countryside where walking long distances to school was a daily occurrence, but others were less able, and it proved a jolting reality check for those eager but out of shape.

Time passed quickly and on Sunday morning the battalion paraded in the grounds of Holland House for the last time. The lawns were cleared of tents and equipment and the men stood in company formations with rifle and pack awaiting an address from Lieutenant Colonel Lewis, their commanding officer. At a quarter to six he stepped out of the grand old house and the battalion was brought to attention.

"Gentlemen, I won't keep you long for we have a long march ahead of us and we must get on," said Lewis, projecting his voice without shouting in the manner only a Commanding Officer of his quality can. "I just wanted to say how proud I am of you all for being here and for embarking with us on this most noble of quests. It is my great honour to lead you and I pray to the Lord I can lead you well. I would like to make a special welcome to those new Kensingtons among us today, you already look like fine soldiers and you are most welcome. Let's march now out of London, heads held high and in good spirits!" His address increased to a shout as he raised his right arm and brown-gloved fist high into the air like a Roman General. Eric was moved and felt part of something big, a great rousing cheer came from the men around him. Lewis turned and walked back into the courtyard of Holland House where his senior officers were watching on.

"Settle down now!" called the RSM in his animal like manner. A hush fell over the gardens. "Right, Company Sergeant Majors get your men in position on the road!"

Quickly the battalion were in position and waiting for the officers to take their places at the front of their respective company columns. Eric marvelled at their polished swords glinting in the sun as they made their way to their mark and at five minutes past six, they set off towards Marble Arch where the remainder of the 4th London Territorial Infantry Brigade would meet them for their grand parade. It was a beautiful morning and spirits were high, the cool morning breeze a welcome gift for the soldiers who were in full khaki uniforms carrying heavy packs.

When they arrived at Marble Arch, they were shuffled into position in front of the gathering crowd, a band at the head of the procession could be heard rehearsing as they stood waiting for their orders to march away to training and war. Stuart, Eric and Basil were in the same line at the rear of B Company and they stood together marvelling at the occasion and support from the people of London. So far there was nothing to suggest to Eric that this would be anything but the amazing adventure he had envisaged, it wasn't hard for any of them to maintain a smile.

At nine o'clock a church bell sounded and after its chimes the band started up in fresh vigour and the crowd started to cheer. As the formation turned to the left and marched away, boots smashing the floor in unison, Eric felt the tickle of soldierly pride on the back of his neck and he scanned the crowd, five people deep in some places, for faces he knew. As they passed Connaught Street, Eric was sure he had spotted Kathleen waving her arms madly and shouting from behind an old lady shocked by her shouts, ducking from the noise. "E! B! Stuart!" she shouted, following them down the road. Eric saw her jostling awkwardly through the crowd while trying to maintain eye contact.

"There! There's K!" said Eric nudging Basil by his side and making sure Stuart was looking in the right direction.

They all looked at her with wide grins of delight, waving their hands and blowing kisses as she dropped back, trapped in the melee of well wishers. Eric could see in her eyes the swelling of tears and the way her body drooped at their leaving made his heartache. He saw her turn away and disappear out of view, but he and the boys marched on. They were part of a fighting machine, a weapon set in motion with a purpose and destined for glory.

Abbots Langley, Hertfordshire – 19th September 1914

LIEUTENANT Sewell and his new wife emerged from the church to cheers and applause, confetti and khaki caps were thrown into the air in celebration as the couple made their way to their carriage. Training had been intense, but the wedding of their platoon commander gave the Hanham boys, and the remainder of A Company, a well-earned day of relaxation. After waving the happy couple away in their carriage the mass of khaki uniforms, suits and summer dresses walked leisurely to the reception along country lanes baked hard under the sun of late summer.

Basil and Eric walked with Davison and Barker, two men Basil had introduced to Eric on the first morning and who had now become good friends. They stopped on a grass bank to the side of the road watching the crowd pass, smiling at those who looked their way. Eric lit a cigarette and passed it to Basil then lit another for himself before trying again to catch the eye of the young ladies here as guests. Most of them acknowledged him and turned back towards their conversations or to concentrate on the uneven road. One however, a lady with brown hair, pink and peach coloured flowers in her hat, seemed to smile at Eric who looked back at her unsure whether he had interpreted her actions correctly.

"She's keen on you," said Barker with a nudge to Eric's arm.

"Do you think so?" Eric looked back at just the right moment to see her turn away.

"She is too good for you, E," teased Stuart as he passed in front of his brothers and their friends on the bank. Eric looked down to see his older brother with an elderly lady on his arm, supporting her in the transition from church to reception.

"And she for you, old man," said Eric, laughing. Stuart smiled as the four men jumped down from their lofted position to join the procession.

Stuart, still escorting the old lady from the church, was one of the last to arrive at the reception. He had listened to her the whole way and quite enjoyed her ramblings, he was in no rush. Eric and Basil had long left him to the task alone, running ahead with a smirk when they caught sight of the pub, thirsty and excited at the prospect of ale.

The Royal Oak and its garden was particularly inviting. The white washed walls were shining brightly in the early afternoon sun and the red roof tiles were bold and clean. Bunting had been hung along the side of the building and flowers had been placed along the picket fence. Hanging baskets dripped from their morning watering, the vivid flowers within bursting with colour, flushed with pride. At the side of the road in the shade of a large oak tree waited the carriage, the driver had dismounted and was brushing down the handsome black horse now eating hay from a leather bag strapped to its head.

Stuart entered the garden and the bride opened her arms widely to embrace her grandmother. "Thank you so much" said Mrs Sewell to Stuart. "I hope she hasn't been too much trouble?" She looked back at the old lady with a motherly, patronising look. Her Grandmother raised her hand dismissively, Stuart smiled knowing his companion would not have appreciated that.

"This is Corporal Hanham, dear, he's one of our best men and a law student," said Sewell proudly to his new wife. Stuart was flattered by the comments and Mrs Sewell looked impressed.

"How wonderful, my father and uncle practised law. It is truly a fascinating world."

"It is indeed, ma'am," said Stuart, unsure of how to address her so opting for formality. "Perhaps I might get chance to speak with them?" Sewell made an awkward face.

"Alas they are not here, my father died a few years ago and my uncle a while before him." She was smiling through a little pain at her absent father on her wedding day. Stuart now remembered she had walked down the aisle alone.

"I am sorry."

"It is quite alright. Please have a drink," she said, gesturing towards the table where glasses of fruity mead had been poured. Stuart took one out of politeness and smiled, he had abstained from alcohol shortly after his eighteenth birthday, said his thanks and walked over to where Basil and Eric were talking amongst friends. On his way over to them he regarded the garden. Barrels of beer had been set up in the shade and a man in a white apron was spinning a pig slowly on a spit over some coals. Family members and close friends mixed with soldiers, the garden was alive with laughter and celebration.

Stuart gently elbowed his way into the group chaired by Green. Basil, Eric and the remainder listening intently to Green's story about another wedding he had attended.

"Is that a drink in your hand?" asked Basil with an inquisitive frown. Stuart had forgotten he was holding it.

"Ah yes, I couldn't bring myself to say no. Especially after saying it would be nice to talk with Mrs Sewell's father who it turns out is dead," Basil winced and Green smiled as he patted his arm.

"You won't be wanting this then?" said Eric taking the glass from Stuart.

"All yours E but be careful, you don't want to embarrass yourself in front of the battalion this early on."

"Relax old man."

"Well not too much. We don't need another Christmas Eve 1913," joked Stuart, a wide smile at Eric.

"Bugger off!"

"I sense a story," said Davison, running a hand through his thick dark hair. Basil jumped in immediately to tell the story of the time Eric had drunk too much and stumbled into the wrong house on their road, falling asleep at the wrong kitchen table.

The afternoon drifted along splendidly in the sun and the garden became one swaying sea of happiness and conversation. The day remained warm and bees, humming furiously, were gorging themselves on the wild flowers in the hedge. A cool breeze would lift on occasions and provide welcome relief.

After a short while, Sewell came over to their group, a young lady by his side. She looked shy and small next to Sewell's lanky frame and had removed her hat to reveal curly brown hair that floated down around her shoulders. Eric saw them approach so stood tall, Stuart noticed Eric's eye wander and turned around to see Sewell a few yards away, looking directly at him.

"Good afternoon, sir, you've certainly been lucky with such a lovely day," said Stuart looking up at the sun.

"Indeed it is, Corporal Hanham." Sewell nodded at the others who had stopped their conversation.

"Corporal Hanham, this is Miss Emily Church. She is my wife's cousin and their fathers practised law together. She is also the granddaughter of the lovely lady you escorted from the service." Sewell pointed through the crowd to a picnic bench where the old woman sat, enjoying the shade and a long drink. She waved at Stuart and gestured them over.

Stuart waved back and then turned his attention to Emily who was looking straight at him, her eyes wide and kind. "A pleasure to meet you Miss Church, what a wonderful grandmother you have. I very much enjoyed her company, brief though it was."

"And she yours, Mr Hanham, she has not stopped talking about you," said Emily, gently shaking Stuart's hand. Stuart looked directly at her, one eye bluer than even his and the other bright green. He didn't know which one to look at, he was memorised by both. His body was tight in teenage shock.

"Well I didn't say much and please, call me Stuart,"

"Emily is a very knowledgeable lady when it comes to the law, I said you might be the only man here able to keep her attention." Sewell had a soft spot for Stuart and great respect.

"Well I don't know about that, sir, but I will try my best." Stuart was embarrassed by his praise. Sewell smiled and looked around to answer a call from his wife.

"I shall have to leave you now, look after him Emily." Sewell turned to the others, "Food will be ready shortly chaps."

There was moment of silence as Emily turned to the group of soldiers stood there. Stuart took charge, "Emily may I introduce to you Basil, Hamish, Alfred, Eric and John. We are all in Mr Sewell's Platoon." She smiled and delicately shook hands with them all. Emily then looked at Eric and Stuart and then to Eric again. She had noticed the same brown hair and signature Hanham family bags under each bright blue eye, they also had a similar athletic build and strong jaw line.

"Are you two related?"

Eric laughed. "Yes, Miss Church I am afraid we are, though I am the younger more attractive version."

"If you say so," said Emily with a wide smile. Her comment was greeted with hoots and cheers from the small crowd of men now slightly intoxicated by ale and sun. Stuart laughed and gently laid a big hand on Emily's back.

"This gentleman is also my brother and he's the best of us all," said Stuart with a sincere smile guiding her to Basil.

"Ah yes, I can see the resemblance. You all have the same eyes." Basil gave a shy smile.

"Miss Church, what relation did you say you were to the bride and groom?" asked Green.

"I am Mary's cousin, we grew up together and that's our grandmother." She pointed towards the shade and the old woman still sat on her own. She waved her over once more, so Emily turned back to Stuart and grabbed his arm, Stuart tried to flex his muscles slowly inside his tunic. "Speaking of whom I must return to her, but she said I was to bring you too. I think you made quite an impression." She looked at him encouragingly, flirting. Stuart's heart rate increased, and he felt his stomach tighten.

"Well we mustn't keep her waiting," Stuart held out his arm for her. Emily linked her arm immediately and they strode over to the table in the shade.

"Nice to meet you, gentlemen," said Emily, leaning back towards the group of men left silent by her departure.

At three o'clock a photographer arrived and set up his camera in front of a hedge still bright green and thick with leaves, its wild flowers a ceremonious white. Stuart had walked over arm in arm with Emily, they had been talking excitedly about life, politics and law. The spell of the wedding combined with the heat of late summer ignited in Stuart a fire that would never stop burning and as they walked to where the photograph was to be taken Stuart knew this woman would change him forever.

A few days later Eric bought a postcard of the photograph taken that day and sent it home to Eva.

> '*Dear Mater,*
>
> *Thank you for your letter just received, I was glad to have it, and thanks for the socks. I am writing you a letter as soon as I can get time. We three boys are in this photo, which I will explain later. Stuart looks pleased about something, doesn't he? I am glad that K is home at last, she will be good company for you. Take care of yourself and God bless you Mater,*
>
> > *Your affectionate son, Eric.*'

76 Amesbury Avenue – 20th September 1914

SEPTEMBER had turned wet and cold, the sunshine of the last few days a distant memory. Green leaves still adorned the trees but in places they had started to turn brown and gold with the onset of autumn and the rain was heavy as Eva hurried the last hundred yards to the safety of home. She opened the door and fought with her umbrella before finally getting over the threshold and allowing herself an exaggerated sigh. She looked down at the hem of her dress and at her shoes, they were filthy and wet.

"You look like you could do with a cup of tea, Mother," said Kathleen, watching the saga unfold. Eva looked up in fright, she hadn't expected her home.

"I thought you had rehearsals today, dear?"

"I did but the director was very happy with our two sessions this morning and a few of the cast were a little unwell. He didn't want to push them with big numbers expected tonight."

"I see, well that's good," Eva removed her damp hat and jacket.

"So, a cup of tea?"

Eva looked at Kathleen, her head tilted and shoulders slumped in fatigue. "Yes please, thank you dear."

A short while later Eva entered the kitchen in dry clothes with her damp grey hair tied up in a tight bun. Kathleen was sat at the table reading Saturday's paper smoking a cigarette. She said nothing as Eva sat down beside her and poured herself a cup of tea from the pot Kathleen had prepared. "I do wish you wouldn't smoke those things dear, they are not lady-like."

"You sound like all the so-called *gentlemen* in the city." Kathleen did not look up from her paper but took another confident pull from her cigarette.

"Well I am sorry but on this one rare occasion I am inclined to agree with them, and I am allowed to be old-fashioned now and again."

"I suppose."

They sat in silence for a short while. Eva had her hand cupped around her tea, enjoying the warmth. She was now in her fifties and her circulation was poor.

"It says here we are doing well over there. Says we are halting the German's with ease, despite their numbers," said Kathleen, extinguishing her cigarette in a small glass ashtray. She folded the paper and laid it down in front of her, leant back in her chair and reached for her cup of tea. Eva didn't answer and Kathleen could tell she didn't want to talk about politics or the war, but she felt strangely empty of other subjects, head still freshly filled with what she had read in the paper. She bludgeoned through. "Probably be over by the time the boys get out there." She took a drink from her tea. There was a time she would have changed the subject or endured the silence, but Kathleen was a grown woman now so would talk about what she liked. Still silence from her mother, eyes fixed on the table, cold and unflinching.

Eva remained hauntingly silent, there was no acknowledgement of what Kathleen had said so a stalemate evolved around the table, old matriarch and eldest daughter in a battle for conversational supremacy. The moments ticked by slowly and the grandfather clock in the hall added to the tension by chiming its hourly song. It rang deep in the heart of Kathleen who had endured enough of her mother's game, "So how was church?" she asked, defeated.

Eva's fixed gaze broke. She leant back in her chair placing the cup onto its saucer. "It was lovely dear but the rain was hammering so hard on the roof the poor reverend had to stop and wait for a moment to be heard."

"Is this at St Paul's?"

"No dear, I went to St Mark's today. St Paul's is too far to go every week, especially in this weather. You should come with me sometime."

"I will, Mother, but I was working this morning. These Sunday evening performances are getting really rather popular."

"I understand. Have you any extra speaking parts now?"

"No but I'm enjoying this role. It is challenging in other ways and I am on stage quite a lot. Besides, I have an audition next week for a revue put on by George Graves. If I get that it will be more pay and more performances in a much bigger theatre."

"Oh wonderful, well good luck."

Silence filled the room.

"Did you send Eric a letter for his birthday?" asked Eva.

"Of course, I write to them whenever I can. You know I was just looking at this ashtray, I think I bought this for him on his birthday a couple of years ago," said Kathleen, spinning the ashtray on the table.

"Yes, I seem to remember you did." Eva paused, "Do you know if the Boundfords wrote to him?"

Eva was looking directly at her daughter with a wide grin across her face, she was attempting to extract information about Kathleen's relationship with Howard and at the sound of his name Kathleen turned her head sharply to her mother, eyes open wide with embarrassment.

When she saw her mother looking at her knowingly, smile wide across her face, she wished she had been calmer and more reserved in her reaction.

Kathleen flushed deep pink, looked away and Eva laughed. Kathleen stood up and took her cup to the sink and started to laugh with her mother, there seemed to be no hiding it now, but she attempted to gain some balance. "I don't know, you shall have to ask when you see them next."

"I suppose I shall," said Eva, her laughter ceasing. "But do be careful dear, that boy has always been trouble."

Kathleen placed her cup and saucer in the rack to dry and turned towards her mother. "Well people do change. Anyway, I have to go back to the theatre now, you'll be ok for the rest of the day?"

"Of course I will." Eva looked shocked by the question.

Kathleen walked behind her mother towards the front door but stopped on the higher of the stone steps leading out of the kitchen. She turned around slowly and saw Eva had tilted her head to read the headlines of the paper folded on the table. "You know, Mother, you'll have to talk about it sometime. You cannot ignore the war until they return."

Kathleen did not wait for a response, instead she headed out into the pouring rain.

*

Kathleen walked through the front door of 76 shortly after midnight, the rain had ceased, and the air was humid and close. She sat on the stairs to remove her shoes, her feet were tired, hot and swollen from dancing and walking. She placed her shoes on the rack, leant back with a sigh, wiped the sticky hair from her brow and took a cigarette from her waistcoat pocket. Retrieving the matches from her jacket, she struck one that lit the dark hallway.

"How was the show?" asked Eva from a chair in the dining room. Kathleen dropped the match and the cigarette fell from her mouth, she yelped in shock and put her hand on her chest to soothe her racing heart.

"Goodness Mother! You scared the life out of me," said Kathleen, gathering her nerves and picking up the cigarette that had landed on her lap. "What are you still doing up?"

"I wanted to speak to you, I didn't mean to frighten you."

"Well, sitting in the dark quietly and calling out like that will have that effect on a person."

Kathleen walked into the room and turned on the light. It cast a soft orange glow and as she turned to look at her mother, she could see Eva had been drinking scotch. Kathleen sat in the chair beside Eva and attempted again to light her cigarette. She took a big smoky breath and sunk into the chair. Eva slid her a glass and Kathleen poured herself a drink.

"So, what did you want to talk about? Am I in trouble?" She looked at her mother sarcastically. Eva took a deep breath.

"Do you remember me telling you about the time I fell into the loch when I was just a girl?"

"Yes, yes. Your mother saved you."

"Well that day changed me. I had always believed the world was a powerful place and that we who walk upon it are capable of extraordinary things with our mind." Kathleen said nothing, focused now on the smoke twisting in the still air. She thought her mother was drunk, rambling again. Eva continued. "…That day when I fell in the loch I spoke to my mother, not with my mouth or my voice but with my mind and my heart." Kathleen noticed tears roll down her mother's face as Eva recalled feelings of distress and the pain of icy water. "…My mother couldn't have heard me because I was too cold and afraid to speak but she sensed something and turned to me even though no sound reached her." Eva paused, wiped the tears from her eyes and took another drink from her glass now nearly empty, tawny gold in the soft light.

Kathleen regarded her mother. She looked so old, so grey, her face was fat and round and her hair was a dark mess with long streaks of silver. She seemed hunched and feeble.

"Go on."

"Well, my mother would never admit to it, but we were able to reach one another that day telepathically." Kathleen laughed. "I knew you wouldn't believe me, your father never did, but I want you to understand or at least just hear what I have to say."

"Fine." Kathleen suddenly thought her mother might not be as drunk as she had first thought.

"It is what I believe, and I have the same strange feelings with Basil. I know instinctively when he is sick or in pain. When he fell out of the tree aged seven, I knew he was hurt before I even heard the screams and saw the tears." Eva took another drink from her glass, finishing it easily. Kathleen thought for a moment and took another draw on her cigarette.

"Just Basil?" There was a tinge on jealousy in her question and she felt for herself, Stella and the other two boys.

"I love you all the same and I shall worry just as much about Eric and Stuart but he's the only one I have that bond with. You and Stella are so different to me and Stuart and Eric so much more like your father. Basil's illness as a child and him being the youngest have forged a link between us. That's all."

Eva looked deep into her daughter's eyes, but Kathleen looked away like she was being disciplined.

"So, the thought of Basil and my boys going off to war, where men aren't just being hurt but being killed, is torture for me and if Basil feels pain or gets hit, then so do I." Eva leant back in her chair and focused on the window across from her and the quiet darkness outside.

Kathleen sat in silence and took a couple of final pulls from her cigarette before finishing her scotch in one. She had never thought what it must be like to be a mother and have such a bond with a child and she had not contemplated how hard it would be to see your own three boys going off to fight and wait quietly at home for any news. To her they were brothers and she assumed they would be all right. They were strong and courageous but so were all the others going off to fight and some had to be killed, it was the nature of war. It suddenly hit her in that moment that they may not come home. Tears fell silently down her cheeks.

Eva stood slowly, using the wooden arms of her chair to haul herself to her feet. She steadied herself and walked out of the room silently.

Kathleen sat for a while alone. She looked at her packet of cigarettes and thought about having another. Instead she let her mind process the idea of being able to feel and know when your children had been hurt or worse. She wondered what that would be like and for a moment she believed it possible. After all, her mother, who she respected and loved more than anyone, believed it so why shouldn't it be true? Maybe it was possible to know telepathically the pain of others, particularly if you were the one who gave them life. Her grandmother had felt it when Eva had fallen into the loch and so perhaps there was some hereditary gift. It was too much for Kathleen to think about this late, she was emotional and fatigued. She closed her eyes and sunk into the chair where heavy sleep engulfed her.

Abbots Langley, Hertfordshire – 3rd November 1914

REVEILLE sounded at five o'clock and was met by groans and cursing from men who had been dreaming of places far away. It was a cold morning, so Eric struggled to detach himself from the warm air of his blanket and was quick to change into his uniform once he had braved the chill. He and the rest of the men then rolled their blankets up and took them down to the classroom of the school that had been made into the company store.

It was only a short march to the mess tent, a familiar one they had completed almost every day for the last ten weeks, so it was conducted in silence. Only the sounds of the crunching gravel under their feet, the squeaking of boots and a sporadic cough, sneeze or noisy shiver ran through them. It was crisp and the stars were only just fading in the purple morning sky, breath from the men filled the air as they halted just before the entrance to the mess tent. It was blissfully quiet until someone from the middle of the company farted loudly. His comedy timing impeccable, it started the men laughing and Eric, like his comrades, was now fully awake.

After a breakfast of bacon, scrambled eggs and coffee, the company assembled again to march back to their billets. The slowly rising sun had chased away the last remaining stars and the bright horizon to the east promised a sunny morning. Eric washed and shaved quickly and was rewarded with the task of watching over the rifles and packs stacked neatly outside while the others cleaned the part of the old school that had been home these past months of training. He sat on his pack, lit a cigarette and took in his surroundings. It was still cold outside and there was a frost clinging to the shaded areas around the school, the sun had risen higher in the sky and its rays hit the grand clock tower in the centre of the building. The bricks shone in the morning light and areas of roof that had frosted were now moist and glistening in the sun.

Eric couldn't help but feel slightly nostalgic about leaving this place. Today they may be heading off on the great adventure, but he had enjoyed his time here. He was a natural soldier and his wit, sense of humour and intelligence had made him popular with all the men in his Platoon and Company. His brothers had helped him fit in, but he was confident he had carved his own path, happy amongst his new friends.

Lost in thought, Eric failed to notice Captain Dickens, Officer Commanding A Company, and the Platoon Commanders arrive at the entrance of their billet. "Morning Private Hanham," said Dickens, his young, handsome features did not reflect his rank and authority.

Eric, caught off guard, cigarette smoking, sprung to attention and saluted the group of officers, "Morning, sirs!"

"Away with gods there, Hanham?"

"Just marvelling at the building, sir, I've so enjoyed my time training and preparing for the fight I thought it only right I took a moment to say thanks," replied Eric. He knew how to play the game. Any mention of 'King and country' or 'relish for the fight' when caught in a sticky situation would, more often than not, get him out of trouble. Dickens smiled and returned his salute before walking inside. Eric sat down again on his pack and retrieved the cigarette from the floor, pleased to see it was still lit.

After the billet had been assessed as clean, A Company paraded outside but this time the parade was more formal and Company Sergeant

Major Hockley took charge. As the officers came out of the building Hockley brought the men to attention for Dickens to address them.

"Well done, men, that was the smooth departure we had hoped for. I suppose all those dress rehearsals have been of some use." There was a slight ripple of laughter but most groaned in annoyance. The many false alarms in setting off and cancelled orders had angered them all over time. "But I can say with some confidence that this time we are really heading off." Eric smiled at Basil stood next to him and there was an excited cheer. "...And when we do get the chance to show our worth, I know we will. The London Scottish have recently conducted a glorious charge towards the enemy, they have suffered heavy losses and I hope we should do the same." A confused silence descended as Dickens turned towards Hockley. "Sergeant Major march the men down to the alarm post for an address from the Commanding Officer," ordered Dickens formally, unaware of any faux pas.

"As you wish, sir," replied Hockley.

As the officers walked away Eric noticed one of the platoon commanders explain to Dickens what he had said. Dickens turned on his heels and shouted back to the gathered men. "You know what I mean, men!"

"We do indeed, sir," said Hockley, attempting to help.

"You'd think he'd be better with words given his heritage," said someone behind Eric and it received a laugh. Captain Dickens was the grandson of Charles Dickens and a very popular officer who had the welfare of his men at heart.

"Quiet now!" snapped Hockley with a furrowed brow, the big black moustache on his face growled with him.

*

A Company arrived on parade last and took their place in the battalion square. Shortly before half past seven the Regimental Sergeant Major marched smartly out into the middle of the square.

"Looks like we might actually be off this time," whispered Eric to Basil. Basil tried to acknowledge Eric without moving or speaking, annoyed that Eric seemed not to be taking it seriously. The Regimental Sergeant Major bought the battalion to attention, the cold air and still morning added sharpness to his voice as the Commanding Officer marched to the front to address his battalion.

"I can confirm that I have received the order for the Kensington Battalion to deploy this morning." A cheer came from the men and some, including Eric, foolishly threw their hats in the air. "We have always been known as a disciplined battalion and I hope you will ensure that reputation continues, though I must stress we might have some unattractive work to do. But I know you will take on any challenge set before you with the good grace you have shown thus far. God be with us all." A cheer rang out again.

A and B Company had orders to board the train in Watford at eleven o'clock, it was a rush for them to get themselves prepared to march away at nine. Stuart, inheriting the role of primary letter writer to Eva, managed to write one informing his mother they were all well. At nine o'clock they stepped out from the school yard into the streets of Abbots Langley for the last time. For nearly three months they had been a familiar sight here and were made to feel most welcome. Villagers would stop in the street to watch them pass by on physical training marches or with full packs off to conduct tactical exercises in the surrounding countryside. Khaki clad young men swinging their arms in time with the rhythmic crunch of army boots down autumnal lanes would not quickly be forgotten by residents.

As the band played and the battalion marched through the town Stuart saw Wilkie, a young lad of ten who had helped the men of A Company run errands during their time here, standing outside the hardware store. Stuart handed him four letters he had written earlier for Wilkie to post and tipped his cap to the young man who had sadness in his eyes.

"Four letters?" asked Eric with a grin, nudging Stuart's arm as they marched. He looked quizzically to the sky and counted his fingers. "So that's Mother, K, Stella and…" Eric touched his chin comically and then smiled at Stuart.

"Very funny, old man. You just concentrate on keeping the step" said Stuart, but the image of Emily had entered his mind. With the band in full swing, his brothers by his side and the cheering crowds lining the streets Stuart allowed himself to recall the wonderful few months she had been in his life. How quickly they had fallen in love and how now the world seemed brighter, his purpose obvious. During a recent furlough, they had talked about marriage and excitedly discussed moving to Canada and starting a farm on cheap land the Canadian government was offering western settlers in Saskatchewan and Alberta. The breaking world around them had shaken loose a soul mate and now he couldn't imagine life without her and was desperate not to be separated. The adventure the war had been was now a horrid inconvenience and he resented the way it tore him away from his new love.

Andrew Wood

*

The Kensingtons left Abbots Langley and made their way slowly towards Watford Station. Stuart, among others, noticed the pace was slow and not the normal marching rhythm they were used to. The officers leading realised a little too late which meant the final two miles were set at an uncomfortably fast pace to ensure they made the train. Even the strongest in the ranks were sweating profusely and felt their packs grow heavier. The arrival at the station and boarding of the train with ten minutes to spare was a blessed relief.

As the train jolted into motion Basil, with his back towards the direction of travel, looked out the window and Eric lit a cigarette from the pack in his tunic.

"Do you want one, B?" Basil took a cigarette without a word and Eric lit it with a match.

"How long do you think it will take Basil?" asked one of their friends from the bench opposite.

"A few hours, I should think."

"A few hours of sleep then boys," said Eric laying his head back and blowing smoke into the empty space above his head.

"Some boys are way ahead of you, Eric," said another Kensington sat opposite. Eric looked around at the men already asleep, mouths wide open against their packs, bench frames and windows. He smiled and turned back to Basil who was still staring out into the world sailing past. Eric noticed his blank stare.

"Are you ok, B? You're very quiet," Basil's stare was broken by the question. He took a moment to adjust and noticed his brother looking at him in concern. Suddenly he remembered the question as if it had taken time to stick in his mind.

"I'm fine, just tired." He took one last draw from his cigarette and stamped it out on the carriage floor. "Just tired," he said again lowering the peak of his cap over his eyes and adjusting his position to lean on the wooden frame of the window. In the same movement he opened his elbows so that his arm lay reassuringly on top of Eric's. He closed his eyes and tried to sleep. Eric adjusted his position, so his head was resting on Basil's shoulder, pulled his hat down over his eyes and slept easily.

Stuart was in the next carriage along. It was smaller and darker, had fewer windows and the wood fittings were a stale brown, but the seats were padded with red leather. Stuart thought it might once have been first class but now it was dusty and old it seemed fitting for the group of soldiers occupying it. Stuart, sat facing two other corporals, had a long seat to himself, their rifles were on the floor under their feet and their large packs provided comfortable foot rests. On the far side of the carriage there was long seat that stretched ten metres from door to door and it was along this the remaining six occupants tried to make themselves comfortable.

Stuart was unable to sleep so he watched England pass by as they made their way through Willesden Junction, Addison Road, Richmond, Twickenham, Staines and out into the countryside. He marvelled at the people he saw conducting their daily business, some seemed shocked to see a train full of troops at their platform as if unaware Britain was knee deep in an already costly war. He envied their lives, their ignorance and their blank faces made his adventure seem insignificant. Stuart let his mind drift to thoughts of his mother, his sisters and of home but mostly he thought of Emily. Their goodbye had been the hardest for him and he felt he hadn't lived nearly enough of a life with her. He had only a few memories of his new love and that small number troubled him. He wanted more, he wanted a lifetime of them. Stuart needed to focus his mind on other things so went to go and find his brothers in the next carriage.

Shuffling through into the next car Stuart received some angry looks from soldiers trying to sleep. He saw that in here too the men had given up on the benches and opted for the cool stability of the carriage floor where they resembled lions sprawled out after a feast. He looked over and saw Basil leant on his pack, staring blankly out of the window and Eric on his shoulder, sound asleep with his mouth open like a trap. Stuart stepped carefully over to the bench opposite his brothers, its previous occupants had also vacated it in favour of the floor. He jumped the last foot and lifted his feet up onto the bench under his chin, back against the window and the Hampshire countryside speeding past.

Basil looked up at him and raised his eyebrows in acknowledgement. "Who's your friend?" asked Stuart nodding towards Eric who had released a long line of drool from his mouth onto Basil's tunic.

"Ah for fuck's sake, E!" said Basil pulling his arm from under Eric's head. Eric nearly fell onto the floor and had to use the man resting under his feet to stop himself from sliding off the bench. The man below him growled as Eric sat up and wiped his chin.

"What's all that about?"

"You've made a mess all over my arm," said Basil, pointing out the line of damp along the pressed edge of his tunic. Eric wiped his face and rubbed his eyes.

"Stupid bony shoulders anyway, it's like sleeping on a gate."

"Well it seemed to work for you."

Stuart laughed and Eric stretched his arms high in the air and clicked the vertebrae in his neck with two powerful movements of his head. The three boys were silent for a short while. Basil took a packet of cigarettes out of his pocket and offered one to Eric who accepted. He offered one to Stuart, but he waved it away, Eric lit Basil's cigarette and then his own.

"I bet you'll be drinking and smoking by Christmas," said Eric with a smile, blowing smoke towards Stuart.

"Ah before then," said Basil, doing the same. Stuart waved the smoke from around his face with his hat.

"Well some of us actually have some restraint," replied Stuart.

"Is that so?" asked Eric, lowering his head and looking through his eyebrows menacingly.

"Yes, that is so."

"Ok." Eric nodded and savoured the moment by taking a long, dramatic draw on his cigarette. "So how was the lovely Miss Church?"

Stuart blushed red with mention of Emily and placed his hat over his face as Basil started to laugh.

"Will you lot shut the fuck up!" said one of the men lying on the bench behind them. Eric looked over to see who it was then, confident it wasn't a senior rank, leant over and pinched the man's ear lobe between the nails on his forefinger and thumb.

"Ah! Fuck off, Hanham!"

"Relax, old chum, we are nearly there," said Eric, returning to his seat. Stuart stood up and made his way over sleeping bodies back to his carriage. Playfully he knocked Eric's khaki cap from his head as he passed.

*

Southampton dockyard was a hive of activity when the boys arrived. Soldiers and sailors were working together to get men, horses and vehicles onto ships. Messages were shouted from high up on deck to men on the dock and relayed to a large building, the apparent brain of the operation. Smartly dressed men inside this central hub handed pieces of paper to shabbily dressed sailors who would sprint away with the orders. Many of the horses, nervous about their first trip to sea and war, were rearing up and sounding their displeasure at having to walk up flimsy gangways and into the holds of large unfamiliar vessels. Some had left steaming dung heaps along the main routes that soldiers, marching as a formed body, struggled to avoid. Eric commented how pleased he was that he had only his pack and rifle to look after and not any large, powerful animals too.

The Kensingtons turned onto wharf number three where a naval man pointed them towards a huge ship moored. As they neared the great steamer the boys could see men on deck hauling large ropes, boxes of equipment and provisions. The great rump of the ship towered above them and the boys felt insignificant in her presence. Written across the black stern in shining gold lettering was her name, *S.S. Matheran*. A giant iron beast, long but elegant with one large funnel painted white from base to tip except for a band of black a few feet wide at the top where dense smoke was exhaled in long menacing breaths. This would be the giant lady that carried the boys to foreign lands, an adventure like no other. All the men were hushed in respect as they ascended the flimsy gangways flexing under their weight.

At ten o'clock roll call was conducted aboard S.S. Matheran and the men were dismissed until the next morning when they would be served breakfast of tea and biscuits on deck. Most disappeared to find the best place to lie down and sleep, but Stuart left the warmth of the lower decks to head out into the night. As soon as he emerged into the cold night air, he regretted not unpacking his greatcoat, the hassle of re-packing had seemed not worth the effort, but the air on deck was bitterly cold and his breath hung still in the eerie darkness. He looked around and saw a few men and officers in small groups smoking and others were alone writing letters and diary entries in the peace provided by the cold. He noticed Sergeant Major Hockley wandering around menacingly, he was carrying a rifle and bandoleers of ammunition which Stuart had not seen before, usually the Company Sergeant Major carried just a stick and he hadn't reckoned he needed much more than that even in battle. Seeing this hulking man with his weapon and ammunition was a thudding reality check, he took a deep, stinging breath to compose himself.

Stuart made his way over to the railings on the starboard side of the ship and looked down at the water. It was a dense, ominous black and still like a pond in summer. He could see clearly the reflection of the moon and stars and the lights from another ship only fifty metres across the water. Still leaning hard on the cold metal, he lifted his head to look at the ship opposite and immediately caught the eyes of an enormous Indian soldier. His turban exaggerated his great height and his shoulders were broad under his battered tunic. He had a dense black beard and his eyes were burning gold like that of a leopard. His left arm was tight in a white sling, mottled black in the moonlight with the dark crimson of his blood. It was clear he had been recently wounded.

The Indian stood there smoking a cheroot and for a moment Stuart thought he hadn't been seen until the Indian nodded in his direction. Stuart twisted left and right to make sure he was the intended recipient and when sure he was the gesture was returned. The huge man then flicked his burning cheroot into the dark water, turned and walked away. Stuart watched him until he disappeared into the darkness.

"Tough bloody bastards those lads," said a voice from behind him. It was deep and resonated through Stuart like the base drum of a marching band. He turned slowly to see the Regimental Sergeant Major, looking out over the water at the hospital ship, eyes still fixed on the lights as he took a long draw from his cigarette.

"I'm sorry, sir?" The RSM looked at him, eyes snake black under his hat. All soldiers were supposed to be afraid of him and Stuart certainly was at that moment.

"The Indians, boy, bloody tough soldiers and don't let anyone convince you otherwise." It felt like an order.

"Yes, sir." Stuart straightened up from his hunched position on the rail.

"Have you served with them, sir?"

The RSM walked into the soft light being emitted from the bridge and turned to lean on the railings a few feet from Stuart. He was carrying a rifle and bandoleers. Stuart felt sorry for anyone in the opposing army that came across him in battle.

"I did, Hanham," Stuart was happy he knew who he was. "In South Africa. They are tough bastards I can tell you. I almost feel sorry for the Hun that comes face to face with one of them on a dark night. Tough bastards indeed." The RSM took another exaggerated pull from his cigarette then flicked it over his shoulder into the water. Stuart watched it land and heard the hiss as it hit the mirror surface of the sea.

The RSM turned and eyed Stuart, "Go and get your fucking greatcoat on if you're going to stand up here, Hanham! The last thing we need is a good man like you getting sick when it can be avoided. You need to set the example. Do you understand?"

Stuart tried his best not to smile at the compliment bestowed on him, but he failed and let out a twitchy grin. "Yes, sir."

When he reached the stairs to the lower decks, he looked back to see the RSM leaning over the side of the ship looking at the water like he had been moments before. He wondered what that man was thinking and would have paid handsomely for just a small glimpse into his mind.

*

Shortly before midnight the engine rumble grew loud and increased vibrations could be felt throughout the ship, the great lady was waking and would soon be set to sea. Eric woke to the sound and nudged Basil who was lying next to him. His first attempt to wake him received an annoyed grunt but the second more of a reaction, Eric's last jab had hurt.

"What?" said Basil in anger, twisting his shoulders to look at Eric.

"Don't you want see her cast off?" Basil said nothing but rubbed his eyes and prepared his body for movement, the cold floor was hard and it had made his young joints stiff. While Basil was getting up, Eric walked over to the other side of the room where Stuart had found a small place to stretch out. He reached down to nudge him awake but Stuart spoke before he could.

"I heard you, E," it shocked Eric a little.

"Good man." Eric returned to his kit and collected his rifle as Basil was packing away his greatcoat.

"You'll need that, B. It is bloody cold out there and the RSM gave me an ear full earlier for not wearing mine on deck." Basil nodded and removed the coat from his pack. Eric already had his on and was buttoning up the front.

Stuart, Eric and Basil headed up the three sets of metal stairs to the open deck where the air was freezing on their warm faces, steel rivets on their boots clanking and scratching on the iron walkways. Once on deck they saw that a lot of men had come up to wave goodbye to England and they received friendly nods as they looked for space to sit. They found an area on a few crates over-looking the port side and jumped up onto them, their backs against another crate of the same size stacked up double behind. Eric fumbled in his pocket and produced a packet of cigarettes and handed one to Basil who had sat in the middle. They looked out in silence at the docks that seemed to be as alive now as they were during the daylight hours but on board the ship it felt peaceful. The night was still and the blanket of cold around them made them feel invisible.

Eric slouched casually with his head back, looking up at the stars, his rifle was laid across his lap. A cigarette was hanging from his lips and he smoked it without using his hands. Basil had his knees up under his nose, greatcoat over his legs like a heavy dress. He was looking down at the dock and the men scurrying around, shouting commands and raising their hands to signal the completion of a task. He felt superior to them, he was off to war and they were not. Stuart sat to the right of Basil, his rifle propped up behind him next to Basil's, he had one leg dangling over the crate on which he sat and the other pulled up towards him. He was looking straight out towards the open sea while fiddling with a button on his greatcoat.

The three brothers sat there in silence until twenty-five minutes after midnight when the ship started to roar with the promise of movement. They had got used to her noise, so it was a shock to hear her raise the volume and the vibrations increase under them.

"We must be getting off now," said Eric, as the shouting from the men on the dock increased in ferocity and their movements hurried. A senior sailor came over and stood in front of the boys. He took a long look down at the dock and along the whole length of the ship. He extended his right hand to the men below with thumb raised in thanks and then turned and looked up to the bridge. His face was stoic and professional, but he smiled when he saw the three boys sat there quietly.

S.S. Matheran then let out a steaming shrill and there was a cheer from the men who had come up on the deck to watch her sail away. Eric raised his arm and put it around Basil's slight shoulders in the patronising way only an older brother can.

"That's it now, B, off for the fight," said Eric through gritted teeth.

It made Basil feel small and weak, so he shrugged him off and stretched out his body from under him, no longer tucked up like a child. The air was cold against his legs that had been warm under his coat.

The ship lurched slowly to starboard and then righted herself as she moved slowly and smoothly from the wharf. A lot of the men had come over to the port side to wave down at the dockworkers and sailors who were waving back to them with enthusiasm. Matheran made smooth, steady progress through Southampton Water until she turned west around the Isle of Wight. The water of the Solent felt slightly different below, but she chugged along gracefully, a steady rumble from her depths. The boys, now awake with the excitement of departure, were talking excitedly with no thought of any harrowing reality. Even Stuart, who was now in love and had an exciting new life planned after the war, got lost in boisterous conversation. Like all soldiers they did not imagine anything bad would happen to them.

"What do you think Mother is up to now?" asked Basil.

Stuart checked his pocket watch, "She'll be fast asleep, snoring the house down and keeping K awake." Eric and Basil laughed, their breath in the air like smoke.

"Depends how much she's had to drink," said Eric, still laughing.

Stuart nodded and smiled, "God love her."

The laughter died down and Eric turned his head to Basil. "Come on then, B, get your fags out," said Eric, nudging his younger brother.

"Last two," said Basil. He showed Eric his empty packet and screwed it into a ball before dropping it on the floor. Immediately it caught in the wind and spiralled gracefully away towards the end of the ship but before it could sail out to sea it struck an officer in the cheek. He rubbed his face and turn to the boys with a frown.

"Sorry sir!" said Basil apologetically as the officer turned away. Stuart started to laugh. In his fatigue he found the moment hysterical. Eric and Basil looked at him confused for a few moments, but Stuart's continued laughter became infectious and their faces broke into smiles.

Matheran continued west alongside Hurst Castle and then south past the Needles. Out to the east was the ghostly silhouette of an escorting destroyer. As she turned slowly towards France the boys got up from their seat and found a space towards the stern. Stood together, the Hanham brothers watched the brilliant white of the Needles and their last glimpse of home fade away in the darkness. The glowing wake of the S.S. Matheran trailed ominously behind.

Andrew Wood

Camden Town, London – 10ᵗʰ November 1914

KATHLEEN was early for her audition so wandered across the road to buy a cup of tea. A young girl in a dirty black apron smiled sweetly, Kathleen forced a smile back before finding a seat by the window. Her day had not started well, and she cursed the long journey on the underground and a bus from 76 when some of her previous dwellings were just around the corner. She had to remind herself that staying with her mother while the boys were away was for the best.

Taking a pleasing sip from her tea she focused her attention on the theatre entrance. Posters for a *George Graves Production Coming Soon* were plastered all over the large red door, overlapping each other clumsily. In the panelled windows above, sections of broken glass had been boarded and the strings of lights around the building edges looked old, wire sagging in places. Rusty gutters had left orange-brown stains from fixings on the once white walls. She hoped the theatre was grander inside and imagined it was, George Graves was a big name on the London stage scene so surely wouldn't choose a rotten place for one of his revues. Shabby building or not, Kathleen wanted to be a part of this show so when the time came for her audition she strode confidently across the road as if someone was watching. She pulled open the heavy door and it took a moment for her eyes to adjust to the dim lighting inside. The carpet was bright red and the entrance was bigger and grander than she had imagined. In front of her were curved steps draped tightly in the same bold carpet, pinned at the base by thin brass runners. She walked up the stairs and the foyer opened out further. It was wider than she thought looking in from the street and it bordered on magnificent.

Frosted glass advertising mounted in light oak frames guided the way towards two regal box offices, either side of which were big brass turn styles. She liked the place immediately.

Kathleen walked towards the box offices in the hope someone would be there to guide her through to where she needed to be, but they were empty and the floor inside each was a mess of tickets stubs and golden cigarette ends. She pushed through the turn styles and saw a chalk sign saying *Three Sisters Auditions*, a white arrow pointed towards a felt lined door to the right. She opened the door into a dark passage way and followed the slopping corridor to the sounds coming from the end of the hallway. As she neared a set of stairs, she noticed some double doors had been left slightly ajar. A girl could be heard singing from the other side of them along with the heavy wooden crash of her dancing feet on the stage. Kathleen peeked through the doorway and saw her on stage performing, she was tall with blonde hair and her long skinny limbs were being thrown around gracefully. Kathleen watched for a moment, recognising the choreography she was about to attempt, before continuing towards the stairs. At the top there was a heavy curtain she pulled to one side.

Beyond the curtain it was bright and loud, she was adjacent to the stage and could feel the vibrations of the dancing woman through the boards and her voice echoed around the open space behind the stage. A man in a white shirt and grey waistcoat, leant up against a supporting pillar just out of view from the gallery, looked at Kathleen with a blank, emotionless expression. She froze as the man raised a finger to his pursed lips then smiled and pointed to where she had to go. Around the corner, sat under the orange light of a small lamp, was a young woman reading a newspaper, heroic headlines, bold across the front page. Kathleen approached slowly and leant in front of the women to make her presence known. She looked up at Kathleen and smiled warmly, her beautiful big blue eyes flickered like sapphires in the light and her red hair, tied in a ponytail that reached to the small of her back, framed her porcelain face. She wore a white blouse that was tight around her waist and a long grey skirt covering her legs. Quickly she stood up and placed the folded paper down onto a table that was messy with make-up trays and the tools of her trade. Kathleen was struck by her beauty and rendered speechless.

"Kathleen Hanham?" she asked bending down and whispering in Kathleen's ear. Kathleen felt a rush of blood to her chest and the hairs on her arms and neck rose to the sound of her voice. She nodded her reply as she was shown to a chair in front of the mirror.

"Great, I'm Harriet, I'm just going to do a little bit of make-up for you. You're auditioning for the elder sister?" She leant over to check her list.

"Yes," Kathleen smiled nervously into the mirror.

"You still have a few minutes, so relax."

Harriet removed the clips from Kathleen's hair, her face was professional and emotionless. Kathleen could hear the young girl on the stage had finished her lines and was now being asked questions by some men sat in the front rows. She tried to listen to the conversation and the questions being asked but she could only focus on Harriet who was gently running her hands through Kathleen's hair.

"Harry, we are going to take a break. Have the next one ready in ten minutes," said the well-dressed man on the stage. Kathleen saw Harriet acknowledge him and he disappeared in the reflection of the mirror as the girl from the stage walked past Kathleen and Harriet to behind a screen.

"See, lots of time," said Harriet, whispering again into Kathleen's ear.

A few moments of silence followed as Kathleen tried in vain to concentrate on her audition to come, all the while attempting to catch Harriet's eyes in the mirror and force a smile that made Kathleen's body tighten and yearn. Harriet continued to play with Kathleen's hair and eventually tied it up in a tight bun. She then showed Kathleen the costume rail where she roughly measured a long black dress with a light, flowing hem against Kathleen's frame. The sequins on the chest were in the form of an elegant heron that gave it an oriental feel. Kathleen held it up and smiled at its quality.

The young girl emerged from the screen in her own clothes. "See you later, Harry," she said, pouring her long blonde hair into a neat white hat.

Harriet indicated Kathleen could change behind the screen and as she began to undress Kathleen peeked through the slight gap at Harriet who was leaning over her make up trays. She felt like a teenager and convinced herself that Harriet had tried to steal a glance but quickly she returned back to the moment and shook her head, embarrassed now by her stupid adolescent behaviour and shocked by her feelings toward this woman. As she pulled the dress up tight over her chest, she began to focus again on the audition moments away and ran through the choreography in her mind. She was nervous again.

"Let me know when you need it tied up." Harriet's words were so well timed that Kathleen had wondered again whether she was watching, the thought that she might be made her stomach tighten and her body react in a way unfamiliar to her.

"Now would be good." Kathleen faced the wall and raised her arms high in the air in anticipation of Harriet's hands on her bare back. She felt her gently and slowly take up the slack.

"Ready?"

"Yes." Harriet pulled hard on the fastening cords, Kathleen let out an audible breath and held her chest. Harriet was a professional and tied her dress perfectly, not too tight nor too loose.

"All done." She patted Kathleen softly between the shoulder blades. "Come and sit back down and I'll fix your make-up."

Kathleen returned to the seat and sat down but she found it a struggle in the tight black dress. Harriet bent down in front of her with a tray of white powder in her left hand and a large soft brush in her right.

"Close your eyes." Harriet smiled and Kathleen thought her heart might jump out of her chest, but she obliged and flinched slightly at the first touch of the brush as it moved swiftly and gracefully about her face and neck. She felt Harriet powdering the visible tops of her breast and the deep cleavage between. As she felt Harriet finish her work, she opened her eyes slowly and saw Harriet smile.

"Well I can tell you that Mr Graves is going to like you," said Harriet with a nod towards Kathleen's bosom. Kathleen was grateful the make up Harriet had just applied covered any obvious signs of blushing. For the next few moments Harriet continued her work and they both sat in silence, though Kathleen was sure her heart was beating loud enough to be heard and after what seemed like an age a voice called from behind them.

"Miss Hanham? We are ready for you now."

"Good luck," said Harriet as Kathleen took a deep breath and walked towards the stage.

*

Kathleen left the stage after her audition and expected to see Harriet, but her station was empty. Her jacket and the newspaper were gone and all her make up trays had been closed and stacked to one side. Disappointment hit Kathleen like a bat across the belly and suddenly she was not thinking of the audition or how well she had done. She got changed slowly and with mixed emotions. She had performed well in front of George Graves and the short fat man in a dishevelled tweed suit who it seemed was either the director or producer, she couldn't tell which, and had been asked back for a second audition the next day. She had not let Graves' aura and reputation affect her performance and in fact, the sight of him sat in the shadows a row behind the producer, arrogant and aloof in a shiny grey suit and surrounding cloud of dense cigarette smoke made her laugh inwardly and relax into her performance. Despite the success of her audition she left the theatre confused and saddened and failed to see the cyclist tearing up the cobbled road towards her. He had to swerve quickly to avoid a crash.

"Watch it, ya' stupid ol' crow!" shouted the man as he regained his balance and sped off up the street. Kathleen stepped back to the safety of the pavement embarrassed, confused and now weeping softly under her hat. She turned and walked quickly in the direction of Stella's flat in hope her sister was home, even more so as the heavy clouds opened, and fat rain fell around her.

The rain was incessant and cold, soon Kathleen was soaked to the bone, shivering wildly. Her weeping had turned to hysterics and she became short of breath. She was confused by strange, uncontrollable feelings for a woman, but she couldn't erase Harriet's face from her mind and the thought of her witnessing Kathleen in this state made her feel pathetic and angry. She was normally such a strong and courageous woman, but she felt small and childlike, which, combined with the near miss and the freezing rain, had driven her momentarily to madness. Performing so well in an audition she had been so nervous about was currently scant conciliation. She needed family, warmth and a stiff drink.

Suddenly, the deluge seemed to cease and as quickly as it had begun the sun appeared through the grey-black clouds. Kathleen's eyes adjusted slowly and she stopped in her tracks to look up towards its radiance and threatening warmth. Quite uncontrollably she started laughing, her make up was a mess and sodden strands of hair stuck to the smooth skin of her face. She arrived at Stella's flat a few minutes before one o'clock and nearly slipped down the steep stone steps leading to her front door. Kathleen was emotionally drained, and her strength was fading, she didn't know what she would do if Stella were not home, but the door quickly opened and her sister's welcoming smile greeted her. Stella's dark hair was long and messy, but she radiated warmth. The broad smile on her face disappeared instantly when she saw Kathleen's despair.

"Goodness, K, what has happened to you?" asked Stella as she gathered Kathleen in from the cold.

Blendecques, France – 12th November 1914

BASIL was first to hear the bugler sound morning reveille and for him it was blessed relief. He had been lying awake in pain for the last few hours, his head throbbing angrily with every beat of his heart. He could feel blood coursing around the thin veins of his skull like poison and his face was tender to the touch. He wanted to sneeze or blow his nose, but he was worried the pain might kill him, instead he listened to a few more drops of water fall from the rotten wooden roof of the loft before sitting up slowly, feeling for his boots at his feet. Every movement felt like the hardest thing he had ever done, his painful fumbling removed the shared blankets from his brothers who were lying either side of him, the straw beneath them now dry from the heat of their bodies.

Eric slowly opened his eyes, but the loft was as dark as his sleep, so he wondered if his eyes were open at all. Stuart stretched languidly but quickly withdrew his feet back under the blanket after thrusting them out into the dark, freezing air.

Basil found his tunic and put it on, the pain hadn't caught up with his movements, he took advantage of the break to pull his boots on. Halfway through fixing his laces the gremlins inside him reacted and excruciating pain paralysed him. He let out an involuntary squeal and rested his head on a cocked knee, hands poised ready to continue the job of tying his laces once the pain had subsided.

"Are you ok?" asked Stuart, now sat up shoulder to shoulder beside his youngest brother. "Are you feeling rotten?" Basil nodded as best he could.

"You should go and see the doc." Stuart was rubbing his back tenderly, Basil wished he wouldn't but had no strength to stop him.

"I'll go with him. I want him to have a look at my ankle anyway," said Eric, lighting a cigarette.

"I told you to go yesterday and stop fucking smoking around the straw!" roared Stuart angrily.

Eric looked at him, ready for brotherly confrontation. He couldn't see Stuart's eyes in the darkness but became suddenly aware that they were not the only men in the dank loft, most of A Company were in there too, quietly packing away their sleeping equipment, coughing and sneezing in the cold morning air. The wind was howling outside and rain could be heard on the side of the barn. Just the day before Stuart had pulled Eric to one side and asked in a respectful, mature fashion that he not undermine his authority in front of the platoon, he was a corporal after all and had a job to do. If Eric could have seen his eyes that morning they would have been pleading with him to remember that conversation, Eric stalled his attack and extinguished the cigarette apologetically. Stuart was grateful, he knew the restraint that would have required.

"Careful Eric, you might dry the straw out," said Davison sarcastically from the darkness and spirits in the rat-infested loft were momentarily raised.

Basil finally finished tying his boots and wrapped his muddy, sodden puttees around his ankles. He shrugged his great coat onto his shoulders and picked up his rifle. It was still pitch black, but Basil had conducted most of his actions that morning with his eyes shut tight in pain, so it affected him little.

"Sick parade is at six," said Stuart, rolling the blankets and stacking them against the wall.

"Come on, B, let's get there and be first in line." Eric was fixing his webbing belt around his waist, fumbling with the steel buckle. Basil, saying nothing, made his way over to the stairs in the centre of the loft that led to the ground floor and outside into the cold, rifle slung awkwardly over his right shoulder. There was a small orange light that glowed dimly above the door to the barn that he caught sight of when he was at the top of the stairs. Carefully he made his way down, each step was difficult and he made slow, heavy progress like that of a drunk leaving a bar. Eric limped after him, rifle held in his left hand.

"Where are you two going?" asked one of the platoon sergeants in the doorway. Basil was leant against the banister of the last step trying not to fall. Eric exaggerated his limp.

"Sick parade, Sergeant. I've fagged my ankle and B here looks like he might die at any moment." The sergeant leant forward to look under the peak of Basil's hat and, satisfied with the obvious discomfort in his face, pointed to the far corner of the farmhouse away to his left.

"The doc has moved. His previous quarters weren't big enough for all you sickly creatures." His words hurt Eric.

"That's exactly why I didn't want to get bloody sick," whispered Eric to Basil as he limped out into the cold. Basil followed on slowly and, reluctantly releasing the safe support of the banister, stepped outside into the cold wind that stung his face. He held his hat firmly on his head and ducked his head, so the sharp needles of rain did not stab his eyes. Eric hobbled quietly at his side to take the brunt of the weather.

As they rounded the corner of the farmhouse Basil was blown off balance, but the grey-stone wall supported him. He took a deep breath, steadied himself and pushed off the wall with all his strength. His rifle strap slipped off his shoulder and he nearly dropped his weapon in the mud but caught it at the last second. Eric had not noticed his brother stumble, he was concentrating on the ground under his feet, attempting to find harder, stony areas and avoid the thick, squelching mud. He was aware also of the freshness of the air that filled his lungs, only after leaving the confines of the stinking, wet loft could one really appreciate its squalor.

When they reached the edge of the building they could see inside the house and the dark khaki shapes of men. As Eric opened the door the wind and rain blew furiously into the room. Only when his eyes relaxed to the bright light and his face had flushed to the warmth of the room did he appreciate the sorry scene. Men of all ranks were hunched on a long wooden bench that had been set up against the far wall and others had found areas on the floor to sit, their legs tucked up under their chins like children, rifles by their side. Some stood leaning against each other, eyes closed in futile attempts to rest.

There must have been thirty sick men in the room so Basil sighed when he couldn't see any place to rest. Eric shuffled one of the men hunched on the floor to one side and helped Basil into a seated position next to the door. Eric then propped both their rifles in the corner and, keeping the pressure on his good left leg, leant against the wall next to his brother.

A few minutes later a young medic entered the room from one of the two rooms at the far end that Eric assessed would have been a food store in years past, he was small and had a boyish look to him. The men looked up longingly, each trying to catch his eye and make their case to be seen first. He held a small clipboard in his hands and worked his way around each of them, taking their names and asking their symptoms as he passed. He made notes on his sheet and looked at visible injuries with quiet professionalism. Eric had to nudge Basil into life when the medic got to their corner.

"Basil, you don't look so good," said the medic who knew Basil well. It took Basil a moment to gather his words from the lost part of his brain.

"And I don't feel so good, Batesy." Basil knew Charlie Bates well.

He wrote Basil's name on a fresh sheet of paper and then proceeded with his questions. "Vomiting and diarrhoea? Soreness of joints? Tight chest? Blocked sinuses? Headache?" Basil shook his head slowly at all the symptoms bar the last. He nodded wearily, trying hard to exaggerate the extent of his pain but unable to do so. "Ok, the doc will be here soon."

Bates then stood and looked at Eric.

"Name?"

"Hanham. Private Eric Hanham."

"You're the newest Hanham, aren't you?" Eric nodded.

"Complaint?"

"Buggered my ankle a couple of days ago, not getting any better," Eric pointed down to his bad ankle as if to prove the point. Bates nodded and wrote on his list.

"Ok, let me have a look."

Eric bent down, gingerly untied his puttees and pulled the laces of his boots open. He struggled to kick the boot off using his other foot and grunted in pain at the attempt. Bates knelt and put his clipboard on the floor, he loosened Eric's boot so he could slide his foot out. When it was free Eric lifted his foot and pulled off his wet sock in one swift motion. His ankle was purple and black with bruising and along the bridge of his foot there was obvious swelling.

"That's a good one," said Bates, placing Eric's foot gently back down on the floor. Some of the men listening craned their necks to see.

"The doc will see you soon."

At six o'clock precisely the medical officer arrived from the cold. He was tall and svelte, looked unsteady on his feet and carried with him a tangible arrogance. His black moustache twitched with annoyance at each man he passed and his stiff officers' hat barely reached his rodent like ears. Bates, his triage finished, was waiting for him in the doorway of the examination room.

After a few short moments Bates called out into the room, "Lance Corporal Hanham!"

Eric nudged Basil into life and handed him his rifle. He nodded to the door held open by Bates and Basil slowly rose to his feet and made his way solemnly across the room of men now jealous of the man deemed sick enough to be seen first. Basil hadn't noticed the looks and didn't care, Eric slumped down hard into Basil's space on the floor, apologising to the man next to him for dropping a heavy elbow onto his shoulder. He sat quietly on the floor of the waiting room until enough men had cleared the benches for him to sit. Outside the sun was rising and he could hear the noise of the battalion preparing for the day, upstairs muffled voices and heavy footsteps were getting louder and the tone of their voices led Eric to assume that was where the officers were billeted. He noticed the wind had died and the rain stopped so stood gingerly to look out of the window at the glorious morning sky. It was glowing bright red, pink and orange and Eric felt warm at the prospect of a beautiful day. Awkwardly he went outside for a cigarette.

It was fresh and the cold air invigorated Eric, he lit his cigarette and leant casually against the wall, eyes fixed on nature's glowing gift to the east. He reflected on the last week while he smoked a harsh *Woodbine* cigarette that the men were now being issued. He thought about the crossing from England and the last sight of home. The first night in France where he had been picked for guard duty in the rain, exhausted to the core. He thought of the French crowds who had welcomed them so fervently in their broken English and the courteous owner of the cider farm they now found themselves billeted with. He wondered what had happened to the Scottish Battalion that had left on the train before them and he shuddered at his own memory of the ghastly journey from Le Havre to St. Omer, the rickety old train was cold, dark and not suitable for cattle but deemed acceptable enough for soldiers off to the front. He thought of home, of his mother and sisters, and of his brothers out here with him, of Stuart running around organising the men and Basil who he hoped would be himself again soon.

The thought of poor Basil brought him back into the moment and he looked through the window to make sure he hadn't missed his turn with doctor, satisfied he returned to his thoughts and what it would be like at the front. Perhaps the red light of morning was significant, he laughed at his own poetic commentary and threw his cigarette to the ground. As he did so he heard his name called from inside and opened the door to see Bates scanning for him. As Eric hobbled over to the examination room the rumble of guns started to the east and his ears twitched to the sound.

*

The doctor had deemed severe dehydration to be the cause of Basil's pain, so he remained under observation, allowed to rest and was properly fed and watered. Eric was simply advised to stay off his feet where possible so, annoyed he had even bothered to report sick, he left the farmhouse and returned to his section. As he reached the edge of the farmhouse he stood and observed the commotion of morning routine in the large courtyard. He thought it best to avoid the possibility of being tasked with clearing latrine areas, or some other loathsome job, but the long way around meant walking behind the large machine store where the senior ranks had been billeted, a risky venture as Eric knew it was out of bounds to private soldiers like him.

It was a risk he deemed worthwhile, but the route was incredibly muddy, which made his journey treacherous. Worse still, as he made his way around the corner, he caught the attention of Sergeant Major Hockley who was shaving in a tin bowl and Eric immediately wished he had risked the courtyard. Hockley, with his shirt off and his braces loose around his hips, turned slowly toward Eric who was using the building wall to help him negotiate the precarious bank, greasy with wet mud. As their eyes met, Eric froze. He had been caught in an obvious attempt to avoid the main square and was at this moment unshaven and dishevelled, having dressed in the dark. His rifle was in his left arm and the muzzle dangerously close the thick mud where it would clog but to turn back would show fear and that, for Eric, would be worse.

"Morning, sir. Don't mind me, just making life hard for myself," said Eric with a cheeky grin. He focused again on the task of getting himself to the safety of flat ground. Hockley, looking at him in silent amazement, remained transfixed on the hobbling soldier, arms cocked in the action of shaving and his large body hunched over the bowl, face white with soap.

As Eric limped past, he slipped and fell on his backside but managed to raise his rifle in the air away from the mud. He got up quickly and made better speed on the flat ground and, as Hockley turned his head to watch Eric from over his right shoulder, Eric stole a glance. Hockley's back was large and he was covered in coarse black hair that gave him the look of a bear, his skin was loose and hung from the muscles of his once lean frame. Eric focused again on his path and grinned sheepishly at Hockley as he neared the corner. He was sure he would receive some extra duty or punishment because of this so he thought he might as well jump in with two feet.

"Let me know if you want me to do your back, sir!" said Eric, laughing as he turned and hobbled as quick as he could towards the loft, a broad smile on his face.

Eric was giddy as he entered the barn, he took one quick look back to make sure he wasn't being hunted down and in doing so ran straight into his platoon making their way down the stairs from the loft. Eric looked straight up into the eyes of Sergeant Long, his platoon sergeant, and saw they were serious and emotionless. Eric's mischievous grin vanished.

"What have you been up to, Hanham?" asked Long, his gruff face and ageing eyes threatening a smile.

"Sick parade, Sergeant. Fagged ankle."

"And that's funny?"

"No Sergeant, I…" Eric nearly told the story but thought better of it. "…I was just smiling at the weather."

His cover was convincing, Long said nothing and looked skyward to see what was so amusing. The remainder of the platoon filed past with tins and mugs out ready for their breakfast. Some looked at Eric suspiciously and another gave him a friendly jab to the ribs with their mess tin.

Stuart was towards the back of the line and carried two mess tins and two mugs. He handed Eric his set. "Good timing, E, just off for breakfast. Where's Basil?"

"I think he's being treated. Dehydration the doc says." Stuart rolled his eyes and shook his head.

"That's his answer for everything. Surprised he didn't blame that for the state of your ankle."

"What's the plan today? The doc hinted it might be hard for me to stay off my ankle," said Eric. His question was aimed towards Stuart but loud enough for all around him to hear. A few men turned and nodded at Eric with excited eyes.

"Well, old mouse man is right, it will be hard today," said Barker, his chubby face broken by a deep grin.

"You think a mouse? I think he's more rat-like," said Davison, thrusting his teeth forward and squeaking like a rat. His impersonation increased the laughter around them and Eric smiled but he was still none the wiser to the plan for the day.

"So, what are we doing?" he asked again, shrugging his shoulders. Eric, just like all soldiers, hated nothing more than not knowing their immediate future. He and his chums resented the officers and senior ranks when they kept plans and orders to themselves. This uncertainty would charge the rumour mill, which could destroy morale or falsely raise spirits. The most recent rumour was that the Americans had entered the war and the Russians were almost in Berlin, two unfounded pieces of information that simultaneously worried those who wished to see action and pleased those already missing home. Stuart put Eric's mind at ease.

"We're moving closer to the front, E, setting off at eight thirty."

"Good stuff," said Eric with an exaggerated nod, removing his hat from his head and tucking it under his arm. He adjusted the leather strap of his rifle higher onto his shoulder and ducked under the mess tent into the heat and smells of breakfast. He was excited by the prospect of taking his turn on the line, but Stuart was torn between experiencing war, seeking the glory he imagined as a boy, and returning home to Emily.

At eight-thirty the men paraded fully laden with packs. Basil was back in the ranks having been released from the sick bay, he had been allowed two hours of sleep and had been fed salty food and plenty of water. Colour had returned to his face but the exaggerated bags under his eyes and the heavy, sedated way in which he moved around showed he wasn't quite yet back to his normal self. Stuart made sure he marched on the left of Basil and Eric on the right, if he was to struggle on the march, the length of which was frustratingly unknown, they would be there to help him.

Hockley took his place at the front of the assembled company and looked skyward at the darkening clouds, sniffing the air to assess its future intentions. If he could tell what was to come it didn't bode well as he furrowed his brow and blew loudly through loose lips, his thick moustache danced under his nose. Eric attempted to hide himself from sight in the rear rank. After his morning exploits, he knew he would be a target, but Hockley caught his eye as he scanned the men in front of him. He winked menacingly and Eric who, unsettled, looked away sheepishly. He knew he would not get away with his earlier detour so expected extra guard duty at some point in the near future.

The dark clouds sniffed out by Hockley were soon overhead and Eric, now cold from being stood around, felt small drops of rain on his face and exposed hands as Captain Dickens arrived to address his men.

"We received orders late last night to head further east towards the front. It won't be long now before we are giving the Hun a good taste of Kensington fight." A Company cheered. "Our final stop will be Estaires, but we'll stop around Vieux-Berquin tonight which is still quite a slog, so we best get moving."

Captain Dickens took his position at the front of the column with Lieutenants Sewell and Leigh-Pemberton either side. A Company and the Kensington Battalion marched away from the cider farm that had been home for the past few nights and waved a fond farewell to the proprietor and his family who were stood by the road. He and his young wife blew kisses and waved cheerfully, his two small sons danced around him, unaware of much except the brown puddles under their feet.

Estaires, France – 18th November 1914

STUART woke slowly and prepared himself for the cold. He could hear Eric snoring happily on the other side of Basil who was wriggling for warmth in the middle. Stuart yawned and stretched his arms above his head, his breath was a thick fog in front of his mouth that hung menacingly. There was no wind and it was still dark outside, but the moon was large and low, Stuart could see the white blanket of early winter through the wooden slats in the barn. He paused for a moment, transfixed by its beauty, before getting up and into his uniform. His fumbling, and the noise from others, woke Eric.

"Here we go again," said Eric, snatching the blanket from over the top of the three boys and sitting up abruptly.

"For fuck's sake, E!" said Basil who was now exposed in his undergarments to the cold, the warm air around him immediately dispersing into the darkness. "You do that every morning!"

"And you get angry every morning." Eric quite enjoyed making Basil feel uncomfortable, it was his job as older brother.

"Pass me my kit." Basil reluctantly let Eric have his fun again.

Once dressed they stacked their blankets in neat piles and Stuart went over to join his platoon. A few days ago, he had been moved out of Eric and Basil's platoon to become a section commander in another and was still not happy about it. He had joked before his posting that if he was to *"be potted"* out here he couldn't think of finer bunch to be with. Now he found himself with a new group and, whilst still in A Company so he could billet with his brothers, he missed them.

Stuart washed and shaved in painfully cold water and waited to be called forward for breakfast. He listened to the early morning gossip that today was almost exclusively about the actions of a small party from C Company who had been detailed to head out towards the reserve lines under cover of darkness and dig further defences. Their task hadn't been glamorous, but it was the closest any of the battalion had come to the firing line and there were rumours that enemy marksmen had sniped at them and that one man was wounded. Just before breakfast it was confirmed by the rumour mill that there was a man wounded but he had fallen on his bayonet whilst clambering around the sticky mud. Stuart felt for the man, as he, in time-honoured traditions of British soldiers at war, became an unfortunate point of fun for everyone that morning.

Breakfast consisted of boiled pork and jam, quite a luxury and a welcome change to biscuits and bully beef, so spirits were high but as the sun chased away the darkness a strong wind picked up and the cold was penetrating. Stuart and the whole of A Company huddled together in the mess tent to stay warm. He quietly ate his breakfast with his new platoon but glanced over periodically to where he could hear Eric's voice and see Basil laughing. He wished he was back with them, they helped him focus his mind. When he was left alone his thoughts would inevitably return to Emily and she was someone he did not want to think about too often. Her presence in the world made him weak and he needed all his strength.

After a few minutes there was a loud voice from the far end of the tent. "Corporal Hanham!" called the Orderly Corporal. Stuart and Basil stood up. The Orderly Corporal saw the confusion he had caused. "Corporal Hanham Senior," he said as he ducked out into the cold, beckoning Stuart to follow him. Stuart turned towards Basil, shrugged his shoulders and without a word headed out to join the messenger.

The Orderly Corporal was waiting outside, hunched away from the cold with his chin lowered to his chest and his hands tucked under his armpits for warmth. His rifle was slung on his right shoulder and his eyes were closed against the harsh wind. Stuart approached him and adopted the same stance.

"What's up, Fish?" asked Stuart. He and John Fisher were not friends, but they knew each other well.

"The Adjutant wants to see you this morning." Stuart was confused and was about to ask why but Fisher intercepted his enquiry, "I don't know why but follow me, you can wait in the orderly room." Stuart followed Fisher as a blizzard raged around them.

Fisher relaxed once inside the warmth of the orderly room and offered Stuart tea from a mug perched on the large table he was using as a desk. Four men were sat around the table and nodded their welcome to Stuart.

Stuart looked around the room and decided it was one of the old factory offices. Pictures of large machines and charts were visible on the wall behind the maps, rosters and other important documents put up by the Kensingtons. He looked up at the plaster ceiling that had started to flake away and reveal the dark wood of the roof above. Under his feet the large stones were uneven but solid.

At eight thirty Captain Thompson opened the door to the adjacent office and looked straight at Fisher, engrossed in his paperwork.

"Corporal Fisher, I thought I asked you to get me Corporal Hanham?" said Thompson in an inquisitive manner, confused and worried he might have forgotten. Fisher was quick to answer.

"You did, sir." Fisher nodded towards Stuart who was hidden from view. Thompson looked around the door and feigned surprise when he saw Stuart standing there.

"Morning, sir," said Stuart, raising his right arm and saluting the adjutant.

"Morning, Hanham, do come in."

Stuart followed him through the door and Thompson closed it behind him. The Regimental Sergeant Major was sat in a chair to the left of the desk, his large frame made the armchair look small and his legs were crossed in a gentlemanly fashion. He looked unimpressed as Stuart entered the room, his wide dark eyes emotionless and his mouth, set tight, gave nothing away. Stuart braced to attention at the sight of him.

"Stand at ease, Corporal Hanham," said the RSM.

Stuart stood at ease but still he did not know the purpose of his visit that morning so eyed the adjutant with suspicion. Captain Thompson was a charming man, he had a Yorkshire curve to his accent, but he was very much a London gentleman. He was tall and slight with dark brown hair that even in the field was neatly parted on one side and slicked back smartly. His face was clean, and, despite a thin moustache, he looked younger than his years but had served the battalion well and was widely respected. He sat in his chair and eyed Stuart up and down, his arms behind his head in a relaxed posture.

"The RSM and I have an issue, we are one platoon sergeant down at the moment and after a long discussion last night, we have your name at the top of the list to take that position."

Stuart couldn't help but smile. The RSM nodded at his reaction and lit a cigarette.

*

Stuart found Eric and Basil in A Company stores, they were counting blankets and helping the Company Quarter Master issue rations. He asked politely if he could steal his brothers away for a moment so the two men next in the queue were detailed to take their place and the boys went to the far corner of the store to talk. Basil seemed concerned, but Eric had a smile on his face that was wide and genuine.

Stuart leant his rifle in the corner and stood stamping his feet against the cold. Eric and Basil stood opposite, Basil brandished two cigarettes from his tunic pocket and handed one to Eric who lit them both with a single match.

"Have you heard? We're off to the front tonight!" said Eric, patting Basil playfully on the shoulder. Basil feigned a smile, he was scared and cold and missed home. Stuart nodded and smiled back, he was jealous of his brother's genuine enthusiasm and thought he might share it, had he not thoughts of Emily, Canada and their future.

"I've heard, E, it will be mighty exciting."

"What's wrong?" asked Basil after taking a big draw from his cigarette.

"Well, I've just been asked if I'd like to become an acting platoon sergeant in B Company. They've given me an hour to think it over and talk to you both." Stuart looked at his brothers who were listening intently. Basil was smiling and Eric had his head cocked.

"They couldn't find anyone better?" asked Eric. He was trying to keep a straight face but failing dismally. Stuart laughed modestly.

"Why would you need to consult us? It's a great opportunity and you should be proud," said Basil, seriously.

"Well, it will mean I am no longer with you two in A Company. I'll be with the boys in B."

Eric nodded and looked at the glowing end of his woodbine, Basil looked away. All three brothers were quiet for a few moments. Eric finally broke the silence.

"Well, you are in a different platoon at the moment anyway. I can't see it makes much difference, you'll still be in the same half of the battalion, so we'll be in the line and back here at the same time." Eric shrugged his shoulders and Basil nodded his agreement.

"Alright, I shall take it. I'll write to Mother tonight and tell her." Stuart smiled, Eric and Basil grinned back warmly.

"Better make it soon old man, we're off to the line at five." Eric flicked his cigarette out into the yard and suddenly Stuart remembered one thing he wanted to say.

"And don't worry, I'll come and billet with you two when we're off the line. And we can grub together too." There was genuine affection and sincerity in Stuart's voice and Basil smiled, it made him happy to hear that. Eric was happy too but masked it well.

"Whatever gets you going, just remember that B here is not Miss Church," Eric started laughing. Stuart flinched at the mention of Emily's name but shook his head with a smirk. He was still smiling as he headed back to accept the offer.

*

The rest of the day was frantic and for Stuart especially ɛ
and B Company had orders to take their turn at the front so ⸺ ⸺ᵥᵥᵘˢ
much to do in preparation and he as a brand-new platoon sergeant had a
lot to learn. He was helped along by some of the others he knew well,
their assistance enabled him to write a letter home to Eva. He thought
about writing to Emily, but they had decided before he left that regular
correspondence was not healthy for Stuart and his sanity, a decision he
was already regretting but he stayed true to his word as always.

During the day, rumours were being spread about the death of Lord
Roberts. Only six days before, on their long and strenuous march from
the cider farm in Blendecques, they had been passed twice by his
motorcade and on both occasions, he stood and saluted the Kensingtons
in a most dignified fashion. Lord Roberts was a veteran of India,
Afghanistan and the Boer Wars and was a recipient of the Victoria Cross,
the most prestigious award for bravery. Stories of his exploits spread
around the men and his soldierly spirit inspired them through their
fatigue. Now they heard he was dead and without word of how he came
to pass stories inevitably started to spread. Stuart's favourite was that the
eighty-two-year-old had died gloriously while charging a machine gun
post, but Eric preferred the version in which Lord Roberts had visited a
seedy French establishment and *"shagged himself to death"*. Basil found
out from one of the officers that the actual reason was pneumonia but
regardless, the Kensingtons felt enormous pride that they were one of, if
not the last, unit in the army to have seen this great soldier alive. It fed
their egos and their confidence grew.

At five o'clock, as the darkness of late afternoon turned to night,
Stuart, Eric and Basil, along with their friends and comrades in A and B

Company, were cheered away toward the front by the remainder of the battalion who were to replace them in four nights. The road to the front was long and winding and Stuart could see the grizzly effect of war all around them. They negotiated deep craters big enough to fit a London bus and men frequently fell on debris strewn across their path, debris blown from the skeletons of houses that lined their route.

The moon was high and bright so Stuart could easily identify the pockmarks of rifle and machine gun fire on the grey walls of ruined homes, evidence of the war raging only a short distance ahead. On occasions, flares climbed high into the air which forced Stuart and his men to lie down on the muddy road or rush for cover in the craters and houses around them. For him, and the men around him, war was becoming very real and, in the silence of the march, their fear was palpable. Stuart worried about his brothers somewhere ahead in the long line of men, Basil, especially, who had never been fond of the dark or the unknown. Sporadically, the large guns from both sides would roar into life and deliver a salvo and Stuart quickly understood that the quieter, muffled explosions were the enemy guns some distance away. Their noise, whilst not as shocking as the British guns closer by, was far more menacing and it forced the men to scatter like rats into the crater holes and scant cover around them.

At around ten o'clock Stuart's platoon entered the reserve trenches. They had the way pointed to them by sullen soldiers, hunkered away out of the cold, from a Berkshire Battalion that had been fighting at the front for some time. When enemy snipers attempted pot shots at the Kensingtons moving in from the reserve lines, the Berkshire men didn't even flinch but the Kensingtons, who were new to the fray, all dropped to the muddy ground instinctively. Stuart was no different and soon he was soaking wet and caked in stinking mud like the rest of his men.

"Relax lads, they have no idea where you are at night. As long as you don't spark up a fag, you're dandy," said one of the Berkshire boys. He was, ironically, smoking, so was promptly told to extinguish it by one of the Kensington officers who stood above him like a school bully.

Just before ten-thirty Stuart's platoon were in their allocated trenches and an exchange took place between the officers. Men from the Berkshires stayed on watch at the parapet, but the remainder lined up on the left of the trench ready to march out through the reserve lines and a few days of rest. Stuart and some of his section commanders did their best to enquire about their position and seek advice from the men they were relieving. Some were helpful but others remained quiet and, even in the darkness, showed clearly the signs of fatigue and stress. The dark brim of their soft caps highlighted the menacing shape of their faces, eyes black and sunk into dark recesses like ghouls. Quickly the men on watch were swapped and the Berkshire men left giving quiet condolences.

Stuart was allocated a section of trenches adjacent to A Company, which made him happy as he was closer to his brothers. Quickly he ensured the watch list had been briefed to the men and with his platoon commander he walked the line to ensure all gaps were filled with men and rifles. He had not had many exchanges with Lieutenant Harding, but he found him to be efficient and professional. Stuart estimated his age at about twenty-three but to look at he could have been younger for he had the smooth face and soft fair hair of adolescence. He was a little shorter than Stuart but a childhood of public school sports had made him strong so he moved gracefully through the quagmire of the forward trenches. As Harding sloped away Stuart realised that height was not an advantage in the trenches and cursed having to crouch everywhere.

Harding was quickly content with the disposition of his men so made his way to the primitive dugout that was to be his platoon headquarters, a small flap of sandbag provided an adequate screen that allowed him to light a small candle and compile his orders. Stuart assessed his platoon stores and separated the bundles of wood the men had carried to the trenches. He would issue them out in the morning so his platoon could light fires to keep warm.

After completing this task Stuart walked the line again and could see the men were already suffering in the freezing cold, the air was still but the icy temperatures were already unbearable. Sweat from the physical exertion of the march was showing on the backs of the men and steam from their bodies was visible in the pale moonlight. He issued words of encouragement as he walked by, but the men seemed fine, happy to at last be at the front and doing the job for which they had been trained. His thoughts turned to his brothers who could not be more than one hundred feet away from the far end of his platoon. He smiled at the thought of Eric enjoying himself but worried again about Basil who was dreadfully susceptible to the cold and would be afraid of the darkness. Basil always tried to hide his fears, but Stuart knew his brother too well.

As Stuart headed back up the line the first shot was fired by a man on his immediate left, it was quickly repeated along the line and shouts of *"Enemy Front!"* were passed down excitedly.

Stuart hopped up onto the firing step to look over the trench and could indeed see grey, menacing shapes moving frantically towards them. He gave an order and the intensity of fire increased and spread like a wave down the entire British line in a deafening crescendo. Stuart continued to observe over the trench wall and saw with grisly satisfaction some of the approaching grey shapes jolt upright, animal-like, in reaction to bullets striking them. Bits of flesh and uniform bursting from their bodies, caught in the moonlight. Stuart fired an entire magazine into an area he saw a man descend and felt sick when he did not appear from it. He was sure he hit him at least once so a wave of painful guilt swept across his body. He had taken human life and it had happened so fast, within the first few hours of being at the front. He continued to look at the area in the conflicting hope the soldier would stir or rise and run away back to his lines. His mind was dark and whilst part of him wanted the man to be unhurt he was strangely excited by prospect of shooting him again. His nausea had quickly been replaced by fear of the man and a deep loathing.

In his conflict, Stuart had remained up for too long and his position above the parapet had been identified. A bullet slammed into the mud bank a few inches from his face, the shock and surprise made his stomach turn and he instinctively jumped back off the firing step. His mouth and left eye were full of tangy mud and his ears rang with the sound of heavy, metallic rifle fire. He fell heavily into a deep, muddy puddle at the bottom of the trench and his proximity to death hit him like a punch to the gut. He vomited violently onto the dark ground.

Stuart quickly mastered himself and, grabbing his rifle which lay by his side, he stood up, wiped his eyes and spat out the mud and vomit from his mouth. He became aware of the increased ferocity of rifle fire being heaped upon the Kensingtons. Large splashes were thumping with alarming regularity into the raised portion of trench behind the firing line. The higher bank was there to disguise the silhouettes of men on watch but in that moment, it seemed to be a target for the enemy rifles. He ran down the line barking orders and support.

"Keep firing! Let them have it!" His platoon responded to his encouragement. "Keep moving position!"

When he reached the end of his platoon, he jumped back onto the firing step and fired five rounds at the muzzle flashes he could see in the distance before dropping back down and running the line again. On the way back, he bumped into Harding who was shouting encouragement to his men from the other end, their combined efforts were working well and their men on the step kept up a rate of terrifying fire.

After twenty furious minutes, the firing ceased in intensity and become sporadic. The ghostly grey figures of the enemy returned to their trenches like eels backing into the safety of their rocky holes. They fired wildly as they went in an attempt to protect themselves. Some weren't so lucky and the occasional shriek of delight from a Kensington would indicate a strike on the retreating enemy. At eleven thirty-five the firing ceased completely, runners were sent around to collect casualty reports and replenish the ammunition stocks. Stuart was relieved to hear no men from either A or B Company had been wounded. He reported to Harding. "All men accounted for, sir, and ammunition is being handed out." Harding stood towards the back of the trench congratulating the men closest to him.

"Excellent Hanham, well done... What happened to your face?" Harding was looking at Stuart who had sat on the firing step in front of him, in the bright moonlight his wound was obvious. Stuart forgot for a moment his close call and touched his face. It was moist to the touch and painful around his eye. He could now feel the sting of sweat in an open cut.

"Just a close call, it's ok. Why the attack tonight, sir?" asked Stuart, changing the subject. Harding sat beside him to get out of the way of some men moving ammunition boxes up the line.

"They no doubt got wind we were changing over the troops in the line, often they will put an attack onto men fresh in," said Harding, like it was nothing.

"Rotten bastards," Stuart spat grit from his mouth.

"We will do the same, sergeant," replied Harding, attempting to check his pocket watch in the moonlight. "Anyway, well done. More of the same from you and we'll be just fine. Tell the men they did well when you're on your rounds." Harding stood and walked towards his dugout. Stuart said nothing but was humbled by his words, Harding was younger than him, but he was charismatic and Stuart was impressed. Harding stopped suddenly and turned to Stuart who had stood to walk in the other direction.

"Oh, and Hanham, at first light go to get your face seen to."

*

The dawn sun brought blessed relief as the night had been deathly cold and there was no way to thaw. There was no wind, the freezing blanket of winter was suffocating, and no amount of clothing could protect the Kensingtons from its vice-like grip. Everyone's feet were soaking wet and had turned into painful blocks of ice, so it was truly a relief to see the sun and bask in its warmth. The morning light also meant fires could be lit in barrels to warm men when not on watch and it afforded them the chance to smoke. Men like Eric and Basil, who were addicted to the satisfying sting of smoke on their lungs, lit up with desperate relief, no longer the target to enemy marksman they were in the dark hours.

Stuart had spent the whole night prowling the line to ensure the men were remaining vigilant. He massaged legs cramped with cold and rubbed the backs of men on watch to create frictional heat and give them some relief. His efforts during the firefight and in the long hours of darkness were not unnoticed and the word among the men in his platoon was they were lucky to have him around.

By nine o'clock hot food and coffee was delivered to the forward trenches. Most had sacrificed their eating equipment to allow space in their packs for ammunition and fire stores, so Stuart saw men eat stew straight from the pot like animals, shared spoons their only means of getting warm food inside their frozen bodies. It was a horrid affair, but all were grateful of the sustenance. Coffee too was passed around in a single mug. It served to raise spirits so that when some senior officers from the battalion inspected the lines with Captain Prismall, B Company Commander, the trench was buzzing with excitement and stories of the night's action. Stuart and his men were congratulated for fighting so well during their *"Baptism of Fire"* and cigarettes were handed out.

At half past ten, with Harding now overseeing the line, Stuart wandered down to find his brothers. He did not have to travel far as they were only two sections of trench away, sixty yards in all. Basil and Eric were both sat on the firing step smoking, Basil had one leg raised and

Eric was aggressively massaging his brother's bare foot. Basil was wincing in pain, his foot red-raw and swollen. Neither Eric nor Basil saw Stuart arrive.

"Stop complaining, B, I have to get the blood flowing again or it'll be fagged," said Eric, the cigarette in his mouth bounced as he spoke.

"I know but it bloody hurts," replied Basil through gritted teeth.

Stuart watched the scene for a few seconds, he was happy they were together, and he knew Basil would be too proud to let anyone other than one of his brothers help him in this fashion. He would have suffered in silence until it crippled him rather than look weak in front of other soldiers. Stuart had told him on many occasions that not seeking help is weakness in itself, but it seemed to fall on deaf ears.

"Feet giving you some grief, B?" asked Stuart, leaning casually against the wall of the trench. Eric stopped what he was doing at the sound of Stuart's voice and looked up with a smile.

"I'm afraid so. They are like ice this morning and hurt something awful."

"Do you have some dry socks?"

Basil shook his head embarrassed and Eric looked up at Stuart and rolled his eyes. Basil saw him do it. "Bugger off, E! You don't have any either!"

"Well my feet aren't fucked like yours!" said Eric, pushing Basil's foot off his lap, onto the greatcoat laid on the trench floor. Basil yelped in agony as his foot made heavy contact with the coat and the cold hard ground beneath. He punched Eric hard in the arm, Eric flicked his cigarette onto the floor and prepared to brawl, but Stuart put a stop to it.

"Relax! B, you can use my spare pair, they are dry, and my feet are alright at the moment." Stuart handed Basil a pair of socks from the pocket inside his greatcoat. Basil accepted gratefully, face still flushed red with anger, he regarded Eric out the corner of his eye.

"Just try and keep them dry." Stuart gestured Eric to move to one side so he could sit between the two and prevent any further childish antics.

"What about last night then?" asked Stuart, handing over a full packet of cigarettes to Eric who nudged him appreciatively.

"Bloody rancid cold," said Basil, bending down to put on the dry socks and tie his boots.

"Cold yes, but what about our *baptism of fire?*" Stuart put a big hand on Eric's knee and squeezed it hard in the tender area just behind the joint. Eric flinched in pain and pushed him off.

"Yeah quite a display," said Eric, a big smile broke upon his face and Stuart was a little taken aback by how much Eric had genuinely seemed to enjoy it, "Worth the wait for sure, B here was a regular marksman."

Eric looked around Stuart to catch Basil's eye. His compliment on Basil's shooting was an olive branch to his brother and Basil's smile suggested acceptance. Eric handed Basil a cigarette that he took gladly.

"Really B?" Stuart thought back to how he had killed a man and the feeling was there again, a hollow pain in his heart and stomach. He forced a smile, but his eyes would have betrayed him. Basil, still buoyed by the compliment from Eric, happily played up to the role.

"Well I certainly reckon there's a few Hun that won't come at this part of the line again." He looked up and winked at Eric. Stuart swayed left and right between his brothers giving them each a proud, loving nudge.

"I don't doubt that."

The boys were quiet together for a few seconds while Eric smoked his cigarette and Basil fixed the putties around his boots. It was a macabre silence as each of them thought about the horror of what they had seen on their first night on the line. If it had been a single occurrence that would have been enough for Stuart and Basil, but Eric seemed unaffected by it all. He was first to speak after taking a long pull from his cigarette stained brown from muddy hands, "Did you hear them this morning too? Groaning out there like sheep giving birth."

Stuart nodded solemnly, and Basil laughed but it was fake, he was horrified by the noises of dying men and on one of his watches had been hiding tears from the man on duty by his side, the groans of wounded humans in the darkness and his own freezing feet had been too much for him. He hoped it would cease and he could go home or at least that he would become used to it all soon.

After a few more thoughtful moments of silence Lieutenant Sewell turned the corner of the trench, his lanky frame stumbling on the mud and icy pools of dank water. He saw the three boys sat together quietly.

"Sergeant Hanham. Have you come to check on these two?" asked Sewell in jest.

"Just making sure they are behaving." Eric smiled and leant back against the trench wall smoking casually but Basil was stone faced and embarrassed.

"Well I can tell you they gave the enemy a good taste of British fortitude last night," said Sewell, brandishing a list from his pocket. "But alas I shall be needing them again. Private Hanham you are next up on position one and Corporal Hanham, report to Sergeant Long, he has some tasks for you."

Both boys jumped down into the mud that was stiff with cold. Eric knocked the hat from Stuart's head with a smile before slinking away down the trench, his rifle trailing low in his right hand. Basil gathered his great coat and looked Stuart in the eyes, for the first time he saw the wounds on his face.

"What happened?" Basil cupped Stuart's chin and turned his head gently to have a closer look. Sewell leant over to see.

"Its a scratch. Just make sure you regularly change position."

"Will do." Basil patted Stuart's shoulder and hobbled away on painful feet. Stuart stood to return to his section of the line, but Sewell called him back quietly. He bent down to Stuart's ear and whispered.

"I had a letter from Mary yesterday before we came out." Stuart pulled away and looked into his eyes, he knew the next sentence would be about Emily. "She met with Emily and, whilst she understands if you don't want to write all the time, she asks if you might consider it once in a while?"

Sewell looked embarrassed so he turned professional once more. "Anyway, I shall leave it with you, Sergeant Hanham. Must dash."

As Sewell turned and stumbled awkwardly away Stuart stood in empty silence, he was frozen by her name and thoughts of how much she missed him. He hadn't thought about her for a while but now he wanted nothing more than to be back in London. He wanted to smell her skin and feel the softness of her breath. Quickly he banished these wonderful thoughts from his mind with a heavy sigh and turned to make his way back to his platoon where he hoped for his first bit of rest in nearly two days.

*

The next day Basil and Eric stood warming themselves by a fire after another freezing night on the line. Eric had a cigarette hanging from his mouth and his hands were thrust deep into the pockets of his great coat. Basil stared at his brother, he could see the fire flickering in the pale blue of his eyes and the heavy bags underneath, but Eric looked calm and Basil envied his resolve, even after just two nights on the line he was feeling the strain and was constantly uncomfortable. His feet were in terrible pain and all the muscles in his body would flinch at any sudden sound. The nerve shredding chorus of rifle fire the Kensingtons had unleashed towards the advancing enemy during the last two nights still swarmed around him like a dark cloud and the thought of another night made him nauseous.

The cold however was proving more potent an enemy than the opposing army. Basil had seen men freeze to the butts of their rifles, water in their metal bottles froze solid and many were taken ill, their bodies unable to cope with the conditions. Basil was proud not to have been one of those men but numbers in the line had already started to dwindle, more pressure was heaped on those resilient enough to cope and increased the level of fatigue. Mistakes had started to be made and the constant harassing of German sniper fire accounted for a few near misses as men forgot to crouch through unprotected areas or got too cocky in an attempt to locate the marksman making their life a misery.

As Basil stood in pain and thought things could not get any worse his ears caught the sound of muffled explosions far off to the east. Eric's eye snapped from his gaze and he looked instinctively up to the sky.

"Get Down! Find some cover!" screamed a man from atop the firing step. The thought of this new deadly menace made Basil's knees weak and his body took a moment to react, enough time for Eric to pull him down into a small hollow and lay awkwardly on top of him.

The first shells landed close behind their positions and Basil, laid on his back looking up at the sky, could see snowy mud and debris fly high into the air. It soon began to drop around him, so he closed his eyes and tucked his head tight into Eric's body. The next barrage landed in front of the Kensington line and its proximity made the ground under Basil shake and rumble uncontrollably. He could feel Eric's grip on his arms tightening and Basil did all he could to make himself smaller, but they couldn't hide from the barbed wire, metal stakes and heavy mud that fell upon them. The barrage must only have been a few seconds in duration, but it seemed to last an age.

As Eric levered himself up through the debris that had surrounded him, he looked at Basil and smiled, "Well that's what artillery feels like then," he said, wiping grime and tears from his face.

Basil watched him stand and dust himself off and then accepted his arm as Eric pulled him up. Some men had already mounted the firing step to halt any attack the enemy might have launched under the barrages cover but Basil stood and looked around him for his rifle, lost in the mud and debris. He found it next to where he had been lying and pulled it from the wreckage caked in sticky clay. As he furiously started to clean it he looked at Eric who was now laughing with others around him trying to repair the trench wall. He felt his heart swell and acknowledged a new bond between them. Not only were they brothers close in age and spirit, but they now also shared the invisible, unyielding love for each other that soldiers did in times of war. Basil, as he had been all his life, was glad Eric was by his side.

It was a miracle that only one man from the battalion was seriously wounded in the barrage. Eric and Basil shared a look of worry as the man was carried through their trench on a stretcher, moaning in pain. If the deadly reality of their situation was not already clear, it was made apparent in that moment.

Later that morning Eric was sharing a moment with Private Perry around a barrel fire raging before them. They were both taking a break from repairing the trench defences and waiting their turn on the firing line. They were in good humour, laughing in the resilient way British soldiers do in times of strife. Perry was a large stocky man with a huge heavy head, the strong features of working man and at thirty-eight was a lot older than most of the other private soldiers in the battalion but he carried it well and was extremely popular. He and Eric shared a cigarette as Perry was called to take his place on the line. He rolled his eyes at Eric who, knowing his time would come soon, smiled and shrugged his shoulders. Perry passed Eric the last bit of Woodbine and went to take his place.

Eric watched him walk over to the position a few yards away and conduct a short handover with the man hunched behind the loophole on watch. As Perry jumped up onto the firing step, Eric heard the single crack of rifle fire and saw Perry jolt upright, all the muscles in his body clenched tight as his nerves fired their final pulse. He made no noise but there was squelching thud of metal into his skull and his soft peaked hat was blown from his head in an explosion of white skull and pink, misty blood. The man crouched by his side opened his arms in stunned awe, his face and tunic were sprayed red and white with fragments of Perry's skull. Eric felt sick but as he ran to help his friend he signalled at the crouched man to concentrate on trying to locate the enemy who had fired the deadly shot.

The left half of Perry's large face was missing from brow to mouth, his right eye was open in shock. Eric cocked his head and looked deep into the eye of his friend lying awkwardly, his legs still clung onto the firing step and his great frame lay in the mud of the trench floor, chest toward the sky. There was nothing he could do for him except cover what was left of his face from the world. Sergeant Long arrived quickly and gestured to Eric to mount the parapet and help in the search for the marksman who had taken Perry's life.

Eric stepped up carefully and looked cautiously out into No Man's Land but, together with a few others, could see no sign of a sniper. Davison arrived, took off his hat and mounted it on his bayonet, he slowly raised it while Eric and three other men observed. A sharp crack was quickly heard and the bank behind them spat mud and snow where the heavy bullet had hit. Green had seen the flash and indicated to Eric its position with his own rifle fire. Eric and Green emptied their magazine into the position with frustration and intense anger until Davison pulled them from the lip of the trench, so they did not expose themselves to more enemy marksman. When Eric looked round, Perry, husband to Annie and the first fatality suffered by the Kensington Battalion, was being carried away on a stretcher, both his arms hung pathetically down from the canvas frame.

A and B Company were relieved late on Saturday after three nights and days on the line and marched in darkness back to their billets. It was a horrific ordeal, the wind stung their faces and their fatigue was such that men fell asleep on their feet and did not wake until they hit the ground. It was a few miles to the factory and their billets, but it seemed like a never-ending journey, many were hallucinating and calling out wildly in panicked states of sleep and stress. For the boys it was the hardest march they had ever done and the welcome sight of the large factory building was heaven-sent. The hard, cold floor of the factory store, pathetically insulated with straw, could have been the softest bed in all of creation. The Hanham boys lay together and slept the peaceful sleep of little boys.

Camden Town, London – 7ᵗʰ December 1914

DESPITE the war raging on the other side of the English Channel there was festive cheer around London and for Kathleen, life was fresh and exciting. She naturally worried about her brothers at the front and reports of terrible losses scared her so much she often struggled to sleep but she had been offered a major part in George Graves' production and was enjoying living at home with her mother. Other things were happening in her life, exciting things, over which she had no control.

Kathleen hadn't expected to see Harriet again so when rehearsals began in earnest, she was shocked to see her backstage surrounded by her make up pots and array of brushes. Kathleen was relieved no one had seen her stop still and blush bright pink at the sight of Harriet, grateful too of the time to steady herself and appear casual. Harriet did not have the same time to prepare, so Kathleen saw her stutter awkwardly and blink furious embarrassment, her large blue eyes darting guiltily from side to side. If Kathleen was unsure of some mysterious chemistry before, she wasn't any longer, and in the weeks after something had been developing between them. Something new, unspoken and powerful. It occupied Kathleen's mind almost completely until finally, she managed to pluck up the courage to ask Harriet to join her for a drink in a quiet Camden bar, it was here she waited.

The dark outside world was rushing past in a feisty gale and rain lashed down in cold, angry sheets. Kathleen's eyes flicked from the glass of single malt in front of her to the door and back, she was nervous waiting for it to open and thought Harriet might not enter at all. Her invitation had been awkward and interrupted so she debated whether

Harriet had even understood. She reasoned that the shock in Harriet's eyes and the way she had turned and accepted in adolescent embarrassment was indication enough that she had.

Kathleen tried to break her thoughts from Harriet, if just for a second, so she looked around the bar to try and find something to take her mind elsewhere. The room was long and slender, dull brass work adorning the bar and mirrors gave it an aged look. She studied pictures hanging on the wall and marvelled at the eclectic mix. Some, with skiers hurtling down mountains, looked like they would be more suited in alpine chateaus and other more modern portraits of actors and musicians gave it a bohemian feel. The dark wood of the furniture and fittings reminded Kathleen of a train carriage and she tried to remember the last time she had left London. Two men in the corner of the room were sat together reading the paper and she estimated they were a similar age to Eric and Basil. At the thought of her brothers she looked down in sadness and wondered what they would be doing on a night like this, so cold and sinister. She studied the cloudy mirror behind the bottled spirits on the shelves in front of her and wondered whether the grey appearance was an effect of design or lack of cleaning. She tilted her head to get a better look and was so engrossed in her investigation she hadn't noticed the door open and a cold wind blow through the bar. Her brothers, the array of bottles behind the bar and the thought of that ghastly mirror occupied her completely. She was only broken from her gaze when a familiar figure appeared behind her. She swivelled on her stool to see Harriet by her side.

Harriet was soaked. Her flimsy hat had not been strong enough to protect her from the heavy rain so her red hair appeared dark brown and dishevelled. Her green coat looked black and was heavy with rain, in her hand she held the pathetic carcass of an umbrella, destroyed by the wind and deluge. Despite this she had a radiant smile and her eyes were bright and full of life. Kathleen tried not to laugh but failed, Harriet joined her, and the pair embraced.

"My poor dear, let me get you a stiff drink," said Kathleen. She turned towards the small, shrew like man behind the bar who had approached the pair in anticipation of an order.

Kathleen ordered two double whiskeys then turned to Harriet who had opened her jacket to assess how wet her remaining layers were. She wore a cream dress, now dirty brown around the hem, and a tight tweed waistcoat that accentuated the shape of her hips. Kathleen had to stop herself from drifting into a longing gaze as Harriet's body was presented to her, so turned and asked the barman if he had a fire going. He struggled to break his gaze from Harriet before arrogantly pointing towards the back of the bar where a sign on the wall indicated the lounge bar.

The lounge bar was small and poorly lit but there was a fire glowing brightly against the back wall and two red leather armchairs faced each other in front of the fireplace. Harriet rushed over and stood in front of the flames to dry, Kathleen placed the drinks on the small wooden table between the chairs and sat down. She noticed a man sat in the corner of the room, he was reading a newspaper under the soft glow of a brass reading lamp attached to the wall. He had a regal grey beard and regarded Kathleen accusingly from over the top of his thin spectacles. She looked at him and held an emotionless gaze until he returned to his paper.

From her chair Kathleen watched Harriet enjoy the warmth of the fire, neither spoke for a few minutes. Harriet was stood directly in front of the flames, head fully reclined and her eyes closed tight in warm relief.

She held her jacket open, arms stretched out to catch the heat from the fire. Kathleen marvelled at the shape of Harriet's body and wondered where her mind had gone in that moment, she so desperately wanted to know.

Harriet then let out a deep sigh and lowered her head slowly to look at the flames. Kathleen switched her stare to the swirling glass of scotch in her hand. Harriet laid her jacket on the floor in front of the fire to dry, took her thick red hair in her hands and gently hung it over her right shoulder towards the fire. She sat down gracefully, took the glass of scotch from the small table, lifted it up to her lips and drew a deep breath through her nose. She opened her eyes and looked at Kathleen who had been observing her in fascination.

"Thanks for the drink." Harriet raised her glass towards Kathleen who returned the gesture and gently tapped her glass against Harriet's. The moment was perfect.

"So, are you excited about Thursday?" Harriet's smile was genuine and her blue eyes flickered golden in the light of the fire. Kathleen had to look away from her to answer, such was her spell.

"I am, very much, I just hope I don't make any mistakes. I don't want to be in trouble with George."

"I don't think you have to worry about that, you're one of the best in the show." The compliment came naturally from Harriet and it was sincere. Kathleen caught her gaze but again had to look away, she worried she was blushing.

"Thanks, but I don't think that's true."

"Well you are, and Eddy thinks so too." Harriet took a sip of her whisky. It stung her throat and she coughed awkwardly which made

Kathleen laugh. "Goodness me! What is this?"

"It's the best they had I'm afraid. Only the first one will hurt." Kathleen tried to control her laughter.

"Let's hope so." Harriet laughed and for the first time she regarded the establishment they were in. She gazed around the room and caught the eye of the old man in the corner who had already had enough and was leaving the room with a growl. Harriet smiled at Kathleen.

"What made you choose this place?" Kathleen couldn't tell whether she was impressed or not.

"My brother in law told me about it, very unique and quiet he said. Except on Fridays when they play American music." Kathleen tried to convince Harriet it wasn't somewhere she frequented. Harriet turned to look at Kathleen.

"So how is Howard? Last time we spoke you were concerned about him." Harriet looked directly at Kathleen, cradling her drink in two hands. Kathleen had to put a hand on her chest to stop her heart leaping across the room. She had mentioned Howard a great deal in an attempt to convince Harriet, and herself, that whatever was happening between them was nothing. The reality was Kathleen hadn't seen him over the last few weeks and had not thought about him a great deal either. Recently she had seen an angry, disjointed side of him that she did not much like and thought she might only have been with him as it was convenient and that was not her style. She had also noticed jealousy in his letters and sensed worry in his voice when they had last met. She paused for a second and then decided she would allow herself to walk down the path not yet travelled. She looked up into Harriet's large blue eyes and this time Harriet looked away.

"He's worried I think." Harriet looked back at Kathleen in concern. Kathleen shifted her focus to the glass in her hand and wished she had more whisky. "Maybe he is worried I have found someone else?" Kathleen drained the remnants of her glass.

"And have you?" Harriet had genuine concern in her voice and Kathleen wondered whether she had understood, she looked up into Harriet's eyes. They looked heavy but hopeful. Her mouth was set firm and her red lips, full and enticing, seemed ready to break into smile.

"I don't know. Have I?" It was the biggest leap Kathleen had taken in her twenty-seven years. She gazed hopefully at Harriet, longing for a smile, any flicker of loving reciprocation.

Harriet took a deep breath and sunk into her chair, her face illuminated by a broad, happy smile. Her hair glowed terracotta and her pale face flushed with colour. She held her gaze at Kathleen and nodded her head slowly. Kathleen could feel her heart beating in every corner of body, her breasts firmed under her tight dress and she felt a stirring like never before. A euphoric feeling in places she had not been aware of in all her life. She was stunned into silence as Harriet drained the rest of her whisky and stood in front of Kathleen.

"I think I might need another drink." Harriet took Kathleen's glass and walked gracefully out of the door, leaving Kathleen alone in the room. Kathleen sunk into her chair and looked towards the dancing flames of the fire. She could still smell Harriet's presence and the spitting flames seemed to kick harder into life. Kathleen started to imagine, with increasing pleasure, the possibilities of what might be.

*

Harriet returned from the bar with some friends that happened to be seeking refuge from the weather and together they all drank until they were asked to leave shortly after eleven. Harriet's friends had offered to show them some new, exciting places in town, but Kathleen and Harriet declined and walked drunkenly to Stella's flat where Kathleen had been staying while her sister and Frank were away. The night, whilst still cold and windy, had become clear and stars could be seen through thin layers of fast-moving cloud.

They arrived at Stella's flat and Kathleen, having supported Harriet from falling drunk most of the way home, helped her into a chair in front of the fireplace and removed her jacket and shoes. She pulled some blankets from the chest along the far wall and laid them across her lap. Gently she tucked the blankets under her feet and behind her back so she wouldn't feel the cold.

Kathleen sat opposite and watched Harriet for a short time, she looked so angelic in the darkness, her smooth pale skin was like a soft light in the gloom and her breathing was regular and calming. She contemplated how out of her depth she was and marvelled at how life had seen her to this point. How the daughter of a minister had ended up in the theatre to begin with and how now she had come to fall in love with a woman. She had worked with beautiful women on many occasions but never had she felt the electric chemistry she did with Harriet. Perhaps their connection was something that broke the barriers of gender and society. Perhaps they were kindred spirits that had found each other quite by random, solitary animals of the same species that had stumbled upon one of their kind in the wild. She did not know but the mystery of what might be excited and scared her in equal measure.

Suddenly Kathleen became aware of her own fatigue. She made her way into the bedroom and without undressing got under the heavy sheets. She thought one last time about the events that evening and said a prayer that her brothers would be safe, wherever they were. She thought about Howard sleeping alone and felt guilty but the flame burning bright inside her had replaced the initial excitement and feelings she had had towards him a few months ago. Finally, before the warming embrace of whisky carried her to sleep, she thought again of Harriet, beautiful, amazing Harriet sleeping in the next room. Kathleen was delirious with happiness.

Sleep had only taken Kathleen for an hour or so when she was woken by sounds in the living room. Her head was pounding, and her eyes adjusted painfully to the dank light. She froze, fawn like, until quickly she reminded herself where she was. She thought Stella and Frank might be home but remembered joyfully that the figure entering the room had to be Harriet. She smiled at the thought, her body tensed in anticipation and desire.

Kathleen felt the bed lurch as the weight of another joined from the opposite side. She felt the sheets tighten around her as they were lifted and the cold air from outside the cocoon was a pleasing shock. She remained still with her eyes shut tight in pretend sleep as Harriet shuffled closer under the sheets and pushed her left arm under Kathleen's in a tight embrace. Kathleen could feel Harriet's long legs adopt the same, foetal position and her forearm nestled between her breasts. With her free hand Kathleen held Harriet's hand, now gently placed under her chin, and squeezed it as Harriet kissed the exposed back of her neck. Kathleen turned slowly towards her. Even in the darkness she could see her eyes were open and were focused deep into her soul. Kathleen's heart was racing, and she became aware of the tightening of her stomach and the pulsing of blood around her body. She didn't stop to think before kissing Harriet passionately on her lips, she could taste stale whisky, but it was sweet around her mouth. Harriet's response was immediate, there was no turning back.

Estaires, France – 24th December 1914

THROUGH his periscope Basil watched bright shards of sunlight creep slowly across No Man's Land towards him and he imagined the warmth instantly relieving him from the tortuous clutches of the cold. He and the remainder of the Kensingtons on the line had packed the firing step for their morning 'stand too', which, as the day was brightening, would soon come to an end. Basil, like all the men strewn out across the great lines of trenches, was excited about a fire's warmth and the chance to smoke, sources of relief forbidden during the hours of darkness.

Shortly before eight-thirty the call to stand down whispered along the line but Basil was detailed to remain on watch. His heart sank but, wincing at the crippling pain in his feet, he stood firm on the line and kept a keen eye on the area in front of his trench. The snow of a few days ago had melted or turned rusty brown so it no longer covered the horror of No Man's Land. Barbed wire was strung out in thick coils in front of both sets of trenches, held firm by menacing pickets that Basil thought looked like medieval blockades. There were deep, frozen puddles in crater holes and bodies of men from both sides lay silent and stiff in the positions they had drawn their final breaths. The mud was thick and black and a rat or bird, brave enough to perch on one of the shattered tree stumps, the only sign of life. It was a deathly spectacle, but it was not the reason he had tears in his eyes. His trench foot had become so bad that he could hardly stand, he longed to remove his socks and attempt to dry his feet.

At nine o'clock he handed over his watch and as he gingerly stepped down off the firing step he tried not to yelp or scream. Eric, who had been observing him in concern from his position in the trench some feet away, made his way to where his younger brother sat. He dropped beside him and handed his lit cigarette to Basil who looked up at him, eyes full to the brim with tears of pain and suffering.

"Come on B, let's have a go at those feet of yours," said Eric, patting his lap invitingly. Basil looked at him helplessly.

"I don't think I can get my boots off."

"It will hurt but they'll feel better after a rub." Eric patted his lap again before taking another cigarette from his packet and lighting it. Basil nodded and carefully placed his right foot into Eric's lap.

Eric unwrapped Basil's puttee and untied his boot, he asked Basil if he was ready before removing it fully. As Basil nodded Eric whipped it off swiftly from the heal, Basil gritted his teeth to muffle the sounds of pain.

"You fucker!"

"Best to do it quickly." Basil knew he was right but was still angry and in immense pain.

Eric slowly removed his sock. It was soaked with sweat, muddy water and there were dark patches of blood on the thick wool. These were sticky and made removing the sock a delicate process. Eric's stomach tightened and he turned nauseous as he saw the state of Basil's foot. It was swollen bright red and in places the skin had swelled and creased to such an extent that the deep recesses had cracked and sticky, pussy blood was seeping out. Basil was crippled by pain. The freezing air against exposed skin was agony, like red-hot knives prodding his foot.

Eric steadied himself, gathered his nerve and wiped tears from his eyes. It saddened him beyond measure to see his brother in such pain, but he was also amazed Basil had managed to survive on these feet for so long. He choked on his emotions.

"Ready? I'm going in." A false smile broad across his muddy face.

Basil smiled, took one last pull from his cigarette and flicked it away. He stuffed part of his leather rifle sling in his mouth to bite down on, he did not want to scream among his friends and in ear shot of the enemy, and then nodded at Eric to begin. Basil was raged by pain and he nearly fainted with the intensity of it, but he bit down hard and squeezed fistfuls of cold mud to help him stay conscious. He couldn't stop the muffled squeals and tears from creating dark channels down his grubby face.

Once Eric had completed his treatment on Basil's feet, he bandaged them up lightly, fitted him with a pair of his dry socks and fastened his boots and puttees. Basil gave his thanks as best he could, but he was exhausted and delirious. Eric, helped by Davison, propped Basil up into a corner and both men sat either side of him to keep him warm. Every man in the trench had a bad day so no one thought any less of Basil, it was his turn to be cared for. He had fought as hard as anyone over the last couple of months, so others were happy to take his watch on the line while he recovered and rested his feet.

*

Shortly after ten o'clock Captain Keen, the medical officer, made his way through the trenches. Most were suffering from symptoms of trench foot as there was no escaping the cold and very little one could do about keeping feet dry, but Eric made sure Keen came and had a look at Basil.

"It's really bad sir," said Eric, showing the way to where Basil sat.

"Let me see, Corporal Hanham," ordered Keen.

Basil slowly and painfully removed the puttee, boot and sock from his left foot. Eric stood by Keen's shoulder and nodded encouragement to Basil struggling in pain. When his foot was exposed Keen took it gently in his hands and sighed tellingly at its pathetic state.

"You need to come off the line, Corporal Hanham," said Keen. He looked towards Sewell who had joined the growing inspection team. Eric nodded his approval and looked excitedly at Basil, but he was frowning and shaking his head, determined to stay.

"No, sir, please I can't leave just now," pleaded Basil, genuine in his desire to remain at the front. Eric looked at him angrily and shook his head, but Basil ignored him.

"You need medical care," said Keen looking at Sewell, who shrugged his shoulders. Basil wasn't the first of his men he had lost to this condition and he wouldn't be the last.

"Can't I stay, sir? At least until tomorrow? I can keep dry until then." Keen was silent for a while, Sewell looked at him, hopeful he might let Basil and his rifle stay on the line for one more night. They didn't know what to expect this Christmas Eve, so every man was essential, Keen knew that too. Eric stared angrily at his brother, he had his chance to get behind the lines, attend to his feet and be out of danger but he was being stupid and stubborn.

"Fine, but you'll be on the first trip back to billets tomorrow and on the carts, do not walk on these feet if you can help it."

"Yes sir," Basil smiled. He was happy he would stay with his friends and he knew he would be respected for being brave through his pain. Sewell smiled proudly, patted him on the back then followed Keen on his rounds. Once the two officers were out of sight Eric clipped Basil hard around the ear, knocking the khaki hat from his head.

"You're a fucking idiot, B!" said Eric, walking to his post. Basil started to put his boot back on but felt sad at Eric's reaction. He wanted Eric to be proud and happy he had stayed with him up at the front. He wanted to share Christmas with his brother so was confused he wasn't pleased he had stayed.

Through the morning Basil took his place on the line when required and helped as best he could with fatigue parties and crucial elements of trench repair. His inability to walk meant he wasn't much use to those working hard to fortify the positions, so he spent most of his time on watch and, despite the constant pain from his feet, was in good spirits. He had seemed to grow in stature with the decision to stay and on more than one occasion he was congratulated for being tough, word on the state of his feet had spread and many respected his fortitude. It was adulation that Basil had rarely had in his life, so he enjoyed it immensely.

Early in the afternoon Stuart arrived to see his brothers and wish them a happy Christmas Eve. Eric was quick to tell tales and scorn Basil for not taking the opportunity to leave the trenches and have his feet seen to. Eric was twenty-two and Basil had only just turned twenty-one earlier in December, but both saw Stuart, at twenty-six, as a father figure. Stuart, diplomatic as ever, soothed both egos and they all sat down to share some biscuits and bland tea from Stuart's tin mug.

"Received a letter from Mother yesterday," said Stuart, reaching inside his jacket to pull out the letter. He handed it to Basil who was eager to read it.

Hanham

'Dear Stuart,

Thank you so much, dear for the last letters or rather, card and letter card, to be exact, which I received on Monday – I was delighted. It is such a comfort to have something direct from you – I am afraid here there has been nothing but rain all the time but Monday turned out sunshiney and so has today. I cannot be quite exact but I think I am safe in saying it has rained almost continuously for, at least, a fortnight. I think it really must be longer than that I have thought about my dear boys in those muddy trenches, and have so prayed that God will be pleased to protect them and keep them safe from harm, and bring them safely back.

There have certainly been some wonderful happenings, and what did you think of the book I sent? I am so hoping you will get your Xmas things in good time, and in good order.

Kathie is hard at rehearsals now. She thinks it is going to be a very pretty thing, but it is very exhausting as a dance. I wrote on the envelope about the parcel and I enclose their answer. I do hope that perhaps by now, you may have received it. I am sending a few papers – and some Punch – to the three of you, I hope you will get a chance of having a little leisure time to enjoy them.

I am so happy you have written to the Rev. Duval but I am afraid there really isn't any news dear. Do tell me if there is anything you are especially in need of that I can

get or make – you will won't you? <u>*Please.*</u> *It is a little*
satisfaction for me to do something for you.

I don't think we shall get to many theatres this season.
You see, owing to the war – the price of seats has been
reduced, nearly everywhere – and in consequence the
managements do not feel like giving tickets away. K's
card will allow one to the picture places, but I don't care
to go alone and of course she is occupied now. I can
always find something to do, I read and am therefore
quite content by my own fireside! I have had several of
Anthony Hope's novels from the library lately. I am not
quite sure if I like them, but they are very good for a
woman my age anyhow!

Well my dear, once again, God bless you all and keep
you, I pray, always the love of your affectionate Mother.

"She seems well," said Eric as he lit another cigarette.

"Say E, have you got one of those for me?" Stuart's question
caused Eric to look at him confused, his brow furrowed.

"Ha! I knew you would break," said Basil, slapping Stuart hard on
the back. Eric smiled and passed Stuart a Woodbine from his pack.

"Well it helps pass the time." Stuart accepted Basil's eager attempts
to light it.

"I'll bet you've been accepting the rum ration too?" Eric's eyes
widened but Stuart was quiet for a moment, he looked up at the blanket
of low grey clouds moving slowly and menacingly across the sky as he
raised his cigarette to his mouth.

"Only on the very cold nights."

Eric laughed hard and loud and ruffled Stuarts hair like a child. Stuart shrugged Eric off but accepted his loss, he was indeed smoking and drinking before Christmas and no longer the teetotal man he had been a few short months ago. The transition amongst the stress and freezing horror of the front had been a lot faster and easier than he expected.

"Oi! Keep the fucking noise down!" screamed a voice from around the closest bend in the trench. The boys fell silent as the Regimental Sergeant Major came into view, "You'll have the Boche over here asking what all the fuss is about!" The RSM looked the boys up and down, "The Hanhams, I should have known."

"Sorry, sir, I was just coming to say hello," said Stuart, standing from his seated position on the firing step.

"Well, wrap it up. Come and see me if you have nothing to do. It'll be just like the Hun to have a go at Christmas." The RSM sniffed at the sky angrily. Even he was not sure if there would be an attack over Christmas, tensions were high.

"Yes, sir. I'd best be heading back anyway, we are also short on manpower so I've been on the line as well as trying to run the platoon. I can tell you, I'm bloody fagged out!" said Stuart, taking another draw from his cigarette.

Eric and Basil nodded as Stuart slung his rifle on his shoulder and looked away down the trench. The route was a quagmire and the pathetic attempts to line it with planks of wood and sandbags were laughable. The water table and constant rain crippled their efforts. Stuart turned back to Basil, "Do try and keep your feet dry, B, and make sure you head back tomorrow for some treatment. I hear some chaps are having their feet removed they are so rotten." Basil looked up at him in shock, a child again and not the man he was a few moments before. Basil looked at the ground as Stuart headed down the line, but he suddenly stopped and turned back towards his brothers after only a few paces.

"Oh, I almost forgot." He rummaged in the pocket of his greatcoat and produced two small boxes. Each box was wrapped in brown paper and had a small drawing of a sprig of holly next to the name of the recipient. "A gift from the Boundfords." Stuarts threw them to his brothers.

"Merry Christmas," said Stuart as he walked away down the trench, trying as best he could to avoid the freezing water and mud thick as treacle.

Basil watched Stuart leave. He felt a stir inside him, a deep love and respect for the man who was not only his big brother but a father since their own had passed away nearly a decade ago. He felt safe at his side and longed for him to be near always. He hoped for a moment Stuart might look back, but Basil only just caught a glimpse of the side of his face, then Stuart was gone.

"Ah that's proper." Basil turned to look at what Eric was so impressed with. He saw in Eric's hand a small oval tin. Silver in colour, it stood out like a jewel against the darkness of the trench and the grey, wintery lifelessness of the day. Basil's eyes lit up. "I'll bet you got the same."

*

Towards evening there was an increase in sniping and a member of the adjacent platoon was hit in the shoulder. He was lucky and disappeared to the aid station with a minor flesh wound but the incident revitalised the British line into finding the culprit, or at least a German on whom to exact revenge. Basil looked on as they searched intently through their periscopes and, as the afternoon light began to fade, fired shots into suspicious mounds of earth in the hope of exposing a German. Soon the enemy across the deadly wasteland got involved and quickly it descended into one of the more dangerous trench games. As Eric and his team experienced a near miss they jokingly pointed to, with the end of a bayonet, the exact point where the bullet struck the bank. Davison then raised a bully beef can on the end of a stick and another shot was fired. The shot missed the tin by a whisker and was greeted by laugher and ironic cheers. The third shot hit the tin and forced Davison to drop the stick and hit the floor, still laughing. The bully beef tin was blown far behind the Kensington trench and this time the laughing and jeering came from the German side. They had won this particular episode in their constant battle with the monotony of trench life.

Shortly before last light Basil was detailed off to keep watch over a position in the second trench. It was not an enviable position because it was in the corner of that particular section and had an exposed right flank. Efforts were constantly made to shore up this area because the position offered such good observation and fields of fire but the weather and concentrated attention from the enemy would weaken it over time. There had been a couple of men from other battalions killed whilst on watch in this position, so it had been labelled *"The Coffin"* in an attempt at humour.

Soon the call for stand too came down the line. Eric jumped up next to Basil and looked up at the weather threatening to turn, dark black clouds promised snow at any moment. Eric, looking through the periscope out into the darkening No Man's Land, was quiet as Basil shuffled into position a little closer to him along the trench wall. Quietly he whispered, "Merry Christmas, E."

"Merry Christmas to you too," said Eric, grinning back. As he did the first snowflakes fell and Basil moved his position slightly to ease the tension on his back foot that was throbbing in wretched pain. It was at that moment the shot came.

The sparks as the bullet hit the loophole made Eric jump in fright and the moment immediately after was deathly silent. Basil looked down in shock and utter bewilderment at the part of his chest the bullet had entered. He hardly acknowledged the pain as it pierced his body like a hot knife, but his legs quickly buckled, and he fell down onto the dark, dank floor of the trench. Breathless, and now in startling agony, he looked around for help and tried to scream but no sounds came.

Against the dark sky of Christmas Eve, he saw the large silhouette of his brother jump down and grab his great coat. Basil could see his mouth moving and the fear in his eyes but could not hear or feel a thing. Behind him shots from his friends lit the darkness in aggressive volleys of frantic firing but unable to cope any longer the lights in his mind burnt out.

In London, Eva felt her heart break and, howling in motherly anguish, she dropped like a stone to the hallway floor. The plates she carried shattered around her. Kathleen ran frantically from the front room.

"Mother! What on earth has happened?"

76 Amesbury Avenue – 6th January 1915

KATHLEEN was sat with Stella at the kitchen table drinking coffee and eating stale bread with blackberry jam when the letterbox opened, and a bundle of letters drop to the mat. They hadn't heard from the boys in a while and since Eva's premonition on Christmas Eve they had been sick with worry. Kathleen rushed towards the door to inspect the delivery. As she passed the living room, she looked inside to check Eva was still fast asleep in her chair. Eva had not slept properly since Christmas Eve, she was sure that her intense, telepathic bond with Basil was the reason for her episode and was convinced Basil had been gravely wounded or worse. She had found normal rest impossible so would nap in her chair only when drink or delirious fatigue took hold of her. She and the girls waited anxiously every morning for word but still none had come.

Kathleen picked up the mail, shuffled through the few letters quickly and immediately the inclusion of an official post card she hadn't seen before made her stop still in shock.

The Royal Crown sat at the top of the postcard and in bold, capital letters were the ominous words *'POST OFFICE TELEGRAM'*. Underneath in official type was the message Kathleen could barely make herself read. Her mind raced and her heart stopped beating. She took a deep breath and steadied herself:

'PRIORITY - MRS E HANHAM, 76 AMESBURY
AVE, STREATHAM, LONDON.
I REGRET TO INFORM YOU THAT YOUR SON,

CPL B. A. HANHAM, HAS BEEN SEVERELY
WOUNDED AND IS EN ROUTE TO JARROW
HOMESTEAD HOSPITAL, BROADSTAIRS, KENT.'

Kathleen shuddered and fell back to the banister. She leant there for a while, her hand covered her mouth and tears rolled down her face. Stella took a step towards her from the kitchen but remained hunched in the hallway like a child.

"K? What is it?" she asked, her face poised for despair and her bottom lip tucked under the top row of her teeth. Kathleen turned to her and held the postcard to her chest, Stella braced herself.

"It's Basil, he's been severely wounded." Kathleen's voice was trembling, and her face was porcelain white. It was harder for her to say than she ever imagined it would be. Stella placed her hand over her heart and Kathleen thought of her mother asleep. Slowly she walked into the room and crouched down in front of Eva.

"Mother," Eva's eyes opened slowly, the wait for news was killing her. Eva's hair was a tangled grey mess and her skin was pale. Her eyes adjusted to the light as she focused on Kathleen.

"Mother, a telegram has just arrived." Kathleen went to continue but Eva raised a hand quickly and closed her eyes. Kathleen looked wide-eyed towards Stella who had sifted through the other letters in the doorway and now held one up from Stuart, silently she mouthed his name. Eva held her hand out and Kathleen rested the telegram on the palm of her hand. She held it close to her chest and Kathleen watched as she slowly pulled it up to her face. As she read it Kathleen saw her mother's eyes moisten. Eva took deep breath.

"Poor boy, he'll be so scared. We must write immediately," said Eva as large tears rolled down her aged face.

Immediately Eva wrote a letter to her youngest son and addressed it to the Matron of Jarrow Homestead Hospital. Stella ran out to post it as Eva read Stuart's letter and penned a reply.

> *'My Dearest Stuart,*
>
> *I am sorry that I was unable to get my usual few lines off to you yesterday, but now that I have received yours, there will be more to write about. Thank you so very much for your letter dear. It was so welcome. I am quite greedy about letters and can never have enough.*
>
> *This morning's post bought me a telegram referring to Basil – telling me he was on his way to Jarrow Homestead Hospital, Broadstairs – nothing else, but of course he was wounded – but it was a printed official postcard with the name and addresses only filled in – so I at once wrote to the Matron of the Jarrow Homestead and enclosed a note for Basil. I should have gone down at once, but, unfortunately, I have one of my winter colds and felt it would not be right to run the risk of communicating it – especially if he is in the convalescent stage – poor dear old boy. It is so strange, but I knew of it instinctively! I have had some very eerie experiences lately, which you would perhaps laugh at – but which have more than ever convinced my belief in mental telepathy – did it occur on the 24th? Do tell me please. I*

am so thankful that God in his goodness spared his life. It might have been lungs or heart – and I can ill spare any of my children. I do thank God with all my heart and I pray you both be preserved from harm, if it be his will and return home to me – and soon. According to the papers life is still good in some far-flung parts of the world – I am so thankful you are both keeping, so far, well and fit. I am so glad you have received Mr. Davy's and Mrs Marshalls things. I do think it was so good of them but have you received nothing yet from the Boundford family – they are disappointed not to have heard that their packages have reached you. Jerry and the sisters sent you, each, tobacco tins. Have you had them? It is strange about that packet of Nov 18th – you were not Sergeant then you know – and in spite of the forwarding agents entering the parcel as London Regiment. K addressed the parcel itself for me both on the package itself and on a tie-on label as 13th Battalion London Regiment so I cannot understand. But what the chocs and biscuits, potted meats and so on will be like, by now, I cannot imagine. If what I hear is true about the new army and the Canadians and so on – they surely ought to give you a rest at home soon. Kitchener seems pretty optimistic anyhow! Won't I do some cooking when you come, please God. God bless you and keep you dear I pray, always the love of your affectionate Mother.

Hanham

*

A few days passed while Eva recovered from her cold, she had so desperately wanted to visit Basil but knew these young men, bodies broken, could not take more infection. Now, feeling better she had made the journey and sat quietly with Kathleen in the waiting room of Jarrow Homestead Hospital. Kathleen could tell her mother was bubbling with excitement under her calm exterior. She too was thrilled to be seeing her brother, the long weeks they had been away at war had felt like years and everyday the newspapers reported on the sacrifices being made. Each new headline ignited fresh concern and raised the stakes for those with loved ones fighting across the sea.

Frustratingly Kathleen and Eva had been asked to wait for the doctor before they were allowed see Basil. Eva fiddled nervously with the small bag of chocolates and home-made biscuits she had for him while Kathleen inspected the penmanship on the envelopes of letters from Stella, unable to attend due the onset of her own winter cold, and others who had sent their wishes. She tried not to think about what ghastly wounds Basil might have and how much he could have changed from the kind, loving boy he had been only a few months ago. The telegram had said '*severely wounded*' but that could mean so many things. Kathleen prayed he had the same zest for life and the youthful sparkle in his eyes that made him her little brother.

Kathleen was lost in a distant gaze when the door behind them opened and, preoccupied with the paintings and tapestries adorning the dark mahogany walls in this once regal dwelling, she failed the first time to hear the doctor call Eva's name.

"Mrs Hanham, I am Doctor Peterson," said the doctor as he extended his hand to Eva who stood to greet him. He was tall and his slicked back hair made him look wealthy and comfortable with his standing in society. He smiled kindly but it was not the genuine smile of a friend, rather the professional welcome of a taxman. Kathleen's stomach started to knot in worry as she took her place by Eva's side.

"Hello doctor. I'm Evangeline Hanham and this is my daughter Kathleen" said Eva, as calmly as she could. Her hand was shaking as she took his.

"Pleasure to meet you both." He spoke well and with slow precision. Peterson didn't wait for the question he knew would be asked. "Lance Corporal Hanham has suffered a great deal." Eva's shoulders started to drop and Kathleen's grip on her arm tightened in dreaded anticipation. "I hope in time he will make a full recovery." Eva breathed a sigh of relief and Kathleen smiled.

"That said, he has a way to go. Firstly, he has terrible trench foot, but he was lucky, the left especially was in awful condition and was nearly removed." Eva took a deep breath and swallowed hard. Kathleen couldn't control tears from running down her face, but Peterson continued in his exact manner. "He has been shot in the chest just below the heart and above the lung. It is rather a nasty wound and the bullet is in a place where we cannot retrieve it without a serious chance he will die of infection. We must hope his body does not reject it but there is a chance it could."

"Reject it?" Eva's voice was a whimper.

"Yes." Peterson put a reassuring hand on Eva's shoulder. "It is in an area too close to the major organs so the surgeons cannot remove it. I have seen these wounds turn septic fast. He will have to remain close by medical aid for some time and certainly he cannot do anything strenuous while it remains there."

"Can I please see him?"

"Of course, he's right this way but there is one more thing, Mrs Hanham." Eva looked up helplessly at him. "Just be warned that he may not be the child you remember." Peterson looked at Eva with his eyebrows raised and his lips tight in serious concern. He turned and led the way into the ward.

Eva stood frozen for a second. She took a deep breath and then followed Peterson onto the ward, Kathleen on her arm.

The medicinal smell of the ward was harsh against Kathleen's senses as they were led slowly between the two rows of beds, observed as they went by wounded soldiers in varied states of ill fortune. Kathleen wished herself invisible but their loud steps on the dark wooden floor shattered the silence and all the men that were able looked in her direction. She tried not to catch their eyes initially but a young man in one of the beds with a broad smile and friendly nod broke her spell and she felt foolish for being so nervous around them. They were all young men like her brothers and were probably very glad to be home. She grew taller as she moved through the room and nodded good morning to those who smiled at her.

At the end of the row the doctor stopped at an empty bed and looked quizzically at the nurse changing the sheets. "Lance Corporal Hanham?" asked Peterson with slight accusation. The nurse looked at him calmly, continuing to fold.

"By the veranda doctor," she said, returning to her work. Peterson shook his head and exhaled in dismay.

"You know they say it isn't bad for them but as a medical professional I am not convinced pulling smoke into ones lungs is a good thing and your son smokes too much, Mrs Hanham." Kathleen smiled at the thought of Basil breaking the rules. Peterson showed them to the end of the room where two large wooden doors led out to the cold murky day.

Eva thanked Peterson, but she and Kathleen were bursting with excitement and Kathleen had to stop herself running through the doors like a giddy child. Slowly they pushed them open and Eva let out a muffled squeak of joy when she saw her son. Basil was sat quietly in an old Victorian wheel chair facing away from them. He was wearing the blue ward uniform and from the waist down was covered by a thick tartan blanket. His hair was neatly swept back and the smoke from his Woodbine made him appear mysterious as he gazed out into the world.

"Dear Boy!" said Eva loudly. The familiar voice Basil had not heard for months made him turn in his chair and he smiled instinctively at the presence of his family. Eva rushed over to him and embraced him hard, too hard, and Basil grunted in agony.

"Sorry my dear, I forgot," Eva released her grip to look into his eyes. She held his head by the jaw and kissed his cheeks many times until he turned away in childish embarrassment. Kathleen placed her hand on his arm and looked at his face lovingly. She and Eva couldn't help their tears.

"What, Mother, did you forget that I had been shot?" said Basil, partly in jest but wincing in genuine pain.

"I'm sorry dear, I couldn't help myself." Eva was now stroking his hair and looking intently at his face. His once boyish contours had the fine, hardened lines of a man and his blue eyes were heavy and sad. The bags under them, common among Hanham men, were darker and deeper. Eva was lost for words, so Kathleen spoke.

"How are you B? Apart from the obvious," Basil took a long pull from his cigarette as Eva sat on the bench beside him, both hands tight around Basil's one free hand resting gently on his lap.

"I'm ok, thanks. The bullet in my chest a minor annoyance compared to my feet." His words were laboured, "Although, that too is really rather sore." Usually such an excitable boy, the man version of her brother seemed troubled. Kathleen thought she must keep the conversation from stalling. Eva, sat by Basil's side, looked at her son in silence trying not to cry.

"Stuart and E. How are they?" Kathleen was trying to remain upbeat. Basil flicked his cigarette into the garden.

"They were well when last I saw them. Eric is getting on well and Stuart is doing a very good job, but he was sad to leave his chums. Say K, have you got any decent wiffs? These ones we get given are awful." He half smiled and some of the old spark appeared in his eyes.

"Yes of course." Kathleen fumbled manically in her bag to find them, grateful for the chance to help her brother. "Here, keep the pack."

"Thanks."

Basil took two cigarettes from the packet and handed one to Kathleen and she accepted gratefully, the packet had seconds before belonged to her but it felt like Basil was giving her something of immense value to him. Basil took a match from the tin in his top pocket and lit both cigarettes awkwardly. He did not have any movement in his left arm and the fingers on his hand were less dextrous than before. Kathleen let him fumble without intervening then leant down to his level and allowed him to light her cigarette.

"Is that the tin the Boundford family sent you all?" asked Eva, unsure of what to say.

"It is." Basil dropped it back into his top pocket. "I know Stuart uses his too. He's started to smoke as well." Basil grinned, it was close enough to a joke to make Kathleen giggle.

"Really?"

"Yes, and he's been drinking too." Basil enjoyed telling tales on his older, wiser, stronger brother.

"Really?" Kathleen started laughing. She thought it was funny but exaggerated her reaction in an attempt to raise spirits and it seemed to work as Basil's smile widened.

"Yep, Eric bet him on the train from Watford he'd be drinking and smoking by Christmas and he won." Basil remembered fondly the moment he had shared with his brothers on Christmas Eve, the day he had been wounded. He then recalled Stuart walking away and the traumatic moment when he was hit, the last time he had seen Eric. His smile slipped, and he gazed at the line of conifers at the far end of the garden. His blue eyes turned pale grey. Kathleen saw Basil's tone change so addressed her own accordingly, she shifted the conversation to include Eva who was still silent by Basil's side.

"That's brilliant, E knows how to wind up Stuart. Doesn't he, Mother?"

"He does dear, all too well." Eva turned her attention again to Basil. "Shouldn't you be inside? It is ghastly cold out here and your feet must be feeling it."

"I can't feel my feet at the moment Mother, so we needn't worry." He smiled at Eva, but it was the horrid, painful smile of the condemned, so Eva turned away. Basil regretted his actions, "Besides they will come and get me soon enough, they are just changing my sheets. I spend my life in bed it seems."

"Quite so, you need to rest and get well again," said Kathleen. She touched his shoulder, but Basil said nothing for a moment.

"What's the point?" Basil took another pull from his cigarette. "They won't let me back out there with a bullet in my chest and weak feet." He was morose and near tears. Kathleen pulled away and tried to stifle the shock at her little brother's reaction, she was confused and upset that he wished to return to war so soon. She too took a long pull form her cigarette and focused on the garden.

"Basil! We've been worried sick about you all for months and only a few days ago we had to read a telegram from the War Office with your name on it. For goodness sake child, God has spared you and I doubt it was so you could return back there straight away."

Basil remained silent in his chair. He appeared emotionless, Eva couldn't remain strong enough to win the battle. "I am so sorry to raise my voice dear, I am just so glad you are safe from harm. We'll get you better and then whatever the Lord has in store for you will be his will." She stroked his face gently, "When will you be home?"

Basil looked deep into her eyes, his own were now close to his usual blue and he had the look of a child once more. He leant his head heavily into the palm of her hand and Eva stood to embrace him, her thick frame comforted him like it had done through his childhood. Kathleen flicked her cigarette away and joined the embrace. Basil's body shook until he was released a few moments later and he relaxed back into his chair. Eva and Kathleen wiped their tears away and Basil breathed in heavily to regain his soldierly composure, he shut his eyes tight and exhaled loudly.

At that moment a sturdy, grey haired nurse opened the door to the veranda and issued her orders, "We will need him back in here now please." She turned on her heel without waiting for a response.

"She's a moody one," said Kathleen. Eva giggled.

"One more wiff before the old bat gets her way," said Basil with a smile.

*

For the next hour Eva and Kathleen were allowed to stay by Basil's bedside. They watched him helped back into bed by a couple of nurses and it was here that Eva and Kathleen saw the extent of Basil's injury. He could not move his left arm very well and every movement was traumatic for him. His feet were bandaged up into padded white socks and he needed help standing when not seated in the chair or on the bed. Once he was laid down in his bed it took him a full five minutes of slow breathing to deal with the pain. A young nurse stood beside him and mopped his brow with a moist flannel to aid his comfort. Tears were rolling down his face and it was too much for Kathleen, she had to turn away. Eva watched the whole process, holding on tight to his right hand. The nurse then removed his blue ward jacket and cotton shirt gently to expose his chest. It was tightly bandaged like a vest and had heavy padding in the area around his heart but, despite this extra padding, there were brown stains of stale blood and the nurse indicated to her senior colleague that fresh blood had appeared.

"We will have to change your dressing again shortly," said the nurse. Basil nodded slowly.

Once Basil seemed comfortable Kathleen pulled up a chair next to her mother and they told him all about what had happened over the last few months. She told him about her play, of Stella and Frank and gossiped about the people he knew. Basil's mouth would twitch a smile on occasions, but he remained focused on the oak beams above him. Listening to the familiar voices of his family soon soothed Basil to sleep and Kathleen and Eva were advised to leave by one of the nurses who had been keeping an eye on him. They left his letters on the side and Eva kissed his forehead. Kathleen touched his hand softly and both women left with their heads low, exhausted and overwhelmed.

Back in London, Kathleen left Eva at home and went to visit Stella to tell her all about Basil. Shortly after seven she arrived at Harriet's flat and fell into her arms when she opened the door. Kathleen was so weak and drained she needed to be helped to the bed where she cried herself to sleep. She did not even have the strength to tell Harriet about Basil and what it was like to see him, nor how she was so afraid for her other two brothers still out there in the cold, stood at their posts. Harriet held her tight and laid a blanket on Kathleen when eventually she drifted to sleep.

Andrew Wood

Estaires, France – 12ᵗʰ January 1915

THE night looked like it would be another freezing ordeal and heavy showers during late afternoon meant all the men were soaked heading into it. There would be no chance now to dry by the fire, night was falling, and everyone was needed on the line. Stuart paced from trench to trench keeping an eye on his men. They had been in the same area now for nearly two months but there wasn't much of an improvement in trench quality or its ability to deal with the Flanders water table. Pallets and *duckboards* were utilised where possible but quality and lasting improvements could not be made while it continued to rain. Stuart and Eric, like all soldiers, had simply to endure.

Stuart, like most, was suffering with trench foot but hadn't been affected badly enough to be pulled from the line like many others. He did his best to alleviate it with regular massaging and the use of whale oil until he was back behind the lines, but it was a constant annoyance. The horrid squalor was also a breeding ground for fever, sickness and diarrhoea that, spread by rats and human contact, quickly ran through a unit at the front and decimated its fighting strength. The Kensingtons were losing more men to trench foot and illness than they were enemy action, although that, too, was taking a heavy toll. The death of Lieutenant Leigh-Pemberton, a much-loved officer from A Company and the best man at Sewell's wedding, from a sniper's bullet the day before, was still fresh in all Kensington minds. Any romantic notions that Stuart and the great swathe of volunteers had when they set sail were now well and truly dead. Survival in these torrid conditions was a constant battle.

The pressure of leadership in such a demanding environment was also taking its toll and Stuart was exhausted but he was staying strong. He felt battle hardened at last, what remained of his Platoon was in good working order and Harding trusted him completely. Stuart's bravery, intelligence and pragmatic approach had impressed him a great deal, so they had a good relationship and the platoon was respected because of it. Often, he was the first choice to lead night raids onto the German lines and whether the task was to capture an enemy soldier for information, conduct reconnaissance or simply harass the enemy and prevent them from conducting their own night attacks, Stuart could be relied upon. Tonight, was one of those nights. He had been asked to lead a raid, this time the objective was to simply harass the enemy, inflict casualties and cause as much fear, panic and pandemonium in the German line as they could.

"Of course, sir, but we don't currently have sufficient numbers, not to cover the line as well," said Stuart when told by Harding he was to lead another raid. He felt the usual feeling of nausea at the thought of heading across to the German line, but he had a more concerning feeling in his gut. Despite the cold he had been sweating all day and his stomach was tight, he worried he might be coming down with diarrhoea but dismissed the idea and put it to the back of his mind. He had no time for that now.

Harding removed his hat and scratched his head in thought. Stuart couldn't see his eyes in the fading light, but he knew he wasn't questioning Stuart's comments. "I shall ask Sewell for a couple of his men to join us. Wait here," Harding made his way through the squelching mud toward A Company, as his platoon commander walked into the darkness Stuart had a tightening in his stomach again. He suddenly felt a desperate need to visit the latrine and cursed under his breath in the knowledge he was soon going to be incapacitated by severe diarrhoea. He hoped he would not experience associated vomiting.

Harding returned a few moments later. "Sewell is sending a few volunt- Good God, Sergeant Hanham, what's wrong with you?" asked Harding as he observed Stuart bent double in the trench. His arms were crossed around his belly in agony.

"I reckon I've got bout of the shits coming on, sir," Stuart had dropped to his haunches, white teeth visible in the darkness as he bit tight in pain.

Harding thought for a moment, "You stay here Hanham. Watch the line and visit the latrine as you need to. I'll task Corporal Harris with leading the patrol." He sent one of the men listening close by to go and fetch Corporal Harris.

Stuart worried Harding thought he was feigning illness to avoid the patrol, but he needn't have. On many occasions Stuart had led patrols when he wasn't required to and was known by his men for being utterly resilient. If he was suffering it was because he really was in turmoil. A few moments later Harris appeared.

"Evening, sir, Tinker says you want me to lead a patrol because our brave sergeant is too afraid?" said Harris in jest, his slender frame hunched against the cold. Harris and Harding laughed quietly and, whilst an obvious joke, it hurt Stuart's pride. He tried to smile but his stomach was too painful. "Go on, man. Go and let the latrines have it," said Harris as he patted Stuart on the back with a gloved hand.

"He's right, Hanham, don't suffer here."

Stuart nodded and stood awkwardly. He used the trench wall to support his ascent, turned to his right and stumbled away. His arms were still folded around his stomach, his body hunched.

"Give em hell, Stu!" called Harris as Stuart moved away into the darkness, the men around him laughed under their breath. Stuart even managed a smile at the comment.

Stuart passed through the next platoon but kept his head down, he was focussed on his destination, the thought of easing his discomfort made his bowels feel loose and he had to tense his stomach painfully to prevent embarrassment. He turned off down the first communications trench towards the latrines and had to work incredibly hard to keep going, sweating profusely with the effort. He would rather have gone on the trench raid than be in this predicament.

As he approached the latrines, he started to remove his clothing frantically. He propped his rifle against the mud wall and flung his great coat on a wooden box to his right. Then he removed his hat and threw it on top of his coat, but it rolled onto the floor and into a puddle. He didn't care. He pulled open the buttons on his tunic, hoping that none were snapped from their thread in the process, and hastily removed his braces from his broad shoulders. In one swift movement he turned, dropped his trousers and sat on the coarse wooden box that had been crudely fashioned into a toilet seat. When finally he relaxed, the evacuation from his bowels was traumatic and he felt immediate relief.

For a few moments Stuart remained delirious and groaned under his breath at the effort it had taken to get here but quickly his senses returned to him he was reminded of what an awful place the latrines were. He felt he might be violently sick when the putrid smell was acknowledged and was grateful at least it was pitch black so he could not see their disgusting state. Desperately trying to find some fresh air above his head, his mind was a blur and he struggled to remain sat upright. It was first time he had been ill, the first time since being in France he had become a serious victim of sickness or injury and he was embarrassed by his state. In his delirium he imagined the men back in his trench laughing at him and he felt a deep, guilty sense of selfishness at not being able to fulfil his duty that night.

Once back at his trenches Stuart had regained a little strength but he still felt weak and lethargic and had discovered while dressing at the latrines that his uniformed soft hat had fallen into a puddle of stinking faeces so he wore his wool hat against the cold, and tossed the former into No Man's Land. As he neared his platoon headquarters, he saw the ten men of the patrol stacked up against the trench wall waiting to leave. Harris was checking them over to make sure they had nothing on them that would weigh them down, rattle or shine. Stuart walked past the men casually but stopped when he heard a familiar voice among them.

"I'm told you can't trust a fart," said Eric from the line of men going on patrol. Stuart smiled and turned to where the comment had come from. Eric's face was blackened with charcoal, but Stuart could see the whites of Eric's eyes and the shining ivory of his smile. He reached and touched his shoulder.

"I could go and get some of it, E, you know, to camouflage your teeth?" He hoped he hadn't taken too long with his comeback, there was a chuckle from the men around them and Eric shook his head with a smile.

"I'd rather you knocked them all out with a shovel," replied Eric, laughing. Stuart stepped back and watched their final preparations.

Since Basil had been wounded Stuart and Eric had seen less of each other. There were fewer men on the line so Stuart did not always have the time to visit with Eric and, unlike Basil, he knew Eric would be fine without regular visits from him. Stuart though had noticed a change in his brother. When Basil had been wounded Eric was first on the scene and had watched his brother leave the trench, gasping for air and life. After Basil disappeared on the stretcher, Eric had to be held down by three men as he attempted a suicidal charge onto the enemy line. Stuart had since learnt that Eric was a regular volunteer for trench raids and relished any opportunity to seek revenge for Basil, his brother and best friend. Stuart wished Eric would not put himself in such danger and he was worried a part of Eric had snapped the night Basil had been hit. The part of him that was kind seemed to be more distant and now Eric was again preparing for another raid. There seemed a piece of Eric that had been broken for good, and his hatred for the enemy boiling constantly.

"E, can I have a word?" Eric looked up at him and stepped out of line. He, like most, had fashioned his own wooden bat, nails protruded from the end like a medieval mace. It was far more effective than a bayonet in the ghastly close quarters of trench warfare.

"What's up old man? Run out of smokes?"

"No, I'm fine, I just want you to take care." Eric reeled away, insulted.

"Don't worry about me. It's the Hun who needs to take care." Eric turned back towards the patrol now in the final stages of preparation.

Stuart grabbed his arm, "E! Basil will be fine. Don't get yourself killed trying to avenge him when he's at home safe and sound." He was angry and gripped tightly but Eric easily pulled his arm from Stuart's grasp, weak with illness.

"You just worry about not shitting yourself." Eric returned again to the line of men waiting for the signal to scale the ladder and make their way towards the German lines. Stuart looked down at the ground. He didn't know what else to say, he hoped in time Eric's rage would cease and he would be his old, comic self again.

Eric was at the end of the line of men as they started to silently climb the ladders out into No Man's Land. He looked towards Stuart who seemed a sad figure in the darkness and he regretted his comments a moment before. He knew every second out here could be his last, so he stepped back out of the line and embraced Stuart around the shoulders. Stuart's arms were down by his side and his body was weak because of the virus in his system. Eric's bear hug was strong, and Stuart felt like a child, but he was grateful. Within a second though, Eric was gone. Scaling the ladder before him with the swift ease of a cat, he disappeared into the night. Stuart felt morose and alone as he watched his brother leave but these feelings were quickly replaced by the angry churning in his bowels. He turned and rushed back to the latrines.

*

The patrol moved as quickly and quietly as possible through the thick black mud of No Man's Land, but every step was a tremendous effort. They tried to use the low ground of shell holes to hide their silhouettes from the enemy but in every crater was a deep, freezing puddle of stinking water that made movement even harder and created more noise. Instead they stayed low and did the best they could to keep quiet, crawling flat on their bellies where the ground forced them higher.

Eric was at the rear of the ten-man patrol snaking its way across the mud, it was his task to keep an eye on the ground they had covered and ensure that an enemy patrol didn't pass them or catch them from behind, to be trapped in the open would be a disaster. In some places there was only two hundred yards separating the trenches, so it wasn't long before the patrol commander indicated a halt. They formed a circle around the rim of a shell hole and waited a few moments to make sure their presence was undetected. A cold wind from the east carried whispers from the enemy in nearby trenches to where Eric waited.

After a few moments of quiet the patrol commander used the light of the moon to check his watch and then signalled with a kick to the man next to him that the next phase was to begin. The signal was passed around the others in the shell hole and the six men detailed to assault the trench lined up on the side closest to the enemy while the remaining men closed the circle as best they could. Here they waited for the exact time when, all along the Kensington line and beyond, small groups would enter the enemy position and cause as much violence as possible.

Eric was one of the men that would enter the trench. He waited at the back of the six-man team in water up to his knees. It was cold and painful on his tender feet, his back was aching, his left elbow was rested on a hard rock and was extremely uncomfortable, but he couldn't move. He focused his mind and waited anxiously for the signal. For him it was another a chance of retribution for Basil, still suffering at home, and the others he knew that were killed or wounded. Eric started to sweat and grind his teeth, he felt like an animal and was a stark contrast to the man in front who was weeping quietly.

After a few more moments of hateful anticipation the signal for the men to advance the final forty yards towards the enemy line was given. Eric, struggling to free himself from the quagmire, was way behind once he had managed to do so. Away to his right about five hundred metres a machine gun opened up and along the line flare guns fired illumination high into the darkness. In this fizzing orange light Eric could make out the small teams of Kensingtons and Royal Irish Rifles entering the enemy lines and closer to him he could see the spiked helmets of his enemy. He was worried the icy puddle had held him too long so was relieved to make it to the enemy trench as heavy lead wasps cracked above his head.

The first three men turned off to the right, Eric and two men went to the left and were immediately involved in brutal hand-to-hand fighting. The man in front of Eric was performing a deathly tango with a large, heavyset German. The German was winning the fight with the Kensington man, so Eric instinctively lowered his rifle and fired a shot from the hip. It exploded into the big man's chest and he fell backward like a giant tree. The man Eric had rescued wasted no time in delivering a killer blow to the man's neck with the sharpened end of his shovel. Eric didn't stop to look at the ghastly scene left by the improvised axe but pushed past for the next prize.

A short way further on was a dugout and the other member of Eric's trio who managed to avoid the big German. He was stood above the still flinching body of another he had just killed, eyes rolled back, mouth foaming in the throes of death. Eric knew there would soon be men emerging from the dugout, so he indicated for the man in front of him to keep watch on the trench ahead and for the man behind to watch their rear. He steadied himself for a fight and felt his heart beat all around his body like a base drum, he began to salivate and snarled as he waited. He had little fear, just a primitive desire to inflict pain and death. He heard his enemy starting to emerge, their heavy boots on the wooden boards that led the way underground and their panicked voices rapidly approaching. Eric lowered his rifle to his hip again and braced himself. When the voices were close, he fired into the darkness of the dugout entrance. The soft thud of lead into flesh and screams from a wounded man indicated he had hit his unseen target, so he drew the bolt back on his rifle and fired twice more into the darkness. Still he could hear shouting and at least one man coming fast up the gangway towards him so Eric threw down his rifle and took from his belt his ghoulish spiked hammer. Now the German artillery had fired large illumination shells into the air and the world was a bright, flickering orange. Eric stepped to one side of the opening as a shot was fired form the darkness, it smashed into the bank as a man emerged from the dugout, his jaw was clenched in fearful fury and his eyes wide and menacing. Eric swung his ghastly club with all his might and struck the side of the man's head with such force it killed him instantly. A second man emerged behind Eric's quarry and lunged at Eric, he had a knife in his hand and was attempting to plunge it into Eric torso, but his actions were wild and erratic. Eric was defenceless, he had no time to lever his crude weapon from the dead man's skull and the blood on the handle caused it to slip out of his grasp. He was on his back, fending off the rabid German like an attacking wolf. He thought for a moment he might be overcome but a shot from his right made the man lurch backwards and Eric was able to throw him away to his left. His foe groaned, gurgled and died.

Eric stood, grabbed his rifle and pulled his homemade weapon from the skull of his victim just as the signal sounded for them to return. Quickly they clambered out of the enemy trench and made their way back towards the British lines. The flares in the air were just about to die but new ones exploded, and Eric could hear German re-enforcements entering the trenches behind them. There was only a short window for them to get back or they would have to find cover in No Man's Land and wait for quiet to crawl back. Eric did not want to lie in a puddle all night so he ran as fast as he could, his lungs were burning but the adrenaline in his body kept him strong. He kept to the same path they had used on their advance and, glad his return journey was not one harassed by the enemy, he and his patrol flung themselves into their trenches one by one. One of the Irish patrols was not so lucky, word spread quickly that they had lost half their number on the return journey.

*

Stuart's night was vastly different to Eric's. He had to visit the latrines four times in the couple of hours the patrol was away and Harding had ordered him to lie down in their platoon dugout. Stuart put up little fight and fell into a feverish sleep, only opening his eyes to make a dash to the latrines or stagger outside to vomit. He had been vaguely aware of the firing during the night and had heard the excited voices of the men arriving back from the patrol, but he was so delirious it felt like a dream. He eventually woke a few minutes past eight o'clock in the morning and felt an instant panic when he saw it getting light outside, the dank interior of the dugout a nasty reminder of where he was. He took a moment to settle himself and prepared to get up from the hard box he had been using as a bed but the effort required to raise his head was testament to how weak he was. He had no strength in his fingers and his core felt rubbery and useless. He took a few moments to compose himself once he had struggled up into the seated position. It was at this moment that Harding lifted the sandbag flap to check on him.

"Ah Hanham, you're up. Good man. Now grab your kit, the med chaps are here to take you back." Stuart looked towards Harding in a pathetic attempt to argue his health, but he was slow and dazed, Harding cut him off, "No arguments please, you look like shit! Come now and you won't have to walk." Harding ducked out and returned to the dawn.

Stuart rolled off the box he was sat on and stooped out of the dugout, he was unsteady on his feet so bounced through the opening. It took a few moments for his eyes to adjust to the light but the sight of the men in front of him gave him a little strength. It didn't last for long though and he fell back onto the wall of the trench, Eric was there to hold him.

"Bloody hell, you look like shit!" said Eric, heaving Stuart to his feet. Stuart steadied himself and looked at his brother. Eric had a cigarette in his mouth and his face was rugged and hard. It was splattered with mud and blood and his eyes were heavy with life. Stuart tried to ask why Eric was here in his lines, but Harding interrupted him again.

"He wanted to make sure you weren't dead, Sergeant Hanham. Now hurry up or you'll miss the cart." Harding shooed Stuart along.

"I'll take him, sir," said Eric, handing his cigarette to the man next to him. Harding nodded and turned back towards the line where most the men were on the firing step observing, steam rising from their bodies. A few others prepared a fire.

Eric kept hold of Stuart's left arm and in one swift motion hoisted his brother up onto his shoulders. Stuart groaned at the pain of Eric's rifle pressing into his chest. "Ah stop complaining."

Stuart was heavy in the saddle and felt awkward strung over Eric's shoulders but didn't have the strength to adjust his position, so Eric had to stop and bounce him up higher when he started to sag. Despite this Eric made steady progress through the mud and Stuart was impressed by his strength. Stuart was not a small man, but Eric seemed to cope with him easily. He grunted his thanks as best he could.

"Just try not to shit on me," said Eric, breathless with exertion. Stuart managed a smile and when finally, they reached the end of the communication trench Eric laid Stuart down on the cart hidden from enemy view by a high bank and whose route back to the casualty clearing station was covered by the empty shells of houses. A large chestnut mare stood quietly in the harness looking down at the ground. Stuart had no energy to speak but looked up at his brother who was stretching his back from the effort of carrying him. Eric then turned to a medic and explained Stuart was feverish and had been suffering all night with diarrhoea and vomiting. The medic nodded and turned away, content that Stuart was in a sorry state. Eric looked down at his brother and smiled, placing his rifle on his chest so Stuart didn't drop it.

"A few days rest will see you right. Don't rush back will you?" Eric laid a hand on Stuart's chest and Stuart held it as tight as he could. "Send me an update when you're set." Stuart smiled as Eric turned away.

"E!" Stuart attempted to call Eric back, but his voice was a pathetic hiss. He was sure Eric hadn't heard so he was relieved when Eric's face appeared above him again, kind and soft despite the mud and blood that dirtied it and the vicious warrior within. Stuart tapped the top pocket where he kept his packet of cigarettes. Eric understood immediately and removed the packet gratefully. "Take care," whispered Stuart coarsely and Eric winked at him as the cart bumped away. Stuart watched him leave then immediately fell asleep.

*

Hanham

A couple of days later Eric received a *Correspondance Militaire* from Stuart, a short distance away in Estaires,

'Dear old E,

I am at the '24th Field Ambulance'. They sent me here instead of to the billet. I am being well dosed with 'many things' but am not quite right yet. I do hope you will be able to get our old cover when you get in tonight. I have been thinking of you all the time, out in the vile rain.

Soon be back to you, Love from Stuart'

Eric was glad to know Stuart was doing better, he felt lonely out on the line without him and found that these last few miserable days had forced his thoughts to drift home. He longed for a comfortable bed, Eva's cooking and he dreamed of dry feet and the warmth of the log fire, but these images of home pained him too. He couldn't imagine what it would be like to go from this place of horror and ghastly acts to the sanctity of his normal life. He wondered if he would ever be able to enjoy the simple things again without images of his time here to haunt him. Was he broken? Would he ever be the same Eric Hanham he had been a few short months ago? Surely in time the images of his brother lying helpless on a stretcher and memories of dead friends and foe would fade. Eric would not allow these melancholy thoughts to plague him for too long, weakness could be the end of him out here, so he converted his sadness to anger and kept going.

The next night A and B Company were relieved and trudged back through the wind and rain towards their billets. The journey was still a ghastly one, but Eric had grown used to the fatigue and his muscles had hardened to the task. Painful feet the main discomfort, now and always. Eric had another letter from Stuart the next day.

> *'Dear E,*
>
> *I hope you got my other post card. I am expecting to be discharged in a day or two. I hope you are going on all right. Will you try and get any letters etc that may come for me so as to prevent them getting in the 'Hospital Bags'. I am writing mum from here, so she does not question where I am.*
>
> *Love Stuart'*

Eric requested a pass that morning to leave the billets and go and see Stuart in the field hospital. He was granted three hours so walked the couple of miles to its location on the other side of town. As he passed through Estaires, Eric could see all around him the scuff marks of war and even though shells had destroyed the majority of buildings they were full of life. Most had been converted into billets or coffee shops selling sandwiches, potted meats and jam. Eric acknowledged a few men he knew in the town but didn't accept any offers to join their foray for wine. Instead he headed straight for the field hospital to look for Stuart.

The field hospital was hidden behind a street of houses, so Eric smelt it before it came into view, the pungent aroma of disinfectant sour in his nose. Under the flaps of the large tent he could see nurses and medics moving with purpose and in the entrance a group of engineers were doing their best to lay decking and make a walkway, but it was a losing battle.

The mud was too deep and churned up so badly that only a prolonged period of warm, dry weather would help.

Eric stood for a while and surveyed the scene while he smoked a cigarette, the last thing he wanted to do was ask the wrong person a question and be reprimanded, that would only annoy him and he felt in good spirits today. Instead he waited for the right moment and eventually he spotted a young medic making his way towards him from the tent. He had a smile on his face and was laughing about something he had just heard. Eric accosted him respectfully as he wore the three stripes of a sergeant.

"Excuse me, sergeant, where might I find my brother? He was admitted with fever and diarrhoea a few days ago," asked Eric, politely. The Sergeant regarded him up and down like an inconvenience but then smiled casually. He turned and pointed to the right side of a large tent.

"Down there most likely though he might be in quarantine if he's feverish," said the Medic, his strong Geordie accent made Eric smile.

Eric thanked him and made his way towards the area he had been shown. He reached the end of the tent and looked into the darkness, there was not much movement inside and most were laying on canvas cots fully clothed under blankets, mud still caked to their boots, trousers and great coats. He finally found Stuart some five beds along the row to his right. He was about to call out to him but was stopped by a voice to his left that shocked him into silence.

"Can I help you, lad?" asked another Medic Sergeant. He was mean looking and his coarse Scottish tone, combined with heavyset facial features, made him very intimidating. Eric stepped back instinctively.

"I'm here to see my brother Sergeant Hanham." Eric pointed to Stuart who had heard the commotion and was smiling at Eric.

"Like fuck you are, young man! This is an isolation ward," said the medic angrily as he gestured Eric away.

Eric walked a few feet and turned back towards Stuart who was leaning up on his elbows and smiling. Eric smiled back, shrugged his shoulders and held up a packet of cigarettes, Stuart nodded with wide eyes and Eric threw the packet at his brother, relived to see them fall close to Stuart's bed. Stuart waved his thanks and picked up the packet from the floor. Eric turned and walked back through the town. He was not sure what to expect when he had set out that morning and it surprised him how truly happy it had made him to see his brother looking well. He really did not know what he would do without him.

Camden Town, London – 23rd February 1915

"DO you want one of these? They are quite strong, but I find they help preserve my voice." Victoria smiled kindly as she offered Kathleen a paper bag of hard sweets. Kathleen took one gratefully and popped it in her mouth, moving it from side to side with her tongue. After a few seconds she felt the hot, medicinal sting and the sweet kiss of sugar. Kathleen instinctively scrunched her face and sucked hard to keep the rush of saliva in her mouth.

"Oh, they have quite a tang to them," said Kathleen through closed eyes. She looked up at Victoria, tall and beautiful, laughing quietly.

"Yes, they take a little bit of getting used to." Victoria was smiling, her shining white teeth perfectly set but quickly her face hardened, and she nudged Kathleen, so she didn't miss her cue. Kitty, the youngest of the three and playing the younger sister of their trio, was alone on the stage coming to the end of her solo. Victoria and Kathleen would soon play their part in the scene.

Kathleen, realising she must get rid of the sweet, slid it gracefully to the right of her mouth and bit down hard with her molars. The noise was ghastly, like the crunch of gravel under a heavy foot and the pain searing and instantaneous. She spat the sweet out onto the floor with creamy white shards of her own teeth. Victoria held her hand to her mouth in shock. Kathleen's eyes were shut tight and she covered her own mouth with both hands to mute her screams. "Are you ok?" asked Victoria.

Kathleen took three deep breaths through her nose and opened her eyes. Tears obscured her vision and she could taste blood in her mouth, a foul tang with the remaining taste of sweet sugar.

"We only have a few seconds." Kathleen took a deep breath to steady herself but the air on her exposed nerves was as intensely painful as the initial fracture. "We have to go! I'm so sorry Kath."

Kathleen recognised her cue, spat onto the floor a gruesome mix of bright red blood, pearl white saliva and more shards of tooth and sweet. Victoria said nothing but followed Kathleen out into the bright spotlights. No one in the audience was aware Kathleen was in excruciating pain.

After the scene Kathleen rushed to a mirror to inspect the damage but she could not find the angle to see the tooth she had broken. She was crying and shaking in pain.

"Let me have a look," said Victoria, grasping her head by the jaw and opening her mouth with the skill of a nurse. Kathleen looked at her bright blue eyes assessing the damage. Both women were glowing with a thin sheen of sweat from the dance they had just completed, Victoria's blonde hair wild and messy, "I am so sorry. Do you think you can continue for the last few scenes?" Kathleen nodded through tears. Victoria apologised again and started to change for their next scene as Harriet appeared from the rear of the stage and smiled at Kitty who was brushing her mousy brown hair into a tight ponytail.

Kathleen was bent down changing her dress then stood to her full height and looked at Harriet whose smile immediately vanished, "What's wrong?" Harriet placed an arm on Kathleen's bare shoulder. Victoria looked round as she was tying her hair into a tight bun.

"I gave her a sweet, Harry, and she's cracked her tooth badly. She has soldiered on though bless her. Again, I'm so sorry, Kath." Victoria's apology was sincere. Kitty looked over and winced her concern at the thought. Kathleen raised her hand in acknowledgement and in acceptance of Victoria's apology.

"Here, let me help you," said Harriet as she moved around Kathleen to brush her hair and set it for the next scene. Kathleen continued to dress but her eyes were flowing with heavy tears and the pain from her tooth had started to spread to her face and neck. She wanted to lie down and cry into Harriet's arms, she was a professional though and would finish the show. She had to.

After the curtain Kathleen was delirious with pain and Harriet would not let her travel home in such a vulnerable state. Kathleen didn't have the strength to argue and was grateful for the company. They arrived at 76 a little after eleven thirty, Kathleen's mouth was throbbing wildly, and she was unsteady on her feet. Harriet opened the door and Kathleen pointed towards the kitchen, gently she removed herself from Harriet's grasp and made her way to the end of the house using the walls for support. There was a soft glow coming from the room at the back of the kitchen where Eva recently had a fire installed, in there was her favourite chair and a small couch.

Kathleen tried to pour herself a glass of salt water to wash out her mouth but Harriet stopped her and forced Kathleen towards the fire. She entered the snug and dropped heavily onto the small couch, tilting her head back dramatically. After a short moment of recuperation, she looked forward expecting to see her mother in the chair, but it was Basil, he looked confused.

"Are you alright K?" asked Basil. He had been reading a book in the light of the fire and had a thick blanket around his legs and feet like an old man. His face flickered handsomely in the orange light and his eyes shone bright.

Kathleen couldn't speak so she pointed to the side of her mouth stuffed with white tissue, her cheek bulging like a hamster. Basil furrowed his brow, he was still confused as Harriet entered stirring a glass of salty water with a spoon. "Here, swill this around your mouth and spit it out," said Harriet, handing Kathleen the glass and removing the spoon.

Basil swivelled in his chair as far as his chest wound would allow and regarded the stranger in his house. Harriet looked like a giant in the glowing light of the fire and in contrast to the low ceiling of the snug. Her hair was a deep red and her pale skin shone like white silk in the low light. Her big eyes flickered yellow.

"You must be Basil," Harriet extended a hand. He laid his book down on his lap and shook her hand gently, his eyes fixed on hers.

"I am," he said, sheepishly. "And you are?" Harriet looked at Kathleen who casually waved at her indicating she was to conduct her own introduction.

"I'm Harriet, I work with Kathleen."

"What's happened to the old girl?" he asked, looking towards Kathleen who was noisily swilling the salt water in her mouth, eyes shut tight in pain.

"One of the girls gave her a boiled sweet at work and she's broken one of her teeth chewing it." Basil laughed and placed his book on the floor. Kathleen kicked the leg of the chair and Basil laughed again.

"Well I shall leave you to it, K," said Harriet, looking awkwardly towards the exit.

Kathleen's wide eyes screamed, and she shook her head vigorously.

She patted the seat next to her demanding Harriet come and sit down. Harriet did as she was asked.

The next morning Kathleen and Harriet walked downstairs towards the sounds and smells of Eva preparing breakfast in the kitchen. Kathleen could tell Harriet was nervous, but she assured her, as best she could with a thick wad of tissues wedged in her mouth, that her mother would not assume them to be anything other than colleagues and friends and that she would be grateful Harriet had assisted her.

"K my dear, how are you?" said Eva rushing over to Kathleen. She tilted her head back and opened her mouth like a child to assess the damage. Kathleen removed the tissue she had protecting the nerves from the cold morning. "Goodness me it's completely smashed. You'll have to go and see someone to have it removed or it will go bad." Kathleen nodded solemnly.

"And you must be Harriet. Thank you so much for helping K home." Kathleen turned to allow Harriet's entry to the room and accept her mother's greeting.

"It was my pleasure Mrs Hanham, she's a very determined lady," said Harriet, proudly. Eva smiled and indicated Harriet should sit at the table opposite where Basil was sat reading yesterday's paper. He smiled politely as she sat down.

"Now we don't have much dear, but I can offer you tea and some eggy bread."

"That sounds lovely," replied Harriet.

"Now K, go and see a man I know on the Bristow Road, he is meant to be quite good. A friend of mine went to see him when she had trouble with her teeth and she said good things," ordered Eva as she plated the first portion of eggy bread and placed it in front of Basil.

Harriet cocked her head to read the headline while Kathleen poured them some tea. It read: *"KING COMMENDS FIGHTING IRISH".* Harriet broke the short silence. "You must be happy to be home Basil?" A broad smile of sincerity across her pretty face.

Eva pulled a deep breath from the air above her head and Basil twitched a false smile towards Harriet. Like a lot of men who had returned home wounded he was pleased to be alive, but Basil had a crippling feeling of guilt inside him that he couldn't ignore. He wanted, needed, to be back out there with his brothers and his battalion and felt pathetic sat at home while others continued to fight. He dreamt the dreams of a soldier and could not see why he had been chosen, spared or punished in this way. He didn't know what he had done to be so devoid of the glory he had sought as a small boy. He thought the end to his fighting ignominious and he hated himself deeply for being so pathetic. He found himself spiralling into a world of self-loathing and depression and he was a long way from the boy who had left for the war. He was now an angry man, his eyes lifeless and sad.

Eva broke the awkward silence, "Well he's happy to be having good food again." She gently touched his shoulder as she lay Harriet's breakfast in front of her. There was silence again, Kathleen noticed Harriet's face was flushed pink in embarrassment, so she changed the subject.

*

Kathleen struggled through the next couple of days in constant agony. She had managed little sleep and the infection from her damaged tooth was causing a painful throbbing, but she had managed to perform well enough for her issue to go unnoticed. The show however was causing her, and the other members of the cast and crew, added concern. A lot of the stagehands had been dismissed and the props and scenery scaled back. All of them knew that funds were running low and Graves had been seen showing three female friends around the theatre and explaining to them the new structure of the revue. This started a rumour amongst the cast that Kathleen, Victoria and Kitty were soon to be replaced. Currently Kathleen wasn't thinking about work, she was totally focused on the pain in her mouth. Her legs were shaking in anticipation and her stomach growled in nauseous worry as she waited for the dentist. The waiting room was a faded green and grey and the exposed brickwork showed no one had given any thought to appearance.

"Miss Hanham?" called a voice eventually from a small room to her right. She looked round the poorly decorated waiting room to the man stood in the doorway. He beckoned her over with a flick of his head, so Kathleen shuffled nervously into the room and dropped slowly onto a reclined chair under a bright lamp.

"What is the problem then?" There was no introduction and Kathleen felt like a hindrance. He tied a cotton mask to his face but not before Kathleen caught in her nostrils the sharp aroma of stale alcohol. She thought about cancelling but the shooting pain resumed and reminded her why she was here.

"I have broken my tooth and it is mighty painful," said Kathleen, looking towards the ceiling and the bright light. The dentist nodded and grunted his understanding.

"Open wide."

Kathleen obeyed and the dentist had a good look inside her mouth. Forcefully he pulled her head around instead of moving his own for a better view, snorting his assessments as he went. Kathleen looked uneasily at his greying hair and could see plainly the ugly pockmarks of his adolescence many years ago. His eyes were pale green like the waiting room décor.

"I shall have to remove that broken one for sure and maybe the one next to it, but I won't know until I see the roots," said the dentist, in a matter of fact way.

"Will it hurt?" Kathleen was not a determined, sprightly woman anymore. She was a little girl, afraid.

"I should think so, but it will soon improve." Kathleen thought she saw a smile in his eyes. "Lay back please." Kathleen laid her head back and opened her mouth wide. She closed her eyes but not before she caught a glimpse of the gruesome instruments the dentist was about to use. One had a wooden handle two inches long and a sharp metal point with a flat edge, the shape of the stem reminded her of a corkscrew. In his other hand were powerful forceps.

Kathleen started to cry as he entered her mouth. She could taste the cold tang of metal on her tongue, so she clenched her fists until her fingers were throbbing red and her knuckles were white. She flinched as the forceps grasped the painful remnants of her broken tooth and whined though her nose as he dug away at the root with the other implement. He pulled hard, but the pincers slipped off the stubborn tooth.

"Keep still!" he demanded.

Kathleen braced herself for more pain. This time the intrusion was deeper and the shock more profound. Tears were pulsing out of her eyes and mixing with the bloody saliva on her cheek. She thought she might pass out when he pulled hard again without success.

"Well the good news is the root is still strong, so I'll only have to remove this one." He said it in a playful way, which unsettled Kathleen. She opened her eyes wide enough to see him through her tears and was sure he was enjoying his work.

He entered again, this time the tooth came out with an audible, excruciating rip. Blood spurted from the gaping hole and she was almost violently sick as a large amount of it slipped down her throat. It was warm and bitter. He stuffed her mouth with white padding and instructed Kathleen to bite down hard on it to stop the bleeding. She opened her eyes and he passed her a towel to wipe her face and neck.

"All done."

Kathleen crashed through the door of 76 an hour later and ran to the arms of Eva who was upstairs tidying her room, she was hysterical and sobbed wildly. Eva lifted Kathleen's chin to look at her and frowned when she saw the blood on her face and the tears in her eyes. Had Eva not known where she had been her concern would have been greater as Kathleen looked as though she had been in a street fight or set upon by a London mob.

"My love, what on earth did he do to you?" asked Eva. Basil was now stood at the door of his mother's room, the commotion had roused him from troubled sleep.

Kathleen opened her mouth and removed the blood red padding. Eva yelped at the mess that had been made of her daughter's mouth. All her teeth were stained brown with blood and the black hole of her exposed root was oozing slowly. Kathleen pulled a fresh wad from her jacket pocket and Eva stuffed it into her mouth. Kathleen was then led away to her room and laid her down on her bed. Basil watched his brave sister in silent concern.

*

Over the weekend the pain in Kathleen's mouth subsided but things were not going well at the theatre. It looked more and more like she, Victoria and Kitty, would be replaced by three of Grave's friends struggling for work. Most concerning though Harriet had not been at the theatre one evening and it did not take much for Kathleen to discover she had been let go. She couldn't wait for the show to end that night and, after changing quickly, she ran the few blocks to Harriet's flat.

It was raining lightly and cold, but Kathleen didn't pay much attention to the weather. When Harriet opened the door, she looked happy and smiled at Kathleen in obvious joy. Kathleen entered, removed her wet hat and jacket and when Harriet shut the door Kathleen turned and kissed her passionately.

"Someone is feeling better," said Harriet, her beautiful smile lit a candle in Kathleen's heart and a wave of happiness flooded through her body, but Kathleen quickly turned serious.

"I've come straight from the theatre. What happened?"

"They can't afford me anymore." Harriet turned and walked towards her small living room and the light of a single lamp, "But I'm not fussed. Do you want a drink?"

"You're really not upset?"

"No, to be truthful I was expecting it and I think you should too. Those girls are there to replace the three of you, I'm sure of it. There isn't a great deal of stage work around because of the war and George can pay them less than you and keep his friends working," explained Harriet, pouring a glass of sherry for herself and one for Kathleen.

Kathleen was quiet on the couch, she had thought that was the case and was now angry she hadn't taken one of the roles offered to her over the last couple of months. She made a mental note to check back on them during the week.

"Besides, I've been thinking about doing my bit. You know, for the war effort." Harriet's comment broke Kathleen from her own selfish concern. She looked up sharply at her lover, Harriet's face was golden in the low light of the lamp and her wide eyes were shining bright.

"What? What will you do?"

"I think I will train as a nurse," Harriet took a delicate sip from her sherry and came to sit down next to Kathleen. She placed her glass on the small table beside the couch and held Kathleen's right hand tenderly. "Seeing our boys, like your Basil, around town with their injuries makes me want to help. I could really be of use, you know."

It sounded like her decision had been made and she was convincing Kathleen of her choice. Kathleen though needed little convincing, she had also thought about such work but believed that her work as an actress and making people happy through theatre was very important too. It was what kept her going when her feet were blistered or her voice hoarse and painful. She placed her glass on the floor and turned to face Harriet, "You will be such a wonderful nurse and it is such important work," she paused and thought of Basil, "It's just I will miss you so much." Kathleen levelled her gaze at Harriet. This war was responsible for so much anguish, much of it unseen or undocumented in the papers.

"And I you but you never know, I might be based in London." Harriet's eyes lit up in hope.

"I hope so." Kathleen laid her head on Harriet's chest. She could feel Harriet's smooth skin through her thin night dress and closed her eyes to remember that moment and all the fun times they had had over the last few months. She was lost in her scent and in the warmth of her body. Harriet said nothing but held Kathleen tight to her, she took deep heavy breaths that made her body rise and fall in sensual grace. Kathleen raised her head slowly and kissed Harriet, the sweet taste of sherry was fresh on her lips.

In the morning Kathleen attended rehearsal while Harriet went to enrol as a nurse. They met for lunch at quiet place near the canal. Harriet struggled to tell Kathleen she was to leave in two days time for her training in Bristol and couldn't possibly know where she was going to be after that. Kathleen had hoped for more time before Harriet had to leave so was shocked and unable to control her emotions. She felt foolish for falling in love and it angered her. She had been so strong until this woman had entered her life and now, she felt weak, suddenly alone in the world. A lost soul in a battle with only herself, a war she couldn't hope to win.

They arranged to spend the night together and in bed they explored each other slowly and lovingly as if for the first time. Every moment had the heightened feel of it being their last and painful thoughts of loss made their love stronger. They communicated through flickers of sadness, twitching smiles of longing and deep breaths of shuddering pain. Kathleen felt like she was being pulled away from her soul mate by an immovable force, an evil disease sweeping across the world that couldn't be stopped.

They said their final goodbye outside of Harriet's flat in the cold, bright light and Kathleen felt sick with fear and loss as Harriet walked away down the road. Her breaking heart was thumping hard in her chest and she longed to see the face of her beloved one more time, but Harriet did not look back. Kathleen turned and walked away. London felt silent and ghostly. The sounds of the city were slow and laboured as she focused on placing of one foot in front of the other. She had to think hard about where she was and where she had to be, it seemed nothing mattered.

*

Kathleen was thirty minutes late for morning rehearsals so was relieved to see they hadn't begun as she arrived at her rail behind the stage.

"Where have you been?" asked Victoria, smoking a cigarette casually. Her eyes were narrowed in jovial accusation. Kathleen was glowing with the stress of tardiness, she looked guilty and childlike and her eyes were red raw.

"I've just been - "

"Relax, George and the money-man are still talking in the front row. I think I know who pulls the strings around here now," said Victoria, peeking around the back of the stage. Kathleen moved to take a look, she needed something to take her mind away somewhere, anywhere.

"What do you think they are talking about Kit?" Kitty was stood opposite Victoria mimicking her stance, she even held her cigarette in the same classy way Victoria did. Kathleen started to change behind them, she was crying again so splashed her face with water to hide her tears.

"I don't know but I'd love to listen," replied Kitty. Victoria lowered her voice and impersonated the money-man and Kitty giggled playfully.

"Looks like they've finished." Kathleen said nothing but turned to face the two girls. She was now in the same dress as Kitty and Victoria, but her hair was dishevelled and her face was wet with water and tears.

"Are you ok?" asked Kitty, sincerity etched across her freckly young face. Victoria extinguished her cigarette and put a long arm around Kathleen.

"It'll be ok dear, whatever it is we can work it out." Kathleen pulled away gently and straightened herself. She brushed herself down and started to put her hair up in a bun.

"I'm fine, just a late night." Kathleen attempted to shrug her emotions away.

"Vic! Is Kathy back there please?" asked Graves from the stage. Kathleen hated being called 'Kathy' but went out and stood in front of Graves. Behind him was the fat man he had been talking to moments before.

Graves looked neat and tidy in grey trousers and matching waistcoat, his white shirt was open at the collar and he regarded Kathleen with his dark, shifty eyes. His hair was slicked back as usual and he didn't waste his time, "I am sorry Kathy, but we will be letting you go."

Kathleen stood in silence and looked at him. Within the last hour she had lost the greatest love of her life. Her heart, which seemed beyond mend at this current juncture, could not process more loss.

"For what reason?" Kathleen's eyebrows raised nonchalantly, her eyes bright with recent tears and her growing fatigue, her face was red without make up. Graves thought for a moment, he clearly wasn't expecting such an inquiry and did not have an answer to hand.

"You're just a bit too fat," he said, after a short pause.

Kathleen's eyes widened and she looked towards Victoria and Kitty who were listening to their conversation. She saw Victoria's face harden like steel and turn angry, but Kathleen had no fighting words. She was broken and whilst this foolish man was not worth her dwindling strength, but she wasn't going to let his comment go unpunished. As she turned and walked away, she stamped on Grave's closest foot with the heel of her shoe and, ignoring the hateful words spilling from his mouth, went to change and go home. Kitty had her hand over her mouth in shock as Kathleen passed her, but Victoria stormed onto the stage in a tirade.

When Kathleen turned onto Amesbury Avenue in the early afternoon, she saw Basil hobbling up the road towards 76 so ran to catch him. As she got close, she could hear him whimpering like a beaten dog so knew immediately he had just returned from the Millbank Hospital where he received his daily *electrical massage,* an excruciatingly painful procedure designed to help his feet recover. She bent down to support him.

"B dear let me help you," said Kathleen, tucking her shoulder under his arm. As she did so she looked into his eyes and saw they were streaming with tears, his nose was leaking with effort and his brow was dotted with heavy, shining beads of sweat.

She didn't know what to say, she had experienced the worst day of her life but seeing her youngest brother is such pain and anguish made her forget for a moment her own worries. Her heart was bleeding for him, and she felt a maternal desire to take away his pain and transfer it to herself.

"Nearly there." Kathleen looked up the hundred yards to the front door and refuge for the soldier in her arms.

Eventually they made it to 76 and Kathleen helped Basil to the chair in the back room by the fire. Eva came down the stairs when she heard the commotion and immediately went to tend to her son.

"Dear boy, is it getting any better?" asked Eva. Kathleen stood behind her and saw Basil could only shake his head.

"You are so brave. Isn't he so brave, K?" Kathleen nodded.

"Did you feel the pin this time?" asked Eva. Basil shook his head again. He still had a long way to go and methods to improve trench foot felt more like torture than care. Basil even stated he would rather be shot again than suffer any more with his feet and the whole experience was taking its toll. His already slight frame was weaker and more skeletal than ever. Added to this he still had a German bullet inside him, and he needed to be positive and healthy to fight any internal infection that might occur.

After a short moment of silence Basil closed his eyes in exhausted sleep and Eva turned her attention to Kathleen who was now preparing some tea.

"How are you, K? I haven't seen you in a few days." Eva wore a face of worry, only ever smiling when looking at Basil, she was constantly waiting for news. Kathleen paused to think about the last couple of days and took a deep, shuddering breath to steady herself. She feigned a smile and turned to her mother.

"I'm alright. Though I have been fired for being *Too Fat.*" She felt that was reason enough for her sadness and would hide well the harsher, crippling pain she was feeling about her lost love.

"He said what?"

"It's ok, it is just the reason he used to let me go and replace me with one of his friends. Victoria was apparently *too tall* and Kitty *too thin* so we've all been cast out."

"That's awful dear." Eva thought for a moment "Are you sad about Howard too?"

His name shocked Kathleen. He was so far from her thoughts of late that it made her jump to hear mention of him. For a few months she had been considering a life with him but now, after feeling what true love really felt like, she wasn't sure he could give her what she needed.

"Howard? What about Howard?"

"Yes dear, he's signing up. I would have thought you'd know that." Eva looked accusingly at Kathleen. Her eyes were steady and her brow furrowed in confusion. It made the wrinkles on her forehead deep and dark.

"No, I didn't know that. I haven't seen him for a couple of weeks," said Kathleen. Eva pulled away in deep thought.

"I see. Well he reports for duty on the 27th. Are you two not seeing much of each other?"

"I've just been so busy," Kathleen did not want this line of questioning, not today, so she stood to make tea as the kettle sang but as she reached the stove she could feel her heart breaking afresh, her stomach was churning and dark clouds of sadness grew thick around her. She felt a fool for falling in love and hated herself for the distance she had let grow between others in her life. She had neglected her mother and done little to help Basil since he returned home. She had alienated Howard who had been kind to her, and she had thought little of Stuart and Eric still at war across the sea. She had subconsciously used an exciting new love affair to cover sadness all around her and now it was gone, she was falling through the cracks. Darkness and helplessness suddenly overwhelmed her. Heartbroken, embarrassed and scared Kathleen collapsed to the floor, unable to cope.

Neuve Chapelle, France – 10th March 1915

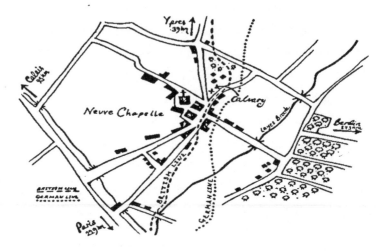

ERIC sat with his back against the wall of the trench and tried to steal a few moments of sleep but was unable. He took a cigarette from his packet, placed it in his mouth lit it with a match from the tin he kept in his tunic pocket.

"Nice tin," said the young man to his right. Eric smiled his thanks and lit a second match, the first having been unsuccessful. "I'm Harry, have you been a runner before?" He extended his hand to Eric. Eric felt a little sorry for him as he shook his hand. Eric was only twenty-two, but Harry was about eighteen and his face was smooth, having never seen a razor, and his youthful eyes did nothing to hide his apprehension.

"Once or twice," said Eric, offering Harry a smoke from his pack. "You've just got to make sure you remember the message and find the right officer."

Eric shrugged his shoulders. He was fit and strong, could make decisions without direction and was intelligent enough to remember routes back and forth but most importantly, the message he was carrying. No one could risk orders on paper falling into enemy hands, so runners were crucial, and Eric enjoyed the role.

"I know. I just worry about getting lost."

"They wouldn't have chosen you if you were not the right man, Harry." Eric mustered the most reassuring manner he could.

Harry nodded and looked up as the big guns opened up from behind them. It was seven-thirty in the morning and the salvo intended to destroy the enemy positions in the village of Neuve Chapelle had begun. The village was an advantageous position the Germans currently enjoyed and was to be attacked and taken by the Brigade. Eric rolled the cotton wool he had been issued between his fingers and stuffed it into his ears, but the noise remained deafening.

At eight thirty the guns fell silent and Eric heard whistles and shouting from the men in the first wave clambering over the top. The almost immediate response from the German machine guns, and the sharp crack of concentrated enemy rifle fire was a harrowing indication that the shelling had not destroyed their lines as intended. Eric winced as he heard the weight of fire and some of his fellow runners questioned how anyone had survived to fight back. Eric was comforted slightly by the knowledge the Kensingtons were in reserve, so Stuart and his friends were not on the receiving end just yet.

Eric and his posse of runners waited on edge to be called into the headquarters and given orders to deliver to their commanders at the front. Their proximity to the fighting was such that they could hear the shouts of the advancing troops and feel the crack of bullets as they flew menacingly over the top of the trench. Shortly before nine o'clock a young staff officer lifted the sandbag that sealed off Brigade Headquarters and looked towards the waiting group of runners.

"Royal Irish Rifles!"

"Sir!" A young Irishman dashed past Eric and entered the headquarters to receive his orders. A few minutes later he emerged and turned left up the communications trench towards the frontline. The officer appeared again.

"Lincolns!" Harry jumped from his seat next to Eric, picked up his rifle and ran towards the sandbag flap.

"Good luck!" called Eric as he left.

A few moments later Harry appeared again, head now full of information he must retain and his mission weighing heavy on his young mind. He winked at Eric and headed off in the same direction as the Irishman minutes before.

It was not until shortly before ten when the call for the Kensingtons came. Eric flicked his cigarette away and picked up his rifle. He ducked under the sandbag flap and saw for the first time the Brigade Headquarters. It was a large open space that had been carved into the side of a trench. Officers of all ranks swarmed over maps and orders, there were detailed lists pinned to the walls of the trench and some junior officers were furiously scribing notes. At the back of the headquarters sat the Brigade Commander, he looked relaxed in his chair, but his eyes were heavy-set with worry. He looked at Eric and managed a light smile before a senior member of his staff shouted a question in his direction. The young officer that had called Eric started talking so he focused his attention on him.

"You need to find your Commanding Officer and tell him he needs to release a company to support the Royal Irish Rifles in the northern sector of the village. Do you understand?" Eric nodded and repeated the instruction verbatim back to the officer who was showing the signs of severe stress, Eric assumed the morning had not gone entirely to plan.

"Good man, off you go and hurry back."

Eric made his way as fast as possible to where he knew the Kensingtons were waiting. The weather towards the end of February and in early March had been mainly dry so the trenches had hardened and he made good progress. As he darted down a line of trenches that had been the frontline that morning, he started to see faces he recognised and those that knew him smiled a friendly hello. Eric had no time exchange pleasantries.

"CO? Where is the CO?" demanded Eric as he ran past. Hunched over with rifle trailing in his hand he looked professional and important so was shown the way by a long line of outstretched arms. As he neared the Kensington Headquarters, he was passed by the Irishman he recognised from earlier and they nodded at each other.

Eric finally reached the Commanding Officer. He was sat on a box talking to his Senior Major, the Regimental Sergeant Major was crouch next to him, growling to himself like a bear. Eric interrupted their conversation with the orders, "Morning, sir. You have to release a company to support the Royal Irish in the northern sector of the village." The Commanding Officer furrowed his brow and thought for a moment. He then turned to his own runners gathered next to him.

"B Company!" The B Company runner stepped forward. "Tell Captain Prismall he is to take his Company and support the Irish in the northern sector of the village." The runner repeated the order and set off in the direction Eric had come to find Captain Prismall. "Anything else Hanham?" asked the Commanding Officer. Eric shook his head.

"Back you go then. Good work."

Eric turned and ran back towards brigade headquarters. He smiled at the men he knew, wishing them good luck, but as he reached the end of the line, he heard a voice he had known all his life and it stopped him in his tracks.

"I hope you have come with good news, E?" asked Stuart.

Eric stopped and smiled at his brother who was fixing his bayonet to his rifle. All of B Company were now preparing to head out to the village where the fighting was fierce.

"I am afraid not old man. It seems the Hun are stubborn bastards!" Stuart laughed. He looked enormous in his great coat, his face was rugged and hard, the bags under his eyes looked like muscles and stubble framed his powerful chin.

"Well these boys are obviously the exceptions," said Stuart, nodding behind Eric at the line of prisoners being escorted by Irish soldiers through the Kensington lines.

Eric turned to look at them as they walked past, he expected some men might react nastily to seeing the enemy so close but only one man spat in their direction and was quickly reprimanded by a corporal next to him. Eric stood tall as they walked past. He had killed some in the darkness during trench raids and from distance on the line but never had he seen them so close in the light of day. He was impressed by their size and sturdy build and the way they moved with grace and purpose. The officers had a regal arrogance about them that was hard to dislike and their uniforms, while muddy and splattered with blood, were well fitting.

They wore them with pride, brass buttons shining in the sun and imperial spiked helmets were detailed and majestic where their canvas covers had torn. Even the wounded among them suffered in quiet grace. Eric then remembered that it was men like this who had shot his brother and his blood boiled.

"Relax E, their war is over now," Stuart sensed Eric's rage so put a strong arm on his shoulder. Eric broke from his rage and turned to Stuart.

"Must head back." Eric was sad to leave his brothers' company, he hadn't seen him for a few days and was missing him.

"Good luck." Stuart patted him hard on the arm and knocked his hat from its place atop Eric's head.

"Good luck to you too." Eric picked up his hat, punched Stuart playfully on the arm and sloped away out of sight.

"Hanham! Are you ready?" called Harding. Stuart looked left and right at his men and raised a thumb to indicate he was. B Company then climbed the ladders and entered the Battle of Neuve Chapelle.

*

Stuart and his platoon were at the far right of B Company as they advanced towards the village. The Irish dead lay on the ground in ghastly forms of the recently deceased and the wounded held out bloody hands for assistance, but Stuart and his men couldn't stop to assist. This area of land was still under fire from the enemy so they could not stay to help. As they reached the village B Company waited in ditches on either side of the cobbled road and runners were sent forward to find the Irish commanders. One of the runners was cut down immediately by a burst of machine gun fire and he died instantly on the old road, in full view of his friends. Stuart kept talking to his platoon to occupy their minds. Bullets were whizzing all around them, buildings were spitting stone when hit by shells and only a stone crucifix, with the Son of God languid in his dying form, at the entrance to the village remained eerily untouched.

"Stay down men, keep low and move with purpose!" barked Stuart above the din of battle. He could see the fear in their eyes, he was scared too but leadership kept him focused.

B Company eventually moved forward to defend the northern edge of the village and occupy a group of houses that had been reduced to mere carcasses of their former selves. Harding gave Stuart the northern most house to oversee and half the platoon to defend it. Wounded Irishmen crawled from their positions with the assistance of their able-bodied comrades and when Stuart asked one of them where the enemy was, the scared young man could only point out towards the horizon in the east.

Stuart and his men were instantly under intense fire from the outskirts of the village and two of Stuart's men were wounded in the first few minutes of the engagement.

"Keep moving positions!" yelled Stuart. He stole a glance at the enemy line, but a deathly hiss and crack made him retreat back into cover. He had seen enough and went to Harding with an option, "Sir, we have to move on their flank! We are sitting ducks here!"

Harding thought for a moment and then called a section of men over to him. He ordered Stuart to lead them around the houses to where the enemy were located. Stuart shouted for the rest of the platoon to increase their rate of fire and immediately they obeyed.

The volley was terrifying and perfect cover for the small group to move behind. Stuart made his way up the ditch on the side of the road until he dared go no further. He signalled to the men behind him to spread out along the edge of the last pile of rubble where the main street split into a forked road. He climbed over the remains of a kitchen and peered around the corner to look down the street where he saw a dozen enemy soldiers firing from the raised line of destroyed houses, a machine gun was spitting angrily from the middle. Stuart called his men up to him and spread them out as best he could among the bricks and debris. He gave the order and they fired into the flank of the enemy.

At least four were hit instantly, the remainder, surprised by the deadly fire, turned and ran down the street. They were only fifty yards away and presented easy targets for Stuart and the section so were cut down quickly. The machine gun in the middle tried to turn its fire onto Stuart but the two men operating it were killed by the remainder of B Company, the limp body of the gunner slumped protectively over the gun that had been causing so much devastation just moments before.

Quickly Prismall and the rest of the Company arrived to occupy the houses on the northern edge of the village but were immediately engaged by machine gun and rifle fire some six hundred metes away. The Irish fought up the centre of the village alongside Indians and Gurkha's beyond them. For the moment, Neuve Chapelle was in allied hands.

*

Eric, back at Brigade Headquarters sat quietly with the other runners. Since his first duty early that morning he had twice been back to his Commanding Officer and relayed orders for him to release more of his men to assist other units in the fierce fighting in and around the village. Now, shortly before three o'clock in the afternoon, he found himself again called to carry an important message.

An older major who bore the red collar insignia of the General Staff had replaced the young officer and the Brigade Commander stood around the large map in the centre of the headquarters pointing aggressively, his voice was loud and serious. The officers around him were silent and sullen like children being scorned by a father. Eric listened intently to the order he was given.

"Yes, sir, dig in north east of the village." Eric pointed to the precise area he was shown on the map. The major nodded and Eric ran out into the afternoon and the misty rain that had started to drift from the sky.

Initially Eric followed the same route to where the Kensingtons had been waiting in reserve but there were now only a few of them left there so, without a thought for the danger, he scaled a ladder and started running towards the village he could see smoking almost a kilometre away. His rifle was low in his right hand and he ran as fast as he could across the fields strewn with Irish dead and wounded. The area has not yet been muddied and scarred by shelling and the brave Irish had cut the barbed wire defences in numerous places, so he made quick progress across the open space that had been the end of so many. A few men moaned pathetically as he passed but Eric could not stop to help, he assured himself he would offer them a smoke on his way back and inform the stretcher-bearers of their location, for the moment though he had a message and it needed to get to its recipient quickly.

As Eric reached the edge of the village, he noticed an increase in dead men in the surrounding field and on the cobbled road leading into its centre, the remains of the church tower still slightly higher than the damaged buildings around it. The dead were stiff in the attitude they left the world, but Eric continued towards the end of the main street where he found a couple of wounded men he knew. One had his arm in a bloody sling and the other had a muddy bandage around a thick thigh, his exposed lower leg stained red and brown with blood and dirt.

"Reg, where is your commander?" asked Eric. The soldier looked up at Eric and smiled in recognition.

"He's up at the top of the village with the CO from the Irish," replied Reg, squinting into the sheets of misty rain. Eric patted him on his good arm and set off up the street using the ditch as cover. There was currently no shelling or fire onto the village, a small lull in the battle, but he didn't want to invite any his way.

As Eric reached the far end of the village, he could see a group of officers assembled in one of the houses. The roof was destroyed, and the front of the house had collapsed into a rubble heap, but the top floor remained and was providing them with shelter from the rain and cover from enemy fire. Eric dashed across the road to where they were gathered.

"Sir! I have orders from Brigade." The Irish major holding a map against the wall looked at Eric with tired eyes.

"It's your runner, Prismall," said the major to Captain Prismall who was stood to his right.

"They are for you all, sir," said Eric. He had no problem speaking clearly in front of officers unlike a lot of enlisted men. In fact, he enjoyed the way he could be demanding around them, a trait that made him a good runner.

"Let's hear them then, lad."

"You are to dig in north east of the village," said Eric, pointing confidently to the map being held against the wall.

"Yes, thank you," replied the major sarcastically. Eric steadied himself for one of the occasions where the messenger got the full force of the recipient's anger. "Tell them that I would dig in there if the bloody Hun wasn't being such a nuisance and hanging on!" Eric nodded and turned to return with the message.

"Wait!" The major waved him back. "Tell them I hold the village but will need significant reinforcements to be able to attack and hold that area. Tell them I cannot do it at present." Eric nodded his understanding. "…Tell them also that I believe the enemy are seeping through our line and making their way back into their trenches. In short, I am rather out on a *bloody* limb here. Will you remember that?" Eric nodded and Captain Prismall backed his fellow Kensington.

"This lad will remember Willy, he's our best runner." The comment made Eric warm with pride.

"Well that's good to hear. Off you go and hurry back with orders of what I am to do next. I think my runner has *had it* out there," said the major, nodding towards the open expanse of ground at the base of the village where a vast number of his men lay dead and dying. Eric thought for a moment of the young Irishman from the morning out there in the field, wounded or worse, and it made his heart ache. He didn't know him but felt like he had.

"Anything else?" Eric shook his head and went to leave but stopped and turned to Prismall.

"Sergeant Hanham, sir, is he well?" asked Eric. Prismall smiled and nodded.

*

Eric ran back down the length of the village in good spirits, he thought of Stuart fighting hard and it made him happy to hear he was alright but when the row of houses came to an end he paused and looked out towards the old British frontline and the expanse of land between. The misty rain had dissipated but the air was still moist with the chill of early March and the clouds were darkening with the onset of evening, they had in them the evil promise of rain. Bodies of Irishmen, Indians and other young men were dark mounds in the fading light. Eric then looked to his left and straight into the open eyes of a dead German sat up at the edge of the house. His end had been a harrowing one and his eyes, now lifeless and grey, reflected that in their wide, pained expression. His large moustache was heavy with rain and his face had been washed clean by the mist. Eric looked at him for a moment before setting on his task back across the field, but he got no more than three metres before the ground around him was raked violently by machine gun fire. He slid on the thin film of mud created by the rain, gathered his footing and just made it back to the relative safety of his previous position as bullets splintered the bricks around him. He looked at the dead German again who seemed now to have a smile on his face. Eric hated him afresh.

In his dazed state Eric regarded himself and, pleased to see he had suffered no wounds, remembered the Irish major's concern that the enemy had slipped back into their lines. He realised immediately his return journey would be harder and it angered him. He was pleased to hear Irish shouts and a heavy volley of rifle fire in the direction from which the machine gun had engaged him, but he determined that a return trip over the open ground was not an option. Instead he darted across the road and entered the old German front line that spread away to the north and made quick progress down the trench. Periodically he would peek above the parapet towards the British line, so he did not lose sight of the place he knew and his desired destination.

So concerned was Eric not to get lost he did not notice the German voices in the trench ahead of him until it was almost too late. When he became aware of them around the corner he froze. He was convinced they had heard his heavy steps on the boards but the normality in their voice indicated he was still undetected. He thought for a moment what to do and suddenly realised he was trapped. He couldn't return the way he had come for fear of detection and the enemy machine gun that had so nearly accounted for him moments earlier. He could not dash across the open field for he would certainly be spotted by whoever occupied the line and become an easy target. He was left with one choice and the thought excited him. He would have to investigate the noises ahead and deal with it, he had the element of surprise after all and relished the fray.

Quietly he stalked closer, raising his rifle to his shoulder he could still hear the voices as he peered around the trench wall. He was sure he had heard only two different voices and was happy to be correct. Two German soldiers were stacking boxes of ammunition onto a cart, they obviously had a safe route back to their new front line, so this ammunition was to be used against Stuart and the Kensingtons holding Neuve Chapelle. Eric could not let this happen, so he carefully and quietly aimed his rifle at the larger man with his back towards him. He wore a soft grey hat with a red band around the rim and he had insignia on his epaulettes denoting rank. The other man helping him with the boxes was young and had the scared look of a boy. He glanced nervously around him and over to Eric but failed to see him crouched in the mud.

Eric levelled his sights into the centre of the big man's back and pulled the trigger with excited anger. His back exploded in a deep red splash and his soft hat was dislodged from his head as he fell forward onto the stacked cart like a wounded buffalo. The younger man was covered in bright red mist from the exit wound on his comrade's chest and was paralysed by shock. It was enough time for Eric to reload his rifle and fire a second shot into the boy's torso. He fell back against the trench wall and lay writhing on the trench floor like a landed salmon, his cries of pain high pitched and haunting.

Eric emerged quickly from his hidden position and stood over the howling boy. He levelled his rifle at his head to fire the killing shot but felt inside him a revolting anger that gripped his very soul and turned him from human to beast. The boy looked at him in terror, a small stream of bright blood running from his mouth down his cheek. He was young, maybe nineteen, but Eric did not see a terrified boy and instead saw the face of an angry wolf, a vision of evil with bright blue eyes of hatred. Eric turned his rifle over in his arms and struck the boy on his left cheekbone with the curved metal end of his rifle butt. The boy's cheek shattered under the hefty strike and a dark hole replaced the left side of his once handsome face. Eric was possessed with rage, white teeth now exposed he hammered down twice more into the boy's skull until he saw the pale pink cushion of his brain. The right side of the boy's face was still intact, his one eye pleaded with Eric to stop but Eric was broken and so far from himself in this moment. His final strike ended the life of his young enemy. His spirit destroyed with his youth.

Eric stood still, he was panting heavily. His face was splattered with blood and his eyes were swollen with tears. He stood and observed the once human mess in front of him. His anger was fading and he felt the judgmental presence of his father and of God. He wanted to break down and cry, he wanted to crawl into the underworld and never be seen again but excited German voices close by pulled him back into the living world. He looked around quickly and, in his haste, scaled the parapet to dash across the open field towards the British line and safety.

Instantly he was under fire from behind and away to his left where the previous machine gun fire had harassed him, but he kept low and moved as fast as his feet would allow. He used small thickets and walls for cover, but the fire became so intense he had to slide to a stop and lay flat for a moment in a small fold in the ground to avoid being killed and to gather his wits. His lungs were burning, and his chest was tight against his tunic, the cold air was stinging. He could hear the angry voices of the enemy coming towards him, the enemy that would no doubt seek to put an end to him in a manner similar to the way he had destroyed the young boy, or worse. Darkness would not come to his aid so Eric had to make another run for it. He stood as quickly as he could, leaving his rifle to move at greater speed, kept low and darted from side to side. He paused again behind a small mound and then became aware of British voices close by, "Run lad! You're almost there!" shouted a friendly voice from a hundred yards away.

Eric felt renewed strength in his failing limbs and went for one more charge, but German voices raised again behind him and he stumbled in some dark, heavy mud. As he gained his feet again, he felt the hard hammer strike and it was immediately followed by hot, searing pain. The force spun Eric around and threw him onto his back, the impact of his weighty frame on the hard ground knocked the air from his lungs. For a few seconds the world slowed, fell quiet and deathly still, the shouts of the enemy were no more and his body was overcome by crippling numbness. He felt like he might be caught in a terrible dream and fought to stay conscious, but his world turned black in breathless panic.

Shortly after dark Stuart was in the centre of the village with Lieutenant Harding to receive orders. The Irish were there too, and it was their senior major who delivered them the plan.

"Right men, the runners are having a terrible time getting here with orders from Brigade. I've lost two today and that Kensington lad hasn't returned so I guess the Boche got the better of him too. No matter, we are best placed to make the decisions anyway."

The major continued his address, but Stuart was no longer listening. His heart was breaking, his breathing laboured and angry he looked like he might charge the enemy alone. Harding noticed his reaction and led him away, but Stuart's feet were failing him and he started to fall. Harding needed help from another man to get him up and carry him away.

"What wrong with him?" asked the Irish major, no sense of compassion.

"Our runner was his brother," said Prismall.

Hanham

Bac St. Maur, France – 19th March 1915

'Dear E,

I was relieved to receive your two post cards. Strangely enough I got the first one last. I heard, the next day, of your wound, I hope it hasn't caused you a great deal of pain. Up to the present I have come off quite safely.

You know how 'warm' it was on the day you were hit, well it continued like that for two full days more. You will have seen from the papers how successful it has been. I hope by this date, E old chap, that you are in 'Blighty' – I am sending this to mum to send to you when she hears of your address. I hope you will get a nice big bit of 'sick furlough' home.

We are just back to billets after nine days in the trenches and as you may imagine are feeling well 'whacked'. I shall be glad to hear of your experiences when you get a chance. I do hope you will get home to '76' on 'sick leave' for a bit. I wonder if I shall get my leave now after this very strenuous period.

Please tell B that the Drum-Major says his parcel has gone off all right. I will pack your stuff off to you as quickly as I can, old chap.

Cheer up. Writing again later on,

Yours affectionately Stuart'

Stuart placed the letter in an envelope, took a cigarette from his pack and lit it. He laid his head back and gazed thoughtfully up into the branches of the young oak tree he was sat resting against. The recent warm weather and promise of summer had encouraged fresh green leaves from their buds and Stuart, enjoying a few days of rest behind the line, was happy.

He and the Kensingtons had fought bravely during the Battle of Neuve Chappelle and enjoyed the respect they earned but they had paid a heavy price for it. Six of their officers, including Stuart's Company Commander Captain Prismall, were killed and one hundred and fifty men were either killed or wounded during the battle. Eric was one man in that number and Stuart thought of him now. He had been distraught when he had heard the news his brother had not made it back to the British lines and with no word whether he was alive or dead he had assumed the worst. It was only after another day and night hard fighting and their eventual withdrawal from the village that Stuart heard Eric had not been killed. He smiled through tears of happiness when told about how Eric had made it back to the British lines and was strangely unsurprised to hear how lucky Eric had been. The bullet struck him directly on his tobacco tin and, though badly wounded, the tin had undoubtedly saved him from a life-threatening wound and likely death. Stuart, with his eyes closed, felt his own tobacco tin is his hand and marvelled at how luck and judgement bounce around so randomly in this place. He was so pleased both his brothers had made it out of this place alive, he wondered whether fate or God had a role in it all or whether they were all just feathers floating in the wind, some landing on soft grass and others in dirty puddles. With these thoughts in mind and small birds busy in the thicket Stuart drifted to sleep.

The sound of artillery woke Stuart a short while later. He had been dreaming the random, skittish dreams of half sleep and had a confusing moment while he remembered where he was in the world. As his eyes adjusted slowly to the bright sun, he steadied himself to write another letter, this one was to Emily and would be infinitely harder to write. Every time he wrote to her feelings surged inside him and would become too powerful for the bulb in his mind, it would burst, and he would be consumed by darkness and by thoughts of never seeing her again. He then had little control over his mind and plagued himself with thoughts that she would have found someone else to love, wouldn't recognise him or that he was being foolish, and this was just a passing fancy for her. He tortured himself with the belief that someone like Emily would never marry a man who lived in a little red brick house with his mother off Streatham Hill. Slowly though he soothed these wild notions and began to write.

*

"Mind if we join you?" asked Harris as he walked towards Stuart sat quietly under the tree. He was squinting as he ducked into the shade, his dark brown eyes hidden under bristling eyebrows. In his hand he had two dark green bottles of red wine and a loaf of fresh bread. Taylor, walking next to him, had another bottle of wine and a cloth parcel of cheese. Stuart quickly wrote his loving goodbye to Emily and folded the letter into his pocket.

"Just writing a letter or two." Stuart hoped he had not been crying.

"Don't worry chum, I'm not interested in your love letters to Basil," said Harris, sitting next to him. Taylor laughed as he propped their rifles into a tripod to keep muzzles free from dirt, he sat down opposite the two men as Harris passed Stuart a bottle of wine. Taylor's youthful face was happy and friendly in the speckled sunlight breaking through the branches.

"What's this for?"

"Your promotion to Sergeant. Well, your *official* promotion to Sergeant."

"Ah I see, thank you very much." The three men clinked bottles and took large pleasing gulps from the bottle. Stuart wiped the excess from his mouth, "You know it's just the same as being an acting sergeant."

"We know, but its official now and we wanted a drink," replied Taylor with a smile. He was new to the platoon, but Stuart had liked him immediately.

"So, were you writing to Eric? Quite a lucky fellow isn't he." Stuart thought for a moment, no one apart from Eric, Basil and Harding knew about Emily and he wanted to keep it that way.

"Err, yes he is a lucky chap."

"Do you know where he is currently?"

"No, I'll just send it home. My mother will post it on from there when she knows where he is. So, what's the word on the rumour mill?" Stuart took another cigarette from his packet.

"Not a great deal, we start training again in a day or so and the battalion is shifting its man power around after that."

"Well let's enjoy the quiet while it lasts," said Stuart, cutting Taylor off. He didn't need to be reminded of Neuve Chapelle.

"Quite so!" said Harris. "Say, did he get to keep the tin?"

"Well I should bloody hope so! It is not every day something like that happens." Stuart shook his head and raised the bottle to his lips, "...Lucky Bastard!" The three men laughed for a minute.

"Say, is it true you used to be tee-total?" Taylor nodded towards the bottle in Stuart's hand and the cigarette in his mouth. Stuart laughed.

He certainly had changed a great deal. When war had been declared Stuart had been readily swept up in the feverish wave of patriotism and was excited about the coming adventures. Stories from the Boer War, strangely romanticised since its end a decade before, were widespread and in the first few weeks of training he had thought himself to be in an enviable position. He was strong and physically robust, intelligent and well liked by fellow soldiers and officers but perhaps most crucially he had his two brothers around him and no wife or children at home. He was free to soldier and free to live, young and solely focused on the task at hand and he relished the camaraderie. That was until he met Emily, since that day he had something at the back of his mind to consume the quiet moments and to vex his heart. He had been able to detach himself from the thoughts of her when his brothers were close and focus on their well-being, especially Basil, but now they were both away from the fray and recovering on the safe side of the English Channel he had space for painful dreams of Emily and of home. He found himself dreaming of summer walks around the green areas of his city and long hours of silence with her by his side, the prospect of a new life in Canada excited him but it was dangerous, hope brought him strength, but it also injected weakness into his mind. He cursed the existence of happiness and sometimes resented ever meeting the woman whom he now could not do without. Any glorious notions of war were drowned a long while ago in the squelching mud, trampled by the painful feet of uniformed men.

Stuart had been in a quiet trance for a time when Harris spoke and broke the tension. "Ah well, this place changes us all." Stuart nodded silently.

Green Hall Hospital Belper, Derbyshire – 3rd April 1915

ERIC had been moved quickly through the various stages of the medical evacuation system and within a couple of weeks he was in Green Hall Hospital in Belper, Derbyshire. He had been incredibly lucky. During his mad dash back to the safety of the British line he had been shot in the hip and although the bullet had hit him hard and penetrated his body, creating a ghastly wound, it had only entered an inch or two as it was slowed dramatically by a direct hit onto the tobacco tin he carried in his tunic. He was knocked over and had been rendered unconscious by the weight of the shot and his fall but had landed safely in a small hollow where he was out of sight from the enemy marksmen. The men in the British line overwhelmed his pursuers and forced them back with at least one less in their number. Eric was dragged to safety and awoke an hour later on a stretcher in the aid station.

Since the moment of his wounding he had been carried over a comrade's shoulder, bounced along the trench on a flimsy stretcher, dragged on a horse drawn wagon to a field ambulance, taken by stretcher again and boarded onto a train and finally driven in a motorised ambulance to a hospital in Boulogne where he spent nearly two weeks. He then boarded a ship and steamed across the channel to an English port he could not recall, was driven again to a railhead where then he rattled along the Midlands countryside to another motorised ambulance waiting the other end. Eventually he reached Green Hall Hospital and a bed with freshly starched sheets. It was quite a transition, but Eric was most amused that during all those miles on land and sea he had not once set foot on the floor. He had been carried the whole way in one fashion or another and even his calls of nature were conducted from his bed. It seemed like a blur, moments of clarity and then large gaps where pain and fatigue had forced him into deep, dreamless hours of unconsciousness. His leg was badly damaged and his wound severe, but he would live.

He knew also he had been operated on at some point, but he wasn't sure when, he thought it must have been quite soon after being wounded as he certainly had his tobacco tin and bullet with him while in Hospital in Boulogne. It was quite remarkable, the heavy slug had made a neat little hole on the lid of the tin, only denting the thin metal lightly, the spring mechanism still worked, and the lid snapped shut as it had done before. On the back of the tin there was more damage and, much like the exit wound from living tissue, it was wider and ugly. Sharp shards of thicker metal casing were forced into the unnatural shapes of war, but they had diverted the bullet and driven it down into the fleshy parts of Eric's leg rather than deep into the vital organs of his abdomen. The matches inside were undamaged.

Eric enjoyed fondling the small heavy cone of lead that had so nearly been the end of him. It made him angry to think of one of these ugly, deadly wasps still inside his younger brother and he couldn't help but imagine the one inside Basil was alive and moving to the devil's beat. Other times he would roll the bullet between his fingers and smile at his own luck. Eric had been a regular at church but over the years his belief in God had started to wane. This incident had made him wonder again but regardless of divine intervention or simple luck, Eric was very happy to be back home for a while and he looked forward to some comforts. From Boulogne he sent a letter home to Eva telling his story but did not yet send his trinket, he did not want to lose the object that saved his live and the bullet intended to end it. Not every man is so lucky to have souvenirs like this and they were now his most treasured possessions.

*

Eric was recovering well but his wound was going to take a long time to heal, even with the help of hundreds of stitches itching incessantly under his ward uniform. The tin had saved his life, but it had altered the angle of the bullet, spiralling from the tin it had created a deep fleshy recess in his hip and leg. So far though he had been devoid of infection, which was excellent news, internal infections were often killing men long after blood had ceased to flow, their broken bodies and struggling immune systems unable to cope with the deadly bacteria coursing through their veins.

"Good morning Mr Hanham. How are you today?" asked the nurse as she pulled the curtain from around his bed. Eric smiled.

"Never mind me, my dear, how are you?" replied Eric, his cheeky grin highlighted the handsome features of his face. He had become rather a celebrity in the hospital. His story had spread, and he was happy to show the damaged tin and bullet to anyone who asked. His character had also made him popular and he was enjoying his rest, but it wasn't all pleasant. He, like most men on the ward, had the unsettling dreams of soldiers and would often wake screaming from torrid sleep when it became too real or the faces of friends and foes too haunting. He was troubled by his trench raids, the thought of his primitive mace made him shudder nauseously. His most common dream and the one that caused him most distress, was when he re-lived the moment where he had brutally killed the young man just before he was wounded himself. In his dream, the man didn't die but lay there disfigured. One side of his face was a black cavernous hole speckled white with fragments of teeth and skull while the other side was clean and pure. It would smile at him, plead and sometimes it would frown in terrible anger. On occasions his face turned from the young boy he had killed into Basil and then Stuart. Eric would wake in screams of terror, wet with sweat and urine but he was not judged. Many men on the ward experienced such dreams and the changing of soiled sheets was not anything to be ashamed of here.

"I am very well. Have you seen what a lovely day it is outside?" Eric looked to the window at the end of the room and smiled when he saw the bright rays of sunshine.

"I should very much like to walk today. My legs feel weak like a little boy and I'm afraid if don't use them more I shall never be able to take you dancing." The nurse, with her mouse like appearance, looked at him with a false veil of contempt from over the top of her spectacles, a thin metal chain attached to them made her appear older than she was.

"You just be careful, Mr Hanham. Too much exertion will cause you more problems." Eric waved a big hand at her. "I'm serious."

"I know, I know. I just want to walk the grounds," said Eric accepting a plate of bread and honey. She placed a mug of steaming tea next to his water jug.

"Don't forget the photo this morning, Gentlemen. We shall be taking it in the garden at ten o'clock." The nurse pushed her cart out of the door and onto the next ward.

After chatting to a few fellow patients and re-reading some letters

Eric hobbled to the ablutions. He then collected his packet of cigarettes, his notepad and pencil and limped gingerly out into the cool freshness of the young day. The April sun was already high in the sky and dew remained on the grass hidden in dark areas of shade. He stood for a moment at the edge of the large wall that surrounded the magnificence of Green Hall. Until recently it had been a preparatory school for boys and Eric was able to imagine the fun that was had here and laughter from the boys felt alive in the air. The large windows framed in white shone gloriously in the sunshine and green ivy hiding the dark stone walls behind was a shimmering green sea. Eric lit a cigarette before making his way awkwardly around the gardens.

Eric missed these lone ventures and, although painful, he was glad to feel some of his old strength return to his legs. He had been laid on his back for the best part of a month, so his legs were visibly weak. When naked he could see the loose muscle of his quads, flabby and pathetic around his once sturdy legs, his calf muscles too were stodgy and wrinkled. He was only twenty-two but from the waist down he felt like an old man. He joked with the men on the ward about dancing and sex, but he was quite certain he couldn't muster enough strength or levels of arousal required for either act. Outwardly he was confident and brash but inside he was damaged and hurting. He was confused and while he didn't have the crippling feelings of inadequacy that Basil did, he harboured a deep hatred of himself for the things he had done and thought he probably had deserved to have been killed. Mixing with these powerful feelings, too developed for someone of his young age, was a desire to do more. He wasn't keen to return to the mud and cold, but he missed the excitement of battle and the chance to steal life from his foe. He didn't like that part of him, and he felt broken.

Eric settled down on a bench at the far end of the garden and started to draw, he was a talented artist and found creating images with pencil soothing. When he had been younger, he had been able to drift away for hours in such drawings, but the trials of life had limited his concentration to smaller spells. He found it easier on his troubled mind to draw what he saw in front of him so today he sketched the great Green Hall.

As he let his mind drift, he thought of Eva and of his family in London. She had of course been up to see him with Basil and Kathleen, Stella and Frank had come too but on a separate occasion. He had enjoyed seeing them all, but he was especially pleased to see his younger brother. The last time he had seen him was on Christmas Eve when Basil had been wounded and it had broken Eric's heart to see his brother carried away, his breathing laboured and gurgling the sounds of a dying man. Their meeting was highly charged and a significant step towards recovery for them both. Eva and Kathleen relaxed once they had seen Eric appeared to be his old self. He didn't outwardly show he had changed like Basil but on the inside, he was screaming. He thought of Stuart and considered what he might be doing, he hoped he was safe and well. His last correspondence from him had been jovial, the Kensingtons were training at the moment but their eventual purpose was unknown.

After half an hour Eric stopped drawing and placed his notebook into the top pocket of his thick blue ward uniform and, desperately trying to avoid scratching the irritating stitches in his side, started a letter to Basil. Eric had decided he would send home his tobacco tin and bullet. He didn't want it around him now but certainly needed it safe.

Hanham

'My Dear Old B,

Thank you so much for the fags, it was good of you to send them and I can tell you that I relished them exceedingly, you know I've grown such a smoker I can hardly do without a wiff, and we are only allowed one packet of 'Wild Woodbine' per day, and they run out so quickly and are such rotten stuff that I seldom have any of them left in the morning. How are you going on? Are your feet better now? I do hope so.

What did you do with yourself yesterday (Good Friday). Wasn't the weather simply frightful? It rained all day, and was so muggy that it wasn't worth going out for a walk.

What do you think of Stuarts promotion? Isn't it good, the poor old boy certainly deserves it, you ought to get another stripe now.

Oh I do hope I shall get my furlough before yours expires, it would be so nice to have a little time together and be able to go to the Pictures or a Music Hall or something of that sort, but you mustn't expect me to come home on Wednesday, if you do not hear from me just before then, as there are doubts whether my wound will be healed by then, it is going on very slowly but is quite healthy. I forgot to tell mater that I am doubtful about furlough next Wednesday, so will you do it for me, please.

You will keep my souvenirs safe (the bullet, and tobacco case) won't you, for I shouldn't like to get them lost as they are worth keeping you know.

There is no news to tell B, old man. I am looking forward to seeing you all and spending a few days at home. Write as soon as you can spare time I should so like to hear from you, it would cheer me up, you know. Always the love and affection of your affectionate brother. Please give K. her letter which is enclosed. Thanks.

Eric.'

Eric started to write a letter to Kathleen but was only a few words in when he was called over for the photograph planned for that morning. He rose from the bench without grace and hobbled slowly towards the gathering of nurses and patients.

76 Amesbury Avenue, London – 24th April 1915

SOME boys were playing football fifty yards from Basil as he sat quietly on the edge of Tooting Bec Common, they were using jumpers for goal posts and what had started as a friendly game had turned serious. The randomly selected teams had temporarily formed the close bonds of youth, their jovial nature long gone and a desire to win consumed them. A small group of girls were sat on the grass a short distance away and Basil reckoned they were the sisters of the boys panting up and down after the ball. He had come out to buy a newspaper but had extended his morning errand to include a short stop on the common. The spring weather was pleasant, and London was singing in the sunshine. His feet were still a long way from healed, but he was now able to walk short distances with just a walking stick for support. The kilometre from 76 to the Common was about the limit of his ability even now, four long months after his last night in the trenches.

His furlough had been extended three times because of his feet but now they were healing it was the bullet inside his body that gave him more concern. He was sure when lying awake in the silence of night he could feel the hot metal moving around his organs like it had life of its own. He had dreams it burst out of his chest and he was left with the ghastly exit wound. Most concerning, he continued to abuse himself internally. He still saw in himself a pathetic excuse for a man and he envied the men still out there fighting. He was a mere twenty-one years old but as a wounded veteran he felt aged and past his prime.

Today though Basil was happy, Eric would be arriving home on sick furlough that afternoon and he was excited to see him. His older brother in a similar predicament to him diluted his inadequacy and he had one less person to envy. He would not feel so alone and isolated with Eric around and he knew Eric's character would raise his spirits and those of his mother.

Basil had been quiet and sullen since his return and it had taken its toll on Eva, she was becoming frailer by the day and he wanted to stop and tell her "*he was ok*" and that she must stop worrying. But he couldn't, so she couldn't. She was doing the best job she could, and Basil was trying his hardest to get his young mind to process the events of the last few months.

Basil left the boys debating whether a goal had been scored, they reminded him of his brothers, and he was happy he would be seeing one of them later today.

*

"Is he here? E?" asked Kathleen loudly, blazing through the door to 76 like a bull. She had got a small part in a play that would soon be released near Covent Garden, it meant she was working close enough to 76 to come home between morning rehearsal and the evening performance.

"Not yet K," replied Stella from the dining room table. Eva was sat there too.

"Where's B?" asked Kathleen surveying the room.

"He's waiting at the bottom of the street. I am surprised you didn't pass him," said Eva. Kathleen was out of breath and flushed with excitement.

"I came from the other way," Kathleen removed her shawl and took a few deep breaths to calm herself. Eva stood up and made her way over to the window and looked down the road in the direction the boys would arrive. She stood there silently for a long time, eyes fixed in hope. Her heart was beating hard and it was clear by her rigid stance she was nervous, excited and beside herself with happiness at the thought of her two youngest boys at home under her roof.

"How's the play going?" asked Stella once Kathleen had sat down and lit a cigarette.

"Its good thanks, they have noticed I'm not a fool so have given me more lines and responsibilities and upped my meagre pay as a result."

"Perhaps soon you'll be the lead?"

Kathleen laughed. "Thank you but I doubt that. The American girl is rather good, and the chaps adore her." Kathleen raised her eyebrows and Stella shrugged her shoulders sympathetically.

"He's here! He's here!" screamed Eva. Stella stood up and followed her mother out of the room and into the street. Kathleen stood behind her sister to look down the road.

Both Eric and Basil were walking awkwardly with the aid of a stick and of the two Basil seemed most able. They were talking with each other, wide grins across their young faces. Eva and Stella burst into tears as Eric looked up at them and smiled. He looked resplendent in his khaki uniform, despite his obvious limp and the need for support. Basil was carrying his kit bag. For Kathleen it became too much when she watched her mother embrace Eric, she looked so small and feeble in his arms and the emotions of the last few months came flooding back. The women took turns in smothering Eric with hugs and kisses.

For the next couple of hours, they all sat around the dining table talking happily. They listened intently to Stella's ramblings and Kathleen told tales about her new play and the previous one she had been *too fat* for. Eric joked he would pay Graves a visit when his leg was better but currently he would be able to run away too easily. Eva sat between her two sons looking at them both with pride and held their forearms tight. Subconsciously she was holding them back from leaving again and no one mentioned the war until Eva gave Eric a letter addressed to him from Stuart.

> '*Dear E,*
>
> *Thank you so much for the papers you sent me. I hope by now you are home and I am directing this there. I wonder if you went to St. Pauls today. It is a 'third Sunday' – we had a church parade this morning. I hope your wound is healing up well old boy, more later.*
>
> > *Yours affectionately, Stuart'*

Basil then handed Eric the letter he had received from Stuart in the same correspondence. Eric was pleased to see it and read his brothers hand. He imagined Stuart sat writing it and it made him happy.

> '*Dear old B,*
>
> *Thank you so much for your letter and for the wiffs, they are fine. It was good of you to send that Easter egg, it was a beauty, and thank you too,*

*old man, for the beef. It was just what I wanted. I
hope you will have an extension of your furlough
till your fit. It wouldn't be good for you to come
out here again while you get those rotten attacks,
old man. More later old boy, from yours
affectionately,*

Stuart'

Later that afternoon Kathleen and Stella said their goodbyes and left
76. They walked together as far as the bus stop where Stella left to catch
her train, Kathleen waited for the bus back to Covent Garden. She had
only been waiting a short while when it came bouncing up the road. The
passenger compartment swayed from side to side with the weight of
people and it struggled over the brow of the hill towards her, the engine
screamed, and black smoke filled the air around it. Kathleen raised her
arm to signal the driver who duly pulled up alongside. She made her way
to the back, paid the conductor and climbed the elegantly curved
staircase to the open seating area on top. It was the first weekend the
open top buses had been out on the streets and the sweet, bright spring
day had enticed people to the upper level. She sat on the bench at the
back and looked out on the world.

It had been a remarkable few months. Two of her three brothers had
been severely wounded fighting overseas and were now back at home
with her mother. She had finished with the Graves production and lost
the love of her life, enjoyed tremendous moments of ecstasy and
experienced happiness like she had never known but she had also been
to the very depths of the darkest emotional holes. Until recently she

hadn't been aware of true happiness or true despair and even the death of her father, tremendously sad though it was, seemed insignificant compared to the violent instability of these last few months. Losing Harriet, seeing Eric and Basil so beaten by life and observing the torrid way in which the war had affected her mother had opened Kathleen's eyes to a greater appreciation. Her love affair with Harriet had showed her that true happiness can be found in the most unexpected of places and, whilst she so desperately longed to be with her again, she wouldn't force anything that wasn't destined to be. If there was a time when they could again be together then she would of course embrace it, and Harriet, with open arms but she wouldn't hold on to the hope that it would. She had said as much to Harriet in a letter sent to her hospital in Dorset and Harriet had agreed, she too wanted Kathleen but was worldly enough to know it couldn't be forced, especially at a time when so much was uncertain.

Kathleen had also spent some time with Howard before he left for training and she forced herself to be happy and excitable around him. She blamed her distance over the last few months on work and the war and Howard seemed to understand but his focus had shifted now to his part in the war. He knew he would soon be working overseas, some men he was training with had even mentioned Egypt. He had talked of marriage, but Kathleen had skilfully avoided the subject. She didn't feel at all ready for that, especially so soon after her heart had been broken and she still had her reservations about Howard. Kathleen's drifting thoughts eventually led her to Stuart, and she wondered how he was. She let herself imagine him in his uniform at the front, strong and brave and she even let herself drift back to childhood and the happy years they had spent growing up together in Kent. As the two eldest they shared a special bond and she held him in such high regard it was almost holy.

Kathleen was so transfixed in her memories she had not noticed the bus come to a juddering halt at the end of its route.

"Are you ok, my dear?" asked the conductor as he touched her on the shoulder. Kathleen woke from her daydream with a start. She turned and looked into his kind eyes and touched her face, it was wet with tears and her breathing was laboured.

*

"More potatoes Eric?" asked Eva holding the plate out to him. Eric nodded excitedly. "Basil, will you have some more?"

"You need some, old boy, you're like a rake," said Eric. Basil looked embarrassed so accepted the offer of more food. Eva was happy to see him eating, she had hoped Eric's presence would inspire Basil to get well.

"I think I'll head down the Lion after this, B. Have you been down much since you've been home?"

"No, I haven't to be honest. Walking until recently was such hard work and I didn't want them to make a fuss of me." He was lying. He hadn't been down because he was ashamed of himself and he didn't want to see anyone who knew him. He foolishly thought they would laugh at him.

"Fair enough. Join me tonight? I doubt we'll have to pay for a beer," Eric smiled, and Basil shrugged his shoulders.

"You boys should go, I think it would be nice to see some of your chums." Eva had suggested it to Basil a few times but sensed his apprehension so had dropped the idea early on.

"I don't know E, I don't feel I deserve any free beer, all I did was get shot and have gammy feet." Eric looked at Basil confused, shocked into silence for a moment by his words.

"What on earth are you talking about? You stood toe to toe with the Hun for two whole months and in the freezing depths of winter! You got shot and still have the bloody thing in there causing you jip. I think you've earned a drink or two," Eric pointed his fork angrily at Basil. Eva smiled, perhaps harsh words from Eric, a fellow soldier, was what he needed. Basil was silent but Eric continued, "You are no coward, B, and you never will be in the eyes of me or anyone in the Kensingtons. I mean, you're a stubborn fool, but no coward." Basil twitched a smile as Eric returned to his meal.

"Perhaps we'll go for one," said Basil and Eva's heart bounced in renewed hope. She prayed Eric being here would help Basil, he was always so lost and alone without him.

After supper Eric and Basil wandered down to the Red Lion, as they stood on the opposite side of the road, they could hear the music and laughter within and see the throng of people through the window. The soft light that was once so enticing seemed ominous and intimidating, especially to Basil.

"Still want to go?" asked Basil. Eric looked at him and smiled.

"Well we've come this far," replied Eric, holding his walking stick up to indicate how difficult the journey had been for them both. Basil nodded, and they crossed the street, limping together.

As they opened the door they were greeted by an unsettling wave of heat and noise from inside and it took a moment for them to adjust to it. Eric was visibly taken aback. The orange light and noise transported his mind back to the trenches and for a split second he was under the glow of flickering illumination shells and could hear the shouts of men. He shrugged the memory away.

Basil followed behind him and they made their way towards the bar. Quickly their presence was registered, and a path was cleared for them. Cheers sounded from the crowd and as they made their way to the bar and those they knew patted their backs. At the large dark wooden counter two older men got up from their stools to allow Eric and Basil to sit, they smiled back towards the clapping, cheering crowd. The barman stretched his hand out to Eric and Basil in turn.

"Welcome home lads. Welcome home! What can I get you?"

"I think a couple of Copper Ales, please, Jack," said Eric, reaching into his pocket for some money to pay.

"Don't be silly, you and Basil will not pay for a drink tonight and I'll have no discussion on the matter." Jack was the landlord of the Red Lion and had been for years. Eric liked him a lot but had a few times been hauled out on his backside by Jack after a few too many ales. Jack wasn't to be argued with, he used to box, and he had fist likes hard pink clubs. He also didn't tread on any rumours that he was well connected to some sinister underground networks in the city.

"What about us?" asked one of the men beside them.

"Come back a wounded hero and you can drink for free too!"

Jack poured two frothy pints for his honoured guests. Eric smiled at Basil who returned an awkward grin as the music started up again and all but the few men around where the boys sat, returned to their conversations.

"So, Eric. Did you teach the Boche a lesson in manners?" asked Jack, leaning on the bar, talking loudly over the din of Saturday night. Eric took a long pleasing drink from his pint jar and smiled to the gathered audience. Basil drank tentatively by his side.

"Well I don't know about me but B here was quite the marksman!" Eric slapped Basil on the back.

"Oh yeah?" Jack seemed a little surprised. Basil smiled coyly, he wasn't overly happy to be the centre of attention but played along.

"Yeah Jack, they couldn't relax around me!" Basil held his pot aloft in a salute to himself. It received a cheer from the red-eyed crowd around him and a pat on the back from Eric who had already finished his first pint. Jack was busy pouring him another.

Eric and Basil sat drinking at the bar and telling stories for an hour or two. They didn't pay for a single drink and only smoked a couple of their own cigarettes. They were treated like conquering heroes but for Basil it became too much, he was awkward and ill at ease with his celebrity. He didn't think he deserved such kind words or friendly treatment so shortly before ten he told Eric he was leaving, blaming his feet for the early departure. He was cheered out the door and was almost across the road before he heard Eric behind him.

"Wait for me old man!" said Eric, hopping across the road and together they walked back to 76. They stayed up for a while talking in the dark about the war until Kathleen returned home from work shortly before midnight. She joined them for a drink before they headed up to bed. Eric, without asking or needing permission got into the same bed as Basil instead of the one made up next to it. He wanted to be close to his little brother again, like they were as children or at the front. Soon they were sound asleep.

In the dark hours of morning, Eva, Kathleen and Basil lay wide awake in their beds. Tears were rolling down Eva's face, Kathleen's too and Basil had a pillow wrapped tightly round his ears in an attempt to muffle the horrifying screams coming from Eric and his dreams. Basil thought it best not to wake him but after fifteen minutes of haunting noises and hurt he couldn't take it any more and was forced to nudge his brother awake.

Eric woke in shock and embarrassment and, with his brow glistening wet with sweat, he quickly checked his crotch for the warm flooding of urine. He signed with relief when he found it to be dry and just a little moist with sweat.

"I am sorry, B," said Eric as he got up, moved into the adjacent bed and tried again to sleep.

Aubers Ridge, France – 8ᵗʰ May 1915

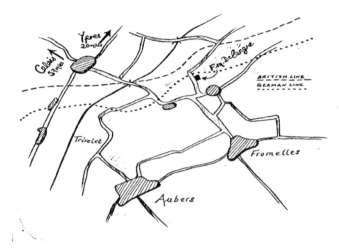

"HANHAM! Where are you lad?" screamed Hockley from the other side of the wall Stuart was resting against.

"I'm here, sir, around the corner," replied Stuart. Hockley stepped out into the sun that was bathing the granite wall. Some of the stones twinkled in the bright sunlight so Hockley had to squint in order to make out Stuart sat there smoking, writing paper on his knees and a pencil in his right hand poised to scribe.

"What are you doing sat there lad? We've still a lot to do," Hockley's gaze was accusing, and Stuart felt uneasy.

"Sir, my platoon is ready. Provisions and ammunition have been issued, I've conducted three kit checks and all corporals and above know to be in the courtyard for the CO's address at four o'clock," said Stuart, remaining relaxed but trying not to be arrogant. "I thought I'd write a letter or two and I've told the lads they can do the same." The last sentence was posed like a question. Hockley thought for a while, his thick dark moustache twitching menacingly. He had recently become B Company Sergeant Major and was a welcome addition, Stuart liked him a lot.

"Quickly then lad, write your letter and then come and find me. I have a lot of things to do and you can certainly help. Be in the barn in" Hockley checked his timepiece, "fifteen minutes."

Hockley turned and walked away and Stuart waited until he was gone before he sighed and returned to his writing. He had wished to write three letters that afternoon but now he was constrained to one or perhaps two if he kept them brief. He debated not writing any, but he was all too aware of the hugely significant offensive to be conducted at dawn and he didn't want to waste this chance to correspond, rushed or not. He let his pencil decide whose name it was to be at the top of the letter and of course it penned *'Dearest Emily'*.

Since his brothers had returned wounded back to England Stuart had felt very alone. There was only so much extra work he could do to occupy his mind before he was forced to think of home and the future. He would wonder what his brothers were doing in the spring sunshine and smiled at thoughts of his mother and sisters enjoying Basil and Eric at home. He had regular letters from them all but would wait for short moments of quiet during busy periods to read them and even then, he would scan them quickly in full knowledge he would again have to focus on the tasks at hand. This way he found thoughts of home and the distant warmth of family consumed him less. Quickly he would then re-read them before penning his reply and he kept his letters short.

Where Stuart struggled most was writing to Emily. Since the Battle of Neuve Chapelle there had been an increase in correspondence between them as Stuart had now realised the need for hope. He no longer wanted to be the lone wolf he was and while he still kept her a secret amongst his comrades, he couldn't wait to read her letters. He would save them for prolonged periods of quiet so he could let himself float away to the future he dreamed of so much. They planned weekends when he returned home and talked passionately about a future together in Canada, the solitude of prairie life and its untouched wilderness was so appealing to them both. He envied the wounded men who had already been sent home and had to mentally reprimand himself on occasions when he thought about ways he might be able to put himself in harm's way and receive a 'blighty wound' that would allow him out of this place. He was sure every man thought the same, but it was never communicated, there was a war to win and it was gravely serious. More so now the enemy employed the harrowing tactic of using gas to kill or maim their opponent before a big offensive. King and country and the lives of the men around him overpowered matters of the heart.

Stuart pulled a post card from his tunic once he had completed a heartfelt letter to Emily and wrote Basil's name on the front with the address of 76 under the official heading *Field Service Post Card*. He turned it over and started to fill in the reverse where allowed. There was no need for him to read the warning *'NOTHING is to be written on this side except the date and signature of the sender. If anything else is added the post card will be destroyed.* He struck lines through the irrelevant sentences until it read,

Hanham

'I am quite well.
I have received your letter dated 4th May.
Letter follows at first opportunity.
Stuart
8. 5. 15'

Under the cover of darkness, the Kensingtons made their way from their temporary billets in Laventie to the forward trenches where they crammed in as best they could. C and D Company were in front and would lead the Kensingtons out into the attack. Some men took their turn on the parapet observing the darkness of No Man's Land and others tried to sleep but most could not. The Kensingtons were the important left flank of a major offensive to take the higher ground of Aubers Ridge in front of them, they knew there would be some hard fighting ahead. Any sleep was restless and filled with nervous dreams.

As night became the early hours of morning sappers from the Royal Engineers scuttled around in the darkness of the forward trenches and down into the deep tunnels they had been digging over the long months. At the end of these dark, damp corridors were the mines that would be set off to signal the attack. The Kensingtons were then to dash across the open expanse of No Man's Land and through the wire that had been freshly cut by other groups of brave engineers. They would occupy the craters and clear the enemy trenches to allow reinforcements to pass through them and seize the objectives of Delangre Farm and the enemy supply trenches stretching up to the east and the top of Aubers Ridge. The scale of preparation and vast amounts of training the Kensingtons had been conducting in the build-up gave them great confidence. They were also buoyed as a battalion by the visit of the British Commander in Chief Sir John French. He had reviewed the Kensingtons to congratulate them on their terrific fighting spirit during the Battle of Neuve Chappelle and they were now a proud fighting unit, battle hardened and respected. They had also heard rumours that their Divisional Commander had remarked, *"The Kensingtons will not fail"* which gave them further resolve.

Stuart was squatting against the back wall of the trench to keep his backside out of the sticky mud. The spring sun had baked much of the earth hard, but some areas of trench were still recovering from the awful winter. He supported himself with his rifle between his legs, hands grasped high up the barrel his head was rested against his wrists like in prayer, but he was only trying to rest his eyes as best he could. Men around him were fidgeting and restless, some tried to write letters home and others had managed to sleep so snored happily in the mud. Stuart envied those asleep, his mind was swimming with fear and gave him no quarter, so he thought through the orders he had received and their objectives for the day. He imagined what he would say along the way to keep the men fighting hard and he thought of what he would do if it didn't go to plan but there was no way he could know that at the current time, still it plagued him. In the raging water that was his mind he would occasionally think back to home and his family and of course, Emily. He imagined her sleeping soundly in her bed, eyes twitching in a pleasant dream filled sleep. It scared him to think of her so he grit his teeth to focus again on the day to come. Stuart was very grateful for the whispers that came along the trench shortly before five o'clock in the morning. "Bombardment will start in a few minutes," said the man next to him.

The bombardment lasted for forty minutes without rest and inspired the men once again. Despite learning the hard way at Neuve Chapelle, all were confident that the ferocity and volume of shellfire would have destroyed the enemy positions and whoever was left there would be a shaking wreck of a soldier unable to fight. At twenty minutes to six the final shell whistled above and there was a brief moment of silence, men were standing in the front trenches as C and D Company prepared to scale the ladders up into the fight. They were waiting for their final signal that came thirty seconds after the last shell landed. The engineers detonated the mines under the German line and a series of deep, earthly explosions rumbled from below ground. Heavy clouds of dust and earth were lifted into the air and cheers came from the men on the British side. Whistles then blew and men from all across Britain, Ireland and India left the safety of their trench and launched themselves into the attack.

Stuart and the rest of B Company moved forward and prepared themselves for the second wave. He watched in tense fear as their comrades scaled the parapets into the soft light of approaching dawn. As C and D Company stood tall and started out across the ground the enemy rifle and machine gun fire began. The terrible weight of it was fierce and it took the lives of so many Kensingtons before they were able to take even a few steps. They fell or were dragged back into the trench and carried away dead or wounded. Some managed to get a few feet before being cut to pieces by barbed wire and fizzing lead, their bodies maimed and disfigured by flying hatred. Screams from dying men soon filled the air along with the snap of deathly fire from the enemy, men of the second wave started to breathe heavy and pray to their god and families. Stuart himself had to run the line shouting support and braying brave words to stop himself falling into unmanageable distress. His heart was beating like a heavy bass drum and his stomach was tight in dread.

"Not long boys! We'll give those bloody Hun some London steel!"

Officers were walking stoically in front of the men trying not to look concerned or scared, smiling at those most afraid. They looked up and down the line until Captain Witty raised a bony thumb up and blew his whistle. It was hard to hear above the shouts of warring men and the dull thud of bullets around them but they all, despite their fear and the cracking fire above them, mounted the ladders and climbed out of the trench. Stuart encouraged his platoon out and across the hard ground now littered with Kensington dead and dying, as he placed his own foot on the ladder to climb up, he looked over and caught the eye of Harding who gave him a friendly nod. Stuart returned the gesture and ascended the ladder.

The scene that greeted him was like nothing he could have imagined. The sun was now peeking above the horizon behind the British objective and illuminating the battlefield in front of him. Men were strewn all around in various states of life and death and those still running towards the craters and enemy trenches were hammered by the relentless sheets of machine gun fire, their dull deadly beat the only sound to be heard above the shouting and screaming of advancing soldiers.

Stuart gathered his nerves from all around him and hunched into a run. He chose a path that appeared clear of barbed wire and ran as fast as he could towards the craters he could see a hundred and fifty yards away. Men of C and D Company who had made it there already were doing their best to harass the enemy with their own rifle fire, but it was having no effect on the intensity of No Man's Land. It was still a seemingly impenetrable wall of stinging wasps, most diving head long into the hard ground around the brave Kensington men.

The cleared paths were narrow, so Stuart had to file in behind another man from his platoon and shouted encouragement as they moved forward. After only fifty yards the man in front of him was bowled over and he slumped pathetically into a lifeless pile on the floor. It happened so quickly that Stuart did not have time to divert his path and was tripped by the man's backside comically thrust into the air. Stuart looked back towards the friend he had been following for signs of life but his blank, open eyes, indicated his world was now dark. Stuart turned onto his front and looked ahead. He was about to stand but a dotted line of bullets splashed rhythmically a foot from his face, so he instinctively buried his head to his chest and prayed to remain unseen. His eyes and mouth full of dirt kicked up by the digging bullets.

Stuart took two deep breaths, wiped his mouth and tried to steady himself. His heart thumped wildly and his brow was soaking wet with sweat, he grit his teeth until they hurt and roared like an angry lion as he stood to run the seventy yards to the crater in front of him. He did not break his stride and swerved between the openings in the wire. The light was now brighter allowing him to see his footing, so he moved quickly over the dusty ground. Angry hisses and cracks were all around him, but he arrived at the crater untouched. Lungs burning and heart racing, he had made it across.

*

Stuart took a few moments to gather his thoughts and assess the situation. Men were laying down at the forward edges of a crater and firing into the enemy positions up the rise towards what remained of Delangre Farm. Stuart could see the flashes of machine gun and rifle fire coming from those places so slid down further into the crater to avoid their glare. He looked to his left and saw a group of German prisoners being forcefully corralled by a few Kensington men. The captured men were in complete shock, they were covered in blood and mud and their eyes were wide in disbelief. They did not look like the regal, proud soldiers he had seen pass back through the lines during the Battle of Neuve Chapelle. These men were scared and visibly shaking in fear, behind them he saw some of his men searching for leadership and this pulled him into life. He ran towards them and beckoned them all to follow him to the very left of the line, B Company's objective that morning.

"Come on lads, follow me! We need to get up to the far side and protect the flank," shouted Stuart as he passed. Grateful for renewed direction they followed him without question.

Stuart and his small party of men made their way into the German trench that had been taken by C Company and moved quickly through to where they were supposed to be. The ordeal of crossing No Man's Land was such that the men were disjointed so Stuart's posse grew with more members of B Company as they filed past. He noticed the volume of dead and wounded, British and German, in the trenches and the craters. It was a harrowing scene and hard to stay focused, Stuart was happy to run into Captain Witty but was shocked to see him badly wounded and laying in the bottom of the German trench.

"Hanham, good lad well done getting here. Torrid affair I'm sure you would agree," said Witty. His usual calm appearance and soft gentlemanly features broken into a dark grimace of pain. Stuart crouched beside him and looked gravely at the wound on Witty's side being tended to by one of his men.

"Don't worry about that, Sergeant Hanham. Now tell me how many men do you have with you?" Stuart turned to look back at the line of men stacked behind him.

"Maybe twenty, sir, but they aren't all my platoon."

"No bother, we're all messed up anyway. Take those men and try and stop the bloody Boche bombing their way back in here," ordered Witty, pointing away behind him.

"Will do, sir." Stuart waved his team forward.

"Good lad!" called Witty after him.

Stuart snaked his way through the network of trenches towards the dull explosions he could hear fifty metres away. They were the distinctive, thumping explosions of German hand grenades so effective in the tight world of trench fighting. Along the way they passed more dead men and Stuart had to stop when he saw one of them. The men behind him nearly ran him over they were following so close, but Stuart didn't budge, he was transfixed by the young bright eyes of Harding, lifeless and still. Stuart looked him up and down and easily spotted the two large holes in his chest where the fatal strikes had entered his body. He was incredibly fond of his platoon commander and it saddened him greatly to see him lying dead on the floor. It was an ignominious end for such a brave young man not yet a quarter of a century old. Stuart closed Harding's eyes with the flat palm of his hand, wished him a safe journey and turned down the trench towards the sounds of fighting and the enemy on whom he would seek revenge.

The shouting grew louder as they approached, Stuart took a moment and ordered the men to fix bayonets if they hadn't already. "We'll go in hard and aggressive boys! Don't give them chance to think or use their bombs. Keep going until they have fled or are dead and don't look back!" ordered Stuart through a snarl.

His words helped even himself and he was soon ready for the fray. "Ready lads!" They all nodded eagerly back towards him, but one man couldn't wait any longer and he dashed past Stuart around the corner into the fight. Stuart followed him and after a few paces had to barge past another Kensington man brawling with a frantic German. Stuart knocked the foe down so his friend could level his rifle and fire a fatal shot into the German's belly. He didn't wait to fire another and instead followed Stuart further down the trench. The men in Stuart's squad were close behind and desperate for their turn.

As they neared the next kink in the trench two bombs came fizzing over their heads and landed amongst the Kensington following Stuart, he turned the corner at a pace and ran his bayonet into the open flank of one of the men who had thrown the bombs. The man he skewered had lost his grey tunic and was wearing only a white, muddied under-shirt. He writhed on Stuart's bayonet like a speared boar, crying in torment as Stuart mangled his internal organs. The second bomber was shot in the chest and face by two men flowing in behind Stuart as the bombs exploded and the Kensingtons behind them cried out in pain, shrapnel piercing their bodies. Stuart placed his foot on the man's chest and pulled hard to remove his bayonet, but the sucking of his prey's body would not allow him to drag it free, so he fired a shot into the man's ribs as he pulled. His bayonet ejected in a savage cloud of blood and fatty white tissue. The muddy white under shirt of his enemy now slowly turned a deep port. Stuart spat at the dying man and moved on, his body was pulsing with adrenaline and fear, but he needed to remain calm, he needed to lead.

Around the next corner he found two of his men beating a fat German to death with the butts of their rifles and a Kensington lad rolling around holding his belly in wretched pain. Three more of his men were firing out into the distance and around the corner of the next trench. Stuart called some men from behind him to pick up the large box of captured German grenades and make their way up the communication trench that trailed off to his right. They obeyed immediately and Stuart ordered the next seven men to follow them. The next along was Major Stafford and he came straight to Stuart for an update.

"Hanham! What's going on?" asked Stafford. He was tall like Stuart so they both crouched down to the safety of the trench floor, away from the fire ripping through the sky just above them. His deep brown eyes searched Stuart for help.

"Sir, we have managed to get these boys on the run for now but I'm sure they will come back." His lungs were heavy, adrenaline was pumping so hard around his body he thought he might explode or faint. His hands were shaking and covered with blood. "I've sent some boys up the communication trench with some bombs, but they will not hold it without more of our lads." Stuart was dizzy and thought he might fall over but a calming hand from Stafford brought him round.

"Well done lad, we'll spread them out and hold the line."

Stafford turned and barked an order behind him and a flood of Kensington men came rushing around the corner with purpose. Stuart relaxed slightly to see them, their dull green uniforms flowing past him like a muddy river.

*

The next few hours felt like days for the men stretched out on the left flank of the Kensington position. Enemy grenades and rifle fire continually harassed them and heavy black shells from trench mortars fell with devastating effect onto their exposed position. These evil shells were visible from the moment a deep, muffled explosion indicated one had been fired and they flew languidly through the sky towards them, as if in slow motion. One could only pray their number was not called each time these shells sunk menacingly from the sky above. Their precarious situation also meant they were constantly at risk from sniping and many men fell to this foe through the morning, so by midday only around twenty-four men remained in B Company.

Major Stafford was commanding the effort and without any officers to assist he was looking to Hockley and Stuart to execute his orders.

"Sergeant Major, I don't need to tell you that if we don't hold this position the day is lost! I need you to hold the northern section as best you can. We should have had reinforcements, but it seems they still can't get across No Man's Land behind us," said Stafford. The three of them were hunkered down in a shelter that had been cut away from the trench wall. Heavy trench mortars were landing close by and the higher pitched squeal of German artillery had started to add to their woes.

"Yes sir," replied Hockley. His face was stern and bloodied from a cut below his left eye, but his moustache was clean and well preserved as always. "About the wounded, sir, they are mounting, and we cannot get them back."

"We have to focus on holding the line. Those that can move should try and make their way back, but we cannot release men to help them. We simply cannot lose this position!" said Stafford. Grave concern and genuine sympathy etched across his weathered face. Hockley nodded his understanding and Stafford turned to Stuart, "Hanham, you must continue your good work up the communications trench. That is the likely approach for a counter attack as we have seen." Stafford was referring to the aggressive attack Stuart and his men had recently beaten away in brutal hand-to-hand fighting. "Try as best you can to build the defences."

"I am running low on ammunition, sir."

"I know, I have some men stripping machine gun belts as we speak, they will ferry the boxes up to you very soon."

"Alright, but I think I need to take further trenches to better secure my position. They are causing us all sorts of grief from it," explained Stuart, drawing into the dirt a diagram of his predicament.

"As you see fit, Sergeant Hanham but don't spread yourself too thin." Stuart nodded his understanding.

"Off you go then men, do me proud."

Hockley and Stuart prepared to leave for their duty, explosions from heavy guns and ragged cracks from bullets all around them. Before they left the shelter of the small dugout Hockley extended a big hairy hand to Stuart. "Good luck," he said with a smile, the ends of his thick black moustache danced in the breeze.

"And to you, sir." Stuart returned his smile. Hockley, crouched cat like, sloped away to his position but had only managed a few feet before his large back exploded in a squelching thud of visceral pink and deep red. The air in his lungs was thrust out of him in a low growl and he slumped to the floor like a slain beast. He rolled awkwardly onto his back only for a second shot to hit him in the centre of his great chest. Hockley seemed to soak it up with ease, but his eyes closed, and he stopped moving. Even in death his thick moustache was prim and stoic.

"Hanham! Snap out of it and get to your post," roared Stafford and Stuart jumped back into the moment. "I'll sort his sector, you carry on!"

Stuart was numb for a second then turned and ran up the slope. The same marksman fired a couple of shots at him, but he was a harder target, so they splashed into the trench around him and soon he was out of sight around the corner.

When Stuart reached his line of men, they were sorting out a newly arrived box of loose ammunition into small piles and handing them out to the men on the line who shoved them quickly into their pockets. There was currently a small lull in the fighting.

"Right lads! We need to take that other position if we are to survive this day. Volunteers?" Stuart looked along the line. He was surprised to see so many catch his eye and nod their heads. "Good. Thorne, Nipper and Browny come with me. The rest stay here and hold out. We'll call you forward."

Stuart gathered the selected men but was not able to finish his orders before the other men around them started firing furiously.

"Sergeant! They're coming again!" shouted one of the men.

"Hold the line lads!"

For thirty minutes Stuart and his men were engaged in ferocious hand-to-hand fighting and aggressive close-range fire fights with the enemy attempting to break through into their position. They lost count of how many they killed but Stuart knew he had lost three of his own number in the contest. He was in the thick of the fighting throughout and, with another large Kensington man, had found a position that afforded them good protection from the bombs, mortars and sniper fire raining down all around them. Here they would wait for the sounds of approaching enemy, turn the corner and fire down the thin trench into the oncoming grey uniforms. They couldn't miss at this range and killed a dozen before the enemy realised the route was blocked and changed the focus of their attack. Again, Stuart and his men managed to fend away the attack with rifle, bayonet and fists but two more men were lost. For the moment though, the line held firm.

*

Early in the afternoon Stuart got word that the Battalion was to withdraw. Reinforcements had not been successful in getting through and the whole line was now a precariously weak limb that could be severed at any moment by a coordinated counter-attack. Stuart acknowledged this order and ran to call his men back. As he turned the corner to recall the last of his party he came face to face with a lanky German. His grey, imperial uniform was tatty and hung ripped from the left side of his torso. His eyes were cold blue, and his moustache dishevelled on his gaunt face. He had a Kensington up against the wall of the trench by the throat and his bayonet, clenched tight in his bloodied fist, was thrust deep into the side of Stuart's friend. Instinctively Stuart lowered his rifle and fired a shot into the man's chest. He heard it thud hard on target and, shattering his thick breastbone, he fell back mortally wounded. Stuart's eyes then opened wide in shock as he saw behind his slain foe another German whose rifle was high in his shoulder and aimed directly at Stuart. He froze in fear until the loud crack of the German's rifle exploded in front of him and he was thrust back hard against the wall of the trench. Stuart watched his enemy cock his rifle again and raise it to his shoulder. He looked deep into the eyes of his killer. They were the calm, lifeless black of a shark as he pulled the trigger. Stuart's world slowed to a hazy crawl and he prepared himself for death. It had all happened so suddenly that he hadn't been able to register the pain on the left side of his chest and he felt at peace, but the pathetic click of the German's rifle brought him round from his haze and he reacted quickest to the situation. His would-be killer looked in shock at his empty rifle as Stuart raised his to his waist and aimed it roughly in the direction of his assassin. The German did not stop to receive his fate, instead he turned and ran back the way he had come and was quickly out of view.

Stuart levered himself up and ran back towards the safety of his own men but had gone only thirty metres before the true extent of his wound hit him and only when he reached up and felt the hole in his chest did his adrenaline cease to anaesthetise the searing pain. He was reduced to a slow walk and had to stop and lean against the trench wall to stop himself falling over. He reached awkwardly behind his left shoulder and felt the hideous, gaping exit wound on his back, it was the size of a cricket ball and excruciating to the touch. He could feel the fatty tissue around the wound and was quickly aware of the steady flow of blood running down his back. The feel of it and the retreating adrenaline made him vomit aggressively onto the trench floor, stinging bile was mixed with bright frothy blood. He was in serious trouble but thoughts of home and of Emily steadied his resolve. He saw concern on her face and then anger at his capitulation, so he clenched his jaw, wiped his mouth with his good arm and stood to walk.

As Stuart made his way through the trench, he awkwardly removed his field dressing from the pocket of his tunic and managed to open it with his teeth. He reached over with the padded section to plug the wound, but the pain and awkwardness of the attempt meant he dropped the dressing onto the muddy ground. Frustrated, and knowing it would now be infested with bacteria and grime, he continued on to find help. During the last few minutes he had been so focused on his wound he had not been aware of his surroundings so when Stuart looked about him to find someone to help a devastating sight met him. There were dead men strewn on the floor but no living men to assist him and he recognised the area of trench from the days fighting. Hockley's body lay just in front of him without colour or life, so he assumed the Kensingtons had vacated the position and returned across No Man's Land. Stuart peeked over the parapet at the British trenches and saw what remained of his battalion retreating all along the line. He watched for a short while and saw more of them cut down by the same rifles and machine guns that had taken so many lives at dawn, it appeared the return journey was just a harrowing and costly.

Stuart slumped down into a seated position against the dry wall of the trench and tried to compose himself amongst the fierce orchestra of war but suddenly he heard frantic footsteps approaching from his left and it was enough for him to regain some strength from his depleted reserves. He looked around for a means of protection and saw an officer's revolver on the floor next to him, its owner no longer of this world. He yanked it free from the lanyard and steadied it in the direction of the approaching sound. A Kensington turned the corner and reared up like a scared horse at the sight of Stuart pointing the Webley at his stomach.

"Bloody hell Sergeant, you scared the life out of me!" said Perriman in shock, gathering his breath. His youthful face was covered with mud and his tunic was dark with sweat.

"Sorry lad, thought you might have been the Hun." Stuart sat back down. Perriman came over to Stuart, eyes wide in grave concern.

"What has happened? Are you hit?"

"Ah yes, I am, but I'll be ok, I'm just waiting for the stretcher bearers. I am sure they will be along soon," replied Stuart. He didn't believe his own words but there was still hope burning inside him, "Say, can I borrow your field dressing while I wait?"

Without a word Perriman started to retrieve his field dressing from his pocket. "Actually lad, you keep it. You may want it yourself soon enough."

"But you need it now, I can get another," Perriman pleaded.

"No! You keep it. I'll find the stretcher bearers," said Stuart, turning away and walking down the trench. "Good luck."

"And to you, sergeant. I'll send them your way if I see them. See you back at our line soon," said Perriman as he left to try to find a way back to the British side.

Stuart walked further down the trench but knew in his heart he would find no one to help him, the Kensingtons had deserted the trench when reinforcements had failed to materialise. He searched the bodies for a field dressing, but he was so weak he could not look for long. Slowly and painfully he realised the futility of his efforts and sat down in sunny section of trench.

The sound of machine gun fire seemed to dull around him, shells were muffled, and the world became quiet and still. He was exhausted, gravely wounded and alone among dead friends and foe. Sat there on the firing step of the German trench he looked up towards the blue sky and the whizzing shells seemed quiet, like birds in flight. With no more strength left in his body or mind he could not stop the thoughts of family and home entering through the back channels of hope. He thought of his mother and father and he felt their love from far away and beyond the grave. He thought of the sunny days of his youth, fishing and climbing trees with his brothers and lunches in the sunshine of the Old Vicarage. He remembered the times he would play supporting roles in Kathleen's productions and walking Stella to school, of her wedding to Frank and how happy and beautiful she was that day. He let himself think of Emily whose love he had had for such a short but wonderful time, the most beautiful creature he had ever known on this earth and their future that was now so far away from this moment he could not imagine it any longer. His dying brain would not allow such impossible notions.

Stuart opened his eyes to the sun and then looked at himself. In his right hand he cradled the pistol now covered in his own sticky blood. His uniform was caked in mud, dust and the stale sweat and blood of war. The entire left side of his tunic was now a deep iron colour and spreading fast, even in the glaring sun he was cold as his life ebbed away. Tears struggled to leave his severely dehydrated body, but his huge breaking heart was indication of his despair. He knew he was looking into a deep abyss.

On the afternoon of the 9th of May 1915, twenty-six-year-old Stuart Aubrey Hanham mumbled one last heartfelt prayer to his God and those he loved, dropped his heavy head and sunk gently into the peaceful waters of death.

Hazeley Down, Hampshire – 2nd July 1915

BASIL sat as his desk in the Kensington Battalion Headquarters looking enviously at the men marching up and down in the summer sunshine, their hobnail boots crunching in unison on the parade square. He was uncomfortably hot in the corrugated iron structure and the open window did little to help. It was a still summer day and there was no hint of a breeze, so Basil was sweating through his khaki shirt. He leant back in his chair, gazed up into the metal rafters in humid contemplation while he waited for the meeting in the adjacent room to come to an end. The voices on the other side of the thin wall were muffled and drowned by the busy efforts of a large bee above his head.

With the bullet still causing him problems, and his history of severe trench foot, Basil was detailed to serve as one of the clerks at his Battalion Headquarters in Hazeley Down Camp, Winchester. Here many of the London Regiment Battalions had their rehabilitation camp, a place where soldiers would continue their recovery, conduct training and learn new skills before being deployed again to the fighting in Europe and beyond. Basil was told he would never return to active service and there was even talk of discharging him completely from the Army, but he was given the job of clerk to Major Hughes who commanded the Kensington Battalion efforts at Hazeley Down. Basil had his eyes closed in thought as the door opened slowly, he was caught by the three majors who had been conducting business next door.

"Are we keeping you up, Corporal Hanham?" asked Hughes, he noticed Basil with his head back and assumed he was sleeping. He too had been sweating through his shirt and was even more dishevelled.

"I'll leave you to it, Sam, and we will talk again Sunday. Hopefully I'll have some news by then," said a tall handsome major who used a long stick to help his limp. The officers too were mainly those who were wounded and who couldn't currently serve at the front.

"Yes, of course," replied Hughes, shaking hands with the two men before they exited into the summer heat. Hughes returned to his desk and Basil gathered the papers he needed him to sign.

"May I enter, sir?" asked Basil, knocking lightly on the flimsy door.

"Yes yes, do come in," Hughes waved a chubby paw at Basil but didn't look up.

"Sir, I need you to sign these papers and then I'll take them across to Division." Basil neatly laid out the typed sheets he had been producing all afternoon.

Hughes didn't say a word or look at Basil as he read through each one at pace and signed his name at the bottom. Basil waited patiently, staring at the bald patch on Hughes' crown that was dappled with beads of sweat, the moisture darkened his thin fair hair. After signing the last sheet Hughes leant back in his rigid chair and regarded Basil. Hughes was an older man of about fifty and had not been to France at all. He was unable to fight but a skilled administrator, perfect for running this aspect of the Battalion. His dark brown eyes never gave anything away and his soft round face was always resting emotionless. Basil had thought these qualities essential in business, but he wasn't a cold man and liked Basil.

"Why are you so keen to go back, Corporal Hanham, and why do you not sit proudly on your service to date? You're doing an important role here, don't you see that?" Basil had to think, he struggled with such a brazen question from anyone other than Eric. Hughes stared at him.

"Well, sir, I suppose I want to do my bit. You know for King and Country. I think I'll be better served in Fra-"

"Don't be such a fool, Hanham! You were nearly killed and if you were my son, I'd give you damn good hiding so you would realise it!" He smiled which made Basil unsure and look down at his feet like a child. "Ah, I'm sorry, Corporal Hanham. I'm just an old man and I suppose I see the world differently to you. How old are you?"

"Twenty-one, sir."

"Too young to understand then. Hopefully you will soon." Hughes stood mournfully to look out the window in silence.

"Sir," Basil steadied himself for the question. "Is there any news on Sergeant Hanham? You said you would tell me if there was."

"Indeed I did, Corporal Hanham, and as promised I will let you know when I hear something." Hughes turned sincerely to Basil, "At the moment he is still listed as Missing in Action, so we must remain hopeful he is in a prisoner camp somewhere. Have you written to the Red Cross as I suggested?"

"Yes, my mother did. There was a response, but they didn't have any records of him." Basil bowed his head.

"Well, these things take time, stay positive for your mother."

"Perhaps the battalion will return soon and there will be some news?" Basil forced a smile, hope in his heart.

"Perhaps, though I'm afraid there isn't much of a battalion left. I've already told you we lost thirteen officers and over four hundred and twenty killed or wounded at Aubers Ridge. Out of just over six hundred you have to call that a disaster and the reason why our battalion is no longer in rotation at the front." Hughes turned sadly to watch the marching troops in the sunshine and Basil remained silent. "…I am truly sorry about your brother and do not give up hope but try and count yourself lucky you weren't there yourself. And try and enjoy your weekend off, won't you?" Hughes gave Basil a smile of genuine affection.

*

"Any news, B?" asked Eric dropping his cigarette onto the station platform and extinguishing it with a large boot, he too was based at Hazeley Down whilst he recovered from his wound. He was a while from being fully fit but was training to be a Lewis Gunner and was attached to the Pioneer Section, so he learnt about basic combat engineering. When he returned to the front, he would certainly be a useful addition to the battalion but unlike Basil he was not desperately keen to return and currently, like all the Hanham family, Stuart was at the forefront of his mind.

"I'm afraid not. Major Hughes hasn't heard anything more. The battalion was awfully hit and will be running the railheads and shovelling horse shit for some time to come," Basil placed his holdall next to his Eric's on the platform of Winchester Station. Eric looked to the sky in contemplation, his furrowed brow moist in the heat of a summer day.

"I think he's dead, B," said Eric, after a moment's contemplation and in the matter of fact way a soldier might. Removing his hat, he wiped his brow with the sleeve of his thick khaki tunic. Basil looked across at him in shock but quickly back to the floor. Eric was right, of course. From what they had heard it had been terrible fighting at Aubers Ridge and the horrific casualty figures were testament to that.

"I think you're right E. Poor old boy." Basil placed a cigarette in his mouth and lit it with a match plucked from his small oval tin. Eric's tin was in the draw next his bed at 76, the bullet sent to kill him safely inside it.

"We'll play the game for mater and the girls though." Eric leant against Basil and stretched an arm high onto the shoulders of his taller, younger brother. Basil nodded and looked at Eric smiling at him, he made no attempt to shrug him away as a screeching whistle came from the west and large clouds of steam puffed white towers above the trees. Many soldiers, until now hidden in the shade of the platform, made their way out into the sun and were joined by civilians heading to London. A rippling stream of dull khaki mingled with the smart dark suits of older businessmen and cream summer frocks of giggling women. It seemed Basil and Eric were the only ones not laughing in the sun that afternoon. Happiness for them both seemed a long way off.

Eric and Basil arrived at 76 shortly before nine o'clock, the sky was still bright and it was warm outside. The noise of children playing in the street accompanied the boys as they came through the door into the cool house.

"Mater? We're home," called Eric as he dropped his bag at the foot of the stairs. There was no reply, Eric looked towards Basil.

"She must be out," said Basil, shrugging his shoulders. Eric levered himself gently onto the stairs and untied his puttees to remove his boots, pulling them off in cool relief. Basil sat in one of the dining chairs and did the same, but he struggled as always. His feet were still very sore at the end of a long day and his boots were cripplingly uncomfortable. Both boys removed their tunics and walked into the kitchen leaving behind them wet, sweaty footprints on the tiled floor.

"Mother!" screamed Basil as he dashed towards her chair in the snug at the back of the kitchen. Her book had fallen to the floor and her thick arms sagged pathetically over the polished wooden armrests. "Mother!"

Eva stirred slowly and looked at Basil confused. He hugged her like a small boy, but he smelt like a man, pungent in summer.

"Goodness me! You smell awful," said Eva, turning her nose high up to the ceiling in the search for fresh air. Eric was laughing behind them.

"You looked like you'd had it, Mater," said Eric, prizing the top off a bottle of ale from the cupboard.

"Just resting. Until I was attacked." Eva lifted herself gingerly from her chair. Basil was embarrassed by his exaggerated reaction so stood quietly. "How are you boys?"

"Fine," replied Eric taking a big gulp from the bottle. "Oh, this is good stuff. Where did you get this?" Eric wiped his mouth on his shirtsleeve.

"Reverend Duval gave it to us when he came to see me on Tuesday, he said you'd like it." Eva adjusted her hair, it was now completely grey and where once it had volume and shine it was like wire and fuzzy round her wrinkled features.

"I'll be sure to thank him when I see him." Eva sat down at the kitchen table with a sigh, exhausted.

"Are you ok?" asked Basil stepping from the gloom. Eva regarded him and tried to smile.

"I'm managing, dear boy. How are you? Any news on your brother?" Her Scottish accent was prouder now, it always appeared stronger when she was drunk, tired or angry and perhaps in this moment she was all three.

"None, but I hear there will be some soon, they are gathering all the records together and we should have them to look over. Well, Major Hughes will, and he'll tell me if there is anything," Basil and Eric knew it was a lie, but they wanted their mother to keep some hope, they both wanted to believe it too.

"I see. Well, let us hope we hear something soon." Eva sensed Stuart was lost but was trying so hard not to give up. "I put an appeal in the Daily Express yesterday, so it was printed today. Your sisters thought it might help." Eva handed Eric the paper open at the page and Basil read it over his shoulder.

'HANHAM – Mrs. E. Hanham, 76, Amesbury Av, Streatham Hill, S.W., seeks news of her son Sergeant S. A. Hanham, No. 1341 No. 7 Platoon, B Co. 13th Batt. London Regt. (Kensington – Princess Louise's Own). Reported wounded May 9th. Any of his comrades who can give tidings please communicate with his mother.'

"Well it's certainly worth a try. Did it cost much?"

"It didn't cost anything, the Daily Express let mothers and wives put a small appeal in the paper at no cost. Do you think we will hear from someone?"

"Hard to say but if someone reads it I am sure they will write," said Eric, placing the newspaper back down in front of Eva. She looked so helpless in the growing dark. It was as though a part of her had died with

Stuart and she was now a shallow representation of her tenacious former self. It unsettled her boys to see their mother so lost for words and broken with life. They felt selfish for rushing off and leaving her alone to wait like they had but what could they do? It was a calling, Britain needed its young men like never before and some were going to pay the ultimate price, though no one knew it would be so many so soon.

"Say, I had a visitor this week. A Miss Emily Church." Eva forced a smile.

Eric looked at Basil who returned his vacant stare, he then looked towards his mother embarrassed and was about to speak but Eva cut him off, "Relax, Stuart told me about her. She just came to see if we had heard anything, but I had to sadly tell her we hadn't. Poor thing." Eva seemed broken again, freshly wounded, "Anyway she left an address if we hear anything. Did you know her?"

"No not really, we only met her once," Eric took another long drink. Basil and Eva remained deathly silent. "I think I'll go and have a wash. Will K be home tonight?"

"Yes, she should be. Leave your clothes out and I'll wash them tomorrow." Basil watched his mother until he caught her eye and she smiled at him as best she could, her big eyes were heavy and dark in the twilight. Slowly she moved towards Basil leant against the kitchen worktop. Eva was so small compared to him she had to reach high to touch his face.

"So lovely to have you both home," she said with a soft hand on his cheek but her eyes were tired and weary with sadness for her eldest son lost to them all.

Hanham

*

A few days later, after Eric and Basil had returned to Hazeley Down, Kathleen sat with Eva at the kitchen table drinking tea and eating a small breakfast of toast and strawberry jam. They sat in comfortable silence, Kathleen was reading about the Gallipoli Campaign in the paper and Eva hunched quietly listening to the birds chirping their confusion at a change in the weather. Part of her was still basking in the happiness of the weekend past and the memory of a picnic on the common with Eric, Basil and both her daughters. It was still fresh in her mind, but her heart was bleeding for Stuart.

"Well I'm glad the boys aren't over there," said Kathleen, folding the paper and placing it on the table. She grasped her tea with both hands and sipped it gently. Eva remained still but the sound of the letterbox opening and letters gliding to the floor woke them both from their trance. Eva's appeal was now four days old and the thought they might get some news on Stuart excited her. Kathleen kicked out her chair and ran to the door, her thick dark hair bounced behind her and quickly she returned with two letters. One was addressed to her and she recognised Howard's delicate writing style and the Cairo Post Office stamp from where it had been sent. The other was addressed to '*Mrs. E. Hanham*' and was written in an unfamiliar hand.

"This one is for you." Kathleen handed Eva the pale blue envelope. Eva studied it and saw the postmark was from Surrey.

"Well it isn't Stuart's writing," said Eva in obvious disappointment.

"Open it and find out who it's from then." Kathleen was trying her best to remain calm, but Eva just turned the envelope over in her hands, afraid of what it might say. Kathleen forced Eva into action by gently placing a clean knife down in front of her mother, carefully Eva cut the top fold of the envelope and pulled from it two pages of neatly pencilled words. Kathleen propped herself up against the worktop to give her mother space to read but watched for signs of hope or distress.

For Kathleen the potential loss of her brother was tortuous. Since moving home to 76 when the boys headed away to war, she had supported her mother and, while she accepted her role willingly, she couldn't help but notice a change in her own character and approach to life. Before the boys had left, she had been carefree, enjoyed the variety of London life and floated on the changing winds of opportunity. She was beautiful, talented and popular so life had been easy for her and she had bounced through it successfully with no regard for its pitfalls and woes. She loved her family deeply and they were always there as a constant and irreplaceable anchor in her exciting life but now she felt completely different. She had loved deeply and lost, been separated from her friends in town and seemingly forgotten by those she used to consider her dearest. She had seen her youngest brothers change into men, men tarnished by a conflict that none except those who lived it could even comprehend. She doubted her own talents and had found deeper levels of emotion she didn't know she possessed. At the end of every day would return home to her mother who, since Christmas Eve and the night Basil was wounded, was a small bird-like shell of the strong widow who had brought five children to London.

Kathleen was also sleeping in the same bed her beloved brother Stuart had slept in for so long. His presence in the room used to give her comfort and strength but now that room seemed dusty, vacant and even in the beautiful light of summer it was dark. It no longer smelt of him but of stale antiquity and his spirit departing her life made her feel so alone it hurt. Without him she would have to change forever and the young version of herself was lost. The joyous times with Harriet a distant dream, so far from her she doubted its truth. She was so low in confidence she wondered whether Howard, who she had decided to try and love, would continue to love her as the older, sensible and broken women she now was. Life was a heavy fog around Kathleen, like a wet jacket, she felt its weight as she watched her mother read the letter from a stranger.

Eva's expression started hopeful and Kathleen's heart began to swell in her chest but halfway down the first page Eva squealed in pain and put her hand to her open mouth with a sharp intake of breath. Tears formed in her old eyes and rolled down her aged face. Kathleen's emotions were full to the brim and she felt like a kettle reaching its screaming finale. She grabbed the first page of the letter as Eva started on the second and read with slow precision. Every word she felt in her heart and her soul.

> *'Dear Madam,*
>
> *In reply to your advertisement in yesterday's 'Daily Express' re your son Sergeant S A Hanham, although I can give you no news of his whereabouts you may be glad to hear of the following information. On Sunday May 9th while I was in the first German trench he came up to me and asked if I could share my field dressing as he was shot – through the body just above the heart. While I was trying to get it out of its pocket he changed his mind and refused to take it saying that*

I should probably want it myself later on. I tried to get him to take it but he refused and walked down the trench saying that he would wait for the stretcher bearers. About an hour afterwards I was wounded myself and went down the same trench for some distance before crawling over the top to our trenches, but I did not see him anywhere. I was surprised to see your advertisement for, up until now, I thought he must have got across to our own lines and was in an English hospital somewhere. I don't think his wound would have proved fatal as he was able to walk and talk fairly well but there is a possibility he was hit again while making his way to our lines. On the other hand he may have gone further down the German trench than I went and been still waiting when the Germans recaptured the position in which case he was probably taken prisoner. I wish I could give you more satisfactory news of him but I am sending the above information in case you have heard nothing at all. I knew Sergeant Hanham quite well and think you will soon have reassuring tidings of him.

Yours faithfully,

(Pte) A Perriman

No 3247 B Company, 13th London Regt'

When Kathleen finished the letter, she wiped the tears from her eyes and steadied herself. She sat down at the table, so she did not collapse and collated the letter. She looked inside the envelope for further news in pathetic hope but after a couple of moments of panic she looked at

Eva. Her mother was vacant, staring blankly at the wall, and her eyes were still and emotionless like that of a doll. Kathleen placed her hand on Eva's shoulder and bent round to catch her gaze. Eva blinked, looked at her daughter and smiled. Kathleen was confused by Eva's reaction at such terrible news.

"Mother, is there anything I can do for you?" Kathleen did not know what to say. Eva raised a cold hand from her lap and placed it gently on Kathleen's still resting on her shoulder.

"You can give me a hug, that is something I would very much appreciate," Her tears followed the same moist tracks of so many before them and Kathleen stood to hold her mother tight, the need to assist strengthened her shaking legs.

"There is still hope. He could still be alright," said Kathleen through violent sobs.

"He may well be, my dear, but I think it is most likely that he sits up there with your father and suffers no more." Part of Kathleen's world fell away from her, permanent like the face of an eroding cliff.

Andrew Wood

Laventie, France – 2ⁿᵈ December 1916

AFTER Eric's twenty-fourth birthday in September the leaves started to wilt and by the time winter had the world in its icy grasp he was in France and on his way again to the town of Laventie. Returning here and to the Kensington Battalion was a strange experience for Eric. Initially, he was glad to be at the front, no longer subject to the training all returning soldiers had to complete and was excited to see some of his old chums but was wary of returning to Laventie. He hadn't set foot in the town since he had been wounded almost two years earlier and the last time he had been here Stuart was alive and the battalion had been full of people he knew well. Now ghosts of his older brother and past friends haunted him. He knew the pain of being wounded and was all too aware of how indiscriminate the war had become. He knew so many who had been killed during the recent Battle of the Somme in which the Kensingtons, like all involved, suffered greatly. The battalion he knew and loved was no more and only a few remained from the group he had trained with in the late summer and autumn of 1914.

Eric's overriding concern, however, was that winter lay ahead. He was grateful to have had a summer in England as another winter on the line was a harrowing prospect for a man who had experienced the torrid winter of 1914/15, more importantly he was able to spend a great deal more time with Basil. Since Stuart's death the bond between Eric and Basil had strengthened. When Stuart had been around the three of them felt like a trio of young brother lions on the African Savannah and life did not pose too much of a challenge as long as they had each other. Now that one had been lost they felt weakened and for the first time in Eric's life he was fearful of the future. With Stuart gone he was now the eldest man in the family and responsibility weighed down on him, it aged him, and he envied the graceful ease in which Stuart had been able to balance it all. Kathleen was doing a fine job as accountant and friend to Eva but once the war had come to an end, if it ever it would, Eric knew he would be charged with running the household. This responsibility stirred in him a fear he had not known before and he wished to see Stuart again so he could ask for advice. He tried to rewind time in his mind so he could watch his brother's methods but quickly Eric realised how embarrassingly little attention he had paid to the running of the family while his brother had been alive. Nightmares continued to plague him but despite these, and the strains of family dependency, Eric remained strong of heart and mind. To those who knew him outside their close-knit family he appeared to be his old jovial self.

*

When Eric arrived at the front, he was relieved to see the forward trenches were very different from the quagmire he remembered. The banks were high and built up into strong breastworks so even a tall man could walk around unmolested by sniper fire. The ground was a sturdy pathway of duckboards and, although there were areas of dark stinking mud and inevitable cold puddles, decent drainage had been established. Corrugated iron dugouts were chiselled into the side of the trenches and were said to be bombproof so men could retreat out of the elements when not on watch. Wood and more corrugated iron protected uniforms from the muddy walls and, whilst by no means comfortable, it was a drastic improvement on what he remembered and had feared returning to. Added to that, Eric was now a Lewis Gunner so instead of a rifle he carried around with him a big heavy Lewis Gun and Webley Revolver, whilst hard work it afforded him some prestige that he quite enjoyed.

Eric sat smoking a cigarette in one of the dugouts and watched the smoke twisting in the darkness. Now back at the front he took a moment to think about his mothers' parting words *"When you come home dear boy, bring with you no demons."* He thought of the soldierly handshake from Basil as he left Hazeley Down to return to France and recalled a last attempt to console his brother still desperate to return. He looked around the grey faces in the dugout, even though Eric was a mere twenty-four, he felt surrounded by youth. A call from a familiar voice brought Eric out from his daze.

"Eric? Private Hanham are you in here?" The flap was drawn aside to reveal daylight.

"Who is that?"

"It's me, you fool. Davison. Come out here, won't you?" Eric laughed and barged awkwardly past the men huddled in front of him and ducked out into the light. He looked at his friend with a smile and noticed two chevrons on his arm.

"Corporal Davison, well I never," said Eric, embracing him.

"I heard you were back. I've been up and down the line looking for you." Eric looked deep into Davison's eyes, they were heavy and swollen with fatigue. His face was scarred from the right corner of his mouth to his earlobe, the canvas cover of his steel helmet was ripped and stained with mud and stale blood. His greatcoat hung loose from his frame and his rifle was slung heavy on his right shoulder.

"You look well," joked Eric and laughing they embraced again. They sat down opposite each other, and Eric handed Davison a cigarette.

"How's Basil?"

"He's miserable, you know how much he wants to get back here but he never will. His feet are still hurting sometimes and the bullet inside makes him ill regularly, I'm afraid."

"It's still inside him?" Davison was shocked.

"It is. No surgeon will touch it. They say it is too close to the heart." Davison grimaced and Eric shuddered involuntarily at the thought of a bullet slithering around inside his brother's body.

"What happened to you?" Eric pointed to the scar on his friend's face.

"I caught a wad of shrapnel on the Somme. I was lucky, the lad next to me had his head taken clean off." Davison smiled and snorted laughter. Eric had forgotten about the necessarily dark humour of soldiers at the front.

"Nice quick way to go I suppose."

"I was sorry to hear about Stuart. He certainly was the best of all three of you." Davison sniggered and Eric laughed with him.

"You're not wrong there. He's sorely missed." There was a moment of mournful silence.

"Say, fancy a raid tonight? I know how you used to like them. There is a rumour going around that the Boche leave their forward trenches at night. We reckon they leave one man we've named *Old Dugout* who runs around at night and fires randomly in our direction to make us think there is a whole trench full. We're going to check it out. Could do with a gun team to come with."

"Why not? May as well get back into it but you'll have to speak to my Corporal. Chase is his name." Eric had a nervous smile on his face. Davison slapped his thigh in cheer.

"Good news, I'll put it to the Platoon Commander but I'm sure he'll be game."

Davison flicked his woodbine to the floor, stood and started to leave. He stopped a short distance away and spoke softly, "I am really very sorry about Stuart."

Eric looked up but Davison was gone.

*

Davison's young Platoon Commander did not take much convincing that a Lewis Gun would be very useful support for the raiding party so Eric's team of five went along for the raid. Davison drew a diagram and explained to Eric and Chase their role, they were to find a good position amongst the rubble of a destroyed building in the centre of No Man's Land and provide support from there in the event of a hasty retreat by the raiding section. Shortly before midnight they all set out into the darkness towards the ruins of the once proud building, their first marker in the darkness.

The moon was bright at three quarters waxing so visibility was good, the clear sky showed the glittering stars, but the lack of insulating cloud meant it was crisply cold and their breath glowed silver in the night air. As they reached the back edge of the rubble, they paused for a moment and Davison passed the signal back for Eric and his team to take their position. They moved to pass Davison as a burst of machine gun fire erupted from the enemy trench to their right, about two hundred metres away. It was a single gun singing into the night, but it was quickly apparent it was not aimed anywhere near the raiding party, regardless they waited a few moments to ensure they had not been located. Two rifle shots then cracked out into the night from slightly closer to them, the bullets thudded impotently into the solid earthworks of the British line.

"See! Old Dugout is making his way down," said Davison in a whisper to Eric and Chase who were alongside him. Eric had the Lewis Gun over his shoulder like a short, heavy log. "You wait. He'll fire from over there in a minute." Davison pointed in the darkness to the built-up mound of a machine gun position on the German line. The deadly slits from where the gun would spit were not visible in the darkness but a few moments later it started to fire wildly into the night. This time bullets came cracking above the heads of the raiding party but it was clear they were not in the gun's sight line.

"He is so bloody predictable, it'll almost be a shame to kill him," said Davison with a snigger.

"Have we been seen?" asked one of the younger members of the gun team behind Eric. He was laid flat in the sticky mud, the others behind also prone and covering their heads.

"You'd know damn well if you'd have been seen, Wilko. Get up!" replied Chase sternly. Chase was a well-built man who had also been wounded in 1915 but had accepted promotion when it had been offered to him in the time since. A Londoner from a tough area near Croydon he was fit and strong with a sharp wit and he and Eric had become good friends in their time training at Hazeley Down.

Slowly Chase led them to their position in the rubble, but it wasn't easy to find a good spot that was not exposed. Around the remains of the building was a swamp and it stank of death. There must at some point have been a dead horse or soldier putrefying in the dank water for it was an aggressive, evil attack on the senses and was waist deep in places. It was so bad Chase thought about moving somewhere else but nowhere apart from this old building afforded them both cover and the view of the trench needed to support the raiding party should Old Dugout not be the only one home.

Eric setup the gun on the right-hand edge of rubble with Chase overseeing him from slightly higher up. The other three in the team, whose job it was to relieve Eric on the gun after prolonged periods of firing and carry ammunition, were a few feet back with no option but to sit in the sticky, swampy water. They all had to clench their stomachs to prevent themselves vomiting.

"There they go!" said Chase when he saw Davison and his party sprint for the enemy trench. They had waited for the firing to start further down the line before they made the run at the last of the wire entanglements.

"Why would they only have one man in their trenches at night?" asked Eric, looking over his sights as the raiding party neared the objective.

"So, they can stay warm I guess. The remainder of them aren't far away, I can guarantee. If we stay too long, we will be potted for sure," answered Chase. "Maybe he snores too loudly?" Eric laughed at Chases' comment as the first man jumped into the German trench. Immediately they heard him swearing angrily and from the metallic screeching and scratching it was clear he had jumped directly onto a stack of German barbed wire, the men supposed to follow him hesitated and looked cautiously down to their chum before they started laughing and looking around for a better place to enter. Another man had split from the group and headed farther to the right of the entry point but started screaming frantically when he found himself caught up in a thick wire obstacle, he had clearly fallen into it and was held fast.

The raid was only a few seconds old, but it was a farce. Davison shoved the remaining men into the trench a short distance away from where the first man entered and they gathered slightly more momentum, a couple of hundred metres further down the line there were a few random shots fired towards the British line. If Old Dugout was alone, he was not aware of the noisy Kensingtons entering his domain.

"Should we help that man trapped in the wire?" asked one of the men behind Eric and Chase perched on the rubble.

"No, stay where you are. If he attracts attention, he'll need us here to give him cover," said Chase, trying to work out where the man was trapped.

"He needs to shut up!" growled Eric "He'll give us all away if he keeps going."

After ten minutes Davison and some of his party appeared as dark shapes at the point in the trench where they had entered. Some others exited from the side of the machine gun placement Old Dugout had fired from and slowly unrolled a long line of fuse they would light from the safety of where Eric and the gun were providing cover. The man on their right was still calling for aid and his cries became more desperate as the rest of the party made it back to Eric. Davison conducted a head count.

"Where is Murray and that lumbering idiot Price? Where are they lads?" asked Davison angrily to his men but they had no response for him.

"One of your lads is caught in the wire about seventy metres to the right," said Chase.

"That'll be Murray, fucking idiot. We'll have to go and get him." Davison was clearly annoyed. "But where is Price?"

"He's there!" One of Davison's party pointed towards the machine gun position as a fuse sparked into life and fizzed fast towards the gun it would destroy, another of the objectives. Price climbed awkwardly from the parapet, but his long arms restricted his movements and his lanky form was unstable. His tin hat was falling off to one side in a comic, untidy fashion and his large feet were visible even in the low silver light of the moon. He stumbled awkwardly towards them in panic.

"He's coming! He's after me!" screamed Price as he made his way through the barbed wire to the raiding party and relative safety. His screams were humorous, he was laughing like a child stealing bread from a bakery, the baker in pursuit.

"Its Old Dugout! He's after Price!" said one of the men, he too was laughing and it all seemed a joke. As Price passed through Eric's sights, he adjusted the aim of his gun towards the machine gun post, the butt tight against his shoulder he waited for some movement or an order from Chase to begin firing. He too was chuckling with the whole affair and Chase also, it was funny and they couldn't pretend it wasn't. The only men not laughing were the three young men sat in the swamp, too new to the war to have been dulled by its horror they sat in the stinking swamp bemused and afraid.

"He's right behind me! He's a monster!" yelled Price. He ran like a giraffe the last twenty metres but in his haste, he trod heavily on the sparkling end of the fuse and extinguished it before it had made it to the explosives packed around the German machine gun. A pathetic hiss and silver-blue smoke the result of his large clumsy feet and at that moment the gun that was the objective started firing onto them. Heavy bullets whistled past their heads and cracked around them. Old Dugout adjusted his aim and fired another burst into the rubble around where Davison and his men were seeking shelter, the soft ground swallowed the heavy bullets easily, but the red bricks and sharp stone spat nasty shards into the air.

Eric responded immediately with his own fire and the Lewis Gun jumped wildly in his grip, but he held it true and the target exploded with the impact of the gun's fury. Eric's mind was clear, and he had no hesitation, some men returning to the front were paralysed by fear or memories of their own pain, but Eric had no such thoughts and enjoyed the deadly interaction like he had done before. His fire was accurate and aggressive and it made Old Dugout cease his tirade for a few seconds so Davison could order some bombs to be thrown but they had little effect at all, most of them falling well short. Had Price not stood on the fuse they could have killed Old Dugout and destroyed the gun in a hilariously successful course of events but tonight neither end would be achieved. Davison ordered their return to the British line. Eric remained firing from his post until they were all a safe distance behind him then he and Chase packed up their gear and followed the remainder of their team in a hunched run towards the safety of their own line. Wild machine gun fire chased after them.

It was only when they slid back into their own trench and caught their breath that Davison remembered Murray screaming from his entanglement out in the darkness. The rest of his team were laughing about the whole affair.

"Shut up! All of you! That was a bloody disaster and we've still a man out there." They all suddenly remembered their friend in the wire.

"There is a man still out there?" asked the Platoon Commander accusingly as he turned the corner.

"Yes, sir, it was a total mess but we're going back to get him now!" The enemy line was now alert and many had started firing at the British trenches.

"No need. Here he comes!" shouted a man looking attentively through a brass periscope on the firing step. Illumination flares climbed high into the sky and exploded in dancing bright light.

"Our man?"

"Yep, unless its Dugout and he wants another go at Price?" The observer stayed focused on the periscope. "To the right mate!" he shouted, attempting to guide his friend to the gap in the wire but he didn't hear him and headed straight towards the shouts. Bullets whistling past his head encouraged him on and far too late he saw the wire of his own line and the dark of the trench below. He vaulted the wire to avoid getting dangerously entangled again and came crashing down onto two of the young lads in Eric's team, knocking them into a groaning pile. Wild machine gun fire from a few enemy guns split the air above them all, the British line was now firing back in reply.

"Where the bloody hell have you been?" roared Davison angrily to Murray who was catching his breath on the wooden floor of the trench. The two men from Eric's team who had broken his fall lay winded around him in the flickering light of another illumination flare.

"Sorry, I was all in knots out there," replied Murray, breathing heavily. "But if you think I'm giving up my extra ration of Raiders Rum you're... Bloody Hell! What's that smell?" The stench from the swamp water staining the uniforms of the men who had broken his fall registered with Murray's senses and the British trench erupted in laughter, wild firing from both sides continued. "Well Old Dugout lives to fight another day."

Eric and Chase were laughing as they trudged back to their part of the trench and the last fifteen months of home comforts, family and the worries of maturity disappeared, he was back in the fray and felt strangely happy. In that moment of laughter and strife there was no place in the world he would rather be.

Winchester, Hampshire – 9ᵗʰ May 1917

BASIL stood on the northern platform of Winchester Station like he had many times but today things were different. Instead of being proudly clad in soldierly khaki, hobnail boots and peaked cap, he wore a charcoal grey suit and white shirt. His jacket was undone and flapping in the warm breeze. There were a few soldiers around, but Basil knew none of them and couldn't bring himself to look in their direction. His blood was fizzing with rage and his heart was pounding hard, his face was flushed red and his pale blue eyes were furious. A leather bag of his possessions sat beside him, jumbled and untidy as the train came steaming into the station. He didn't look up to meet it and even thought about throwing himself on the line to end it all, to end all the embarrassment, heartbreak, insecurity and hatred for himself and now the Army. At twenty-three years and six months he was deemed *"No longer physically fit for War Service"* and discharged unceremoniously. Basil was made even more resentful by the absurdity of this all happening exactly two years to the day from when Stuart had been killed. It felt intentional and it took all Basil's inner strength to suppress the dark waters bubbling inside him.

Over the last two years Basil had tried his hardest to find a place in the world. He realised he would never again take his turn at the front because of his wounds and hated the fact they were invisible to those around him. He despised explaining to people why he wasn't on active service and wished his injury to be a missing limb or a lost eye with gruesome scar so the reasons for his home service were obvious. Then the fools that didn't know about the bullet still inside him would not ask him such accusing, condescending questions. Eric encouraged him to relax and ignore these people, most had never served at all, but Basil had developed a strong, stubborn will of his own and was forthright in his opinions. He was no longer the boy he had been and now he was no longer a soldier. Basil had served the Kensington Battalion for four years, one hundred and eighty-seven days, sixty-three of those in France at the front. He still suffered with illness and pain from the wound inflicted on him by the enemy and had damaged his feet to such a degree they would never be the same again. His eldest brother had been killed and his other brother was back in France with the battalion. Despite all that he felt he was dismissed from the Army like a pair of socks beyond mend. He hated himself for believing he could have made a difference and hated the Army for the way he was now being treated. As Basil sat in the carriage of the train back to London, he fought hard to stop himself erupting into an angry tirade and passengers around him moved to other carriages to avoid his putrid aura. He was sweating through his suit and found no solace in pathetic attempts to sleep.

As he neared home, he began to slow his walk and couldn't yet face the journey up Amesbury Avenue to meet the quiet of home and loving words from his mother. He needed noise and activity to silence the voices in his head, so he stopped in at the Red Lion to quench his thirst.

"Thanks, Jack," said Basil as he took his pint jar over to the window. Dropping his change into his pocket he avoided the landlord's gaze and sat in the window watching the world he knew so well pass by. He recognised a few people in the street but he didn't feel like the same person at all. He felt old and grey like a faded poster on a tired wall and he seemed invisible. Patrons entering the pub after work did not give him a second glance and he was sure his reflection in the window was fading.

Basil thought he craved solitude, but every pint of ale or tumbler of gin made him resent life, the war and the Army further. What Basil truly needed was a confidant or friendly ear, he needed Eric, but he continued drinking until his anger began to boil over and spill hot onto the people around him. His shouting grew louder and more offensive and by the time the sun set beyond London, Basil had outstayed his welcome and was violently ejected from the pub by a couple of younger men, supervised by Jack.

Basil woke the next morning in the small front yard of 76 to Kathleen's soft tones, her voice was low and concentrated in concern. She took a sharp intake of breath when she saw the cuts and bruises on his face and as the day light flooded into his red eyes Basil saw his sister looking over him with panic on her face.

Basil wished he were dead. He wished he had been killed at the front like Stuart, a man, a hero, revered by all. Instead he was a pathetic mess on the floor outside his house with his mother called to rescue him like the child he used to be.

*

Basil entered Tooting Bec Records Office early in the afternoon. The day had turned bleak, windy and cold and he was glad to enter into the shelter of the foyer, he looked around for someone to help him. His head was heavy on his neck and demons from drink were scuttling around his brain making eye contact and conversation a struggle. He fought inside him the urge to settle his nerves with another trip to a pub, the entrance down that dark path closer and more accessible than ever it had been.

"Can I help you, sir?" asked a young woman with a name badge on her chest. He thought how lost and confused he must have looked and what a sorry state he was.

"Ah yes please, I need to see-" Basil checked his notebook, "-Major Tew," said Basil with a smile he regretted. He had no desire to smile.

"This way please," she led Basil to a bench against a light stone wall a short distance from the main entrance. "Who shall I say has arrived to see him?"

"Hanham, Bas- Corporal Hanham," replied Basil, sitting down, relieved to be in the right place at least. The young woman smiled and opened the door behind her as Basil started to assess his surroundings.

The hallway was clean and light, despite the dank day outside, and it felt fresh and welcoming. Along this stretch of hall, he could see there were three offices, each had a light wooden door and a ridged glass window embedded in the top half. He looked at the one closest and could just make out a fuzzy khaki figure inside the room hunched over a desk, opposite him was the dark shape of a man. Above the door Basil read the sign *'Major CB Tew. Discharges'.* Angry bile started to rise in his body again, he had momentarily forgotten where he was and the painful, insulting climax to his Army service. He looked away down the hall, blood boiling under his skin.

Twenty minutes later the door opened and a smartly dressed young man about Basil's age shook Major Tew's outstretched hand. He limped awkwardly to the exit, a wad of paperwork heavy in his arm. Basil looked back towards Tew who was beaming a smile.

"Corporal Hanham?" Basil nodded and Tew extended his hand to Basil. He was a man of about thirty-three with kind brown eyes, his hair was fair and messy, but he carried it well. He had the look of a competent officer and his tunic was smart and clean around his athletic frame. Basil stood and accepted his hand.

"Yes, sir."

"Please come in." Tew held the door for Basil and then made his way to a seat behind his desk, opposite where Basil was now seated. Tew had a terrible limp and his face creased in pain as he hobbled over to his chair. He sat down in obvious relief and began the meeting.

"So, you are to be discharged as no longer fit for war service I see," said Tew, reading Basil's file. It annoyed Basil further to know someone had assembled his file at Hazeley Down, the job that until this last week had been his, he said nothing as Tew continued to read.

Tew took his time and nodded along as he read the history of Basil's service, his eyes widened as he got to the part of Basil's wounding.

"The bullet is still inside you?" Tew looked at him with respect and in moderate horror.

"Yes, sir." Basil lifted his left arm and pointed to where the grisly scar was under his clothes. Tew blew loudly and shook his head in sorry acknowledgement.

"Poor lad. And your feet? Awful business that bloody trench foot. Had a bout myself."

"Getting better, sir." He had thought about pretending to be fit and well, but he knew Tew was only a formality and he couldn't change the decision of the medical board.

"Well I am sorry. Still, better this than to be upstairs with the Lord," said Tew in sombre acknowledgement of those who had fallen.

Basil nearly spoke to say he had rather been killed. The demon spiders in his brain and his turbulent emotional state were bringing him to the edge of madness and he had forgotten about the suffering of others. He felt cheated by life, like he had been given the rottenest of deals and his pain was like no other. He wanted to scream at Tew, for in that moment he saw him as the face of the Army, the Army that had taken his youth and given him such hope and a sense of being. He had been someone, a Kensington soldier and a member of a large family. Now who was he? He was a member of a Hanham family ravaged by war, he had lost his elder brother, his hero, and his other brother and best friend was back at the front. His sisters were weary of life and his mother, the single most wonderful person in his world and the one he held foremost in his heart was a dark shell of the woman who had given him his soul and taught him of the world. Yes, he had rather have been killed and was about to say so when Tew recoiled in tremendous agony. His handsome face went tight, and his teeth were clenched white and straight.

"Sorry Corporal, my own wound seems to be forever causing me problems too." Tew reached down, rolled his trouser leg up and pulled off his prosthetic leg with a deep sigh of relief. He took a moment and placed it behind him against the wooden wall of his office. Basil's anger faded and he turned red with selfish embarrassment.

Tew returned to the paper work, stamping it officially in several places. He then handed them over to Basil who looked at them in sorrow. On the back of one of the sheets Tew had written a few lines on Basil's character which Basil read twice to make sure the alcohol wasn't playing games with his mind. Once processed, Basil read it back to Tew in an angry, sarcastic fashion.

"A *steady* and *well conducted* man. Served in France, there wounded." Basil was looking back at Tew in disgust. Tew looked confused. "Four and half years of service, fagged feet and a bullet in my chest and that's all I get written about me!" Basil threw the sheets of paper back at Tew.

"Now listen here young man!" Tew leant forward in his chair and pointed a sharp finger at Basil, it shook angrily and his eyes turned dark and deadly, "I understand your frustration and you seem like a genuine sort who wants to do his bit but the truth is you can't any more. Be grateful you have all your limbs and you can still walk around this earth!" Basil looked instinctively to the ugly wooden leg next to Tew.

"Be grateful too you are still breathing. There are thousands no longer of this life and I've no doubt you know a few personally. For goodness sake, grow up!" Tew leant back into his chair and gathered the forms on his desk. He found the character summary and inserted *very* into the description of Basil. He handed it back to Basil who felt stupid, childish, selfish and relieved. He thought Tew would change what he'd written to say something scathing, but he had not.

"My brother, sir, he was killed at Aubers Ridge." Basil looked timidly down at the floor.

"Well there you are, consider yourself lucky and live a full life for him," Tew extended his hand across the desk. Basil shook it gladly and folded the papers into his notebook for safekeeping. "Now go and see the pay sergeant at the front desk and he'll explain to you all about your war pension."

Basil stood and opened the door to leave but turned and looked back at Tew. "Thank you, sir. I'm sorry."

"I understand. And good luck *Mr* Hanham."

*

Basil talked with the pay sergeant for a full thirty minutes about the pension and compensation he was entitled to and noted down a few possible employers that might be interested in someone with clerical and typing experience. By the time Basil left the record office the sun had broken through the cloud and a recent shower had given the world outside a fresh scent of summer. Basil felt his mood change and there were glimmers of hope for his future, there was a long way to go until he would truly be at peace, but he had been so embarrassed by his actions in Tew's office it had thrust into him a stark reality. As he walked back towards 76 he no longer thought of his own woes but instead turned his thoughts to Eric away at the front. He said a short prayer for him as he walked in the sunshine and made it as far as the Red Lion before he remembered the state of his face. He endured a few fleeting, painful flashbacks to the night before and became suddenly aware he hadn't seen the bag containing all his belongings he had travelled with from Hazeley Down. He tried to recall where he last remembered having it and could only venture it was still in the pub.

So focused was he on the mystery he hadn't heard the first time his name was called from across the street, only the second attempt registered in his mind and he turned to see Kathleen trotting across the road in a flowing summer dress. Her hand holding a pink floral hat down onto her head against the wind, she was smiling as she embraced him.

"Not thinking about round two are you?" Kathleen had a stern, motherly look on her face and Basil smiled.

"No, I think I left my bag in there but I'm afraid to enter and ask. I think I was quite the fool last night, K," replied Basil through gritted teeth, he winced as he touched the cuts on his face.

"Oh, there's no doubt about it but if I know Jack the best thing to do is apologise straight away. Come on I'll buy you a pint and we'll ask about your bag."

Kathleen took Basil's arm and they walked together across the road. Having Kathleen with him gave him resolve but still he entered the pub a scared little boy.

Brixton, London – 6ᵗʰ July 1917

KATHLEEN stood opposite a large grey stone building watching men and women come and go from the factory beyond the archway, she could hear the machines grinding loudly and shouting from within the walls. The women leaving at the end of their shift were as dirty as the men, their brown drab overalls oily and dark with grime and their hair was tied back under tattered bonnets the same colour. She was in awe of them, in her current production she was playing a munitions worker so had spent a week working in this factory to prepare for the role and learn what it was like. Kathleen was not a famous actress but the women on the workshop floor were happy to have her learning from them and chatted excitedly about the show. She played those fond memories over in her mind so was smiling as she waited for Basil to emerge. She was on her second cigarette and happily exchanging glances with people as they bounced past in the Friday afternoon sunshine.

Kathleen was nearing thirty and she felt every minute of it. Moments like this where she was buoyant with life were rare, so she was embracing her current mood, the beautiful weather helped. Since the outbreak of war, moving home, her short but intense love affair with Harriet, rekindling her relationship with Howard and losing her revered brother Stuart, life had not been the same for Kathleen. She now wore the heavy jacket of responsibility wherever she wandered, and it weighed her down so she could no longer float through life as she once had. With Eric now back in the fighting she, like Eva, just had to wait for news.

Howard was still based in Cairo, but Kathleen knew his work as a pay clerk kept him relatively safe. She worried about him but did not feel she missed him as much as she should. Often she would lie to friends about how much she longed for him after hearing heartfelt words about their partners and husbands away with the war but she did enjoy his letters when they arrived. Friends often asked her if they had plans to marry and start a family. Kathleen thought that process would be inevitable, but she had no deep yearning, she sometimes worried that she had been broken in some way.

Consumed in reflection Kathleen had not noticed the attentions of three men looking at her from across the street. They had just emerged from the factory arch and were sharing a small hip flask of whisky between them, reward for a long day of toil on the great machines making munitions for the front. The oldest of the group noticed Kathleen and was now leading his small posse over to where she leant against the wall smoking casually, her thick dark hair was flowing over her shoulders, and her long cream dress a stark contrast to the dirty stone wall behind her. She was an image out of place in the dark alleys of this industrial quarter.

"Afternoon, love," said the alpha male of the three as he removed his cap and performed an exaggerated bow. Kathleen looked up at the group and flicked her cigarette into the gutter with sassy grace.

"Hello, lads," she replied casually, a broad smile on her face. The two grubby men behind her admirer chuckled and nodded an awkward hello. Their friend and instigator stood to his full height and replaced his hat. His face was soiled like his friends, soot and grease had entered every crevasse of his weathered face and thin red veins ran from his light brown iris' to the furthest extent of his eyes. Heavy black bags the tell-tale sign of a long shift.

"Now what is a fine lady like yourself doing here alone?" he asked, dry lips splitting into a serpent like grin. Kathleen was about to answer him when over his shoulder she saw the familiar figure of Basil emerge from the archway and walk away down the road with his jacket tucked under his arm. He stopped after a few paces and lit a cigarette.

"Sorry, gentlemen, must be off." Kathleen smiled kindly as she left to catch up with Basil.

"Perhaps next time!" called the man after her. Kathleen did not turn back but Basil spun his head around to see who had shouted from across the street.

"K, what are you doing here?" Her hair was jumping around behind her, as she reached him, she linked an arm through his, pulling him away from the watching men.

"How was work then, B?" asked Kathleen once they had turned the corner onto Brixton Hill, she still had her arm entwined with his as they walked in the sunshine.

"It was fine K, I just type what I'm told to type for ten hours and then I leave. Nothing glamorous, I'm afraid." Basil was despondent.

"You always explain it like that, when will you stop being so sour?" She was still in a good mood, so her words did not strike Basil painfully, instead they sounded caring and sincere. He said nothing but looked to the sky.

"Lovely evening isn't it. Do you have time for a jar in the Ship garden?" asked Basil.

"I have time, I'm done for the day."

"Really? No performance tonight?"

"Not tonight. The theatre is hosting a war bonds drive over the weekend. No performances until Tuesday but we're rehearsing Sunday and Monday." Kathleen had mixed emotions, the physical break from the work was welcome indeed but five performances were being sacrificed so she would not be paid much this weekend.

"Time for more than just one, then." Basil smirked, beads of sweat had appeared on his brow and his blue eyes were mischievous.

"Why not? As long as you are feeling better?" Basil had been having an awful few days of raised temperatures and fever. His bowels had loosened, his body rejected much of what he ate and drank, and he had struggled with sleep. All regular symptoms of having a dirty shard of lead slowly poisoning him from the inside.

"I am feeling better thanks, much better," He picked Kathleen up in his arms and swung her round twice to show his fitness. Kathleen giggled as she was spun around, South West London was humming to the rhythm of summer, life for the moment was good.

*

The next morning Kathleen woke early. Quietly she shut the door to 76 and wandered to the bakery to buy some bread and to the butchers for bacon and eggs. The sun was high in the sky and the usual activity of early morning seemed charged with hope. Kathleen enjoyed her fleeting transactions with the proprietors of each shop she visited and, skipping along with one of the neighbouring children, she laughed all the way up the road home. When she opened the door to 76 it all changed, there was a sour smell in the air and an evil fug inside.

"K! Is that you?" called Eva in distress.

"Yes, I'm just back from the shops," Eva appeared in her nightgown on the landing, panic on her face.

"Come dear, poor Basil is sick," Kathleen dropped the bag onto the floor and raced up the stairs to check on Basil. Eva was wiping his brow with a pungent fluid that was meant to calm fever, but it smelt like old medicine and Kathleen was sceptical of its charm. Basil's face was red and soaked with heavy beads of hot sweat. His breathing was shallow and fast, his lips were dry, and cracking and his eyes were closed tight in pain.

"How much did you drink last night?" Eva looked angry.

"We were home by dark mother. It's not the drink."

"Did he eat anything bad perhaps?" Eva's concern grew.

"We had a little fish, but I had some too and I feel fine. He was fine yesterday. He told me himself and he looked really well."

At that moment Basil lurched forward and vomited heavy bile into the bowl Eva had placed on his lap. Large pieces of undigested food mixed with the stinking yellow liquid of his stomach lining. He groaned loudly and aggressively wretched until he had no more to give, he laid back onto his pillow with a sigh of relief. Eva bravely inspected the contents of the bowl.

"I think he must have had some bad fish dear, that's all. Look, you can see it." Eva handed the vessel to Kathleen. She nearly vomited at the sight, smell and sound of her brothers' mess sloshing around inside the bowl but managed to make it to their small back yard where she poured it down the drain. She did her best to rinse out the bowl from the water tank without touching the inside. When she returned to Basil's room, he already looked better, his eyes were open and his face was pale white instead of strained red. He even managed a wry smile as Kathleen placed the bowl back down on his lap. Eva had wiped away the sweat from his brow.

"Must have had a bad pint, K," said Basil, gagging at the thought of another.

"Must have."

"Now you get some rest dear, I'll be up to check on you soon," said Eva as she tucked him up under the sheets. She stood and opened the window to let in some fresh air and then walked out of the room past Kathleen in the doorway.

Kathleen stood and looked at her brother. She hoped it was food poisoning or the result of a bad brew, but she knew her little brother's problem was deeper rooted. She knew the bullet inside him was slowly killing him and she prayed that someday soon a surgeon would be brave enough to conduct the risky operation and remove the bullet.

Before she left the room, Kathleen said a prayer for Basil and then one for Eric too, wherever he was.

Micmac Camp, Ypres Salient – 15ᵗʰ August 1917

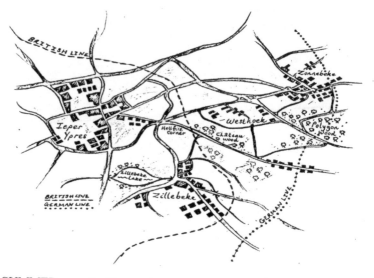

SUMMER was finally starting to show signs it might have been worth the wait. The beating sun had been intense for the last two days and Mother Nature was responding in her elegant way. Wild flowers craned towards the life-giving sun with beautiful grace, Madonna lilies flowered from the banks and ditches strong enough to support their long green stems, the pearl white flowers a welcome contrast to the darkness of war. The hot sun seemed to inspire the Kensington men too, for those that had endured a long winter, unseasonably cold spring and wet summer on the line this heat was life giving and welcome.

Eric had not struggled to settle back into the rhythm of soldiering, but he had become aware of his changing attitudes to the war. His correspondence home was less jovial, he was tired and no longer felt like a boy on an adventure. He and the Kensingtons had been moved around a great deal since Christmas and their tour of Northern France had included La Fosse, Ivergny and Neuville-Vitasse where they were heavily involved in a bloody attack to take the pressure off the Canadians attacking Vimy Ridge. From there they marched to Arras and the surrounding areas of Gommecourt, Simencourt, Tilloy, Berneville, Wancourt, Achicourt and Liencourt. It was on the edge of battle he found himself again as he and the Kensingtons prepared to enter the Third Battle of Ypres.

"Ready Eric?" Chase threw on his pack and Eric was whipped away from his skyward gaze, slow to respond.

"Yeah, ready," replied Eric, hoisting his Lewis Gun up onto his shoulder.

"Away with the gods?" asked Eric's number two on the gun Private Simon. He was a short stocky man with bright blue eyes, he had jet-black hair and thick long lashes like that of camel. Since his arrival he had become a popular member of the Lewis Gun Section under Chase and had become firm friends with Eric.

"Something like that," agreed Eric as they headed out of camp and along the cobbled road toward Ypres.

Only a few times each summer are there evenings so splendid. The sun was high in the sky and its heat was visible. Shimmering, hazy waves highlighted the busy flies in the air and a gentle breeze flicked at the tops of the wild flowers enjoying the sun. There were areas of long grass around the fringes of their billet when the Kensingtons left that evening, an untouched area not ravaged by war. For Eric and those who had trained with the battalion in the English splendour of Abbots Langley it was a fleeting look to the glorious past but as they made their way onto the main road to Ypres the world changed before their eyes.

Large shell holes had mostly destroyed the cobbled road and either side of it laid the wreckage of vehicles, guns and horses. The latter were double the size they were in life as their insides rotted, and gasses stretched their bellies. The empty shells of houses and poplar stumps along the route hinted at what a beautiful part of Belgium this had been before war had come and ruined the peace.

Eric was at the back of his platoon as they made their way to the front. He carried the heavy gun over his shoulder and behind him trudged Simon, Wilkinson and Robertson with two boxes of the Lewis Gun's drum ammunition each. Together the four of them made up half of the Lewis Gun Section that Chase, marching just in front of Eric, commanded. Sporadically shells whistled overhead and each time they sent the men scurrying into boggy shell holes either side of the road. For a while they tried to make the journey using these great swampy pits, but the going was exhausting, and they smelt so bad that the dangerous road was favoured.

By the time they reached their objective for the evening it was nearing ten thirty and the light was fading into dazzling red and gold, its stunning beauty marred only by the incessant firing from both German and British guns laying waste to the sector. The shelling was so regular and intense that only the closest of explosions forced the men off the road and into the rubble filled holes adjacent, a little way ahead the whole of the Kensington Battalion moved into their sections of the reserve trenches.

"Not far now, lads, we'll get some shut-eye soon enough," said Chase as he spun round to encourage Eric and his men the last few hundred yards.

"I do hope our place has a swimming pool. I could murder a dip," said Wilkinson and the comment brought chuckles from the men around him until pleasurable thoughts of being submerged in cool, clean water silenced them all. Their march in the heavy heat of a summer's evening had made them perspire from all parts of their young bodies. The coolness of night was welcomed for once.

"Quite a reception party. That is the Commanding Officer and his two Senior Majors if I'm not mistaken," said Chase after a few more steps.

"You're right mate," said Eric, squinting to see in the growing dusk.

"Do you think they're here to promote me?" asked Simon in jest.

"Ha! You'd be lucky if they aren't here to arrest you." Eric was still laughing when the first shell of an accurate salvo landed close to them and his world slowed. One could usually tell when a shell was heading for them but the ferocity of the artillery fire in the distance, and from the British guns nearby, had hidden its deadly whistles. It landed twenty metres to the right of Eric but straight into the bottom of a deep impact hole created by a previous shell, the explosion however was large enough to knock the men from their feet and onto the sharp rubble. The contents of the hole poured upon them like hateful rain, rocks, mud and stagnant water fell indignantly on the sprawling figures seeking any sort of cover they could.

The second shell in the salvo was long and erupted impotently in the ruins of a house one hundred metres away but Eric saw the third shell land with all its deadly accuracy at the front of the column. It fell on a small area of hard ground to the left of the crossroads where the senior officers were directing men into the support trenches. The shell split into its grim pieces and one large shard clearly hit the Commanding Officer square in the chest, he was spun around in a bloody mess and lay ragged on the floor like a forgotten doll. The other two officers, and some of the men around them, were thrown wildly into the side of the support trenches and Eric believed they must be killed also. The shelling continued in that small area for a further minute, screams from wounded and shell-mad men were the only audible sounds between the nerve shattering explosions.

After the last shell had fallen the hot dust began to settle and Eric's eyes adjusted to the twilight. The scene was horrific. Dazed men were stumbling around like drunks, fighting off attempts from the sober to return to cover they continued searching pathetically for their weapons and one man for his own lost arm, twisted tissue and ragged uniform the only remnants attached to his body. Eric's ears had not yet forgiven him for the noise, his hearing was metallic, disjointed, so he couldn't hear his name being called. A strong arm brought him to life, and he swung around to see Chase, wide eyed and desperate his face was covered in chalky rubble, dust and mud. Eric was so confused it was only when his body hit the ground hard he realised he had been one of the shell-drunk fools out in the open, then the second barrage began. Eric curled up into a ball next to Chase as the ground erupted around them and savage rain of stone, wood, mud and flesh fell onto them.

When the barrage finally lifted, the Kensington men ran the last few hundred yards to the entrance of the reserve trenches and, like rabbits escaping a hawk, dived down into their burrows. When they managed to gather the platoon together there were a few missing and it was quickly established that they were either killed or wounded in the shelling. Word also spread that the Commanding Officer had been killed and the two Senior Majors so badly mauled they were forced to the aid stations with the others wounded in the attack.

"What happened to you, Eric? Looked like you were off to win yourself a Victoria Cross and run back to billets with the old man on your shoulder," said Chase, referring to Eric's stumbling towards the stricken Commanding Officer.

"I honestly don't know what the bloody hell I was doing. Lads, I felt pissed!" replied Eric laughing, he showed them his hands still shaking. Chase and his team laughed with him, the torrid humour of soldiers in such times made funnier by the brutal hilarity of human reactions under such pressure.

"Did you piss yourself?" asked Robertson sat to his right.

"No."

"Then you weren't properly pissed." The trench erupted in laughter again.

*

"Eric. Eric!" Simon woke him with a hefty nudge. "We're moving off mate."

Eric rose to his feet instinctively and looked around for signs of daylight but there was none, the purple night sky lit bright by shining diamonds. "What time is it?" asked Eric still dazed with sleep.

"Just after midnight old boy. Surely thirty minutes is all you need," replied Simon with a snigger but Eric was too confused to laugh. He checked his equipment, hoisted the Lewis Gun onto his shoulder and with his left hand checked he still had his revolver. Content, he shuffled forward in behind the man in front of him.

"Chase. Where are we off? I thought we had some down time till dawn?" Chase turned his head to answer but didn't break his stride.

"We have to get out to our positions along the Menin Road. I'm guessing they don't want us doing that in daylight if it can be helped."

"Fair enough. Who's in command?"

"Not sure. Maybe Venables?"

Eric did not respond but thought about what it must be like to assume command of an entire battalion when the three senior men before you had been killed or wounded in one incident. If one were the second, or even third in line he might be expecting to assume command if the worst were to happen, but Eric was sure Venables was not contemplating having to lead more than his own company and now he had four times the men to worry about. Eric suddenly became a little embarrassed by his own lack of leadership desire and for the first time did not see it as a choice but a charge. He thought if it were offered to him again, he would take it, to be responsible for the well being of a section of eight was no weight compared to what was now being heaved along by Captain Venables.

For two hours the Kensingtons trudged through the reserve trenches like an accordion, stretching out and then bunching together as they made their way east around the shattered remains of Ypres. The trenches had been occupied for a long time so were well established, signposts lead the way to where they needed to be, but the traffic in the support lines was excessive. Stretcher parties were constantly running through wounded men and the battalion had to halt for other units to pass by. It was a horrid journey made worse by the sporadic, harassing shellfire being laid upon. A few Kensington men were wounded and left in the trenches to wait for the next available stretcher-bearers.

So long and painfully slow was the journey through the support trenches that they reached the infamous *Hellfire Corner* as sky was turning from grey into dim colour. The sun was not yet visible but the Kensingtons would have to cross into the forward trenches quickly if they were to get into their positions unmolested, an unlikely feat.

"We're going around to the north to avoid the crossroads men, they are already shelling Hellfire pretty relentlessly," called Lieutenant Edwards as he made his way down the line of his platoon. "We've been given the left edge of Chateau Wood. From there we'll reinforce, and attack as required. Any questions?" His sturdy frame and dark features were a reassuring presence, he took one final look up and down the line before taking his place at the front. Sergeant Wright then addressed the platoon.

"Section Commanders keep your men in check, gun teams secure the flanks and get the guns going if we take any fire," shouted Wright, a handsome man with the stern jaw of a seasoned boxer and the round heavy shoulders of a farm hand. No one knew how he had become a Kensington as he was from the countryside, but they didn't care, nor did they squabble with him. His wide pale eyes and fair boyish features disguised a hard man inside.

Shells continued to rain down menacingly on the area of Hellfire Corner a few hundred metres away and even though Eric and the men were still a kilometre behind the front-line trenches, the tense wait had the feel of a first push. The light of dawn was now about them and rays of golden sunshine could be seen kissing the tops of distant hills to the east. A tense shuffle and a heavy sigh spread down from the front of the platoon.

"Mask up lads!" Eric passed the message down the line and carefully lowered his Lewis Gun so he could remove his gas mask from the satchel around his neck.

"That's all we need! A nice bit gas for breakfast," said Wilkinson. His voice was muffled through his mask, quietly they all looked at each other through the large round glass windows while they waited for the snake to start moving.

The Kensingtons, emerging a few hundred metres from Hellfire Corner, resembled a good formation as they scaled the trenches among the hard rubble of the Ypres suburbs into the squalid, swampy land beyond. From here things started to falter. The mud was thick, dark clay and the land was scattered with shell holes deep enough for a man to be unseen inside. Added to this there were huge mine craters that had been blown by the British in previous actions, in these whole platoons could disappear until they reached the other side. If this wasn't hard enough the shells increased in ferocity on the long line of Kensington men and sporadic, long-range machine gun fire arrived from their flank, more casualties were taken. Each man too was enclosed in his own suffocating mask that forced his breathing to be slow and laboured. The condensation build-up on the lenses blinded the men as it magnified the blazing sunshine now creeping up over the eastern hills. Men were stumbling over pickets, old wire entanglements, their own mud caked feet and British dead. All the while shells and bullets cracked around them from an enemy all too aware of their position and intent. Quickly it turned into a farce.

Eric had managed half the distance when he fell head first into a shell hole. He damaged his shoulder badly in the fall, ripping muscle and bruising bone, and struggled to breathe through the mask and the pain. After taking a quick look around he could not see the tell-tale yellow cloud of poisonous gas, so he reached up and knocked his helmet from his head. Raising his mask slowly from his face, he sniffed the air gently for signs of the nasty substance that had mutilated the insides of so many. When he could only smell the stagnant water under his body and the smell of his own clothing, he deemed it safe to remove his mask completely and open his eyes. As he placed the mask back in the pouch that hung from his neck, he noticed the contents of his pack down the rear slope of the shell hole. His rations, extra field dressing and warm clothing were lying all around. He cursed to himself, shrugged his pack from his shoulder and went to collect his equipment.

Around him he could hear muffled shouting from those still masked and distant cries of a few wounded. Throwing his pack back on and checking the end of his gun to make sure he hadn't stuck it into the mud, he sprinted out of the trench and back into the line that was now pathetically ragged and disjointed. Some men were trapped and couldn't move while others were heading in the wrong direction.

"There is no gas!" screamed Wright from the middle of the platoon line, all those around him stopped to remove their masks, an action that spread slowly along. In doing so one man was hit twice by two wild, unlucky bursts of machine gun fire from the ridge a great distance away. He was dead instantly. The remainder tried to keep walking through the quagmire while they stowed their masks. Some had lost packs and helmets in the clumsy advance but those that had kept moving eventually reached another of the British trenches, protection from the machine gun fire and shells from the east. Here Edwards went to find the Company Commander and Wright did his best to rally the men around him.

"On me lads! Keep coming!" Two stragglers were hit by the same shell. Their cries made all the Kensington men jump.

"Hurry up! Get up here!" Eric looked for Chase and Simon, but he couldn't see them. He looked back across the area they had crossed and was shocked by how hard those five hundred metres had been. The fire was still coming down, but its intensity had dropped.

"The fucking Boche could definitely see us there," said one of the men, adjusting his equipment and wiping down his tunic now covered in thick black mud. "What fools we must have looked!" Eric ignored him but realised he was on the wrong flank so hurried along the trench. He had to put the heavy gun onto his left shoulder as his right was throbbing wildly with pain from his fall.

By the time he had reached the end of the line some control had been gained and the Kensingtons looked again like a fighting unit.

"There he is... Eric!" yelled Simon as he saw Eric approaching.

"I thought we'd lost you out there," said Chase when he looked up to see Eric arrive.

"Nearly, took a dive in a bloody shell hole and fagged my shoulder." Eric lowered the gun down to the floor in obvious pain.

"I'll take the gun mate. Can you manage a box?" Simon handed Eric a box of ammunition to carry in place of the heavy gun. Eric nodded and they made the exchange.

As some of the men from the platoon ran back into the sun and the sporadic shelling to fetch the wounded men Eric and the Lewis Gun Section sorted their equipment and prepared for the next phase. To the north and the east, they heard the sounds of other units attacking the front and could see the movement of troops in the fight some distance away. They guessed their role was to replace those men in the forward trenches and push through as required. They set themselves for the task, but it wasn't until early afternoon that Edwards returned from Chateau Wood with orders. His platoon, and the rest of D Company, headed out to the next line of trenches they could see along Westhoek ridge, some six hundred metres away. The fighting had moved further to the east and they were tasked with reinforcing one of the Middlesex Battalions up on the ridge in the assault onto Polygon Wood, an objective since the start of the battle some days before.

The ground in front of them was less muddied and cratered by the shelling but it still looked horribly impassable. One obvious track led from the edge of Chateau Wood to the trenches they were to occupy, and it was said to be safe to use. Eric was again at the back of the snake as D Company set out in a long line across the open ground to the ridge.

"Turned into another scorcher," said Eric as he wiped the sweat from his brow awkwardly with his damaged arm. In his other he carried a heavy box of circular ammunition drums for the Lewis Gun.

"You're not wrong chap," replied Simon, now marching in front of him with the gun over his right shoulder and another box of ammunition in his left hand. Eric was secretly impressed by the strength and grit of his little friend, but he would never tell him, it wasn't their way.

"Say, how is it we can just amble across here when earlier we were getting whacked from over there?" asked Robertson from the back.

"I don't know but let's enjoy the stroll while we can," replied Wilkinson.

"Just seems odd to me, I think they must have been playing with us."

"No doubt, but we'll soon get to play with them again. We'll be into it when we get over this ridge. You can hear them going at it from here," said Eric as he negotiated a picket lying across the muddy track.

"Yeah, sounds like a lot fun up-" a sudden rake of machine gun fire from a distant ridge interrupted Robertson's sarcastic retort. It fell in the middle of the company line, the unmistakable ranging burst from a machine gun on the higher ground. The line of men panicked and started to run up the winding path to the safety of the trenches on the ridge, now only a few hundred metres away, but as they ran, the guns made their adjustments and a longer, more menacing burst flew across the valley from unseen emplacements.

"I knew they would have a pop!"

"Keep moving!" called Chase as a few bullets and ricochets smacked into the line of men ahead. Eric and the team leapt over their stricken comrades and continued up the hill as best they could. The men below them were writhing around only one hundred metres from the trench and safety.

Eric jumped down instinctively into the trench atop the ridge and they all spread along into positions as directed by the officers. A party of men bravely returned to collect the wounded men from the track but most of D Company were in the trench as intended. It was only now, as they spread out along the expanse of their new position on Westhoek Ridge that the reality could be digested.

The trench they occupied was littered with dead men from both sides.

They lay awkwardly in the crude forms of war and by the state of some they had been here since the start of the Battle two weeks before. Rats took a great deal of persuasion to leave their feast and maggots had starting hatching from the recesses of eyes, ears, open mouths and noses. The soft lips of some men had been pecked and chewed away to reveal the sunburnt gums and ghoulish smiles of the dead. This had clearly been the scene of bitter fighting for dead Germans were entwined with British. No barriers between soldiers at peace.

"These lads have had a horrid time up here!" said Simon, holding his hand to his mouth to block the smell.

"Middlesex." Eric checked the collar insignia of one man sat stiff in the bottom of the trench.

"Poor buggers."

"Do your best to get into position lads! We hold here until called forward! I doubt it will be long, you can hear them giving it a good go down there!" screamed Edwards, grabbing everyone from their morbid trance. Eric and Simon moved under Chase's direction to the far-left flank of the platoon and Eric watched Simon set a position for the gun as he opened the box of ammunition drums he carried. They had chosen a small area that was clear from bodies, they didn't want to see what they could smell.

Eric focused his attention across the valley to the wooded areas. British shells were landing in the distance with alarming regularity, but they seemed to have no effect on the ability of the enemy in the wood, their defence ferocious. The loud beat of machine guns could be heard and the wild crack of rifles drifted with the sounds of war up the ridge to where the Kensingtons waited. Soon enough they would be called to assist or to exploit a gap in the enemy line so costly won by the men currently in the fight. Eric, not for the first time, felt a desire to get involved.

Since his baptism of fire alongside Basil in November of 1914, Eric had enjoyed the rush of adrenaline that filled his body in these desperate times. It was the closest he had ever been to complete, unrestricted euphoria. He felt excitement stir inside him, he knew what it was like to get hurt, to feel pain both physical and emotional and he knew very well that these moments, this trench, and this day would haunt him forever. He acknowledged it all but in that awful, singular moment he didn't want to be anywhere but on the outskirts of Ypres torn to pieces by war. He wanted to fight, and a small part of him wanted to die.

*

D Company remained in the trenches up on the ridge as a patient reserve and was later joined by another two Kensington companies. Fatigue parties did their best to sure up the positions destroyed by shells and cleared many of the dead from the trenches to make their movement, and any future defence of the line, easier. Throughout the afternoon and into the evening the battle in the woods and valleys in front of them ebbed and flowed but its ferocity remained.

Eric's zeal for the fight lasted an hour or so before it was soon replaced by weariness and fatigue was hammering at the door of his mind. He, like the rest of the Kensingtons, had been going hard for thirty-six hours without sleep or quality rations. He felt weak and pathetic when some men, whose dead comrades lay around him, had been fighting for days and weeks. He consoled himself that he had no control over who did what and when. He was just a soldier and did what he was told. Besides, he had seen heavy fighting and was sure that during those battles units had been in reserve watching them do all the work. It was simply the way of things, sometimes you were in the fight and at other times you sat at the back and watched it play out.

They were far from having an easy time of it however. On their small ridge they were exposed to constant fire from German artillery and the poor-quality trenches provided little protection. Most of the time there were the odd one or two shells falling but at other times it rained down devastating fury and it drove some to madness over the course of the day. Large mounds of earth, stone and the bodies of the dead all around them showered the Kensingtons still awaiting their orders. One shell landed in the Battalion Headquarters and caused a great deal of commotion and yet more casualties.

Eventually, just after nightfall, the attack was called off and the Kensingtons were ordered back to Micmac Camp in Ouderdom. The German defence of the wooded areas to the east of Ypres and along the Menin Road was too strong and thousands had been lost in the attempt, swallowed up by trees and swamps.

"Really? Surely that's a mistake?" argued Simon as he processed the message that they would be leaving the area and returning back to billets. "We haven't done anything yet!"

"You're very welcome to go and argue your case!" replied Chase, tired and irritated by Simon's comment. Simon sighed and started to collapse the Lewis Gun. Eric closed the box of ammunition and sealed it shut as best he could. Throughout the day his shoulder had become stiff with pain and he could hardly move it now without piercing agony. Chase noticed his friend struggling.

"How's your shoulder?"

"It's fucked but I'll be ok. It won't get any worse between here and the billets." Eric was grateful for the return, he would not be a bit of use in a fight with a damaged shoulder.

Robertson pulled a knife from his belt kit. "If you want me to take it off, I'll be happy to?" The darkness made Robertson's handsome features appear sinister, but Eric laughed.

"Perhaps when we get back to billets. I'll have a good old slug of rum and a smoke first."

"Maybe treat yourself too. It is never the same with the left," said Wilkinson, cupping the fingers on his right hand into a tunnel and mimicking masturbation. It was enough to start them all howling with laughter and they continued as a few shells whistled overhead and landed in the swampy land behind them.

The route back to billets took them over Hellfire Corner but it was a cloudy, black night so Eric and the Kensingtons passed by unmolested. A couple of casualties were taken when a volley of shells struck them in the reserve trenches on the outskirts of Ypres, but they managed to make it through with relative ease. Only the cobbled road stood between them and their camp in Ouderdom where they would be able to rest and await further orders.

Eric had managed to suffer his agony in silence but was struggling with the weight of the ammunition box in his one good arm, with no box the other side he was unbalanced so worked hard to stay upright as fatigue set in. Halfway down the cobbled road the heavy box slipped from his grasp and he tripped over it onto the road. He let out a tremendous scream that made the whole Kensington line wake from their daze. He had tried to land on his good side but had misjudged the distance to the ground and landed flat on his back onto a large round stone. His shoulder was wrenched from its sling and the pain was so intense Eric's eyes filled with tears and he felt he might vomit but, without a word and from whom he had no idea, a lit cigarette was placed in his mouth. He sucked hard on the end and as the harsh smoke hit the back of his throat it seemed to clear his head and relieve his pain. In one movement he was hoisted up onto his feet with his good arm, another man tenderly manipulated his bad arm back into the sling and they were moving again. Eric bent down to pick up the ammunition box, but another soldier had collected it without complaint.

Eric marched the last kilometre back to the billets without a burden to carry or a rifle in his hands. He walked with one wing bound tight in a muddy sling and with raging tiredness behind his eyes. He was angry and sad, infuriated by his injury and the day they had endured. It all seemed so pointless to him, so wasteful and uncoordinated. He tried to think of home, of Basil and his family but Eric's furious mind would not let him past the moment in which he was living. How had the last thirty-six hours been like this? He and the battalion had marched away on the evening of the 15th ready for a fight, to slay the King's enemies with vigour and relish but now the Commanding Officer was dead, and his senior staff wounded. They had endured a horrific masked stomp through swampy wasteland under fire from an enemy, they could not see or engage and occupied a trench full of dead soldiers, friend and foe. For hours they had watched helplessly a savage battle unfold but like spectators at a bullfight they weren't to be involved. Thirty-six hours, nearly one hundred men from the battalion killed or wounded and not one Kensington had fired a shot at the enemy. What a farce, what pathetic luck of war and what a terrible waste of a summer's day.

There was no singing or cheering as the Battalion entered Micmac Camp, the soldiers quietly found their billets as the sun rose around them. Flaps to tents were closed to the light and Eric, like the rest of the Battalion, fell asleep and waited for their next order.

Hammersmith, London – 30th November 1917

THE doctor prodded the left side of Basil's chest with his cold, sinewy fingers. "Do tell me if there is a tender patch," he said with hoarse professionalism. Basil was laid back on the cold bed with his arms behind his head. The room was chilly so the skin on his torso was goose-pimpled and his nipples were icy hard. "The wound has healed well. Doesn't hurt to touch?" asked the doctor as he felt the dark pink raised scarring on Basil's left side.

"No. It feels ok." Basil maintained his stare at the ceiling.

"Drop your hands and sit up, please." Basil did as he was told.

"When was the last time you were unwell, with fever or anything like that?"

"Last week I had a temperature for a few days and felt sick but it didn't get any worse."

"And the last time you were really unwell?"

"In the summer, I was very ill then. I had a fever and couldn't hold anything down." The memory stung.

"It passed?"

"Eventually. It lasted a good few days." The doctor sighed and felt Basil's throat with hard fingers.

"Ok, you can dress now." The doctor sat in his chair and returned to his notes as Basil threw his shirt on and a thick navy jumper. He pulled his boots over his socked feet and returned to his chair to tie them up. When he had finished, he looked at the doctor, inside he felt like a small boy. Dealings with his health always made him revert back to the child part of himself, so often poorly while his elder brothers were at play.

The doctor looked over his spectacles, his fat bottom lip tucked under his front teeth in concerned thought. Basil steadied himself. "As far as I can tell there is no change. Your fevers, high temperatures and nausea are-" the doctor paused and placed his hand on his chest, "-in my opinion, at least, random cases. Bugs you may have picked up from somewhere. I think if the bullet inside you was the issue, your problems would be more regular and far more severe." The doctor's old brown eyes were tired and expressionless.

"But I can feel its anger, when I'm ill I mean. I can feel the heat around it in my chest," said Basil, pleading to be believed.

"Look, I've seen similar cases and those chaps were seriously ill. You should be grateful your wound has healed, and the bullet isn't causing serious, life threatening infection," replied the doctor with an arrogant, patronising smile that made Basil's anger boil. Basil never liked him, he much preferred Doctor Robinson but he was a busy man, often required elsewhere.

"What explains the illness and the fevers? And the feeling inside my chest?" Basil's voice creaked with emotion. The doctor turned to Basil's notes and flicked through them to make his point.

"You've always been a sickly boy Basil. Some people just are." Basil angered more and felt insulted. His face burned red as he turned his gaze away into the corner to try and shield his annoyance.

"As for the feeling in your chest when you're ill. Of course you will feel pain there, this is where all the organs are. The bullet getting *hot* could be a trick of the mind."

Basil rubbed his eyes and looked out into the world behind the doctor. It was dark outside, and the rain was hammering at the thin glass in icy sheets, driven by screaming wind. "I'd be happy to see you again should anything change," said the doctor, standing from his desk.

"Thank you. I'm sorry it's just I feel so powerless against it all." Basil was instantly annoyed for apologising.

"It is not a problem at all, I am here to help." The doctor's tone made Basil's skin itch.

Basil picked his jacket from the end of the bed and left the room. He was the last patient of the day, so the lights were off in the waiting room and the lady who had greeted him at the reception desk was gone. Basil walked towards the door and shrugged his overcoat onto his shoulders. He pushed it open and the evil cold of winter stung his face.

*

Kathleen had tickets to see her friend's play not far from Hammersmith and it started at seven-thirty, so Basil did not have time to go home to 76. Instead he headed for the warmth of St. Paul's Church, but London was cold and dark so the people moving about that evening did it with haste. Their desire to escape the elements outweighed their social graces so Basil bumped and huffed his way past the throngs heading for home. Vehicles horned their presence loudly and tram conductors hollered their orders to passers-by who hadn't heard them approaching. Basil was happy to see the glowing light of the church windows from across the street and hurried to enjoy the warmth inside but as he reached the door something made him stop. Did he really want to be in there? Did he want to see his chums and talk about the war and politics like they all did so incessantly at the church club?

Hanham

The weather made the decision for him, a cold shiver forced him inside and he was surprised to see the place was almost empty. In the small adjoining building, he could hear a couple of ladies talking excitedly and there was a lone old man hunkered down on a pew at the back of the church, eyes closed in prayer or sleep. Quietly Basil removed his jacket and hung it up on a hook by the door. Candles burnt brightly at the alter end and along the side walls. Some electric lights lit the high beams and the glorious blue and gold ceiling farther down. Silently Basil made his way around the left side of the church to the place where he had used to sit with Eva and his brothers and sisters. He hadn't been this far down the church since his wounding, preferring instead to remain at the back unseen on the few occasions he did attend with Eva. Gently, as if asking permission or waiting for a cry of reprimand from the inanimate objects around him, he lowered himself onto the pew he used to frequent and leant up against the edge like he had as a teenager. Instinctively he looked up the stained glass that had provided him with so much dreamy wonder in years passed and regarded the holy warriors dressed in crimson shawls, carrying holy swords and contemplated what their trials had been like. He wondered if they had ever wished ill of themselves or felt sorry for the way their worlds had played out.

After his wounding on Christmas Eve 1914 he hadn't felt worthy but slowly he was becoming able to appreciate the part he had played and now he felt justified being here, for the first time could see himself as one of them. He imagined talking to them like soldiers in their rows of red and gold uniforms like he had the khaki of his brethren. So different were they in time and quest but so alike in means and struggle. Basil smiled at them and he felt he was being smiled upon.

He regarded the rest of the church and all its splendour, momentarily the wild elements outside were quiet to him and his mind soaked up all he could see, feel and smell. He thought of his ailment and how the doctor did not believe his issues. *Silly old fool!* Of course the poisoning of his body from the inside was the cause of his illnesses, what else could it be? He decided there and then that if he were to fall ill again, he would seek the advice of someone else or wait and speak to Doctor Robertson who was sympathetic to his struggles and open minded.

Basil sat for a full hour with his own thoughts and for once enjoyed the feeling of being alone. Only the loud entrance of a few young men from the behind him broke his trance and he rushed off to meet Kathleen.

*

"What an awful evening," said Basil. He embraced Kathleen in the foyer of the small theatre. Kathleen wore a long green dress and brown jacket against the cold.

"Goodness Basil you're soaked!" Kathleen eyed her brother up and down with concern and felt his sodden jumper.

"I got caught in the rain, K, miserable night." Basil looked around at the venue. He had never been in this theatre before which surprised him, its Kensington location wasn't too far from their old house on Holland Road.

"Nice place, isn't it?" said Kathleen, observing her brother's wide eyes.

"Who got you the tickets? Someone you've worked with?"

"In a way, we have crossed paths on sets before but she's not an actress any more. She knows one of the chaps in this play and they are struggling to fill the seats. Shame really because it's a good little play." Kathleen lead Basil through the turn style, her arm hooked though his. "I guess it's also a little too far out of town to attract the crowds." Kathleen shrugged her shoulders, some of her plays had struggled to fill seats and been cancelled early. Just like before the war there was no predicting the success of certain productions and no explaining the failure of others.

"What did the doctor say?"

"Ah the same old thing. He thinks I'm just a sickly fool. Who knows, maybe he is right," replied Basil shyly, a child once more.

"Don't be silly! You've got a dirty great bullet inside you and until it is removed, you're going to keep getting poorly. Why won't you try again to find someone who will remove it?" Kathleen was clearly frustrated. She seemed angry but Basil was agitated by her obvious observations.

"I've tried K! No one will touch it. Not even the Harley Street boys trying to make a name for themselves. Not while I'm still *OK*." He knew better than anyone that the alien inside him was a nasty time bomb. It scared him daily.

"I'm sorry, B, I just want you to be well," Kathleen held her brother's arm tight and rested her head against his shoulder.

"I know. I know. Any news from Howard?"

"No, I haven't heard anything from him since his last letter. I am still expecting him to be home for a short while over Christmas which will be nice." Howard's absence had made her forget the reservations she had about him and she found herself mildly excited by the prospect of his return. Absence had increased his appeal and her mind distorted not only his face but her feelings too.

"Do you think he'll bend the knee when he returns?" asked Basil with a cheeky grin. Kathleen smiled but did not evade the question.

"Well we aren't getting any younger." The ticking clock in her body was loud and drumming wildly, "Come on, let's find our seats."

The show was well put together, Kathleen was impressed by the actors in the production and would have quite liked to be a part of the play herself. Basil too was impressed. He was hard to please when it came to the theatre so Kathleen made a joke at his expense when he said as much.

"Hold the front page! Mr Basil Hanham enjoyed a production outside of the West End!" exclaimed Kathleen as they stood in the foyer waiting to thank her friend for the tickets.

"K? Is that you?" Both Kathleen and Basil were smoking in silence, but the soft tone of the voice went through Kathleen like a blade and its familiarity ignited a fire inside her body and soul. She froze like a fawn in a thicket as time slowed. She felt the heat of her blood under her skin as she looked up slowly into the warm blue sapphires of Harriet's eyes. Kathleen's face flushed bright pink and Basil noticed the intensity of her reaction so saved her further blushes.

"Harry isn't it?" asked Basil, extending a hand.

"Yes, a pleasure to see you again Basil. How are you?" Harriet turned to him, lighting the room with her smile. Perfect teeth dazzled Basil like the headlights of a motorcar.

"I'm ok thank you. It has been a long time," said Basil, looking to see whether Kathleen would enter the conversation, but she had turned away to extinguish her cigarette on the brass ashtray attached to the wall. Basil could see the shock in the tightness of her body.

"It has. You look all healed? Last time I saw you, you were in quite a lot of pain." She placed a hand on his arm. Her touch was powerful, healing hands of the divine.

"Yes, I'm afraid I'm still on the mend but much better than I was. And you? K tells me you went off to be a nurse?" Kathleen had turned to face them now and Basil noticed in her face a look he had seen before, the tense look of longing he had noticed in Stuart when there had been mention of Miss Emily Church. Suddenly he became aware.

"Yes, I was initially in Dorset but have been moved all about. I'm headed to Harwich next, but I have a few days leave first."

"Harwich in Essex?" asked Kathleen trying, and failing, to sound nonchalant.

"Yes, that's right," Harriet looked at her with a genuine smile, she seemed happy to hear Kathleen's voice, but Kathleen just nodded. She was embarrassed by her pathetic response and by her inability to have taken Harriet's presence in her stride. Basil interjected and rescued his sister again, he had never seen her so vulnerable.

"K and I were going to go for a drink. Why don't you join us?" Kathleen looked at him and her eyes screamed at him to retract his offer, but her heart sang some distant thanks.

"Thank you but I have plans with a friend." Harriet's face now flushed red and the freckles on her pale skin grew darker. She looked to the floor.

"Perhaps they can join us as well?" asked Basil. There was silence for a few seconds that dragged like the long years of war.

"There you are, Harry," called a man from behind Basil's shoulder.

He walked to join the stalled conversation casually and with no idea of the history or significance of the meeting. He beamed a smile to Kathleen and Basil, his handsome features innocent and distinguished. His soft brown eyes were friendly, and his dark hair gently slicked back over his head. He was Basil's height but had the broad shoulders of a rower and was older than Kathleen, perhaps in his mid-thirties. "Hello I'm James." He extended a hand to Basil first.

"Basil Hanham. Pleased to meet you. This is my Sister Kathleen." James smiled wider and shook hands delicately with Kathleen.

"Oh wait! You're Kathleen Hanham? Harry has told me so much about you." Kathleen looked at Harriet who stared back at her with silent intensity. In that look they spoke to each other and Harriet assured Kathleen she had not mentioned their passionate past. Kathleen forced a smile and turned to James.

"Nothing bad, I hope?"

"No quite the opposite. In fact, whenever we discuss the theatre, she always says you're the best in the business. Are you working at the moment?" Harriet smiled and her face reddened further. Basil nudged his sister playfully, but Kathleen remained stoic and she shook her head with slow grace.

"I think Harry may have been drinking too much whisky during your theatre chats James, I am no star," replied Kathleen, modestly. Harriet smiled.

"Ah she's not one to suffer fools so if she says there is something special about you then you can be damn sure there is." James had no idea what his words were doing to the two women. He was simply conducting a meeting in the polite manner he knew but the thought of being special to Harriet made Kathleen sadden and her whole body weakened as Harriet regarded her with those magnificent blue eyes.

"Thank you." Kathleen turned her attention to Harriet for the first time, "You didn't mention you were in London."

"I'm sorry. I've been so busy," replied Harriet, trying not to cower.

"I can vouch for that, she has barely time for me," interrupted James laughing, unaware of the wound he was widening in Kathleen's heart and the deep distress he was causing Harriet. Basil came to the rescue again.

"Well we've all been busy. Such is life at the moment. We should be heading home, K," said Basil, turning to Kathleen. She looked up at him and thanked him with wide hazel eyes, a moist sheen forming on their surface.

"It was nice to see you again, Harriet. K is in a production at the Haymarket if you're around that way."

"Oh really. Well I shall certainly try and come along before I head off." Harriet touched Kathleen's arm. Kathleen felt again her life-giving electricity and words escaped her. She smiled her thanks and held her breath to keep back tears. Harriet sensed her pain and turned and walked away without further words. James said his goodbyes quickly, for the first time sensing it was more than just a random meeting of old friends.

Kathleen held her breath as she watched Harriet dash away into the night. When she and James were out of sight she turned and fell heavy into Basil's arms. He held his sister as she wept onto his shoulder, her body was shaking, and he could feel her heart beating hard like a drum.

"Come on K, let's get you home."

*

Kathleen took her time changing after the evening performance and politely declined offers from cast and crew to join them for a post-performance drink. She said she was tired, which was no lie, but she had an odd sense that there was someone in the audience that night here to see her and feeble attempts to spy through the curtains while the show was in full swing revealed no clue. She suspected it might be Harriet, but Kathleen was sure she couldn't see her again, her heart could not take another meeting, so she waited in the foyer and lit a cigarette while the theatre custodian turned off all the lights. She had taken care with her make-up and made her hair up nicely under her hat just in case, but she was sure that whoever was waiting would have long gone, probably when the last of the production had left.

She took one final look around the foyer and decided she was being silly, no one had come to see her, and she was alone as the foyer lights were turned out, she sighed deeply and headed for the exit. Had she wanted someone to be there? Did she want Harriet to have come to see her? Truthfully, she didn't know but her heart sank regardless.

Kathleen hunched her shoulders and headed for the outside world. As she pushed open the heavy brass doors the chill of winter hit the exposed skin of her face, the dense darkness of a moonless night only dimly lit by soft street lamps. There was laughter and cheer coming from a pub a few doors down.

"I thought I'd missed you," came a voice from the shadows. It was deep and hoarse and not the voice she had been expecting. Kathleen froze and swivelled round to look into the shadows. She was not afraid, but her heart stopped still and her eyes struggled to adjust to the soft amber light.

The figure was tall, svelte and black in the shadows, it grew slowly lighter as it stepped from the wall. A military uniform was now clear to see and Kathleen's mind raced. Stuart? Eric? Surely neither?

"You look like you've seen a ghost," said the figure as it removed its hat and tucked it under the arm of its great coat. Howard's face was framed by the low light, a pleasing smile on his face. His cheekbones and jaw heroic above the turned-up collar of his heavy khaki jacket.

Kathleen's eyes leaked heavy tears that shone like glitter as they ran down her face. Her eyes stayed wide and her mouth set still. She dropped the cigarette down by her feet and buried her head into his chest, the scratchy uniform material rough on her delicate cheeks. She wrapped her arms tight round his body and sunk into the moment.

"I'm so sorry to have kept you. Had I known you were waiting," said Kathleen looking up at Howard.

"It is no problem, I thought I'd missed you so I'm happy to see you now. I wanted to surprise you," replied Howard, kissing her lips.

Kathleen pulled away and smiled through tears, "Well you have certainly managed to do that."

"Beside I haven't been waiting alone, there was a woman here for you too, but she had to leave," Kathleen looked up at him. Her tears ceased and her heart stopped its frantic march. Her stomach clenched, she felt sick, weak and broken.

"A woman?" Kathleen's voice was creaking.

"Yes, we were chatting. Her name was Harriet I think."

Tilloy Sector, Arras, France – 12ᵗʰ August 1918

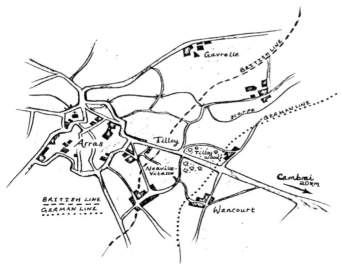

ANOTHER summer was in full bloom and Eric and the Kensingtons found themselves in the familiar surroundings of Arras. He had endured a third winter on the line and in the spring he and the battalion had been heavily involved in stopping the savage German offensives. They took great pride in being able to count themselves among the units that stood firm and, with over two million American soldiers promised, the war seemed to be moving to an end.

Eric sat with his shirt open enjoying the fading light and a moment of peace while Simon purred catlike asleep next to him and Chase wrote a letter home. July and August had kicked the flies into life, but they were tolerated as the passage of seasons steamed slowly by. The remainder of the Lewis Gun Section was spread out along the bank either smoking or dozing in the late afternoon sun. Eric leant forward and buttoned his tunic, "What time are we off Chase?" Chase checked the timepiece on his arm.

"We still have an hour."

"I can't sleep any more, that bloody coffee has me wired tight."

"I told you not to have two cups," Chase chuckled to himself. Eric said nothing but extracted a packet of cigarettes from his top pocket, he handed one to Chase who accepted gratefully. Eric lit them both with a lighter he had bought in Arras. He laid his head back and looked up at the clouds moving swiftly on the wind across a blue sky.

"I think it'll be a blowy one tonight," said Eric as he watched the smoke from his mouth speed away across the line of men using the low bank for a place to rest.

"So, they say."

"Who are you writing to?" Eric turned on his side to watch Chase.

"You know what Eric, you're like a bloomin' woman when you're bored! Do you know that?" snapped Chase. Eric started laughing immediately and Simon broke into a giggle by his side.

"I'm sorry, Corporal, am I annoying you?" Simon turned over and smiled at Eric.

"Now Eric, don't annoy our commander. He might make you do something like go and mount a forward picket in the dead of night," said Simon. He was being sarcastic, that was their task that evening and for the next three at least. Chase smiled and continued to write for a few moments before dramatically signing off the letter.

"Right! Finished. Now I'm all yours, dear, what's on your mind?" joked Chase as he leant on his side and fluttered his eyelashes at Eric. Eric laughed harder and Simon blew some kisses.

"Causing trouble?" asked Davison as he lowered himself down between Eric and Simon.

"Ah we're just passing the time." Eric handed Davison his cigarette. Davison took it from Eric, regarded it then threw it away.

"Hey! I've not got many left!" Eric looked at Davison with bright, angry eyes.

"Relax old man, I have a packet of the good ones I got from an officer. He made a bet with me and lost!" Davison handed Eric and Chase a smooth white stick neatly packed and golden tipped. Simon raised his head to see over Davison's cocked knee and got an offer of one for his trouble.

"Ah the good shit, you are forgiven, old friend," said Eric removing his lighter from his tunic pocket and the four men laid against the grassy bank peacefully smoking splendid cigarettes as clouds darkened the sky above them.

"So, what news?" enquired Eric, inspecting the glowing end of his cigarette.

"Nothing new I'm afraid. All as it was this morning," replied Davison. "Any word from home?"

"Nothing new there, Kathleen's wedding to Howard still set for the autumn and Basil is still a clerk at the munitions factory," replied Eric, taking a long pull from his cigarette. Davison nodded. "And Frank, you know Stella's Frank? He's been posted with the band somewhere in London, which is good news. I think they are on the war bonds circuit again."

"That's great. Say lads, have you boys heard of Eric's sisters? Quite the lookers." Davison smiled at Chase and winked to Simon, the scar on his face creased into fine pink lines. Eric sighed.

"Really?" asked Simon.

"Yes, but they are only interested in artists and musicians. Not short, fat men from the docks!" replied Eric, laughing wildly at his own comment and the reaction on poor Simon's face. Davison, Chase and the men around them laughed with him.

"I'll see you later Eric. Stay safe out there. You know we're just behind if you need us." said Davison picking a quiet moment to extract himself. Eric, still laughing at Simon waved a casual goodbye.

*

As daylight slowly faded the temperature dropped but Eric and the men were soon hot and sweating as they marched to the front, their backs to the town of Arras. The whole front line had been quiet for some days so there was no significant anxiety among the Kensingtons as they moved forward to take their place on the line. They knew the route and it wasn't long before they found themselves passing the aid station at the back of Bully Beef Wood and made their way through the shattered remains of Tilloy to the forward trenches. They were passed along the way by smiling faces of the London Scottish Battalion they were replacing. Whispered banter went back and forth between the two units in the growing darkness, many of the London Scottish handed over their cigarettes to the Kensingtons heading up to the line.

D Company took over the trenches and the sentry positions on the line, but Eric and his section prepared to push further into No Man's Land and occupy their Lewis Gun posts. The sun had now set, and cool darkness was around them like a blanket. The low clouds and wind perfect cover to set out forward of the British line. Chase gathered his team together. Eric carried the heavy gun and Simon, Walker and Jacobs the boxes of ammunition. Walker and Jacobs were young and keen when they had arrived as boys in January, but they had matured and resembled men now. Walker was a tall, skinny boy from the docks near Simon, his boyish features hid a hard life. Jacobs had a privileged upbringing in comparison but was still rough around the edges. He grew up around Brixton where his father ran a bicycle shop. He was shorter than Walker but had the strength of youth and had proven himself a good soldier in the short time he'd been around. Eric felt a lot older than them all, he would be twenty-six in September. He was revered as a 1914 Kensington who had fought in every action the battalion had seen, bar Aubers Ridge and the Somme, and who wore inverted chevron of good conduct on his tunic.

"Keep moving lads, you know where we are going," said Chase as they reached the western edge of Tilloy Wood. The Arras-Cambrai Road ran along the northern edge but both wood and road had been severely destroyed by shellfire over years of war. The ragged stumps of dead trees and sharp broken roots the only sign of the once thick wood, hard chalk foundations of the road the only indication of the thoroughfare it once was. A partially completed German dugout was their home for the next few days and relief of the London Scottish their task that night.

"How are you boys?" asked the commander of the London Scottish as the Kensington men entered the dugout.

"Just peachy," replied Chase. Eric had been here many times so did not stop and look around. He ducked inside the dugout shaft and made his way down into its depths. It smelt dank and stale but a small oil lamp at the bottom of the wooden steps offered a little light, so he was able to make his way down with ease. At the bottom he lowered the gun from his shoulder, leant it against the wall and dropped the pack of provisions he had carried for the last few hours, sighing with relief once the weight was off his back. The tins of bully beef, biscuits and canned fruits had become very heavy and his shoulders felt light without the burden. Walker staggered behind him and dropped another pack next to Eric's.

"Evening, lads," called a voice from the shadows.

"Hello. You'll be pleased to know your relief has arrived," said Walker. The man in the shadows said nothing but offered a cigarette to Eric and Walker. Eric slumped down on the large box next to him and accepted his light.

"Much been happening?" asked Eric as he watched his smoke dance in the orange light of the dugout.

"A few small patrols the other night but they didn't venture far. Gave them a case or two for good measure," replied the man, now fumbling with his kit and kicking his friend on the floor fast asleep.

"Have you been here before?"

"Yeah, a few times," said Walker, crouching on his haunches and stretching his back.

"Well then you'll know not to raise even a finger out there in the daylight unless you want it removed free of charge." The soldier threw on his pack and heaved his Lewis Gun onto the crook of his arm.

"Yeah we know," Eric lifted his feet to allow the man to pass by and ascend out into the night, but Chase's voice came down into the dugout before he could leave.

"Eric! Come on mate. You're first up on the night post." Eric lowered his feet to the floor and extinguished what remained of his cigarette on the panelled wall of the dugout.

"Excuse me, lads." He swung his Lewis Gun onto his shoulder and made his way up towards the purple sky.

When Eric emerged, he was thrown by the brightness of the night. The clouds had been blown away to expose a low moon and it shone like the sun. Eric could clearly make out the faces of Chase and the others in the trench, the world in silver-tinted colour.

"So much for cloud cover," said Simon with an anxious smile.

"Bill here was saying there is a track leading through the wire and along a sunken edge of the wood, you can use it to get out there and relieve the lads in the night post. He's happy to show you if you aren't sure," said Chase to Eric who was taking a hefty slug from his canteen. He wiped his mouth with his sleeve.

"No, I'm happy with the route. Ready?" Simon nodded and rose to his feet, collecting as he did so the two boxes of ammunition.

"Leave them here mate, use what is already out there," said the London Scottish Commander.

"Happily!" replied Simon placing the drums down. He removed his revolver from its holster and checked it was loaded then nodded to Eric he was ready.

"You'll be relieved in three hours," said Chase as he patted Eric on the back. Eric smiled and nodded his understanding, his eyes pale and bright.

Eric followed Simon down an old part of the German trench system now destroyed. The moon was low, so the going was easy along the duckboards that remained in place. As they reached the end of the trench Simon stopped, looked around and then turned to Eric, "Is this the right way?" Eric nodded but could see Simon was a little unsure.

"Here, you take the gun and I'll lead." Eric handed the cumbersome weapon to Simon, checked his revolver and with it cradled in his right hand he continued towards the end of the trench, periodically he peeked above it to check the route. The lifeless stumps of trees surrounded them, but he could see a large pond alongside the road as he remembered, and it shimmered like a silver mirror in the glare from the moon. He waited for a moment until he was sure none of the stumps moved like men in grey uniforms. When he was content, he turned to Simon, "Come on, stay low."

The moonlight enabled them to move fast, even through the heavy mud surrounding the pond. Occasionally they would wait behind stumps of trees and listen with jaws open, ears directed to the east to improve their sense, but the night was quiet. They continued on their way, sweating now with adrenaline and effort. They used shell holes to mask their approach, dipping in and out of them until Eric stopped at a familiar spot. Crossed sticks in the mud and a piece of wood nailed unnaturally to a tree stump was the indication he had reached the night post entrance, so he stopped behind a fat tree stump at the edge of what used to be the wood.

"Lads," whispered Eric in the stillness. He arranged the revolver in his hand ready for an unfamiliar answer.

"Relax, I saw you coming," said a voice in return, closer than he expected. "If we had thought you were Hun, you'd have had it by now." Eric, happy to holster his revolver, crept slowly towards the soldier hunched in the darkness and placed his ear close to his mouth. His breath was foul, but Eric did not shudder.

"We've had to move the position onto the road, got too much attention here the other night." He turned Eric's head to where two men lay prone in the jumbled remains of the road. "Don't fall asleep because you'll be potted for sure if you are here in the light. The baddies are only a couple of hundred yards away. If the wind's right, you hear them snoring in their night posts." Eric winced at the idea the enemy were so close but was happy to pull away from the pungent aroma of his informer's mouth.

Eric assessed the situation and was not happy, "Can you tell my corporal we need more than one gun up here."

"We only have one gun," replied the soldier, confused by Eric's need for a second. Eric said nothing but trusted his intuition, he'd been doing this a long time and he knew Chase would respect his opinion. He and Simon lay on their fronts and crawled over the rubble and mud that used to be the Arras-Cambrai road until they were in position next to the London Scottish. Without exchanging words, and in as near to silence as they could manage, they set up their gun while the other men disappeared into the night.

For hours Eric and Simon lay prone on the hard foundations of the road, a small raise of rubble their protection from the front and measly cover. Quickly their backs began to cramp and the cold of the cloudless night set in. The damp, muddy floor invaded their heavy uniforms from beneath and their elbows were soon painful and dented by the rocks and bricks they rested on. So severe was the pain they took it in turns to lie flat on the ground for ten minutes at a time, arms rested by their sides, while the other observed the enemy lines to the east. Their toes too were soon painfully cold and no amount of frantic wiggling inside their boots could alleviate the discomfort. Minutes dragged by like hours until shortly before one o'clock they heard men approaching from behind them. Eric shuffled down into the shell hole and removed his revolver from its holster. They had expected their relief, but no chances were taken. Eric hunkered down in the shadows pointing his Webley at the approaching noise.

The night was still crisp and bright so Eric could see clearly the shapes approaching from the low ground around the pond using the remains of trees as cover like he and Simon had. They were unmistakably the shapes of his comrades with Chase, nimble and feline, at the front and Walker with his lanky frame stumbling at the back. Eric whispered them over to him the last twenty metres.

"They said you reckon we need two guns up here?" asked Chase into Eric's ear.

"For sure. I don't think we can cover it all with one gun," explained Eric. Chase took a moment and looked around. The position had indeed changed since the last time they were here.

"I agree. I've sent for the rest of the section, so we'll man it tomorrow night in two five man shifts. For now though I'll stay up here with your gun and you two head back to the dugout."

"See you at first light," said Eric as he and Simon sloped off into the moonlight, revolvers ready.

*

Daylight hours were spent in the coolness of the dugout while two men observed No Man's Land from the entrance. There were no signs of activity and it was quiet but the threat from snipers and shelling was constant. During the night half of the section would make their way cautiously out to the night post and lay prone on the road observing the enemy approaches while the other half manned fall-back positions. On their second night of this rotation it rained relentlessly and, sodden, by the third evening Eric and his friends felt as if they had been here a whole week. Unshaven faces were muddied and sullen with the conditions.

"Are we first out there again tonight, Chase?" asked Simon from his seated position in the dugout entrance. The sun was setting so they were preparing themselves for the night ahead.

"Yeah, we'll keep the same rotation," replied Chase, finishing the remnants of his mug of tea. Simon nodded and continued to eat his bully beef from the tin.

"I don't know how you eat that rubbish cold," said Eric, scrunching his face in disgust. "I can barely touch it when it is warm and full of sauce!"

"He's got no taste buds. His mother's milk was so soured with booze she destroyed them when he was a weaning pup," said Chase with a smile. Eric laughed but Walker joined Simon's defence.

"He's from the Docks boys, made of hard stuff down there, aren't we, mate?" Walker patted Simon on the back.

"Youngen here is right, we dock boys just get on with things."

"Well I wished you would get on and finish that tin, the sounds you are making make me want stick my head above ground!" said Chase. Eric laughed harder at his friend's expense.

"You can give it a rest Eric! If I have to smell your arse again it will be too soon," hissed Simon.

"Well you shouldn't be greedy and take two sniffs." Eric's repose was snappy, even Simon laughed at his wit.

"Come on then lads, wake the others for stand too. Let's get on with it," ordered Chase, looking at the time on his wrist and frowning at the sky.

After dark the five men made their way out into No Man's Land, towards the night posts. It was cloudy and there was a strong wind bringing thick drizzle from the west. It was not pleasant but perfect conditions for their purpose; all their sounds were dispersed, and clouds covered the moon to make the night even darker. The enemy might be out in these conditions too, so they moved with caution and shortly before ten o'clock they had made it into their positions and settled in for another few hours of back pain, cold feet and throbbing elbows.

Eric and Simon had been quiet for about thirty minutes when they saw the first flash in the distance. Immediately the second and third ignited the horizon.

"Artillery," said Eric to Chase who was hunkered down to his right.

"At us?" There was no panic in his question. Eric looked up to the sky, but he couldn't hear the shells for the westerly wind was too strong and blew the sounds away.

"I don't -" Eric did not have chance to finish his sentence before the first shell came crashing down onto the ruins of an old building one hundred yards in front of them. The second fell casually into the thick mud the other side but the third hit the harder surface of the road and burst into a powerful mist of debris and deadly shrapnel.

"Yep! I'd say they are meant for us!" screamed Eric from his foetal position.

"Come on lads! That's a ranging burst. Let's go!" ordered Chase from the bank of the road, his section did not need asking twice. They were up and on their way back within a few seconds, just as a second group of three shells fell closer to where Eric and his comrades had been lying. They felt the blast on their backs as they threw themselves to the dirt. Heavy, jagged wads of metal whipped past their cowering heads.

"It's a creeper!" shouted Eric and they all acknowledged the sweeping nature of the barrage so often used against them on obvious features like the Arras-Cambrai Road. They kept running, Eric's lungs were burning by the time they reached the western edge of Tilloy Wood. His legs were heavy with mud, shaking with adrenaline and thick lines of sweat ran down his face and back. Shells continued to creep up behind them, but they were out running the slow progression of the bombardment.

"They are still ranging," said Chase.

"Surely we need to get back to the shelter?" asked Simon in panic as he struggled from a boggy puddle. Walker dragged him out by his collar.

"It might be cover for an advance or a raid. Get into the fall-back positions, that's what they are for!" ordered Chase and with Simon now free the five of them continued their run back to the secondary positions but were suddenly engaged by their own men.

"Fucking hell! It's us, you fool!" called Chase as they all threw themselves into the mud to avoid the flashing bullets. Eric could hear one of the men next to the firer reprimanding him, far from eloquent. "...Is everyone good?"

"Jacobs? Are you alright?" asked Eric.

"Yeah I'm alright. Just landed on a fucking picket." Jacobs rolled in pain, checking his side for blood. "Its ok. I'm ok."

"Come on lads, keep moving. We're coming in!" shouted Chase to avoid more friendly fire.

"Come on up mate!" came the reply from the hidden post that was so nearly the end of them. Chase, Eric and Simon occupied the middle of three positions fifty yards in front of the dugout. Walker and Jacobs in the smaller one to their right and the other guns spread along to the left. Along the road the ranging burst were creeping slowly closer but stopped halfway between them and their night positions.

"Perhaps they were just trying to rattle us?" asked Simon.

"Maybe," replied Eric as Chase barked orders to his men.

"Still could be an advance or a raid! Keep an eye out lads!"

After nearly an hour of silence there was no more shelling or any sign of advancing troops in the darkness. Illumination flares were continuously sent high into the sky by British guns to the rear and Eric felt a calming warmth surround him as he watched them flutter brightly to the floor. He enjoyed the flickering orange light they cast upon the world and he knew he would look back fondly on their glow and the sounds they made.

By eleven Chase had organised a roster to watch the line. He had sent Walker and Jacobs back to the dugout, but he remained in the central position under a camouflaged corrugated iron sheet with Eric and Simon.

"Bit of excitement, eh?" said Chase as he leant against the back of the shell hole they had converted into a gun placement. Eric lay prone behind the gun at the front and Simon a few yards away to his right.

"Yeah, keeps us on our toes I guess," agreed Eric but as Chase nodded his response and Simon snorted a laugh the sky in the east flashed angrily ten or eleven times within few seconds. The wind had dropped so Eric could easily hear the muffled explosions of the guns and this time the deadly whistles were audible, trails of low-lying cloud showed the direction of their flight.

"Shit! They are headed right this way! Stay down lads!" shouted Chase as he curled into a ball and slid down into the base of the large shell hole they occupied. Eric wriggled into the corner of the firing bay that was shaped by some sandbags and Simon lay still where he was a few feet away, his hands covering his ears from the noise to come.

In the few seconds that followed there was nothing else that could be done. Their lives were in the lap of some god of war and there was no time to improve their chances of survival. They had simply to pray their number was not painted on the shell screaming death toward them.

The first few dropped short but were very close and the rumble of the earth was like thunder under them. Every sinew and muscle in Eric's body tensed tight in fear as they were showered with debris and heavy mud. The next couple dropped either side of them but the fifth or sixth dropped into the shell hole Eric, Chase and Simon were in. The blast flashed white and blew the pathetic shelter from above Eric's head as he was thrown forward into the bank of the adjacent crater. All the air was expelled from his body like a popped balloon and he shook with adrenaline and fear, his eyes refused to open and for moment Eric thought himself dead. The barrage around him was unrelenting, louder than any noise Eric had heard in his life as it swept forward and backwards, left and right, Eric's eyes remained shut tight. He felt the earth piling up on top of him and worried he might be buried alive, but this thought assured him that for the moment, at least, he was still of this world.

After what seemed like a lifetime the shelling ceased and Eric dug the loose soil from around his chest and face. He felt the coolness of the night kiss his cheeks and gulped sweet air into his lungs like a drowning man. He wriggled out of his cocoon and counted his limbs. He felt his chest and his head for wounds. His body ached like he had been in a fight with a tiger and his mind was shell-shocked and disjointed, adrenaline coursed through his young body concealing any pain.

An illumination shell rose high into the sky, but Eric did not hear it explode, he gritted his teeth through the intense ringing and painful throbbing in his head. Pathetically he started crawling back to where he had been. His Lewis Gun was sticking out of the mud like a flag and the sandbags showed a trail to the old position as the world around him flickered violent orange. As he hauled himself over the lip he looked around for help and signs of life but was greeted by the vile remains of his friend. Half of Simon's body lay on the lip of the shell hole with a smoking shard of shrapnel the size of a dinner plate protruding from his chest. His legs and left arm were no longer part of him and only his head and chest remained. White fleshy bits of fat and bone shone in the flickering light along with the sad glint of his open eyes. Eric found enough strength to scramble to his feet but was as unstable as a new-born foal. He fell to the ground twice more as he tried to make his way to the dugout and safety. His ringing ears stole his balance and weakness in his legs meant he couldn't carry his frame. Eric screamed as he hit the ground and the sound of his own horrible agony tore at him like a knife.

He could now also feel the searing, wretched pain in his backside and gingerly he felt around the gaping wound on his right buttock.

Another flare went up into the sky and suddenly men rushing to his aid surrounded him. In his panicked, frantic state he tried to fight them away with his fists but was he was weak and dazed, with wide, frightened eyes he spat hysterical rage. One man grabbed his face and looked deep into him, but Eric did not recognise the friend he had known for four long years. Davison threw him onto his back in one swift motion and ran him back to the British line.

Eric looked back toward the shell hole as he hung tight around Davison's neck. The last image he saw before he fell unconscious was the staring, open eye of Chase glaring at him sadly from the ground. The other side of his skull had been blasted away with the left side of his body and his uniform was blown clean from what remained of his bare chest.

St. Margaret's Church, Streatham – 19ᵗʰ October 1918

IT had rained all morning, but the sun was now peeking through the thick grey clouds and the world was bright. The surface of the wet road shone and golden-brown leaves covered the paths. Kathleen had walked in silence with Basil on her arm the few hundred metres from 76 to St. Margaret's Church. Stella followed behind her to make sure her wedding dress did not drag on the grimy path, a job she did with patient grace. As they approached the church Kathleen looked up the steps to the open doors, a young usher ran back inside, giddy with news of the bride's arrival.

Kathleen stopped a few feet from the entrance and regarded the steps up to the open doors. She looked past the glare of the sun on the stained glass high up the bright terracotta brick of the old church. She closed her eyes and turned slowly to Basil waiting patiently by her side.

"You know B, when I was young girl, I never imagined you giving me away." She looked at him with her big hazel eyes, a film of moisture on the surface threatened to become tears. Her dark hair was curled into pretty, bouncy coils and her soft pale face was a wonderful contrast to red lips.

Basil looked to the floor in sadness like it was his fault her father and Stuart were no longer around, "Well I'm sorry K, I-"

"You didn't let me finish... But there is no one in the world I would rather have escort me today." Basil smiled handsomely and nodded his head, his blue eyes developed their own emotional sheen and his hair blew delicately on the breeze. With his arm still entwined in hers he leant over and kissed his sister on the cheek. Their bond had grown in the years he had been home and shared secrets only strengthened their love for one another.

"Right! Before I start to cry-" said Kathleen, turning to look at Stella who had not managed to stay so strong. Dark wet lines had run down her cheek. Basil dried Stella's cheeks with his handkerchief as Kathleen lowered her veil.

"You look beautiful, K," said Stella.

The organ blasted the wedding march from its dusty bowels as Kathleen and Basil entered the church and marched slowly down the aisle, smiling at people where they dared. On Kathleen's side were her friends and the Hanham family and on the right the Boundford clan had done their best to fill the pews. At the end of the aisle stood Howard in the smart black suit he had decided to wear instead of his uniform. He smiled as he watched his bride approach under Mendelssohn's spell.

As Kathleen reached the end of the aisle and the point where Basil would give her away, she looked left and saw her mother smiling proudly, strong and stoic, as always, and for once not dressed in the sacred black of mourning. Next to her Eric leant awkwardly on large crutches propped under his arms. He wore the smart khaki of a soldier, resplendent and youthful, he smiled proudly under a poor effort to grow a moustache. Kathleen looked at them both and Eva blew a kiss to the bride. Then Kathleen closed her eyes and let herself imagine Stuart there with her. It gave her great solace to think of him watching down from some lofty place with their father.

Kathleen couldn't hold her emotions any longer and tears, like raindrops, falling down her face caught in her veil. Basil nodded to the vicar, shook Howard's outstretched hand and kissed his sister before taking his seat on the front row. Howard gazed through the lace of his bride's veil and smiled at her but Kathleen's mind was a tornado. Her thoughts raced over the last four years and all the faces of her past merged into one splendid collage. Harriet, Stuart, Eva, Howard, Basil, Eric, Stella, Frank and many more along the way, all smiling happily at her in the joyous sunshine of her mind. Her pain and struggles over these last tortuous years temporarily forgotten.

76 Amesbury Avenue – 25ᵗʰ October 1919

EVA sat and watched Basil lying on his bed trying to rest, the effort of dressing had weakened him to the point of exhaustion and the last ten days of torrid fever had reduced his slight frame to a dangerous state of malnourishment. Her face was heavy with concern and her hair was tied back on her head in a messy nest as she looked helplessly at the gaunt face of her youngest. The sound of the horn outside made her jump and forced Basil to open his eyes.

"He's here," said Eva as she parted the curtains and peered into the road. She noticed the big black car and saw Eric briefly as he entered the house with a bang.

"I'm back! Are you dressed old boy?" Eric ran up the stairs as Basil struggled to push himself up into a seated position on the edge of the bed.

"I may need some help," said Basil, looking pathetically to his brother in the doorway of his room. Eric, like Basil, was smartly dressed in suit and tie.

"Of course." Eric strode over to Basil and gently lifted him childlike into his arms and carried him out of the room.

"Be careful on the stairs," called Eva.

"Don't worry mater I have him. Christ you weigh nothing B! I can tell you I will not be doing this when you're all well again." Eric forced a smile, but Basil did not have the strength to respond. He was saving his resolve for a time when he would need it.

Once outside Eric opened the car door with his foot and placed Basil gently on the back seat. The soft red leather was cool on Basil's burning brow. "Do you want a blanket?" Basil shook his head without a word so

Eric shut the door and ran around to the other side. "Are you sure you won't come?" asked Eric of Eva stood helplessly in the doorway.

"No, I would only get upset. I know you'll look after him." The sight of one son carrying the other away had brought tears to her eyes.

"We'll be back before you know it," said Eric as he clambered into the driver's seat and revved the engine. "She's a loud old beast but she'll get us there. Mr Shore was happy to lend it when he heard about your troubles." Eric pressed opened the throttle and bounced the vehicle down the cobbled street towards the main road into London, but it took a full hour to get to Condine Street, Eric shouting and screaming at fellow motorists all the way. His attitude to driving was the same he had to life and it made Basil smile when not gritting his teeth through pain and nausea.

"Here we are, B. How are you doing back there?" Eric jumped the car onto the pavement outside their destination. "Number sixty-two," he said proudly to himself. Basil swivelled himself into position and tried to open the door, but the effort proved too much for him and his arm dropped pathetically down by his side. Eric swung it open from the outside.

"Come on then, let's have you out." Basil was unsteady on his feet and unable to support his frame, so Eric wedged his body under his arm and lifted him into his arms again. Basil was embarrassed so mumbled a weak protest.

"I know, I'll let you walk into the room but it's on the second floor so stop your complaining," said Eric, kicking open the door to the building.

After ascending the large marbles stairs Eric saw the familiar face of

Basil's doctor sat on a bench along a wide sunlit corridor. He was wearing a brown suit with a smart yellow bow tie, but his old red face was taught and concerned. He looked up and forced a smiled at Eric.

"Good man, how is he doing?" asked Doctor Robertson as he regarded Basil's face for signs of deterioration or improvement, his white hair smelt medicinal.

"He's still having trouble keeping food down and his temperature is high," replied Eric, lowering Basil gently to his feet.

"Alright, well in that room is a selection of skilled people and hopefully one of them will be able to help. Some are keen to make a name for themselves so let's bank on bravado." Robertson patted Basil softly on the shoulder. Basil smiled and stood up straight. "Ready when you are, Basil."

Basil nodded and Robertson opened the door to a room of assembled experts. Their humming chatter ceased as he laboured into the room and Robertson showed him to a seat at the front. Eric went to sit down on a chair at the side of the room.

"Best you wait outside, Eric," said Robertson with an apologetic smile. Eric looked to Basil who nodded he was all right. Eric smiled awkwardly and left the room feeling helpless and irrelevant. He knew Basil's life depended on the people there and now he was on the other side of the wall unable to exert his own pressure or pleading. He winked at Basil as the door closed.

"Gentlemen, this is Corporal Basil Algernon Hanham and he is twenty-five years old. He took a bullet for King and Country on Christmas Eve 1914, a bullet that is still lodged in his torso, I believe around his lung." Robertson paused for effect and Basil smiled at being referred to as a soldier again.

"He has a history of childhood ailments so admittedly his immune system is not the strongest, but he had been in good health prior to the incident in 1914. Most have seen my letter so know my diagnosis, but I will reiterate for those that haven't."

Basil was saddened by the comment on his weak immune system and he felt nauseous at the thought of the incident again. Every time he thought of the slug-like piece of metal slithering menacing around his insides it seemed to grow in anger and attack him again, like it was a living thing with an evil mind connected to his own.

"He had been seen by another Doctor in my absence, but he recently passed away. Mr Hanham-" Basil wished he had used his old rank again, "came to me with severe abdominal pains and illness in July. I found him then to be feverish with septic conditions of skin, enactive tissue and to be suffering with septic diarrhoea. His general health is much impaired and I believe the bullet in his chest is the cause of the infection. In short gentleman, if he does not have it removed, he will likely die." There was a silence in the room and Basil felt the hot presence again of the bullet inside him. He looked around at all the men scratching their chins and consulting their notes.

"Will you remove your shirt please, sir," asked one of the younger men on the front row. Basil nodded and attempted to open the buttons but struggled with the first one. "Do help him," said the same voice and Robertson leant over to assist Basil.

Once Basil's shirt was removed, he stood in front of the audience and explained slowly and bravely his symptoms to the crowd who made notes and sighed their approval. Some rose from their chairs and came to gently prod the area around his left side. It had swollen tight and the skin around it was hot to the touch, the other side of his torso was grey in the light and malnourished, his ribs, like a whippet's, were clearly visible.

After ten minutes of inspection Robertson helped Basil replace his shirt, sit down and there was tense silence as some of the men avoided Robertson's glare. Basil grew worried he would not find his salvation in this room.

"Well?" challenged Robertson.

"It's badly infected and whatever happens will have to happen fast," said the young man at the front. "There is a lot of bad tissue and I should think inside you will find a puss-filled mess that must be delicately and systematically cleaned. If it isn't, this will flare again in time."

"I agree but will you do it, Mr Kerrigan?" Robertson seemed agitated. Basil sensed the pleading nature in the way he asked and grew fearful his fate had been decided. His hatred for the bullet grew and he despised the man who had fired the shot. He hoped he had met a terrible end during the war and been eaten by rats.

There was silence in the room and Kerrigan consulted his notes. He was younger than most in the room and his handsome features were scrunched in thought. "I will," he said, finally.

"You're a fool, Kerrigan. That man will die on your table," said an older man with a beard in the second row who, immediately stood to leave. Basil was hot with fever and rage. His blood boiled in his body and he found passion and fortitude from some deep reserve.

"No, I won't, sir!" screamed Basil. His eyes were angry and forced his accuser to repent.

"I am sorry, young man. That was insensitive of me I know. You are clearly a fighter and very brave soul. Our country-we-owe you a great debt that we can never repay." He started to leave the room but only three pairs of eyes followed him out. The remainder agreed with his medical diagnosis if not his manner. The older man stopped at the door and turned to Basil's hopeful saviour, "I wish you luck, of course, Mr Kerrigan."

*

Two days later Basil was on the eve of his life or death operation and Eric, still with the use of the car, had driven around London to collect the Hanham family and take them to 76. They planned a dinner together, but Basil was too weak to make it down stairs so they all gathered round his bed and ate on their laps.

"Smoke out of the window, Frank! Poor B doesn't want your wiffs making him feel more ill," said Stella to Frank who bounced up apologetically and went to the open window.

"It's alright, I like the smell. Can't wait to have one again myself," said Basil with a smile. A little colour had flushed his cheeks and he was able to keep water down for now. His face was less ghoulish in appearance and only the excessive bags under his eyes hinted at his crippling fatigue.

"You'll no doubt be keen for a jar or two, as well," said Frank with a smile. Basil nodded and there was silence for a short moment before Maurice started to cry in Kathleen's arms. At only a few months old he was still firmly attached to his mother.

"I'm sorry, B, I think he's hungry again," said Kathleen, staring lovingly at the tiny human in her grasp. His pales eyes were opened wide and his button nose red.

"He's so wonderful," Basil smiled at his nephew.

"What time tomorrow?" Stella aimed the question at Eric.

"Two o'clock," replied Eric, walking over to share a cigarette with Frank at the window. He eyed baby Maurice with the smile of a proud uncle as he passed behind Kathleen.

"Are you wearing that?" Kathleen nodded at the blue suit on a hanger in front of the wardrobe. She was bouncing her baby gently to settle him back to sleep.

Basil turned his head to look at the suit, the same suit he wore for her wedding the year before. "Yeah, if I'm going out, I'm going out looking splendid." Eva was quick to pounce.

"You're not going anywhere! What you mean to say is, you'll be wearing it out of the hospital when you're fit and well again!"

"Yes, that is what I mean." Basil smiled at his mother as awkward, emotional silence filled the room. Stella, Kathleen and Eva looked like they might begin to cry, Eric noticed and decided to break the spell.

"Besides, if you're going out it will be in your birthday suit on a slab of cold steel." Eric burst into hysterical laughter. Frank snorted at the inappropriate nature of his comment and Basil shook his head as a wide, genuine grin spread across his young face. Kathleen and Stella stared in wonder at their brother who was still laughing but quickly they switched their attention to Eva when she sniffed a giggle.

"Mother! You can't let him get away with that!" demanded Stella. Eva gathered herself and looked seriously at her youngest daughter.

"I laugh dear because it'll all be back to the way it should be soon enough. I will not be losing another son this week." She gestured towards the scroll and large brass coin on the shelf above the fireplace in Basil's room. The large brass token and letter from the King bearing Stuart's name looked across the room at them all. Basil wanted them in here with him, he wanted Stuart's spirit to give him strength while he was fighting for his life. Perhaps he wanted assurance of company on the next journey, he wasn't sure.

"Would anyone like more tea?" Eva stood and left the room with a tray of empty plates and cups. She stopped and kissed her grandchild's head as she shuffled out onto the landing.

"I'll never understand her," said Stella, when she was sure Eva was out of earshot. Eric, Kathleen, Stella, Basil and Frank laughed together like they had years before, troubles and strife forgotten in a few moments of joy.

One by one they all said their heartfelt goodbyes to Basil, but he wouldn't let them say lasting farewells. For him this was not final. For him this was the eve of a new and better life. One free from the handcuffs of war and the illness associated with it all but regardless of his orders, they were all shedding tears for their brother and friend as Eric drove them home in the darkness. Maurice seemed to have sensed the mood, he cried quietly in his mother's arms.

*

The next day Basil had insisted he would walk himself to the car. Eric waited outside and Eva, with her emotional reserves depleted, watched him leave. She had stayed in his room all night talking with him and watching him sleep, he had spent a lot of the night praying with her and crying into her arms. By the morning she was exhausted but rallied and managed a squeaky *"cheerio, dear boy"* as she waved the car away down the road.

Basil asked Eric if they could leave early so he could pay a visit to St. Paul's. Eric had agreed and, parking the car in the churchyard, he helped Basil through the heavy doors and down to the front where they used to sit as young men before war had changed them. They sat side by side in quiet contemplation until Basil spoke.

"How forgiving is the Lord? I mean, will he forgive us all?" Tears dropped from his cheeks onto his jacket as Eric put a big heavy arm around Basil's shoulder.

"Brother, there is *nothing* to forgive." Basil closed his eyes and more tears dropped onto his cuff. Eric laid his other hand on Basil's hands closed tight in his lap. "Why do you punish yourself so much? Why do you always think yourself not worthy?" Basil had no words for his brother, instead he leant gently onto his shoulder.

Basil's mind was a violent mess, like the infection in his body had spread to his already troubled thoughts. He was a sickly child who dreamed only of glory from the battlefield and beyond, he longed to be the equal of his brothers and their friends and he longed to be among the number that could hold their heads high in the world after the war had been won. He wanted to be a man like Eric with stories to tell and respect unending but here he was a crippled man dying of a wound received nearly five years ago. In his mind, it was a pathetic wound that only highlighted his inadequacy. Basil's breath became laboured, his eyes and nose streamed with his own self-loathing.

"I have never been worthy, E," he said finally. His voice was mumbled and distorted but Eric had heard.

"Let me tell you this. You are the bravest man I know. You have fought your whole life and not just the Hun, but yourself. I wish I had your heart and I know Stuart was ever so proud of you. He told me on many occasions." Eric leant over to catch his brother's eye, but they were closed in tight sadness, "The lads too, looking down at us now, loved you like a brother, like Stuart and I love you and like you loved them. If you think yourself unworthy Basil Hanham then you're a damn fool and I'll certainly hear no more of it!" Eric held his brother tight in his arms. "Now come on, you silly old boy, let's go and get that angry Boche piece of shit out of you so we can crack on. Let's live for the lads who are no longer here."

Basil took a moment to compose himself, wiped the tears from his face with his sleeve and Eric helped him to walk out of the church. Basil stopped to steal one last look at the holy warriors on the window. He drew from their smiling faces and crimson shawls one last piece of divine inspiration, an aid for his journey.

*

Eric drove Basil in silence to the hospital and helped him down to surgery. Here they were separated so that Basil could be prepared for his operation but a few moments later, a nurse asked Eric if he had a few words for Basil before he was sent through. Eric, unsure he would be allowed this chance, jumped to his feet and ran into the room where Basil was laid flat on a hospital bed. A cotton sheet covered him up to his neck, alien hospital apparatus surrounded him on both sides and Mr Kerrigan the surgeon smiled awkwardly at Eric. Eric then looked at his younger brother and saw the crippling fear on his face. Basil's eyes were wide, and his hair was brushed back, the notable Hanham family bags dark and creased tight. Eric smiled at him. It was all he could do for Basil who lay there like a scared child.

"You look like you've seen a ghost," said Eric, reaching for his hand.

"Not yet."

"And not for a while either, I'll be here waiting when you wake up." A lonely tear rolled down Eric's muscular cheek and dropped onto Basil's hand.

"I know you will, E. I'll see you soon." Tears fell from the edges of Basil's eyes onto the pillow as Eric watched his brother and best friend wheeled through two large white doors into the adjacent room. He returned to his seat to stare at the pale green wall. His legs bounced incessantly for what seemed like days and his brain flooded with crashing waves of doubt and fear. He thought of their life before the war, before the days of training and their great adventure. Of a life before the first horrid winter on the line and the carnage that followed. He thought of Kathleen and her new baby, of Frank and Stella and of course he thought of Eva and Stuart. How would his mother be if Eric were the only man left to her and how upset would Stuart be to welcome his youngest brother to heaven so soon after surviving the Great War, a war that had been over for almost a year. He became aware of his own feelings and thought of his own ghastly wounds and experiences during those years, the worst of his life. He saw the faces of the lost and of the men he had killed. He tried to recall all the names, but he couldn't.

Hanham

Sewell, Barker, Green, Hockley, Robertson, Wilkinson, Simon, Chase, Dickens, Ball, Long, Leigh-Pemberton, Prismall, Wilson, Perry... Hanham. He prayed to God to forgive him for his sins and promised that if Basil would survive then he would never again leave his side and he would devote his life to family.

As Eric heard the door swing open down the hall his heart stopped beating, his breathing ceased when he recognised Kerrigan walking slowly towards him. Eric tried to interpret every movement in the surgeon's gait, but he couldn't. He hated these drawn-out moments of insecurity, helplessness and the draining agony. As Kerrigan came closer, Eric stood tall. His mouth was dry, and he felt nauseas anxiety in every part of his soul.

"Mr Hanham, will you please sit down."

Aubers Ridge, France – 9ᵗʰ May 2018

THE tight black wrapping of the large hay bail was hot to the touch but, once I had climbed on top, the landscape stretched out in front of me, far into the distance. Shimmering seas of lush green grass sloped away down the ridge, hiding the scars of this land. On a post a few feet away, a small, tattered and faded Australian flag fluttered in the warm breeze and behind me was a dense wood. Fifty metres away my father sat in his red Honda CR-V correlating maps with accounts of the battle to gauge where Stuart Hanham had fought and died on the 9ᵗʰ of May 1915. Next to him a modern sign read *'German Front Line 1915'*. Farm machinery moved slowly in the hazy distance and roosters were calling from a nearby dwelling when my father came to tell me that we were most certainly at the spot where the Kensingtons had fought.

I looked around but couldn't imagine how it must have been, it was so serene, so peaceful on a summer's day and impossible to imagine what it would have been like. Even my own experience of war in Afghanistan helped me very little. I know the feeling and the sound a bullet makes as it cracks past your head. I have had shells whistling above me and, many times, felt the earth shake in a large explosion but even knowing this, I could not comprehend what it must have been like for Stuart that day. It was only as we entered the wood behind us, ignoring the crude signs of *'PRIVE'* like naughty boys, did I start to feel closer to those who had died here so many years ago. In the wood it was eerily silent and cool. The ground had not been farmed flat and lines of trenches could still be made out. Crater holes, although a lot smaller than they would have been, were still obvious among the trees and full of stagnant water.

Hanham

Together my father and I had followed the route the Hanham boys took through Hazebrouck, Viex-Berquin, Neuf-Berquin, Estaires and Laventie, where Basil was wounded in 1914. We had walked the streets of Neuve-Chapelle where Stuart and Eric fought and the place where a tobacco tin had saved Eric's life in March 1915. In these places my father, an experienced battlefield tour guide, shared some of his vast knowledge with me but in this small wood on the top of Aubers Ridge no words were needed and stronger forces moved us. I felt the presence of more than just trees and leaves, but it wasn't a dark feeling. It was not the harsh, sour taste of death but simply an awareness of not being alone. It felt like we had entered a garden party late, incorrectly dressed and all the happy guests had turned to look at the new comers, two welcome strangers entering their place of refuge and everlasting peace. I felt no hostility and imagined men like Stuart joking with Germans he and his friends had so brutally fought with. There seemed no concept of enemy in death and I felt no fear. It gave me a strange, haunted peace to be so close to where Stuart Hanham drew his last breath one hundred and three years to the day.

*

Basil, ever the fighter, survived his operation in October 1919 and he and Eric lived with Eva in Streatham until her death in 1937. Thereafter Basil and Eric lived together for the rest of their lives until Basil's death in 1972. Eric died three years later in November of 1975 and I wonder if he was ever truly at peace after things seen and done during the war. Both their names can be found on a stone tablet at St. Paul's Church,

Hammersmith. The stone commemorates those from the area wounded during The Great War.

Howard disappeared in late 1919 and never returned so Kathleen raised Maurice by herself, no easy task in the early part of the 20th Century. She was brave and loving until her own death in September 1956. Stella and Frank went on many adventures after the war and when she eventually died in December 1985 Maurice was the last of the Hanham family. After Maurice the amazing story passed to his stepson, Patrick. It was Patrick who, in the hope someone would make something of it, put the Hanham letters up for auction. My father was the successful bidder and since then the Hanham story has been with us, demanding to be told.

As we left Aubers Ridge and drove to the Ploegsteert Memorial I felt we had found Stuart. I had got as close to him as I ever was going to and seeing his name on the memorial would be the final stop on my pilgrimage. We stopped at a few small British cemeteries on the way and I wondered whether any of the unknown headstones were his. Perhaps what was left of him had been laid to rest in one of these remarkable places but there were far too many to pause over each in case one was his.

On our way to Ploegsteert, my father, never one to let a machine tell him the best route, took us on a painfully slow 'detour' through the town of Armentieres so we arrived at the memorial a little later than planned but in glorious early evening sunshine. We parked outside the café opposite and reflected over a beer. Flies busied themselves around us and 'Knights in White Satin' played from the radio in the bar. Cars rushed by on the road and a Belgian couple argued over a map, their pushbikes resting against the wall next to them. This was the final part of our journey and I was glad I had waited until now to visit. Had I been here before I had begun setting down the story, I may have been overwhelmed but now it was perfect.

Slowly I walked across the road and, feeling the effects of the strong Belgian beer, looked up at the two huge lions sitting proudly at the entrance. Their regal presence guarded thousands of names adorning the curved panels inside. Theses names, from a distance, look like graffiti or some complex computer code but, when seen closer, separated into individuals, each with their own story.

Thanks to my research I knew where to find Stuart's name, but I was afraid to approach straight away. Instead I walked onto the grass in the middle and looked at all the names before slowly I turned and walked to where the Kensingtons were listed. Their panel was bathed in the bright orange light of evening and, shining brightly at the bottom, was the name I had come to see. S. A. Hanham.

I felt insignificant in front of him, like he had done me, personally, a favour by dying so bravely. I felt his eyes upon me, intense and judging so I looked awkwardly at the names either side, above and below. Hockley, Sewell, Green and so many more who lost their lives alongside Stuart that day. It struck me also how terrible it was no one had written books about the other eleven thousand four hundred and forty-six men listed on the walls. How had Stuart's story come into my life and not that of another? Some men had little wooden crosses with poppies dedicated to them but not many. What of the others who were here? Did anyone come and see them? The thought that maybe no one did made me resent the world and not for the first time I understood the reason why the First

World War has such a place in our hearts.

We stayed for a while longer and I went to look at Stuart one last time. Throughout writing this book I have felt the presence of the Hanham family all around me and they have become a part of me. I imagined Kathleen on stage in London and could feel Basil walking down the road to Laventie, a smile on his adventurous young face. When in Neuve Chapelle, I saw Eric running through the streets during the battle but as I ran my finger along the sunken letters of Stuart's name, I felt something more. I felt him stood by my side, looking sadly at his own name and the names of his friends.

All I could do was thank him.

For more information, including pictures of the Hanham family, visit www.hanhamstory.com.

Acknowledgements

I could not have told the Hanham story without significant help from a great many friends and family along the way, but I shall do my best to thank those whose assistance and contributions have allowed me to share with you this wonderful tale.

Thank you Patrick Armitage who, by putting this wonderful story up for auction, allowed the Hanham family out into the world and to my great friend John Holmes who, when he saw this lot up for auction at Duke's Auction House where he works, made sure my father was aware.

Thank you to my editor Edwina Pitcher whose patience, kindness and attention to detail helped refine the Hanham story and to Henrietta Townsend, Joanne Hargreaves, Joanna Jepson-Biddle, Emily Stafford, Rachel Brown, Tim Hutt, Christopher Kerrigan, James Scott, Nick Griffiths and Allan Wood for persevering through my first draft and offering me their insights.

A tremendous thank you to Sarah Foster for her wonderful artistic mind, insight and hard work during the creation of the cover and maps. To Gemma Alcock whose strategic guidance and technical ability have been essential and a mention too for Freddy Paske whose advice and ideas surrounding the release of Hanham have been greatly appreciated. A thank you too for Duke's Auction House and St Pauls Church, Hammersmith for hosting my launch events.

Special mention though must go to my father Allan Wood. He not only bought the lot that allowed the Hanham family to enter my life but his extensive knowledge of The First World War, time given to showing me around the battlefields where our boys fought, patience, understanding, camera duties and unyielding support have been utterly essential throughout my journey to bring this story to life. Without him and my loving mother by my side I would not have had the strength to see this project through.

Thank you all.

Andrew grew up on the Jurassic Coast in Dorset and enjoyed an active upbringing by the sea before joining the British Army. He commissioned from The Royal Military Academy Sandhurst into The Royal Tank Regiment, with whom he served for the best part of a decade. He left in 2016 to follow his childhood dream of becoming a novelist. Andrew remains a tank commander in the Army Reserves and is a lover of all sports, history, conservation and nature.

Printed in Great Britain
by Amazon

17785322R00210